PRAISE FO... ...OGY:

"In the tradition of other ribald, earthy, urban authors like Blaise Cendrars, Charles Bukowski and Henry Miller, Gutiérrez is an exuberant writer. . . . [Dirty Havana Trilogy] is not only entertaining; it's also curiously uplifting as it illuminates the darker places of a society on the brink."

—New York Times Book Review

"The streetwise gutsiness of Bukowski and Miller pervades Cuban poet Gutiérrez's raunchy, symbolic, semiautobiographical debut novel of life in 1990s Havana. Although the title suggests a triptych, the work more closely resembles a mosaic of short stories bursting with vivid images of exhilaration, depravity, desire and isolation. . . . This searing no-holds-barred portrait of modern Cuba, expertly translated by [Natasha] Wimmer into prose strong in the rhythms and vulgar beauty of the city, will attract readers who like their fiction down, dirty and literate."

—Publishers Weekly

"Dirty Havana Trilogy might be the most important work of Cuban fiction in the last thirty years."

—Vibe

"Dirty Havana Trilogy [is] Pedro Juan Gutiérrez's lewd, impious and brilliant novel of contemporary Cuba. . . . [The narrator's] life serves as a kind of exhibit, a corrosive parody of the official, prettified versions of human nature. . . . Dirty Havana Trilogy is an exploration, and often a Sadean one at that, of human nature stripped to its essentials. In the brutality of his honesty, Mr. Gutiérrez reminds one of Jean Genet and Charles Bukowski. He takes us on an unforgettable journey into a world where politics, spiritual anomie and desire make their troubled accommodation."

—*New York Times*

"The depravity, sexism and racism of Gutiérrez's characters should probably disgust us, but his rebellious high spirits and sybaritic determination, like [Henry] Miller's, make us laugh reflexively at our own weak attempts to tame and enjoy life amid easy opportunity."

—*Philadelphia Inquirer*

"[*Dirty Havana Trilogy*] is probably the most honest depiction of life under Castro to have emerged in recent years. In his tale of squalor and petty hustling, Pedro Juan, who presents himself as a cynic and moral bottom-dweller, is in fact a humanitarian who in his own way fans the sparks of solidarity and friendship that Communism would replace with mindless discipline and paranoia. A detailed political treatise could not better demonstrate Castroism's failure to create a 'new man' in the place of the old one, wicked and sinful, yet compassionate and generous as well."

—*National Review*

"*Dirty Havana Trilogy* is a courageous book from someone who still lives on the island, a singular chronicle of the 'dirty' reality of today's Cuban society. Gutiérrez's prose exudes the rage and indignation of a native, and reading him is a memorable experience for those who don't shy away from a little suffering with their literature."

—*Miami Herald*

"*Dirty Havana Trilogy* is an unabashed vision of the worst of Havana, but it maintains a seductive rhythm of survival, desire and tragic beauty. Beneath its crassness, there's a melancholy that makes this novel remarkably enticing."

—*Time Out New York*

Dirty Havana Trilogy

Dirty
Havana
Trilogy

A NOVEL IN STORIES

Pedro Juan Gutiérrez

Translated from the Spanish
by Natasha Wimmer

HARPER ● PERENNIAL

NEW YORK ● LONDON ● TORONTO ● SYDNEY

HarperCollins books may be purchased for educational, business, or sales
promotional use. For information, please e-mail the Special Markets Department at SPsales@harpercollins.com.

First Ecco paperback edition published 2002

Library of Congress Cataloging-in-Publication Data
Gutiérrez, Pedro Juan, 1950–
[Trilogía sucia de la Habana. English]
Dirty Havana trilogy / Pedro Juan Gutiérrez ; translated from the
Spanish by Natasha Wimmer.—1st paperback ed.
p. cm.
Originally published: New York : Farrar, Straus and Giroux, 2001.
ISBN 0-06-000689-7
I. Wimmer, Natasha. II. Title

PQ7390.G83 T7513 2002
863'.64—dc21
2001040807

16 RRD 20 19 18 17 16

I / Marooned in No~Man's~Land

Early that morning, there was a pink postcard sticking out of my mailbox, from Mark Pawson in London. In big letters he had written, "June 5, 1993, some bastard stole the front wheel of my bicycle." A year later, and that business was still bothering him. I thought about the little club near Mark's apartment, where every night Rodolfo would strip and do a sexy dance while I banged out weird tropical-improvisational music on bongo drums, shaking rattles, making guttural noises, trying anything else I could think of. We had fun, drank free beer, and got paid twenty-five pounds a night. Too bad it couldn't have lasted longer. But black dancers were a hot commodity, and Rodolfo left for Liverpool to teach modern dance. I was broke, and I stayed at Mark's until I got bored and came back.

Now I was training myself to take nothing seriously. A man's allowed to make lots of small mistakes, and there's nothing wrong with that. But if the mistakes are big ones and they weigh him down, his only solution is to stop taking himself seriously. It's the only way to avoid suffering—suffering, prolonged, can be fatal.

I stuck the postcard up behind the door, put on a tape of Armstrong's "Snake Rag," felt much better, and stopped thinking. I don't have to think while I'm listening to music. But jazz like this cheers me up too and makes me feel like dancing. I had a cup of tea for breakfast, took a shit, read some gay poems by Allen Ginsberg, and was amazed by "Sphincter" and "Personals ad." *I hope my good old asshole holds out.* But I couldn't be amazed for long, because two very young friends of mine showed up, wanting to know if I thought it would be a good idea to launch a raft from Cabo San Antonio heading for Cabo Catoche, or whether it would be better to take off north directly for Miami. Those were the days of the exodus, the summer of '94. The day before, a girlfriend had called me to say, "What'll we do now that all the men and kids are leaving? It's going to be hard." Things weren't like that, exactly. Lots of people were staying, the ones who couldn't live anywhere else.

Well, I've done a little sailing on the Gulf and I know that way's a trap. Showing them the map, I convinced them not to try for Mexico. And I went down to see their big six-person raft. It was a flimsy thing made of wood and rope lashed to three airplane tires. They were planning to take a flashlight, compass, and flares. I bought some slices of melon, went over to my ex-wife's house. We're good friends now. We get along best that way. She wasn't home. I ate some melon and left the rest. I like to leave tracks. I put the leftover slices in the fridge and got out fast. I was happy in that house for two years. It's not good for me to be there by myself.

Margarita lives nearby. We hadn't seen each other in a while. When I got there, she was washing clothes and sweating. She was glad to see me and she went to take a shower. We had been lovers on the sly—sorry, I have to call it something—for almost twenty years, and when we get together, first we fuck and then we have a nice relaxed conversation. So I wouldn't let her shower. I stripped her and ran my tongue all over her. She did the same: she stripped me and ran her tongue all over me. I was covered in sweat, too, from all the biking and the sun. She was getting healthier, putting weight back on. She wasn't all skin and bones the way she used to be. Her buttocks were firm, round, and solid again, even though she was forty-six. Black women are like that. All fiber and muscle, hardly any fat, clean skin, no zits. I couldn't resist the temptation, and after playing with her for a little while, after she had already come three times, I eased myself into her ass, very slowly, greasing myself well with cunt juice. Little by little. Pushing in and pulling out and fondling her clit with my hand. She was in agony, but she couldn't get enough. She was biting the pillow, but she pushed her ass up, begging me to get all the way in. She's fantastic, that woman. No one gets off the way she does. We were linked like that for a long time. When I pulled out, I was all smeared in shit, and it disgusted her. Not me. I have a strong sense of the absurd, and it keeps me on guard against that kind of thing. Sex isn't for the squeamish. Sex is an exchange of fluids, saliva, breath and smells, urine, semen, shit, sweat, microbes, bacteria. Or there is no sex. If it's just tenderness and ethereal spirituality, then it can never be more than a sterile parody of the real act. Nothing. We took a shower, and then we were ready to have coffee and talk. She wanted me to go with her to El Rincón. She had to keep a vow she made to San Lázaro and she asked me to go with her the next day. Really, she asked so sweetly I said I would. That's what I love about Cuban women—there must be other women like them too, in America, maybe, or Asia—they're so sweet you can never say no when they ask you for something. It's not that way with European women. European women are so cold they give you a chance to say NO at every turn, and you feel good about it too.

Later I came home. The afternoon was already cooling off. I was hungry, which was no surprise, since all I had in my stomach was tea, a slice of melon, and some coffee. At home I ate a piece of bread and washed it down with another cup of tea. I was getting used to lots of new things in my life. Getting used to poverty, to taking things in stride. I was training myself to be less ambitious, because if I didn't, I'd never make it. In the old days, I always used to need things. I was dissatisfied, wanting everything at once, struggling for more. Now I was learning how not to have everything at once, how to live on almost nothing. If it were any other way, I'd still be stuck with my tragic view of life. That's why poverty didn't bother me anymore.

Then Luisa called. She was coming for the weekend. And Luisa's a sweetheart. Too young for me, maybe, but it doesn't matter. Nothing matters. It started to rain, thunder crashed, the wind came in gusts, and the humidity was terrible. That's the way it is in the Caribbean. It'll be sunny, then all of a sudden the wind picks up and it starts to rain and you're in the middle of a hurricane. I needed some rum, but there was no way to get it. I had money, but there was nothing to buy. I lay down to sleep. I was sweaty and the sheets were dirty, but I like the smell of my own sweat and dirt. It turns me on to smell myself. And Luisa was coming any minute. I think I fell asleep. If the wind got stronger and ripped the tiles off the roof, I wouldn't care. Nothing matters.

1·2 / Memories of Tenderness

I was looking for something good on the radio, and I stopped at a station playing Latin music, salsa, *son*, that kind of thing. The music ended, and the laid-back guy with the rough voice started to talk, the one who'll go on about anything, his kids, his bike, what he did last night. His voice is the kind that gets under your skin, and he talks tough and slangy, like he's never been anywhere but Central Havana, the kind of brother who'll come up and say, "Hey, man, what you need? I got a deal for you."

My wife and I listened to him, and we really liked it. Nobody on the radio was doing what he was doing. He'd play good Latin music, say something, pause for a minute, put on another record, and then it was on to the next thing. No long explanations or showing off. He seemed smart, and I'm always happy to come across smart, proud black guys, instead of the kind who won't look you in the eye and who have that pathetic cringing slave mentality.

Well, we'd always listen to him at home, back when we were happy and life was good, no matter that I was earning an unhealthy and cowardly living as a journalist, always making concessions, everything censored, and it was killing me because each day I felt more like I was prostituting myself, collecting my daily ration of kicks in the ass.

Then she went back to New York, wanting to be seen and heard.

Just like everybody else. Nobody wants to be condemned to darkness and silence. They all want to be seen and heard, want a turn in the spotlight. And if possible, they'd like to be bought, hired, seduced. Did I write "everybody wants"? That's not quite right. It should have been: "*We* all want to be seen and heard."

She's a sculptor and a painter. In the art world, that makes her "popular." And that's supposed to be a good thing. It's comforting to be popular. Anyway, she left again. And I was kicked out of journalism because each day I was more reckless, and reckless types weren't wanted. Well, it's a long story, but in the end what they told me was: "We need careful, reasonable people, people with good sense. We don't want anybody reckless, because the country's going through a very sensitive and important phase in its history."

Around the same time, I found out that the guy with the rough, boozy voice wasn't black. He was white, young, a college student, well-educated. But his persona suited him.

So I was very lonely. That's what always happens when you love holding nothing back, like a kid. Your love goes off to New York for a long time—goes to hell, you might say—and you're left lonelier and more lost than a shipwreck in the middle of the Gulf Stream. The difference is that a kid recovers quickly, whereas a forty-four-year-old guy like me keeps kicking himself, and thinks, "Not again" —and wonders how he could be such an idiot.

The fact that it was Jacqueline made it even worse, because she holds an important record in my manly existence: she once had twelve orgasms with me, one after the other. She could have had more, but I couldn't hold out, and I went and had mine. If I had waited for her, she might have gotten close to twenty. Other times she had eight or ten. She never broke her record. Because we were happy, we got a lot of joy out of sex. The thing with the twelve orgasms wasn't a competition. It was a game. A great sport for keeping young and fit. I always say, "Don't compete. Play."

Well, in any case, Jacqueline was too sophisticated for 1994 Havana. She was born in Manhattan, descended from a mix of three generations of English, Italians, Spaniards, French, and Cubans originally from Santiago de Cuba who scattered toward New Orleans and all over the Caribbean, as far away as Venezuela and Colombia. A crazy family. Her father had been in Normandy, was a D-day veteran. Anyway, she's a complicated woman, and too much work for a simple tropical male like me. She would say, "Oh, there's nobody sophisticated left in Havana. People just keep getting tackier, shabbier, more countrified." Something wasn't right about that. Either it was Jacqueline's elegance, or everybody else's tackiness, or my stupidity, because as far as I could tell, everything was fine and I was happy, even if the poverty got worse every time you turned around.

When I was left alone, I had lots of time to think. I lived in the best possible place in the world: an apartment on the roof of an old eight-story building in Central Havana. In the evening, I'd pour myself a glass of very strong rum on the rocks, and I'd write hard-boiled poems (sometimes part hard-boiled, part melancholy), which I'd leave scattered all over the place. Or I'd write letters. At that time of day, everything turns golden, and I'd survey my surroundings. To the north, the blue Caribbean, always shifting, the water a mix of gold and sky. To the south and east, the old city, eaten away by the passage of time, the salt air and wind, and neglect. To the west, the new city, tall buildings. Each place with its own people, their own sounds, their own music. I liked to drink my rum in the golden dusk and look out the windows or sit for a long time on the terrace, watching the mouth of the port and the old medieval castles of naked stone, which in the smooth light of afternoon seem even more beautiful and eternal. It all got me thinking with a certain clarity. I'd ask myself why life was the way it was for me, and try to come to some kind of understanding. I like to step back, observe Pedro Juan from afar.

It was those evenings of rum and golden light and hard-boiled or melancholy poems and letters to distant friends that helped make me sure of myself. If you have ideas of your own—even only a few—

you have to realize that you'll always be coming up against detractors, people who'll stand in your way, cut you down to size, "help you understand" that what you're saying is nothing, or that you should avoid a certain person because he's crazy, a fag, a traitor, a loser; somebody else might be a pervert and a voyeur; somebody else a thief; somebody else a *santero*, spiritist, druggie; somebody else trash, shameless, a slut, a dyke, rude. Those people reduce the world to a few hybrid types, colorless, boring, and "perfect." And they want to turn you into a snob and a prick too. They swallow you up in their private society, a society for ignoring and supressing everyone else. And they tell you, "That's life, my friend, a process of natural selection. The truth is ours, and everybody else can go fuck themselves." And if they spend thirty-five years hammering that into your skull, later, when you're on your own, you think you're better than everybody else and you're impoverished and you miss out on the joy of variety, when variety is the spice of life, the acceptance that we're not all alike and that if we were, life would be very dull.

Well, then the guy with the rough, boozy voice turned up on the radio again, fooling around a little, and slotted in a Puerto Rican salsa orchestra, and I danced for a while. Until I asked myself, "What the hell am I doing here dancing all alone?" Then I turned the radio off and went out. "I'm going to Mantilla," I thought. I roamed around until I caught one bus and then another, and I got to Mantilla, which is on the outskirts of the city, and which I like because out there you can see red earth and the green of the land and herds of cattle. I have some friends in the neighborhood—I used to live there, years ago. I went to see Joseíto, a taxi driver who lost his job in the crisis and now was gambling for a living. He'd been supporting himself gambling for two years. In Mantilla, there were lots of illegal little gambling clubs. The police made a sweep sometimes and wiped out two or three, locked everybody up for a few days, and then let them go. I had three hundred pesos in my pocket, and Joseíto convinced me to play. He was carrying ten thousand himself. He was in it for the big money. We went to one of his lucky houses. And he was lucky. I lost all my money in fifteen minutes. I don't know why the hell I let Joseíto drag me along. I never win anything when I gamble, but he was raking it in from the start. By the time I left, he had already pocketed five thousand pesos. Lucky bastard. With his kind of luck, I'd be riding high. Well, he has a good life in Mantilla, and he always says, "Oh, Pedro Juan, if I'd had any idea, I would've gotten rid of that fucking taxi a long time ago."

I was pissed about the money. It bothers me to lose. I get irritated every time, and it bothered me that Joseíto could make a living so easily, whereas whenever I play a hand of cards or pick up some dice I start losing right away. I'm not a jinx, because I give everybody else good luck. It happens all the time. Once I bought an old, beat-up car and I left it parked out in front of the building for a week, just sitting there; it had two or three things wrong with it, and fixing it was going to be expensive. Well, a few days later, an old Spaniard came up to me to tell me that everybody in the neighborhood was playing the car's license plate number—03657—in the lottery. Laughing, the old man said, "We're going to have to pay you a commission, Pedro Juan. Last night the butcher won three thousand pesos on 57. What do you think about that?"

"What do I think? I think the son of a bitch should at least pay for my repairs. The car's been sitting there for a week because I'm so broke."

"Damn! Everybody making money on your car, and you making shit."

That's right. I'm hopeless at gambling, and at a whole lot of other things too.

When I left the little club where José was getting rich, I had a few coins in my pocket. Enough to take the bus back to downtown Havana. But I needed a shot of rum. Losing had really pissed me off, and I was feeling aggressive. A little rum calms me down. "I'll go see Rene," I said to myself. Rene (I just call him Rene because he's a good friend) is a fine press photographer. We used to work together a lot, years ago. But then he was caught taking nude photos. They were simple photos of naked girls. No fucking, no black dick sucking, nothing like that. Just nude studies of beautiful girls. There was a scandal. He was kicked out of the Party, ejected from the profession, and expelled from the Association of Journalists. The last straw was when his wife kicked him out of the house and told him she had become "disenchanted" with him. Well, that's how it was. Cuba at the height of its existence as socialist construct maintained a virginal purity, in exquisite Inquisitorial style. And all of a sudden, the guy realized that his life was over. He was living in a dump in Mantilla with a fucked-up son who supported himself by selling grass, but who spent more time in jail than he spent in their dump selling the stuff he brought back from Baracoa. He sold coconut oil, coffee, and chocolate too, on the black market, but he made his real money dealing in excellent mountain weed and he brought so much back that he could sell it cheap.

Rene was alone now. His druggie son had left by raft for Miami in the exodus of August 1994. And he had no idea what had happened to him.

"I don't know where he is, whether he got to Miami, or whether he was taken to the naval base at Guantánamo. Or whether he's in Panama. I have no idea. To hell with it, Pedro Juan. To hell with everybody. When he was here, he spent all his time telling me that if it wasn't for him, I'd be out on the street. Everybody can go fuck themselves! I've gotten the shit kicked out of me so many times I'm sick of them all."

He started to cry. He was sobbing. I thought he was probably stoned.

"Come on, Rene, I'm your friend. Cut it out, man. Let's go get some rum."

"There's a little left in the kitchen. Bring it here."

It was rat poison. Half a bottle of cockroach repellent. I swallowed down a shot.

"Rene, for God's sake, you're killing yourself with this *aguardiente*. What the fuck is it made of?"

"Sugar, believe it or not. My next door neighbor makes it. I know it's shit, but I'm used to it now. It doesn't seem so bad to me. Fancy a joint? There are some papers in the drawer."

"Why are you talking like that? Since when are you the big Spaniard?"

"I picked it up from the whores who come here. They're so dumb they talk to me like the Spaniards who hang out with them. They're always saying 'have a *light*?' 'good chap,' 'let's have a word.' They're crazy. So am I. I'm crazy and I talk just like those Spaniards and their black bitches."

We lit the joints and we sat in silence. I shut my eyes to savor mine. That Baracoa weed has a smell and taste like nothing else. But it's strong. I didn't inhale much. I was thinking I should go to Baracoa and bring back a kilo or two. Rene's son would bring back coconut oil, coffee, and chocolate too because the smell of the coffee masked the smell of the weed. I could do the same thing. And I'd make a few pesos. That's what I was thinking when I felt Rene get up, pull a photo album out of a drawer, and hand it to me.

"Look at this, Pedro Juan."

He was already stumbling over his words, after all the *aguardiente* and the grass. He dropped into his armchair again, flattened and hopeless. I had to get the hell out of there. The air in that place reeked of shit and despair. And it's contagious. It's like breathing in a poisonous gas that gets in your blood and suffocates you. I couldn't keep talking to Rene. I needed a buddy who was tough. The kind of guy who could get me out of my slump and away from all my memories of happiness. I needed to make myself hard like a rock.

I opened the album. It was a collection of nudes. There were at least three hundred of them, in every position. Blacks, mulattas, whites, brunettes, blondes. Smiling ones and serious ones. Some were in pairs, kissing or embracing or feeling each other's tits.

"So what is this, Rene?"

"Whores, man. A catalog of whores. Lots of taxi drivers keep photos like this for the tourists. They advertise the product around town, the tourist picks what he wants, and they take him to the right place."

"Then you're shooting pictures of stars! Rene, photographer to the stars!"

"Rene, photographer to the whores! I'm finished, man. I'm washed up."

"Don't talk shit, Rene. If you're making good money that way . . ."

"You know I'm an artist. This is crap, kid."

"Listen, you're driving me crazy. Don't be such an asshole. Take advantage of these whores. If I were you, I'd take the damn photos for the catalogs, and then I'd take good nude shots, powerful ones of whores in their beds, in their rooms, in their world, in black and white, and then in a few years I'd put together an incredible exhibition: 'Whores of Havana.' And you'd be launched with the kind of show even Sebastião Salgado couldn't put together."

"In this country? The whores of Havana?"

"In this country or wherever. Work and then find a place to show your work. Then if they shut you down here, go somewhere else, anywhere. But whatever you do, get off your ass and out of this fucking room."

"Well . . . it's not a bad idea."

"Of course it's not. Try it, and I promise you'll get back on track. Listen, did your son have partners in Baracoa?"

"What do you want to do?"

"Bring back a little weed. I'm cleaned out, Rene. I have to make a few pesos."

"If you go, look up Ramoncito El Loco. He lives on the way out of Baracoa, near La Farola. Everybody knows who he is. Tell him you're my partner, and that this is for me. That way he'll give you a deal. But don't hang out with him, because everybody knows the old man's always been a dealer. You'll get busted."

"All right, brother. Take care of yourself. We'll be in touch."

I had to hurry to Baracoa. After I took care of business, maybe I could find myself one of those big-assed Indian women who make you feel like you've got the sweetest dick in the world. The Indians there have barely mixed with whites or blacks. A little trip would be worth the trouble. The people there are different.

13 / Two Sisters, and Me in Between

They let the house fill up with junk. They had only been living there for a few years, but it already stank of shit from the chickens and pigs they were raising on the terrace. The bathroom was disgusting; it looked as if it had never been cleaned. But what can you do? That's the way it is with blacks. I came looking for Hayda, but Caridad was home by herself. We discussed the issues of the day: food, dollars, poverty, hunger, Fidel, people leaving, people staying, Miami.

A long time ago, Caridad and I had a fling. It was over quickly. We spent a whole day together, waiting for the bus to Havana. When it finally came and we got on, it was already nighttime, and we had a little orgy right there, jism flowing in abundance. We were young, and when you're young, you don't care what you waste, because you think nothing will ever be used up. And that's as it should be. No matter what you do, when you're old there won't be anything left, even if you've tried to save yourself up. When we got to Havana, she expected me to take her to a motel so we could do things right, on a bed. But no. I'm white, more or less, and back then my white man's sense of duty made me lose sight of the most important things in life. My brain had been too well-inoculated with self-discipline, injected with a sense of responsibility mixed with authoritarianism and patriarchal structure. Thank God I got over all that.

Well, in her mind, that was an insult. Women—and especially black women—don't like to put anything off. She thought I was someone who left things half-finished, and she never accepted any of my propositions again. Back then she was an eighteen-year-old tennis champion. She traveled the world, she was beautiful, and she was on her way up, moving fast, not looking back. And so she wanted nothing to do with me.

Then I met her sister, Hayda, and we began a twenty-year affair. On and off, of course. Hayda is completely different: she's a tall woman, very thin. A social worker in a clinic, which has given her inner strength. As a child, she had an accident with a kerosene stove, and she has a burn all down the right side of her body, from her neck to her waist. She's a little neurotic, insecure, full of doubts, and her skin has a strong smell to it. Blacks who are very dark always have an acrid smell. So it was years before I could stick my tongue in Hayda's hole. But she's very hot. Completely uninhibited. She's a total pervert. Anyway, more about her later.

Now I had Caridad in front of me, twenty years after that one-night stand. Actually, we had one other fling: she was married by then, and her daughter had been born, and she was fat and busty, with lots of blubber everywhere, and all she did was talk about her job as a coach and how nasty everyone was to her, how she couldn't travel anymore, and how her husband was a loser who did nothing but play baseball on the weekends. "They treat me like shit, and what have I ever done to deserve it? It's jealousy. They're all jealous."

I endured her stupid harangue because Hayda might show up any minute. Caridad brought out a bottle of guava *aguardiente*, and we had a drink. When we were halfway through the bottle and we were still alone in the house, Caridad was maneuvering a grand history of her championship days out of me, and by then we both had tears in our eyes, so I went over to her chair and I kissed her. She stood up and offered herself to me with a desire I hadn't expected. We kissed each other with lots of tongue, and when I felt her, oh, she was really wet, dripping wet. I couldn't wait. I took her to bed and fucked her there because she was too fat to try it standing up. But it was no good anyway because I was too hot and I couldn't wait for her. I came right away. When I realized what I had done, I tried to keep going, but we both got nervous: if her husband came home, he would kill the two of us with his baseball bat. And the man was a brute. Not very big, but lots of muscle.

Well, we got dressed, sat out in the street again. I had another glass of *aguardiente*, and after a minute, I left.

Then, a little while later, I told Hayda, without giving it a second thought. I've never really imagined I was very important to Hayda. I told it to her as a funny story, because it was the quickest and most disastrous lay I've ever had in my life. Hayda didn't get angry, but later she argued about it with Caridad. She accused her of getting her sister's lover drunk so she could fuck him. Woman's jealousy, that's what it was. I never understand that kind of thing, because it's filtered through the dumb egoism of cheap boleros. A person should only be jealous when something is really worth it, truly important. People shouldn't waste their energy being jealous of everything. But women don't think like that. A woman can be jealous of her husband, her lover, and two suitors all at the same time, and all with the same intensity and force. Women are either extremely versatile or amazingly pragmatic.

The story was buried for a long time among the three of us. But today, Caridad and I were alone together again. Her little girl was playing outside. Her husband was out and about. He fishes now. He's given up baseball. And it occurred to me to say to Caridad, "If we had a bottle of *aguardiente* . . . Remember that time?"

"No. If we had a bottle of *aguardiente*, nothing would happen."

"Why not?"

"Because some people forget to act like real men when they drink. And they can't keep their mouths shut. They talk too much."

It went on and on. She almost kicked me out of the house. According to her, I'm a wretched shit for telling her sister. And it's she who has the most right to me, because she had me first. What a mess. I've never really understood all these ethical issues or the rights and duties that come with them. I'm a cynic. It's easier that way. At least, it's easier that way for me.

Then I managed to turn the conversation in another direction. We talked about Brazil. It had been proposed that she spend a year coaching Brazilian kids in some city near São Paulo. We looked for it on a map. On the map it did seem to be near São Paulo. "I'll give you introductions to my friends in São Paulo. Go visit them, and you'll have a good time. They're great people." And so I calmed her down a little. I got her to take a walk a few blocks down the street with me. To get to Hayda's little house, you had to walk through a lot of slum land on the outskirts of the city. She showed me the way. "You take this path here. When you get to that mango grove, go left and ask for the brick factory."

That's what I did. I was crossing a neighborhood of very poor people, but at least they answered my questions and pointed me in the right direction through the maze of shanties built of tin and rotten boards and pieces of brick and rubble discarded by the factory. When I got to Hayda's shack, she was washing. She came out to open the door in panties and a bra, half-wet, and we barely spoke a word. It was a great fuck. I let her have her orgasms. I gave her the first with my tongue. It's amazing, it always works. She only has to feel my tongue scraping up her clit to rocket off on the first one. I kept going, no hurry. I like that woman. She turned around so I could take her from behind. She's always told me that her husband—she was married three years ago—can't do it. He's black, and he's got the dick of a black man, and that discourages acrobatics.

We were sweating a lot. It's a very small house, with a low roof, two rooms, and a tiny bathroom. At last I couldn't stand it anymore and I came, the same way I always do. I shout and get frantic. It's as if I'm flying high and then falling all the way from the sun. Just like Icarus when he goes featherless into the sea. Oof—we finished. We lay there exhausted for a while, looking up at the ceiling. I was exhausted. She not so much. She never gets tired; even if she has ten orgasms, she wants more and more. But the heat was stifling. She said, "The water's on. Use it while we've got it and wash up a little." I couldn't find the soap. I asked where it was.

"There isn't any soap, Pedrito. I can't remember how long it's been since we had soap."

"And so you just wash with water?"

"Of course. What do you think?"

I tossed a few cans of water on myself. No effect. Without soap, you can't get rid of smells, damp, sweat. I dried myself, got dressed again. She did too, and we sat down to talk.

"I'm going to Havana to work the streets. I can't go on like this."

"Are you crazy, girl? You're not tough enough for that . . ."

"Look at this . . . : All I have is two pairs of panties and they're both ripped. Ruined. No soap, no food, no nothing. It's just inertia that keeps me working at the clinic. I don't even know why I bother. I've had it . . . and my husband, that idiot . . . oh, I can't stand it anymore."

"He's not an idiot, Hayda. These are hard times. It's tough to come up with real money."

"I know it. But you've got to go out and look for it. Nobody's going to bring it to you here. But he won't. He sits out there on the patio, doing nothing. Smoking, drinking rum when he's got it. He gets himself drunk as a dog. Then he can't even fuck me. It's just no good!"

"Damn it all, he could raise a piglet or something. Make a few pesos on the side."

"Nothing. He won't do anything. He won't lift a finger. Sometimes I think he's retarded . . . Really, don't you think if I go hustle . . . ?"

"Listen, don't even think about it. The market's already swamped. The little girls hustling in Havana are twenty years old, and they look like models. They're gorgeous. Vicious, too, and they've got deals going with the police, taxi drivers, hotel concierges. Come on, forget about it."

"Pedrito, for God's sake, what am I supposed to do?"

I gave her a few ideas on the subject of food. The people in Havana were starving. Anything edible could be sold instantly.

"I'll help you, Hayda. I have people who'll pay in dollars for anything to eat. With one little trip a week . . ."

We talked until nightfall. I was waiting for her husband to come home. I would have liked the three of us to get drunk together and dance so that she could get both of us hot. It's what she tells me in bed. That she'd like to sleep with both of us at once so that I could take her in the ass and he could take her from the front. It seemed she'd had only a little bit of rice for dinner that night. That got me down. But I haven't heard anything from her since. Months have gone by, and she hasn't come to Havana. Some people are just paralyzed. They don't know how to make do, and so they starve to death.

1·4 / Tough Guys

Things had been going badly for me for a while, and I thought it might be a good idea to go in for a check-up. Getting out my bicycle, I rode all the way along the Malecón to Marianao. I had half given up on *santos*; América kept encouraging me to go through the initiation ceremony so I would have my own personal *santo* but I didn't want to get in too deep. That's the way it is: when things are good, you let everything slide. When you're in trouble, that's when you remember the *santos*.

América was hauling buckets of water from a low tap on the sidewalk. The water's never on in that building. I helped her a little because she's too old for work like that, and she was sweating. In a few minutes, bucket by bucket, we had almost filled the tank, when a racket broke out at the other end of the building. A woman was having an attack, convulsing in the middle of the corridor.

"The spirit of a dead man is passing through her, that's what it is. Wait here for me while I go help her," the old lady said to me, and she went hurrying off.

All I wanted was to haul a few more buckets, finish up the job, and have my session with América. I couldn't spend all day in Marianao. And it's hard to stay out of trouble when you're hanging around her building. There's always some mess, and the police come right away. Just then, América shouted for me, frightened, "Pedro Juan, come here, child, come here!"

The dead man's spirit still clung to the woman. When I got to the end of the corridor, more women were gathering around.

"Go in there and get him down, child! Cut him down, for God's sake."

I peered into the woman's room. Her son was hanging there, with an electrical cord around his neck. He was naked, covered in stab marks, blood all over his body, a dried, dark blood. Some of the wounds were deep.

"Call the police!" I shouted, as I pulled up a chair and tried to get him down, but he was big and bulky, too heavy. I couldn't undo the knot in the electrical cord. He was as cold and stiff as an icicle, and I was smeared by the blood that began to flow again from some of his wounds.

América passed her hands over the woman a few times and sprinkled her with cold water, but the dead man's spirit wouldn't let her go. At last she fainted and fell to the floor. Just then, another neighbor arrived. He threw his arms around the hanged man and began to cry and cover him with kisses. He asked me to help lift the body down.

I didn't get it. Here was a tough guy from the building—you could tell he was tough—and he was kissing the dead man on the mouth, his eyes full of tears. At last we managed to unhook the man and get him down.

Picking him up in his arms, the guy lay him on the bed, and said to me, "Leave me alone. I'm going to clean him up."

To be honest, I was glad someone else was taking care of the corpse. Now I could go. I had blood all over me, and I wanted a bath. América had finally revived the hanged man's mother. Then I noticed the crowd in the doorway, everyone staring. No one dared enter the room. A few women were crossing themselves and praying. América tried to help the guy, who was already washing the body, but he kicked her out. "I told you all, leave me alone. Go on, get out."

América took me by the arm and brought me to her room.

"Sit down while I make you some coffee. I can't give you a session today. A fresh death gets in the way. And all that blood."

"What's been going on here?"

"The boy who hanged himself was queer. Ever since he was a kid, he got fucked, at the Remedial Center for Minors. And he liked it. He was always handsome, and that made him cocky; he was tough, but he didn't like women. And he was a bitter one. You see what he did to himself. Stabbed with a knife and then hanged. You've got to be crazy to hurt yourself that way. Do you know what he did yesterday afternoon? He was riding a horse on the land out back, but he whipped the horse so hard that it kept bucking until it threw him. Well, then he stabbed the horse in the neck and killed it. After that, he ran off and vanished. I guess he came back early in the morning and hanged himself."

"And his mother wasn't in the room?"

"No. Sometimes she goes out with men and comes home drunk. Sometimes she's gone for two or three days."

"And who was that who helped me get him down?"

"One of the neighbors. They'd been together a long time. I never understood it. The man has a wife and children; he's handsome, the kind of guy who carries a machete and is always getting in trouble with the police. But what do I know? I guess they liked each other."

I drank my coffee. América drew a bath for me, and just as I was starting to lather up, the police came to take us to the station to make our statements. That day I didn't get my session and my clothes were ruined; I had to throw them away because the stains would never come out.

1:5 / Claustrophobic Me

For years I've been trying to dig myself out from under all the shit that's been dumped on me. And it hasn't been easy. If you follow the rules for the first forty years of your life, believing everything you're told, after that it's almost impossible to learn to say "no," "go to hell," or "leave me alone."

But I always manage . . . well, I almost always manage to get what I want. As long as it isn't a million dollars, or a Mercedes. Though who knows. If I wanted either of those things, I could find a way to have them. In fact, wanting a thing is all that really matters. When you want something badly enough, you're already halfway there. It's like that story about the Zen archer who shoots his arrow without looking at the target, relying on reverse logic.

Well, when I started to forget about important things—everyone else's important things—and think and act a little more for myself, I moved into a difficult phase. And it was like that for years: I was on the margins of everything. In the middle of a balancing act. Always on the edge of a precipice. I was moving on to the next stage of the adventure we call life. At the age of forty, there's still time to abandon routines, fruitless and boring worries, and find another way to live. It's just that hardly anybody dares. It's safer to stick to your rut until the bitter end. I was getting tougher. I had three choices: I could either toughen up, go crazy, or commit suicide. So it was easy to decide: I had to be tough.

But back then I still didn't really know how to get all the shit off my back. I just kept moving, strolling around my little island, meeting people, falling in love, and fucking. I fucked a lot: sex helped me escape from myself. I was in my claustrophobic phase. Even in an ever-so-slightly cramped space, I'd immediately feel I was suffocating and I'd take off, howling like a wolf. It all started when I was trapped in the elevator in my building. It's an old machine, manufactured in the thirties, which means that it has a grate, and it's open on the sides. It's American, and ugly, not like those beautiful old European elevators that still run smoothly in the hotels on the boulevard de la Villette and those other old Parisian neighborhoods. No. This elevator is a cruder, simpler piece of junk. Very dark, because the neighbors steal the light bulbs, with a permanent stink of urine, filth, and the daily vomit of a drunk who lives on the fourth floor. You go up or down slowly, watching the scenery: cement, a slice of stairway, darkness, another slice of stairway, the doors to each floor, someone waiting who finally decides to take the stairs, because the elevator stops whenever and wherever it wants. Often it decides to stop without lining up with any of the exit doors. There in front of you is the rough cement wall of the shaft, and you can hear people screaming, "Get me out of here, goddamnit, I'm stuck!"

Like a senile old man, the elevator is forgetful, and it moves up and down very slowly, shivering and snorting, as if it no longer has the strength for so much work. And so, at one of those unexpected stops between two floors, I stuck my hand out between the door grate and the wall of the shaft, knelt down, and felt for the edge of the door on the floor below to line the elevator up properly. That was the only way to get the machinery working again to keep moving up. And I did it: I closed the door tightly, the elevator started again, but there was no time to get my arm out of the way. It was jammed between the wall and the grate, in a three-centimeter gap (in order to write this, I've just measured it). It was horrific: my arm and hand scraping along, at the elevator's leisurely pace, all the way to the seventh floor. I was screaming bloody murder, doubled over in pain, and I was sure my arm and my right hand were a mash of bones and blood and shredded skin. But no. No broken bones. It was a burn, my whole arm and hand raw flesh, bleeding, the nerves scraped into a festering puree of dirt and dog shit. So from that moment on: straight into the pit of hell. Rampant claustrophobia. When I got out of the elevator—or when I was gotten out—I stayed trapped inside myself. And I was trapped for years, trapped inside myself. Collapsing inside.

The claustrophobia was so awful that sometimes at night I would wake with a start and jump out of bed. I felt trapped by the night, by the room, by my own self, on the bed. I couldn't breathe. I'd have to pee and get a drink of water and go out on the roof and watch the dark immensity of the sea, and breathe the salt air. Then I'd calm down a little.

Oh, it wasn't really just the broken-down elevator. The elevator was the last straw. But lots of other things happened before that, which I'll tell little by little. Later. Not now. I'll tell them the way a person talks to a dead man though a *santera*, and dedicates flowers and glasses of water and prayers to him, so that he'll rest in peace and not fuck with those of us left on the other side.

Well then, that's where I was, in a state of claustrophobia, overwhelmed. Squashed like a bug. And I walked a lot, all over the place, anywhere. I was always running away. I couldn't be at home. Home was hell. And one day I went to a seminar for film people. If it turned out to be the right kind of thing, I could write something up for the stupid but pretentious weekly magazine I worked for then.

The seminar, in a film school on the outskirts of Havana, lasted four days. From the very first instant, I noticed Rita Cassia: a golden-skinned Brazilian who wanted to make lots of money writing scripts for soap operas and who had beautiful legs and was eager to get over her recent divorce. Basically, she was looking for a happy Latin lover type to cheer her up.

And that's how it happened. All of her eroticism was concentrated in the looks she gave me. She had almond-shaped, honey-colored eyes, just like in a bolero. And when we looked at each other, it was like kissing with lots of tongue. From that moment on, things moved fast. We ignored a famous Cuban documentary film-maker who made great films but didn't know how he did it. The guy was so intuitive he had no idea where his own intuition came from. Luckily, he never tried to explain anything serious. He was nice, and he told stories. We ignored him anyway, and went to walk in a little grove of trees, making silly small talk until the electromagnetic field between us was supercharged and we kissed without exchanging a single word of love or desire. Then she told me that during Carnival in Rio she puts on her skimpiest outfits and goes out dancing samba every night, which I guess might have something to do with her eyes and her electromagnetism.

It was already evening and the little grove wasn't very dense, and there were people there, because the students were very promiscuous, as you'd expect. Near us, two boys were kissing madly and in an instant they had their zippers down and their dicks out, and they were on the ground, frantic, sucking each other in a sixty-nine. That made me even hotter, and we left. We went to the small apartment Rita Cassia was renting, and I made her suck me before I was even out of my clothes. On the table she had a bottle of seven-year-old rum. It had been a long time since I last saw a bottle of good rum. I made myself a big drink, with ice, and then another, and I was amazed: I was able to give her dick for more than an hour, everywhere, without coming. She undulated her hips and pelvis, getting her kicks, and sprinkled me with rum. She'd take a mouthful and spray it over me and then she'd run her tongue along my skin to collect it. Sometimes rum makes me last longer: my prick stays stiff, but I don't come.

When I finally focused on coming—I was getting very tired—I

managed to accumulate enough will power to pull my dick out in time to shoot my come all over her belly. And there was lots of it. It had been two or three weeks since I last fucked, and there was lots of jism. And Rita Cassia was carried away and she kept repeating, "Lovely, lovely, ahhh, lovely."

From then on it was one long orgy, because after the seminar came the Festival of New Latin American Cinema, and Havana—as far as we were concerned—was paradise: lots of movies, lots of fucking, lots of rum and good food. Cuba was just then at the beginning of the worst famine in its history. I think it was '91. Nobody had any idea of all the hunger and crises still to come. I certainly didn't. All I cared about was my raging claustrophobia and the urge I had to eat. That same year, in just a few months, I had lost forty pounds; the cause, it would seem, being lack of food.

We also amused ourselves by eluding Maria Alexandra, a successful writer of Brazilian soap opera scripts. That fine lady was a big dyke, and she besieged Rita Cassia with a splendid display of seduction tactics: morning, noon, and night she would show up at Rita's room with flowers, she invited her to all the cocktail parties and banquets, and she promised her incessantly that she would help her write a good script—to sell to O'Mundo, no less.

Another of her gentlemanly tricks was to play cold war with me, alternately striking one of two poses: either she ignored me majestically, or she treated me with a fatherly yet distant condescension. Maria Alexandra loved Rita Cassia so passionately that she demolished every obstacle in her path, any way she could. She was sure I couldn't bestow on Rita Cassia even the tiniest iota of the enormous pleasure, sexual and sensual, that she was capable of giving as soon as she got her hands on her. Rita Cassia, in her feminine way, stayed loyal to me, but she would turn kittenish, charming, and witty whenever the dyke with the keys to the golden doors of O'Mundo appeared.

And that's how the time passed. We had fun. I felt happy and ignored the fact that I was a pathetic sponger. A proud and romantic beggar. Well, as I've said, it was the beginning of the crisis and our hunger was getting sharper, but a person always sees the dirt in the other man's eye and says, "Everybody's starving and getting thinner every day." It's hard to tell it like it is, "*We're* all starving, and *we're* all getting thinner every day." Rita Cassia paid for everything, because I didn't have even a dollar in my pocket, and I calmly accepted that she would always pay. My only other option was for me to stay home, bored, eating rice and beans and missing out on all the fun. That's how it was, until one day it was over.

I was on the bed, with the last shot of seven-year rum in my hand. Rita Cassia was getting dressed, so we could go walking along the Malecón and say our goodbyes by the sea, late at night, as two good lovers in Havana should. It had to be a cinematic ending, under the stars, maybe even under the moon. She had already packed her suitcase. She would be leaving for the airport at three in the morning. Then I noticed that she had left some valuable objects scattered around the room: rubber thongs, worn but still in fine shape, half a bottle of shampoo, some jars of jam, notepads, slivers of soap, a disposable razor.

"Are you leaving all this here?"

"Sure. None of it's any good."

"Oh, yes it is. Those rubber thongs, the shampoo, the soap. Everything's worth something here, even if you think it's junk."

"Fine then, let's put it all in a bag and you can take it with you."

A little while later, we were strolling the Malecón, saying our goodbyes. We'd never see each other again. She had already told me that it pained her to witness so much poverty and so much political posturing to disguise it. She never wanted to come back. We sat for a long time, listening to the sea. She could smell it, I couldn't. Maybe my nose was too used to it. I like to listen to the sea from the Malecón, late, in the silence of the night. We kissed and said our goodbyes. I walked off toward home, carrying the bag. Slowly. I felt good. And I kept on slowly, without looking back.

1·6 / In Search of Inner Peace

My life still lacked the right mix of company and solitude. What I mean is, I was still off balance, my solitude seemed excessive.

Little by little, I was approaching my prime. But it was a struggle. Living with me was hard on Pedrojoán, too. We argued; we had some serious fights. In our last battle, to keep from hitting him, I turned all my pent-up violence on the glasses that corrected my astigmatism: I took them off and smashed them with one fist. I still can't figure out how I managed not to cut myself to shreds on the broken lenses. The result was a long period of headaches and drowsiness. In Cuba at that time, there weren't even screws for the frames. Finally I got another pair. From then on, I promised to make peace with myself, and keep cool. "Pedro, either you hate yourself or you love yourself. Figure that out, and you'll be on the way to settling your private little war with the rest of the world."

So I was trying. América was helping me. She wanted to help me clean out my head. When I biked to Marianao to visit her, I brought her things for the ceremony: coconuts, white flowers, rum, eggs, honey, candles, and herbs. On the way back, I had to cross the Almendares River, which was mobbed by people frantic to get to Miami. They built flimsy rafts out of tires, boards, and ropes, and they set out to sea as merrily as if they were on their way to a picnic. That was the summer of '94. For four years, people had been starving and going mad in my country, but Havana suffered most. As a friend of mine always said, "Pedro Juan, the only way to live here is crazy, drunk, or fast asleep." The sanest people came up and tried to reason with the raft people. And they replied, "All I want is out of this shit. A person lives the good life over there, that's all I know." They were desperate, and maybe they were brave. Or maybe ignorant, I don't know. Probably bravery and ignorance go hand in hand.

I was there for a while, nosing around in the crowd. There was even a policeman helping four guys fix up their raft, and he said to them, "It'll be stronger now. Hope you make it." I'll never understand politics. For more than thirty years, anyone who tried to escape on a raft to the United States was chased down and seized, and, on the other side, those who managed to get past the sharks, the surf, and the Gulf Stream were heroes for a day when they made it to Miami. Then all of a sudden, the politicians of both countries decided it suited them to do things the other way around. And somehow people here are still shocked by the absurd, by abstract art, by surrealism. All you've got to do is live a little, keep your eyes open. Am I wrong?

When I was tired of looking around, I got on my bicycle and rode home. Slowly. I like to pedal along the Malecón. Halfway home, I went up to Pedrojoán's high school. Was it a premonition? Maybe. All that went through my head was, "Pedrojoán's not doing so well and I'd better stop by and see how things are going." That was it, I didn't have any other kind of presentiment, but as soon as I stepped into the school's foyer, two boys yelled, "Pedrojoán fell off a bus and they took him to the hospital!"

I had to get hold of myself. I almost passed out. They told me which hospital he had been taken to, and I shot off like an arrow. It was the worst hospital in Havana, the dirtiest and most godforsaken of them all. The boy and a teacher had already been there for two hours, and no one had attended to them. His wrist was broken. He had been hanging out the door of a crowded bus, when he started to lose his grip. He knew he was going to fall and might easily be killed. To the man next to him, he said, "Please, hold onto me. I'm falling."

But the asshole said, "So fall, what do I care?"

And then Pedrojoán was head over heels in the street, the bus still going forty miles an hour. It was a miracle he wasn't killed. Well, I got moving. I found two doctors, and I asked them to please treat my son.

Finally they put him in a cast. They encased his wrist and part of his arm, and we went home, but his wrist was still swollen, and it hurt him a lot. I thought they probably hadn't put the cast on right, that they had skimped on plaster. The next day I'd have to find another hospital and fight for treatment again. I gave him an aspirin, and around noon he slept for a while. When everything was quiet, I went out on the roof, overlooking the sea. I wanted a smoke and a cup of coffee. I was drained. My quest for balance was always unbalancing itself. All I asked was for inner peace. I thought I would read a little from Zen: A Way of Life. But it was no good. I read it, and nothing stuck. I found one of Pedrojoán's notebooks lying around. He had been reading lots of books all at once. The notebook was full of quotes, copied from Hermann Hesse, García Márquez, Grace Paley, Saint-Exupéry, Charles Bukowski, and Thor Heyerdahl. A good mix. That combination, plus rock, will keep a fifteen-year-old boy in a state of constant torment, and he'll never be bored. Which is good, I say. The important thing is not to be bored.

Then María called. She's a writer of strange stories who considers me her personal dictionary and likes to consult me about her semiotic violations, which are supposed to enhance the poetic atmosphere of her narratives. We talked for a while, and I said to her, "Don't pay any attention to literature professors, or to grammar teachers or critics or theorists. They can do you a lot of harm. Just listen to yourself. It'll take time, but it's better . . . Well, it's not that it's better or worse. More that there's no other way."

"And what if a writer gives me advice?" she asked doubtfully.

"Well, listen to him, but not too much. Don't pay much attention to anyone."

That's all I can remember. My wife—by then she was almost my ex-wife—was in New York, practically penniless but happy and trying to find a good gallery for her sculptures, and I was in over my head in Havana and blaming it on everyone else. I think I was full of self-pity in those days, and trying to escape myself. That was the worst of it: I shrank from being alone with myself, from keeping myself company or making conversation with myself. And maybe such a dogged quest for inner peace was bad for me. I don't know who the hell put the idea in my head. To live in inner peace, you've got to be an idiot, right?

The telephone rang, and they told me Aurelio tried to kill himself and was unconscious, in intensive care at the emergency hospital. It's close to my place, and I walked over. Along the way, I was working myself up: "He's lucky if he's unconscious," I thought, "because if he can talk, I'm going to give that faggot a piece of my mind. Why go looking for death when all you need is to get things off your chest? Stupid son of a bitch. All it takes is a bottle of rum and a little conversation with a woman, or God, or a friend."

I ran into Aurelio's nephew in the waiting room. He seemed eager for Aurelio to die and get it over with, I thought. He had no news to give me, and no interest in finding anything out. I went looking for the doctors. They didn't want to help. I was getting pissed off when a nurse—a hot little mulatta, but in a foul mood—read me a few lines of the medical report and asked me, "Are you a relative?"

"Friend."

"Oh."

I caught something in her "oh," and since I was already half-pissed at the shoddy treatment I was getting, I snapped, "Listen, I'm not queer, not even fucking close. What do you mean, 'oh'?"

"OK, take it easy."

"Look, if there's something you want to say, come out and say it."

"It was a suicide attempt, drug cocktail, sedatives and tranquilizers. And he injected air into his veins, too. His stomach and intestines were pumped, and now he's in critical condition, with a generalized infection. And if you want to know why I said 'oh,' it's because that's how fags kill themselves. They want to do it, but they don't have the . . . Real men shoot themselves, hang themselves, or jump off a building . . . So you better pray for your little *friend*."

She turned her back on me and walked off mockingly, swinging her hips. But I couldn't take that sitting down.

"Baby, you've got a nice ripe ass just waiting to be pumped full of juice."

She swiveled, more mocking than ever.

"Yes, I can see it's asses you prefer . . . *baby*."

"Honey, if I get hold of you, I'll have you begging for it front *and* back."

It seemed she didn't hear that last remark, because she didn't answer and she sashayed on down the corridor, back to the intensive care ward. When she got there at last, she stopped and shouted, "Listen, buddy, visitor's hour is at six p.m., so don't come at the wrong time again."

I was there every day at six o'clock. Aurelio recovered consciousness. A few days later, he was transferred to a regular ward. He was still fighting the infection, which was serious, but he could have visitors. His half-sister, his apathetic nephew, and his half-sister's husband took turns sitting with him all day. He couldn't be left alone. There were only two nurses watching over a ward of twenty-five patients. On the second day, I offered to sit with him too, but they had gotten ahead of me and decided that I should stay every night.

He was very weak. He couldn't even move his hand, and he was getting oxygen through a tube in his nose.

His half-sister's husband had already told me he'd been living shut up lately, refusing to see people. He wouldn't open the door to anyone. He was becoming more and more of a recluse. "It was hard to do anything for him. Sometimes I tried to see him, but he wouldn't even let me in. I think he was paranoid," he told me.

Aurelio was a loner. His father, a lathe operator in a factory, was a boring, unimaginative, tedious man, a miser who counted his change to the last cent. His mother, a tormented, empty-headed pianist, spent her life floating three feet above the floor. From his father, he got slaps, and from his mother, sweets. And Aurelio had a little of each parent in him. He was part miser and part spendthrift, part lunatic and part bore, part man and part woman. We met in high school, and I always suspected he was gay, though he seemed more asexual than anything else.

Once we were drinking beer at a beach near his house. When we were pretty drunk, and two girls had glanced at us a few times, I was ready to make a move.

"Let's go after those girls, man, come on!"

But he grabbed my arm.

"No, wait. Let's stay here."

"What's wrong with you? Are you queer, do you jack off, or what's your thing?"

"I'm queer, I jack off, I don't have a *thing*. And what about you? Are you a real man or is it just a front?"

"Hey, hey now. What's your problem? What the hell is wrong with you?"

"Sure, you probably like black dick, and by now I'm sick of watching you pretend to be so macho."

"Oh, go to hell, Aurelio."

It wasn't funny anymore. Like the fag he was, he got upset and left the beach. I went off with the girls, and I can't remember what happened next. But after that Aurelio and I didn't see each other for years. One day, I realized that I didn't care whether the guy was a faggot or not. He could do whatever he wanted with his ass. Bottom line, we had been friends since childhood, and it was my fault we weren't anymore. So I went over to his house with a bottle of rum to try to make peace. I don't know how such a thing might be seen among Eskimos. But in the Caribbean, a young guy is putting his virility on the line if he has a queer friend. Well, I've never worried too much about other people's opinions, and the few times I have, it's fucked me up, screwed me over, and forced me to give up and start all over again.

So I went. I said hello. I didn't apologize. We cracked open the bottle. His father and mother were dead. He had been married for three years. He introduced me to his wife, Lina. That's another story: they were passionately in love in high school, but her family pressured her to break up with Aurelio, calling him a fag, a pianist, skinny, ugly, and hunchbacked, among other things. She left him and married a guy who was everything he wasn't. They had two children and he cheated on her with any woman who would have him until she couldn't stand it anymore and they were divorced. Then the romance between Aurelio, pianist and musical scholar, and Lina, soprano, started up again. They were both in their thirties by then. Aurelio had shed the whipped-dog look he always used to have. Now he was passionately devoted to his wife. We saw each other frequently and for the first time in twenty years of friendship, we were able to talk comfortably about sex. He told me that he fucked on the edge of the bed, in the shower, in the kitchen, in all possible positions. Once he showed me the Ananga Ranga, which is full of contortions too strange for any non-Hindu.

It wasn't just nonstop fucking. Beyond that—and most importantly—he built up a full repertory for her. He taught her to sing in Italian, German, French. He lived for her. They had no children. He had just severed what few ties still bound him to his half-sister, his father's daughter from a previous marriage. He became even more of a loner. He concentrated on Lina, gambling everything on that one card. The marriage lasted nine years. She gave him sex and little smiles, and in return, he made her into an artist.

Lately she was hardly ever around anymore, almost always on

tour, traveling to other cities or other countries. And Aurelio just kept getting lonelier. She was sparkling, happy, carefree. He was withdrawn, depressed, brooding over his failure. I think he enjoyed wallowing in loneliness and defeat, and he wouldn't make even the slightest attempt to say screw it all and rescue himself.

Now he was in bed with an oxygen tube in his nose and saline IVs stuck in his arm, a nervous wreck, too weak to fight the infection creeping through his body, which was resistant to any combination of antibiotics. I had been away for a while, and it had been a long time since we saw each other, maybe two or three years.

He opened his eyes a crack, and when he saw it was me, he tried to smile. He started to talk in a very low voice. I moved closer to hear him. The ward was almost dark, and it was quiet. Every so often, a nurse would come in, turn on a few lights, and distribute pills and medicine to some of the patients. Then everything would be quiet again.

"I think I'm dying, Pedro."

"No, no. Don't say that. It isn't true. And get some rest. Aren't you tired?"

"No. What I'd really like to do is start all over again. Sometimes I think I'm going to die, but deep down I don't believe it. I think about making a fresh start. If Lina would just come back from Spain, it might work."

"Lina's in Spain?"

"Yes. My sister told me yesterday. She went on tour. She's booked in Italy and Spain. I was unconscious, and she went on tour anyway. She had to do it, Pedro. I understand. If she leaves her spot open, someone else will take her place. You don't know how much I love her. She's all I've got."

"How can you say that when she's gone to Europe and left you here dying? Don't let her walk all over you like that!"

"It's just . . . it was so hard on her."

"What was so hard on her?"

Aurelio breathed deeply a few times and started to cry. Tears ran down his cheeks. I let him cry for a while; he was sobbing and mucus clogged up the oxygen tubes in his nose.

"Come on, get hold of yourself. Stop crying and pull yourself together. Those tubes are getting clogged and you're going to die. Take it easy."

"Pedro Juan, I'm a fucking queer."

"What does that have to do with anything? Forget about it."

"The problem is I fell in love with a boy, a tenor who sings duets with Lina. I couldn't help it, he's an Adonis. I liked him too much, and we were together three times. We did everything. He's twenty times more of a fag than I am! But he told her about us."

"What? He told her?"

"Yes. Don't ask me why. He told her. The three of us were at home, rehearsing around the piano, and all of a sudden, the stupid faggot got hysterical and started screaming. He told her that I pushed him down and kissed him and grabbed his dick. He played the victim and cast me as a rapist. Which is a joke, because he lifts weights and he's all muscle. He looks like Charles Atlas."

"Really. Why didn't you pick something up and smash his head in?"

"I couldn't. I wanted to cry, I was so upset. Anyway, Lina didn't give me a chance to do anything. She made such a scene that even the neighbors could hear. She screamed that she had always suspected me, and that I disgusted her. She repeated it over and over, that I disgust her. And she went screaming out of the house to find a lawyer to take care of the divorce. She wanted to go to Europe as a free woman. When I was left alone in that big house, I got too sad and I was so ashamed to think everybody knew . . ."

"Why do you care what other people think, Aurelio? It's your life."

"No, no!"

"And then you poisoned yourself?"

"No. All that happened around noon. By nighttime she still hadn't come back. And I couldn't leave the house. I didn't have the strength to get up from my chair. Then I gathered all the pills I could find in the house and I swallowed them, and I injected air into my veins with a syringe, and I beat myself on the back with a belt. I wished I had a whip so I could flay myself. I wanted to chop myself into pieces, tear myself limb from limb. I don't even like to think about it. I was out of my mind."

"Well, try to relax now."

"I need Lina to come back. I know we can make a fresh start. I'm crazy about her, Pedro Juan, really crazy about her. I don't know why the fuck I had to fall in love with that guy—that hypocrite, that fucking traitor!"

Everything was coming out in great sobbing gulps. He was raving, barely able to speak. Then he was too quiet, lying there with his eyes closed. I called the nurse. He was unconscious again. She took his pulse and went running to find a stretcher. They took him back into intensive care. When they went in with him, I was stopped at the door.

"Wait there! You can't come in."

Inside I could hear people running and a frightened voice shouting, "His heart has stopped, it's stopped! A defibrillator! Where's the defibrillator?"

And then it was all too much, and I broke down and cried like a baby. A woman came up to me, touched me on the shoulder, and said, "You must be strong, my son. Do you believe?" I turned and glared at her. I think she had a rosary and a Bible in her hand.

"The fuck I'll be strong, lady! Go to hell and leave me alone!"

1·8 / Giving Up Good Habits

We talked for a few hours on the Malecón, and the longer we sat there, the more we liked each other. We made jokes and laughed at them together. By one in the morning, it was as if we had known each other forever. We were quiet for a while. Staring at her, I started to get a serious hard-on. Then I put my arms around her and we kissed. I put my hand on me. She squeezed, and I said, "Well, what should we do now?"

And she said: "Let's go to my place." She picked up her little boy, who had been asleep for a while, and we left.

Miriam lived in a terrible dump, dark and foul-smelling, in a building nearby, at 264 Trocadero. There were people in the doorway to the building. The room was ten by thirteen feet. In the back there was a tiny space for a kerosene stove, and I had to stand hunched over, because a wooden platform with a ladder cut the room in half. The bed was on top. She put the boy down in one corner, and we took up the rest of the space, fucking frantically for hours. She liked me to treat her tenderly. Or a little tenderly, at least; she kept telling me that no man had ever fucked her that way. "Most men don't even wait for me to come. They come themselves, and that's it."

Just as we were in the middle of things, stones and dust started to rain down on us. "My god, the place is collapsing!"

"It won't, don't worry. This happens all the time."

I got scared anyway, and I left. I went back to the Malecón. I bought a bottle of *aguardiente* from some guy. I drank a little, and the guy came up to me again.

"Hey, man, if you want marijuana, I have some nearby. I can bring it to you right now."

"Brother, I know you're out here trying to make a buck, but this shit is poison. If the marijuana is anything like it . . ."

"No, no, it's good; the grass I guarantee. Come on, I'll fix you up, you light one up, and if you don't like it, you don't have to pay."

"All right, fine."

By four o'clock in the morning, I was floating, what with the rotgut and the grass. But the black dealer wouldn't let me go. He was waiting until I was so high he could strip me of everything I owned. He talked on and on until I told him to go to hell and I went back to 264 Trocadero. I still had half of the *aguardiente* and one blunt. I woke her up. She drank, she smoked, and we fucked a little more.

Miriam was a mulatta, not very tall, underfed but pretty and well-proportioned. I don't like skinny women, all skin and bones, or ones who are too fat, either. Miriam could have used another five or six pounds. She was thirty-one. She had a two-year-old son and a husband who, as she put it, was "as black as a crow," and who was in jail, serving a ten-year sentence. He'd been there for two years, ever since he tried to kill a policeman. He must have been the boy's father, because the boy was very dark too, much darker than his mother. The best thing about Miriam was her shamelessness. She told me all about the other men she had been with, in full detail.

For a while, she hustled tourists on the Malecón and in the hotels of Central Havana. One day she said, "If only you could have seen me in those days, sugar, I was nice and round, with a gorgeous butt, but I got mixed up with my black man, because I'm crazy about blacks. I really am! And with him, jailbird and all, I had the boy. Don't be mad, but he's my macho; you're very sweet, but he's got something and I don't know what it is . . . I don't know how to explain it. If they give him a pass, you'll have to get out. Sometimes he comes on a surprise weekend visit." After she gave birth, she had no one to watch the baby, so she quit hustling. She was poor again.

Her lack of shame approached vulgarity. And I liked that. I kept getting cruder myself. She liked her black men as black as could be, so she could feel superior to them. She'd tell me, "They're pigs, but I say, 'Black man, get down!' and I'm on top because I'm as light as cinnamon." Actually, she was even lighter than cinnamon and she judged everyone that way; the darker you were, the lower on the scale, the lighter you were, the higher. I tried to explain otherwise, but she wouldn't change her mind. Well, it was all the same to me. She could believe whatever she wanted. I had spent my life as a fucking journalist, imagining when I began that I'd be master of the truth, someone who changed people's ideas, but I couldn't think that way anymore.

For more than twenty years as a journalist, I was never allowed to write with a modicum of respect for my readers, or even the slightest regard for their intelligence. No, I always had to write as if stupid people were reading me, people who needed to be force-fed ideas. And I was rejecting all that. Damning to hell all the elegant prose, the careful avoidance of anything that might be morally or socially offensive. I couldn't keep upholding propriety or behaving properly, smiling and nice, well-dressed, shaved, spritzed with cologne, my watch always keeping the right time. And believing all that was inevitable, believing everything lasts forever. No. I was learning that nothing lasts forever.

I felt at home in that stinking building, with people who weren't the slightest bit educated or intelligent, who knew nothing about anything, and who solved everything, or fucked it up worse than it had been before, with shouts, insults, violence, and fists. That's how it was. To hell with everything.

I was there for a while. I like Trocadero. Lezama Lima lived a little farther down, at 162. He died in 1976. There's a plaque next to the door, but only some of the oldest neighbors could still remember him in 1994. "Oh, the fat old man who lived here? Yes, he was very elegant. He always wore a suit and tie, and his wife was crazy. Wasn't he a faggot?"

Lezama often ate at a pizzeria nearby, Bella Napoles. Now they don't even have cooking fuel. In front of the pizzeria, on a patch of dry ground, they've built an old-fashioned wood stove. They cook a little fish soup and rice there, as best they can. Beginning at dawn, Miriam would stand in line, and by noon she was able to buy some food. That was what we lived on.

When the septic tank overflowed, the room became too repellent for me. The stinking black water crept down the corridor of the building. It was like that for a day or two until it drained back into the tank. The women cleaned up a little, cursing everything they could think of, beginning with the first black man to come through the door while they were there. Miriam's kid began to have asthma attacks. She said it was because he was allergic to the shit in the tank. And she took him to a *santera*, but I never asked what the *santera* told her or what was ordered for the cure. The boy was still around, barefoot and half-naked, living exposed to the shit in the tank and having his asthma attacks at night.

When there were heavy rainstorms, everyone trembled in fear; because the building was so old, it was built of bricks, sand, and lime, no cement. The floods of the Caribbean are biblical. They can last for days, with the rain coming in bursts. And more and more cracks riddled the walls. Pieces of wall fell to the ground. During the rainy spell, I was afraid the whole place would collapse and crush us all. Everyone was afraid, and none of us could sleep. The old ladies murmured prayers under their breath.

I was living there with Miriam because I didn't have anywhere else to go. There was nowhere, better or worse, for me to be. The sex was good. She'd sell whatever she could find, make a little money, and keep us alive a while longer. She worked her way under my skin, that woman. There was something primal about her. She lived exclusively for me and her son. She had the old belief in man as a creature of leisure and woman as a beast of burden. It turned her on when I'd come home sweaty, dirty, unshaven. It turned her on to imagine me as a savage male with a permanent, twenty-four-hour erection. It turned her on just to think of herself as my woman, a woman I had to defend from the covetousness of other men. She dressed provocatively, outlining her mound, exposing her belly button, hinting at her nipples. She liked it when men said vulgar things to her, which she'd later repeat in my ear when we made love, and I'd get turned on too. Then she'd ask me to hit her. She liked to be beaten and when she felt a couple of slaps on her face, she'd come.

She could always get money or food. All I'd have to say was, "I'm dying for a drink of rum." She wouldn't say a word. She'd go out, and a little while later, she'd be back with a bottle and a pack of cigarettes. I didn't treat her badly, but she mistook that for love, and she told me that no one had ever treated her kindly in her life. No one. I was the first to caress her, and I was nice to her and said sweet things to her. I didn't want to fall in love again. I'd had enough of love. Love is all mixed up with submission and surrender, and I couldn't be submissive anymore or surrender myself to anything or anyone.

At last I found a job at a radio station, but they wouldn't let me be an announcer, which is what I would have liked. I just had to write public service announcements which were inserted into the regular programming. Stupid appeals to people to stop smoking, not to drive drunk, to prevent children's household accidents. Educational, public-spirited bulletins, in other words—it drove me crazy to write them. Clearly no one listened to them, because people still smoked, got drunk, and rushed frantically to hospitals with their injured children.

But the director of the station—she was a mulatta and an evil daughter of Ochún, but she spoke German and liked to pose as elegant and refined—would tell me the bulletins were sound and practical. That's how she always described them. And I couldn't stand to hear it.

Ever since then I've hated those two words: sound and practical. They are pedantic and false. They only serve to hide the truth. Everything is unsound and impractical. All of history, all of life, every single era has been unsound and impractical. We, ourselves. Each one of us is unsound and impractical by nature, but we curb our instincts and return to the fold like good sheep, and fit ourselves with reins and bridles.

I had been living a double life for a long time: sound and practical at the radio station, unsound and impractical at the building with Miriam. I still didn't feel free, but I was making progress. The truth is, I have no interest in any kind of straight and narrow life, no interest in anything that moves smoothly from one point to the next, tracing a route that clearly begins in one place and ends somewhere else. No. There's no use trying to be sound and practical or to live along a precisely plotted path. Life is a game of chance.

I spent months hauling bags of cement and buckets of mortar. By the end of the day, I was a wreck, but Miriam would be waiting for me all sweet and with a little rum and something to eat, just like when I had an easier job writing drivel for the radio station. Miriam was a lifesaver. We'd have a little rum, and she'd get me going again, and we'd fuck like two lunatics. I wouldn't shower until late at night. She liked my sweat, my "man smell," she called it. It was a strong smell, because she wouldn't let me use deodorant.

At forty-five, I knew I wasn't going to hold up much longer working as hard as I was in the sun, with Miriam—she was twenty years younger—squeezing the jism out of me once or twice a day, and me eating just a little bit of rice and fish. I could see I'd get sick. My body lets me know when things aren't right. My kidneys started to ache.

Then an old friend from my journalism days spotted me on the street and wanted to help me out. I was strong, but I had a kind of wasted and malnourished look. She said, "Pedro Juan, I want to sell a refrigerator. I'll settle for ten thousand pesos. Find me a buyer." We went to her house to check it out, and it was fine. You could ask fifteen thousand pesos for it. Okay. I'd make five thousand for myself, and that was three years' salary for Pedro Juan, construction worker.

Well, it was either sell it or die of dehydration lugging cement and bricks. I had been stealing all kinds of things from the site: cement, tools, scrollwork, bronze door knockers. Someone once said (who it was, I don't know) that property is theft. It isn't the same to steal from people in power who have plenty, more than enough, and who don't even realize what it is they're missing, as it is to steal a wrench from some poor guy who runs a bicycle repair shop and is as screwed as you are.

Anyway, that helped me survive. I sold those things, and we got along a little better. Then I spent a while hanging around a luxury boutique owned by an Italian queen in Miramar. I don't know who the fuck was buying fancy four-hundred-dollar dresses in Cuba in 1994. But the bitch sold them somehow. My scheme was a bust. No one had the brains to break into such a well-protected store. I was surrounded by morons. Well, that's why they were so screwed: because they were so dumb. And that's why they were so dumb: because they were so screwed.

So I decided to sell the refrigerator. Anyway, it suited me to leave Havana for a while, since while I was lurking around the boutique a policeman kept hassling me, always the same guy, like a shadow. He asked for my ID, checked up on me in the system, and discovered that I had been kicked out of journalism, among other things; that I was practically wiped out but that I was still holding tight to a little scrap of wood in the surf, barely keeping my head above water to breathe. The bastard figured out that I was casing the boutique, not that it wasn't obvious, and he threatened me with preventive detention, which is a great invention; they jail you just because they have a feeling you'll do something bad. It's as if they know it by telepathy. And that way they protect you from yourself.

He was a twisted guy, with the soul of a soldier for hire, someone whose brain had been well injected with the illusion of his own power. It's the only way to turn people into mercenaries: by convincing them they're part of the power structure. When the truth is they're not even allowed to approach the throne. That's why they're chosen from among the most backward types or the most twisted, fucked-up ones. After years go by, they're left with an incredible sense of failure and defeat, of time wasted. They've enjoyed the power of weapons, the stick in the hand, of lording it over their fellow citizens and humiliating them and beating them and shoving them into cells. Finally, some of them understand, with their livers shot, that they're miserable beasts, club in hand. But by then they're so scared, they can't let go.

I left for Baracoa. In those days, people in the country had more cash. There was nothing to buy, and they saved their money up. They didn't realize that their shitty bills were losing value and would turn into a big puddle of salt and water.

I took a few swings through town to get my bearings. There were fewer police than in Havana. It's always been that way. In the capital, they turn the screws tighter. In big cities, people are restless.

By nighttime I was back at Hayda's house. I hadn't seen her for several months. The last time we talked, she and Jorge Luis were already at a breaking point. They couldn't have children. He spent his life consumed by love and possession (two concepts which, in the tropics, are too frequently confused, resulting in boleros and crimes of passion). And he was insanely jealous. "He won't let me live," she told me. Around that time, he caught her talking to a guy in a park who put his arm around her shoulders and squeezed tight. Jorge Luis ran home, got a knife, and came after her in the street, shouting like a maniac. When they made it home, she grabbed another knife, confronted him, screamed at him too, and in that way managed to seize control. It all ended up in bed, because he got turned on when she took the knife away from him, and when she slapped him to snap him out of his hysterics. From that moment on, she was in charge and she did whatever she wanted, no interference. Jorge Luis spent all his time getting drunk and smoking when he could, and he wanted to fuck her three times a day. But she wouldn't let him. She wanted to have fun, but she didn't dare break things off with Jorge Luis. She wanted to go to Havana and whore

around a little, hang around the hotels until some tourist took a liking to her and paid her in dollars. "Pedro Juan, there's no other way
for me to have fun, drink, buy clothes. My husband is no good, and
every day it's worse with that shitty job of his. There's never any
food at home. Nothing, Pedro Juan. Can't you see how skinny I've
gotten?"

She was excited when she saw me this time. He less so. They
were broke, worse off than I was. They had a tiny shack built of
half-rotten boards in a slum on the outskirts of the city. They were
two fine blacks, tall, each about thirty-five years old. They made a
nice couple, and every night a neighborhood Peeping Tom would
sneak onto their patio to listen to their sighs and moans.

They had practically nothing: very little clothing, a table, a few
chairs, a bed, a gas stove, and a bicycle. In the yard they had a two-
or three-month-old piglet and a tiny, skinny black dog, with huge
ears and the face of a grinning lunatic. That was all.

It was a pretty spot. From the patio, past the fence, rolled an
enormous green field. And in the distance was the red dusk, now
that it was almost night. I gave Jorge Luis some money, and he went
off to a place nearby to buy a bottle of *aguardiente* from somebody
who had an illegal still and made quality liquor, from sugar. As soon
as he left the room, the temptation was too much, and we couldn't
resist: Hayda and I embraced, we kissed, we inhaled each other. I
felt her up; she was almost naked in short, tight shorts and a tiny
bathing suit top. It was very hot, and we were sweating. We sat on
the patio again, cooling down, and Jorge Luis came back with the
aguardiente. He had money left over, and he had bought some plan-
tains. Hayda fried them, and all three of us had something to drink.
We danced a little. The bottle was empty, and I gave more money
to Jorge Luis. He brought us more *aguardiente* and cigarettes. He almost caught us kissing, and me with my middle finger rubbing her
clit. The smell of her yearning wetness was driving me crazy.

We kept on with the second bottle. Hayda only wanted to dance
with me. She was incredibly hot, and she had me in a state of con-

tinuous erection. She was rubbing herself up against me. And Jorge Luis kept sitting on the patio, pretending he didn't notice, acting like he didn't care. We were headed for trouble, but I didn't want to mix things up with Jorge Luis. On the contrary, I only wanted the two of them to help me sell the refrigerator, and for them to make a little money too.

But the flesh is weak. At least mine is weak, and sinful. And I suppose it's the same for everyone when it comes to flesh, but it bothers people to realize it, and so they've come up with the concepts of *decency* and *indecency*. Except that nobody knows where the boundary is between *decent* people and *indecent* ones.

And so I was urging Hayda on, whispering in her ear, "All three of us, together. Don't you always say his is too big and you can't take it in the ass? Well, me from behind and him in front, and you'll come like a madwoman."

And she said, "No. No. I'd do it, but he's too shy, and jealous. This is going to end badly. Stay on the patio. Don't come in the house."

She went over to Jorge Luis and caressed him and kissed him until she had him all hot. They went in and right away I heard the bed squeaking and her whispering loudly, so I could hear it in the quiet of the country night, "You're torturing me, sweetie, stick it to me all the way." And then she groaned and came again and again and she begged him to bite her, until together the two of them finished me off. I was stroking myself slowly, listening to them, and rubbing saliva on the head of my prick so it would slide easily. There was one glass of *aguardiente* left. Drinking it down in a gulp, I went in. The two of them were asleep on the bed, naked, drunk, gorgeous, and breathing calmly. I had to hold myself back from slipping into bed with them too. The drunkenness started to play games with me: everything was spinning around. I turned off the light and stretched out on the floor, grabbing a dirty pair of pants that was on a chair to use as a pillow. I fell asleep instantly but woke up a few hours later in the middle of the absolute darkness of the countryside, with the mosquitoes and the heat and the damp. I woke with a jump, with a parched mouth and a terrible feeling of confinement, of claustrophobia, in that tiny airless room. Just as if I were in a small cage, behind bars.

I managed to get a grip, saying to myself, "You're not crazy, breathe slowly and deeply and relax." It happens to me a lot at night: I wake with a jump, feeling trapped, like a wolf. A powerful wolf, exploding with claws and fangs, but immobilized. I think I prayed a little, but a line of Rimbaud crossed my mind and I was distracted from the prayer: "*Je est un autre. Je est un autre.*" In the end I calmed down and slept a little longer. I woke up when the light of dawn began to come in through the cracks. In the shadows I saw them stretched out, too beautiful to be real. I left without making a noise. Scooping a little bit of water from a tank in the yard, I washed my face, rinsed my mouth, and left.

1·10 / Buried in Shit

In those days, I was pursued by nostalgia. I always had been, and I didn't know how to free myself so I could live in peace.

I still haven't learned. And I suspect I never will. But at least I do know something worthwhile now: it's impossible to free myself from nostalgia because it's impossible to be freed from memory. It's impossible to be freed from what you have loved.

All of that will always be a part of you. The yearning to relive the good will always be just as strong as the yearning to forget and destroy memories of the bad, erase the evil you've done, obliterate the memory of people who've harmed you, eliminate your disappointments and your times of unhappiness.

It's entirely human, then, to be engulfed in nostalgia and the only solution is to learn to live with it. Maybe, if we're lucky, nostalgia can be transformed from something sad and depressing into a little spark that sends us on to something new, into the arms of a new lover, a new city, a new era, which, no matter whether it's better or worse, will be different. And that's all we ask each day: not to squander our lives in loneliness, to find someone, to lose ourselves a little, to escape routine, to enjoy our piece of the party.

That's where I was, still. Coming to all those conclusions. Madness lurked, and I eluded its grasp. Too much had happened in too short a time for one person to handle, and I left Havana for a few months. I lived in another city, making some deals, selling a used refrigerator and a few other things, staying with a crazy girl—crazy in the purest sense, unspoiled—who had been in prison many times and was covered in tattoos. The one I liked best was the one she had on the inside of her left thigh. It was an arrow pointing to her sex and lettering that read simply: EAT AND ENJOY. One buttock read: PROPERTY OF FELIPE, and the other: NANCY I LOVE YOU. JESUS was inscribed in big letters on her left arm. And on her knuckles there were hearts enclosing the initials of some of her lovers.

Olga was barely twenty-three, but she had led a wild life: lots of grass, drinking, and every kind of sex. She had syphilis once, but she got over it. My stay with her lasted a month; it was fun. Living in Olga's squalid room was like living in the middle of an X-rated film. And I learned. I learned so much in that month that maybe someday I'll write a *Guide to Perversion*. I went back to Havana with enough money not to have to work for a good long time, but when I got to Miriam's, she was terrified. "Get away from here! He knows everything and he's going to kill you!" She was bruised all over and she had a cut above her left eyebrow. Her husband was released after three years in prison. He didn't serve out his ten-year sentence. And as soon as he got to the building, his friends told him about Miriam and me. He practically beat her to death. Then he found a butcher's knife and swore not to rest until he had slit my throat.

The man was dangerous, so I thought I had better steer clear of Colón until he calmed down. But I had nowhere to go. I went to Ana María's place. I told her my story, and she let me sleep there, on her floor, for a few nights, but the truth was, I was disrupting her romance with Beatriz. I could hear them making love in the dark, Beatriz playing the man's role, and all of that really turned me on. I jerked off until one night I couldn't stand it anymore, and then I went over to their bed with my dick erect and superhard, turned on the light, and said, "Up and at 'em! Let's all three of us get it on now!"

Beatriz was prepared for my attack. She stuck her hand under the bed and pulled out a thick length of electrical cord, the kind with a lead lining, and she threw herself at me like a wild animal. "This is my girlfriend, you faggot, go fuck yourself in your mother's cunt!" I didn't know a woman could be so strong. She hit me savagely. She battered my lips and teeth, she split my nose, and she beat me to the ground, where I lay stunned by the blows of the cable raining on my head. Half-unconscious, I could hear Ana María shouting, begging her to leave me alone. Then they tossed a little cold water in my face and dragged me out into the corridor of the building. They dumped me there and closed the door. Beatriz kept repeating, "Bastard, ungrateful son of a bitch. You can't trust anyone, Ana María, anyone."

I was sprawled there for a long time. I didn't have the strength to get up, and my ribs and back hurt. At last I made an effort and managed to get to my feet. If Beatriz happened to come to the door and see I was still there, she would lay into me again, mercilessly. She was stronger and tougher than a trucker. I walked for a while around Industria, and I stretched out on a bench in Parque La Fraternidad. People thought I was a drunk, and they went through my pockets, looking for something to steal. Every half hour, someone patted me down, but I had hidden my money in a book at Ana María's place.

When morning came, I went to the emergency hospital. They fixed me up a little. I didn't have a penny, and it was too soon to try to get my money from Ana María's place. It seemed best to wait a few days.

By now I was battered, dirty, in need of a shave, and desperate enough to beg. I went to the church of La Caridad, in Salud y Campanario, sat on the steps by the door looking hungry and forlorn, and stretched out my hand. Little good it did me. All the money was going to an old woman who was there already. She had a picture of San Lázaro and a small cardboard box printed with the message that she was fulfilling a vow. When the church was locked that night, I had just a few coins and I was desperately hungry. It had been more than twenty-four hours since I had anything to eat.

I begged at a few houses for food, but starvation was fierce everywhere. Everybody was hungry in Havana in 1994. An old black woman gave me a few pieces of cassava and when she looked me in the eye, she said, "What are you doing like this? You're a son of Changó."

"And of Ochún too."

"Yes, but Changó is your father and Ochún your mother. Pray to them, son, and ask for help. They won't let you down."

"Thank you, mother."

That was how I spent the next few days, until my aches and pains were gone. Then I picked up an iron rod in the street, hid it in my pants, under my shirt, and headed for Ana María's place. It was mid-morning, and I calculated that Beatriz would be at work.

I knocked, and Ana María opened the door. She tried to shut it again in my face, but I blocked it with my iron rod. Pushing my way in, I swept her to one side, and she screamed and went running to get a knife out of the sink.

"Ana María, calm down. I'm not going to do anything. I'm going to pick up something I left here, and then I'll go."

"You didn't leave anything here. Get out! Get out! All men are the same, bullies! If Beatriz were here, she'd smash your head in, you bastard. Get out!"

By then I had the book in my hand, I opened it, and there was my money, shining up at me. I put it in my pocket and left. She quieted down all of a sudden, and I tried to disappear as fast as I could. If she thought to scream for someone to stop me, saying I had robbed her, then I'd be screwed.

The first thing I did was buy a bottle of rum. It had been a long time since I'd had a drink. I went to an acquaintance's house and bought it from him. It was black-market rum, expensive but good. I opened the bottle, and we had a few drinks. He asked me why I was so fucked up, and I told him part of the story. Not much of it.

"Why don't you find yourself some old guy to take care of? Around the corner there's a sick old man who lives alone. He's close to eighty years old and he's a bastard, but if you're patient, you could make him behave. His wife died a few months ago, and he's about to die himself of starvation and filth. Get yourself in his good graces, move in with him, take care of him, clean him up, bring him a little food, and when he dies, you can have the house. You'd be better off there than on the street."

We finished the bottle. I bought another one, and I went to see the old man. He was a tough old guy. A very old black man. Ravaged but not completely destroyed. He lived at 558 San Lázaro, and he spent every day sitting silently in his wheelchair in the doorway, watching the traffic, breathing in gasoline fumes, and selling boxes of cigarettes slightly cheaper than in the stores. I bought a pack from him, opened it, and offered it to him, but he refused. I offered him rum, but he wouldn't take that either. I was in a good mood. Now that I had a little money in my pocket, a bottle of rum, and a pack of cigarettes, I was beginning to see the world in a new light. I told the old man that, and we talked for a while. I had half a bottle of rum in me, and that made me chatty and entertaining. An hour and a few drinks later (finally he agreed to have a drink with me), the old man gave me an in: he used to work in the theater.

"Where? At the Martí?"

"No. At the Shanghai."

"Ah. And what did you do there? I've heard it was a strip joint. Is it true that they shut it down as soon as the Revolution began?"

"Yes, but I hadn't been working there long. I was Superman. There was always a poster just for me: 'The one and only Superman, exclusive engagement at this theater.' Do you know how long my prick was when it was fully erect? Twelve inches. I was a freak. That's how they advertised me: 'A freak of nature . . . Superman . . . twelve inches—thirty centimeters—one foot of Superprick . . . appearing now . . . Superman!' "

"Was it just you on stage?"

"Yes, just me. I would come out wrapped in a red and blue velvet cape. In the middle of the stage, I'd stop in front of the audience, fling open the cape, and there I'd be, naked, with my prick limp. I would sit in a chair, and it would seem I was looking at the audience. What I was really looking at was a white girl with blond hair who was sitting in the wings, on a bed. That woman made me crazy. She would masturbate and when she was hot, a white man would join her and she'd do everything. Everything. It was amazing. But no one saw them. It was just for me. Watching that, my prick would swell to the bursting point, and without ever touching it, I would come. I was in my early twenties, and I shot out such powerful jets of come that they reached the first row of the audience and showered all those bastards."

"And you did that every night?"

"Every night. Without missing a one. I made good money, and when I came in those long spurts and groaned with my mouth open, my eyes rolled back in my head, and got up out of the chair dazed like I was stoned, the bastards fought over the right to frolic in the showers of my sperm like carnival streamers, and then they would toss money onto the stage and stamp their feet and shout, 'Bravo, bravo, Superman!' They were my fans and I was their favorite performer. On Saturdays and Sundays, I earned more because the theater filled up. I became so famous that tourists from all over the world came to see me."

"And why did you give it up?"

"Because that's life. Sometimes you're up and sometimes you're down. By the time I was thirty-two or so, the jets of come weren't as strong and then there were times when I lost concentration and sometimes my prick would droop a little and straighten up again. Lots of nights, I couldn't come at all. By then I was half-crazy, because I had spent so many years straining my brain. I took Spanish fly, ginseng; in the Chinese pharmacy on Zanja, they made me a tonic that helped, but it made me jittery. No one could understand the toll my career was taking on me. I had a wife. We were together for our whole lives, more or less, from the time I came to Havana until she died a few months ago. Well, during all of that time, I was never able to come with her. We never had children. My wife didn't see my jism in twelve years. She was a saint. She knew that if we fucked as God willed and I came, then at night I wouldn't be able to do my number at the Shanghai. I had to save up my jism for twenty-four hours to do the Superman show."

"Incredible self-control."

"It was either control myself or die of hunger. It wasn't easy to make money in those days."

"It's still hard."

"Yes. The poor are born to be shit on."

"And what happened then?"

"Nothing. I stayed at the theater for a while longer, doing filler; I put together a little skit with the blond girl, and people liked it. They advertised us as 'Superprick and the Golden Blonde, the horniest couple in the world.' But it wasn't the same. I earned very little. Then I joined a circus. I was a clown, I took care of the lions, I was a base-man for the balancing acts. A little bit of everything. My wife was a seamstress, and she cooked. For years, that's what we did. In the end, life is crazy. It takes many unexpected turns."

We had another drink from the bottle. He let me stay there that night, and the next day I got him some porn magazines. Superman was a professional Peeping Tom. The only guy in the world who had made a living watching other people fuck. We had really hit it off, and I thought I'd give him a thrill with those magazines. He leafed through them.

"These have been outlawed for thirty-five years. In this country a person is practically forbidden to laugh. I used to like these. And my wife did too. We liked to jerk off together looking at the white girls."

"Was she black?"

"Yes, but she was very refined. She knew how to sew and embroider, and she worked as a cook for some rich people. She wasn't just any old black girl. But she followed my lead. In bed she was as crazy as I was."

"And don't you like these magazines anymore, Superman? Keep them, they're a gift."

"No, son, no. What good will they do me now? . . . Look."

He lifted up the small blanket that covered his stumps. He no longer had prick or balls. Everything had been amputated along with his lower limbs. It was all chopped off, all the way up to his hip bones. There was nothing left. A little rubber hose came out of the spot where his prick used to be and let fall a steady drip of urine into a plastic bag he carried tied at his waist.

"What happened to you?"

"High blood sugar. The gangrene crept up my legs. And little by little, they were amputated. They even took my balls. Now I really don't have any balls! Ha ha ha. I used to be ballsy. The Superman of the Shanghai! Now I'm fucked, but no one can take away what I've had."

And he laughed heartily. Not even a hint of irony. I got along well with that tough old man, who knew how to laugh at himself. That's what I'd like: to learn to laugh at myself. Always, even if they cut off my balls.

1:11 / All-Consuming Loves

I've always lived as if there were no end in sight. What I mean is, I'm continually destroying things and building them back up again. It's never occurred to me that I might end up crazy or suicidal. Maybe because it's not my way to cultivate, preserve, or foresee.

Little by little, the weight on my back kept growing. Too much slag.

And so it was a twisted instinct for survival that got me into the habit of taking advantage of everything and everybody. I always have to be keeping track of things, calculating how much I give out and what I'm paid in return. I used to think I was a decent guy, but my mania for mathematics was getting the best of me and making me miserable. Then a beautiful girl stepped into my life, fixed her green eyes on me, and sent me a telepathic message of love, and I believed in her.

I had to believe. When you're as lonely as I was, you're very quick to pick up a signal like that, and you transfer it carefully to your heart, where you deposit it, and you're happy and you think your problems are finally solved.

Well, I never got very far with her. Every day she'd show up where I worked. She inspected fire extinguishers, and there were hundreds of extinguishers. She was a beautiful woman, dark skin, short hair, languorous green eyes, a firm ass, and big, beautiful breasts.

For several days we watched each other in silence, until I made up my mind to act. She waited felinely for me, then purred a little. I asked her out that very night. We went to a bar, ordered a few drinks, and almost without speaking, we kissed and embraced. I couldn't keep my eyes—or my neurons, each and every one of my neurons—off her big, beautiful, twenty-year-old breasts. My erection persisted, I paid, and we left.

I had a nice place in the neighborhood, and I was elated and impatient. She was too. We began to undress in a frenzy, but when she took off her bra, her breasts hung down to her waist. They were big, flabby, soft, two huge bags of skin, like something on an old wet nurse.

It was incredible that someone so young and beautiful should have breasts like that. I tried anyway. But I couldn't do it. I couldn't even get it halfway up, maybe not even a quarter of the way up. She was terribly upset. I think she was insulted. We got dressed and we left.

After that, she would never go out with me again, but she had to keep inspecting the extinguishers, and little by little, we became friends. It was many years before we could be friends.

1·12 / Marooned in No-Man's-Land

I was back from Málaga, and I was sleeping around a lot. Málaga was a great blow to my heart, but I'd rather not discuss it. Not yet. It'll be a few years before I can talk about what really happened to me in Málaga. All I can say now is that dreams are bullshit. We humans should stamp out our dreams, stand firm, and say, "Fuck, that's more like it! My roots go down deep. Let the wind blow all it wants." It's the only way to get through life with a minimum of breakdowns and without getting swamped—at most you take on just a little bit of dirty bilge water.

So I was on the prowl, drinking lots of rum and barely sleeping. But the truth is, my messing around wasn't doing much good anymore. What I needed was to put down roots and forget about tenderness and the need for someone to love and all that kind of thing. No more. I was tough, I was growing a thick skin, and I knew I had a woman waiting for me in Rio and another in Buenos Aires, not to mention the mulattas and blacks of Havana. In fact, I had complications enough with all those women, after the beating I took in the Mediterranean.

I lay down for a while at noon, but my room is on the eighth floor. There are other rooms up here too, full of people like me. Or people who are even poorer, practically illiterate. Well, that's what

I'm stuck with. Then two girls came out on the roof and started shouting at some black men who were walking along the Malecón, "Let's see it, come on, there's nothing there! It's tiny. Ha ha ha. Let's see it, let's see it . . . Ooh, it's really black. Come on, come on, pull it out again and let me see it so the police come and get you."

They went on like that for half an hour, screaming from the roof down to the street at the top of their lungs. And I couldn't sleep. Then I went to the door and I said, "Listen, why don't you go down there and jerk those two guys off? Let me sleep, fuck it all."

"Ooh, isn't he the shit, Pedro Juan sleeping in the middle of the day. Why don't you go down and jerk them off yourself, fucking baldy, bourgeois pig?"

"I'm not the one spoiling for a fuck. You two'll each get a jab in the cunt from me if you keep this shit up. Quit fucking around and go to hell."

They had a few more things to say, then they went into their room and put on a salsa tape. I think it was NG La Banda, something like that. But pounding. I thought the orchestra would bring the walls down.

My head started to hurt. It was a good thing I didn't have a pistol handy, because at times like this, my criminal instincts kick in. I got up, seething, my blood boiling. Going out onto the roof again, I sat on the wall for a while. The weather was changing. Whatever this weather was, it looked like the real thing, full-blown in half an hour. I went back into my shack and a little while later a boy came with a message from Dalia, my downstairs neighbor. I cheered up, because if the storm blew my shingles off and left me without a roof, at least I wouldn't be there to see it. And that's something, anyway. There's a difference between slow torture and a nice swift kick in the balls.

I went downstairs. Dalia was an old lady, near death. But she didn't realize it. She lived on the seventh floor. She wanted me to fix a rotten, hingeless door for her. The door, which opened onto a ruined balcony, was set in a cracked wall bare of plaster. I fixed the door shut as best I could, but it started to rain hard, in sheets, and water was coming in everywhere.

"Dalia, if it keeps raining like this, the wall is going to collapse on us."

"Holy Mother of God! Don't say things like that, child."

"Whether I say them or not, it's going to collapse. Say a few prayers and let's see if we can make it last a while longer."

"The problem is that the people who live in this building are trash. They've neglected the place and it's falling to pieces."

"Dalia, the building is old, and no one ever repairs it. That's why it's collapsing."

"They've let it fall apart. The government's abandoned it. I can say what I want, since now I'm so old they won't do anything to me. But listen to me, child. You've traveled, and you know. There's no place in the world where the government can take care of every-thing. That's why the neighborhood has become what it is. When this place belonged to the owner, the building was a gem. It was a joy to see. I paid ninety pesos a month in rent, but it was worth it because she wouldn't let anyone fix anything themselves, not even a faucet. Nothing. She took care of everything. But only professional people lived here then, teachers and businessmen."

"Well, Dalia, that was another time. Forget it."

"It has to be that way again. Things can't keep falling apart, peo-ple can't always be without work, getting paid for sitting with their arms crossed. Look, I want to show you something. Follow me."

She led me to her room, opened the wardrobe, and took out a few dresses and pairs of shoes, a purse. All new, just purchased.

"And what is this, Dalia?"

"I sold some jewelry and some china and I bought all this for myself. Do you know why? Because we aren't going to be poor and hungry forever. It's already ending. I know it's coming to an end. And a person has to have clothes ready for going out. Strolling clothes. It's not that I'm expecting to find a lover. I'm too old. But you never know, do you? Nobody ever knows."

"Sure, Dalia, it's possible. The last thing you lose is hope."

"That's what I say. The last thing you lose is hope."

We kept talking for a while. The neighbors said she was a virgin. She was eighty-three years old, but she still believed she'd find a boyfriend and get married. She told me her stories all over again, how when she was young she went to Miami for Christmas and how she bought all her clothes and shoes there, in the best stores. And how she played the piano and did embroidery. And how her father, who owned a huge store, and was a stern, overbearing Catalan, died when he was 104 and never let her have a boyfriend, because her suitors were poor, and the old man was waiting for one with money to turn up.

The wind and the water kept getting worse. I went back up to my room and fell asleep. That morning, just before dawn, the wall came detached and it collapsed, after fourteen hours of wind and rain. The crash was heard for blocks around. Though the building had seemed sound, the wall was full of cracks. When the water softened it, it crumbled. The building was like a dollhouse, the kind that's missing a wall and you can see the furniture and everything inside. It didn't seem real. There was a lot of commotion. The firemen pulled two dead bodies out of the debris. But they let us stay. They said the rest of the building was safe, in good shape.

My room wasn't affected because it was on the opposite side of the building from where the wall collapsed. That afternoon I went down to Dalia's apartment. She was terrified. Half of her little house had gone with the wall, and she was left with just the kitchen, the bathroom, one room, and the front door, with a piece of entrance hall. But it was an impressive sight; next to the door an abyss, and thirty meters down, the street. It was a little eerie. All of a sudden, it was as if I had wandered into a nightmare. The old woman couldn't speak. I left her there, petrified, sitting in a chair.

Then I forgot about her. I kept on with my careless life. A month later I was told the old lady had died. It was another old woman who lived across the hall from her who informed me, "Dalia practically killed herself. From the time the wall collapsed, she stopped eating and she huddled back in there. She sat down to die in that chair and she wouldn't even get up to drink a glass of water. I tried to do something for her once or twice, but she kicked me out of the apartment and told me not to meddle."

I wasn't too bothered by the whole business. I hope I make it to eighty-three with a dream or two intact, even if it's the foolish dream of finding myself a girlfriend and getting married, believing that love is possible and that poverty and hunger will soon be things of the past.

1·13 / Great Spiritual Beings

The Mexican was a believer, and he liked to spend long stretches in Tepoztlán. According to him, people from all over the world went there to charge themselves with cosmic energy.

"I was in Tepoztlán once and I didn't feel anything," I said to him.

"Sure. What's important isn't whether something is being transmitted or not; it's knowing how to receive," he replied. Then he told me that there were three places on the planet that attracted emanations. The guy came to Havana direct from Tepoztlán. He stopped by my place to bring me a letter from some friends in Morelia. We talked for a while. He told me he didn't have much money, and he stayed for several weeks. I assumed he was poor and didn't come from money, though sometimes I suspected he was the son of super-rich assholes, someone who had nothing better to do with his time.

In the afternoon, he would assume yoga positions and meditate, and for the rest of the day, he'd read or stroll slowly along the Malecón, by the sea. He ate rye bread and drank herbal tea made from herbs he had picked himself on the slopes of the enormous rocky peak that towers over Tepoztlán. The simple life. It's nice to have a silent, spiritual young roommate, who feeds himself and doesn't get in your way. That's why I let him stay so long, sleeping on the floor on one of those Indian wool blankets. He wasn't even bothered by the cockroaches. As soon as the light was off, they would come out from every nook and cranny, ready for a stroll, frolicsome and in good spirits. He said that was all right. He had a theory about peaceful cohabitation, and he explained how when he meditated and managed to ascend to beta (or alpha, I can't remember which), he could feel the bugs' positive vibrations.

The guy didn't talk much. He had a few things to say about silence, concentration, and inner energy, but I never paid much attention because there was no way I could keep silent, concentrate on meditation, or wait for inner energy to solve my food and money problems. At the time I had a little business involving empty beer cans. I'd pick the cans out of Miramar dumpsters, especially the ones around the embassies and foreign business offices. Sometimes I'd collect more than two hundred cans in a morning. I'd scrape the top off and sell them for a peso each at ice stands. The stands sold a runny, almost sugarless grapefruit ice, but people waited for half an hour to buy it, and they bought cans from me because the stands didn't even have paper cups; they took the shitty stuff and thanked God for their good fortune, because that ice was like a blessing in Havana in the nineties. In the rest of the country, there wasn't even water to drink. Nothing. Hunger from start to finish. But in Havana there's always more get-up-and-go. Take this can business, for example. People would look at me with disgust when I rummaged through the dumpsters. A few times, Public Health inspectors cornered me. They said that the cans were dirty and hassled me about epidemics and things like that. But I wouldn't fight back. I'm tired of fighting back. In the end, no matter what happens, I always get screwed. I don't fight back anymore. I play half retard, half moron, and I'm left alone. Sometimes I think if you're poor, it's better to be stupid than smart. A little bit stupid and very tough (a clever beggar is either a brilliant candidate for suicide or a far-flung combatant in the world revolution, or both at once). And no complaining. It does no good to indulge in complaints or tears or self-pity. Not for your sake or anyone else's. Compassion for no one. You've got to train yourself, but it's possible to achieve the right state of mind. After being kicked a thousand times in the ass and balls, at last you learn to be a little bit tough and to face things head on and go on fighting, no matter what. There's no other choice. Is it possible to live any other way?

That's how things were. Me with my cans, and the Mexican getting more spiritual every day. His great obsession was the sea. Sometimes at night we would sit on the roof, and he'd explain how he had to learn to pick up the vibes concentrated at the edge of the ocean (he never said "sea"; people from the continent think in grander terms). Picking up the best vibes of the cosmos from a rocky mountain top wasn't the same as picking them up on the enormous warm blue expanse of the Caribbean. He went to the beach for a while. I think he rented a room in Santa María. He told me he'd be fasting and meditating on the sand for a few days, in some remote corner of the beach. I paid no attention. But I did try to give him some helpful advice. "Do what you want. But you're going to fucking starve if all you eat is bread and herbs. Eat something else before you go. Don't you like rice and beans?" He smiled condescendingly, clasped both my hands in his, and left.

Four days later, he was back, accompanied by a pretty little mulatta with a nice smile and a perfect body. He told me she was sixteen, but her heels were as scaly as old chicken feet. "So much for spirituality," I thought. And I was right. Her name was Grace. Then she told me her name was Greis, not Grace, and she showed me her identification, which she kept on her at all times, since the police request it twenty times a day from blacks, and even more often if they look like hustlers.

The guy had brought back a bag stuffed with two bottles of rum, cheese, cookies, chocolate bars, and tinned ham. No more silence, and no trace of the herbs or the rye bread. Grace found some salsa on the radio, we opened a bottle of rum, and an hour later we were all feeling fine. She danced with me, letting slip more than she had until then.

"Oh, if only this idiot would marry me and get me out of here," she murmured in my ear, after asking me to fix her something with ham and cheese. She didn't want to make it herself, "so he doesn't think I'm after him for his money or his food. But I'm starving."

"Ah, girl, don't kid yourself. How could you marry that boy? Can't you see he's no good, can't you see he's practically a moron?"

"He doesn't even know how to fuck, but I'll teach him. The worst of it is that he has a tiny prick. I can't even feel it. But it doesn't matter. He already told me he wants to marry me. He's head over heels!"

"What did you do to him, girl?"

"I drove him crazy. I fucked him up and down. I'm addicted to pricks, sweetie. When I see a prick I like, I lose my head. His prick I don't like, but I psych myself up and get over with it."

We finished the bottle, and at Grace's suggestion, we decided to go to her place to meet her mother, invite some of her friends back with us, and buy more food and drinks for later.

Grace lived nearby, on Industria. The building wasn't very big. Her whole apartment was smaller than my place: one nine-by-twelve-foot room crowded with furniture, plaster dolls on the walls. A wooden ladder led up to another makeshift room where she slept with her mother, a fat, good-natured woman who worked in a pizzeria and treated us like royalty. The Mexican wouldn't leave Grace alone: he was all over her like an octopus. I hate shiteaters. But what can you do? They spring up where you least expect them.

At last Grace managed to disentangle herself for a minute from the leech and she went around to some of the other rooms in the building. A few times, she shouted for me to come to the door. Her little friends looked at me, whispered to each other, and in the end I was stuck without a date. I'm not so ugly. I don't know what the hell they thought was wrong with me that afternoon. At last we said goodbye to the fat lady, who even offered her home to the Mexican. "You can stay here if you want. I'll sleep at the neighbor's, and you and Greis will have plenty of room." The woman's one concern was to get Greis to Mexico however she could, or into some asshole's house, where Greis could sit and wait for dollars to fall into her lap. After we left, she probably made an offering to Ochún, who was sitting up in a corner in her yellow vestments with her wicked gaze, always ready to put her charm and devilry to good use.

When we left the building, Grace said to me, "Keep your eye out for a black guy if you want to fuck, because today you're getting nowhere with the chicks." Just then, another of her little friends showed up, a skinny, sweaty white girl, with dirty clothes and bruised, spotty skin. Repellent. Grace whispered something in her ear. The girl glanced at me and asked us to wait for her. She went in to shower. When she came out a little later, she was almost as dirty as she had been before. No soap, most likely. No matter: even being with that filthy girl would be better than jerking off while listening to Grace and the Mexican fucking like crazy.

We went to the Hotel Deauville. The Mexican and Grace went into the store. Mercedes and I waited on the Malecón. She was in a bad mood, and we didn't talk much. She told me that she had just come from Diezmero, where she went to collect some money she was owed, but she wasn't paid, and she ended up fighting with her cousins. "Now I'm stuck without a cent until who knows when. It's not easy, you know." I got the hint. But I played dumb. Skinny, sour, dirty, bad-tempered, stinking, and asking for money. She should have been the one paying me. Just then the lovebirds came out of the hotel with two bulging sacks. Thank goodness. Even if it were only for one night, I could forget the rice and beans and eat something decent.

Back at my room, we put on music, opened the bottles of rum, and the Mexican said he would make some tortillas with ham. But he didn't want Grace to leave his side. She escaped for a minute to give us a pep talk. Coming over to me, she said, "Mercedes is in a bad mood today because she had a fight with some relatives and her day was shot. But give her rum, because when she gets a few drinks in her, she'll fuck anyone. Black, old, fat—it doesn't matter. Whatever. When she's drunk, she's horny as a bitch in heat."

"Listen, don't piss me off. I'm not black or old or fat. What's wrong with you?"

"But you're a deadbeat . . . Don't get mad, honey, but to fuck you a girl's got to be blind. Ha, ha, ha."

"Ah, go fuck yourself, slut. Go back to your moron."

"Slut I may be, but I'll be living the good life in Mexico soon . . . and you won't be . . . sweetie."

This last she said jokingly, but with feeling.

Mercedes was on the roof, looking down at the street. It was almost dark. I brought her a drink. Then I fixed her a plate of Spanish tortilla, bread, and cheese. I tried to talk to her, dance with her. An hour later, she'd drunk I don't know how many glasses of rum, she'd eaten everything she wanted, and she was still as stubborn as a mule. She wouldn't talk, dance, or let me touch her. Meanwhile, Grace got the Mexican hot and fucked him in my bed. To help get things started, I snuck into the room with them and jerked off. In their drunken state, distracted by Grace's fake screams and sighs, they didn't notice me. I went back to Mercedes on the roof. By now I was really smashed. The jerk-off had turned me on, and rum always puts me in the mood. I pulled her to me so I could get her going a little. Her hair was greasy and smelly, but I didn't care. All I wanted was to find a hole, any hole. It made no difference to me whether I fucked her, Grace, or the Mexican. Or all three together.

"Merci, let's go inside. Grace and the Mexican are already fucking. Can't you hear them?"

"Yes, I can hear. Good for them. Let them fuck all they want."

"Sweetie, doesn't anything turn you on? Come on, let's go in," I said, rubbing up against her from behind so she could feel my prick, as stiff as a rod.

"No, no. Get away from me; I don't want you."

And she pushed me away.

"Listen, I've been after you for an hour. What exactly do you want?"

"I want you to go away and leave me alone."

"You don't. You're not serious."

"Yes, I am; how can I put it so you understand? Go away and leave me alone."

"But when I brought you food and rum, you didn't want me to go away, you piece-of-shit whore!"

"Ah, you're the piece of shit! All of that was the Mexican's. You and your motherfucking dick didn't pay for it."

"But this is my home. And you can fuck your mother up the ass."

And right then and there I slapped her twice in the face.

"Go on, get moving. If you don't get out of here right now, I'll kick the shit out of you and bash your head in!"

She tried to hit me back. I hit her harder. And in the middle of the scuffle, some of my neighbors came out onto the roof. So did the Mexican and Grace, half-naked. Grace tried to protect Mercedes, and I shoved her and she fell to the ground, screaming. The Mexican launched himself at me, babbling something about his woman's honor. He tried to hit me, but he got a few cuffs too. The neighbors cheered me on, "Hit him, Pedro Juan, show them all! Hit him harder!" They were enjoying themselves, but I was beside myself with rage. I grabbed Mercedes and Grace, dragged them to the stairs, and pushed them out.

"Fuck you both! Go to hell!"

The Mexican followed after them, pulling on his pants. I tried to hold him back.

"Listen, forget about those sluts and cool it," I said.

"You have no shame, Pedro Juan! You're a fucking loser. But you'll be sorry you went after them like that."

"Kid, you don't know what you've gotten yourself into. Those two bitches will take you for a ride. You're in deep shit."

"You'll be sorry for this. You'll be sorry!"

And he left. I went back to my room. Closing the door so that everyone who was still on the roof would leave, I sat down to have a drink of rum and a smoke. Half an hour later, there was a knock at the door. It was the Mexican and two policemen. The Mexican had come for his things. He even took a leftover egg and a bottle of rum with just two fingers left in it. When he had everything, the police asked me to come with them. The precinct chief wanted to talk to me.

In the chief's office, the Mexican, stumbling drunkenly over his words, accused me of "provoking public epidemics" with my beer cans, and of being a counterrevolutionary.

"Substantiate those charges, sir," said the chief.

"He picks the cans out of dumpsters and then he sells them as containers for food. That's a serious crime against the people of Cuba. And he's a counterrevolutionary because he always says that life here is hard, and the people are hungry."

"Is that all? Well. Regarding the cans, that's a matter for the Department of Public Health. It's not our business. And as far as the counterrevolutionary charges are concerned, it's true that life is hard and people are hungry. How many days have you been in this country, and what hotel are you staying at?"

"I've been here for three weeks, and I'm staying—or I was staying—at his apartment. I'm a tourist. But this man is a counterrevolutionary and a menace to society. You aren't just going to let him go, are you?"

"We're going to listen to what he has to say. Can you tell us what happened?"

I explained in detail. The Mexican was sent out of the room. The chief told me that Grace and Mercedes "are bad news, they're always mixed up in something fishy." The guy relaxed. We talked a while longer.

"This Mexican seems half-queer to me. I don't know, he strikes me as odd. You did the right thing, pal. What made them think they could drink and eat and then run off and fuck some other guy? I would have done the same thing you did. If it had been me, there'd be some broken bones. Go on, go home. And stay away from troublemakers. Good luck with the cans."

I never saw any of them again. Three years have gone by, and I'm still selling cans. Business is good.

1:14 / Down, but Not Out

Martica was half-hysterical. It had been a long time since she had an orgasm when we were together, and she was getting more sullen by the day. She never came to see me anymore. She had never liked me much, but I went to visit her anyway. It had been days since I saw her, and solitude, especially sexual solitude, makes me anxious. She greeted me coolly, and I realized it was time for us to part, but just seeing her gave me a hard-on. Since she was alone, I pulled it out and showed it to her. I thought it would turn her on. I have a beautiful prick, broad, dark, six inches long, with a pink, throbbing head and lots of black hair. The truth is, I like my own prick, balls and pubes too. It's a sinewy, luscious, hard prick. But no. She got hysterical again.

"Put that away, Pedro Juan! If the little girl comes home, what will I do? Come on, don't be a jerk! Put it away!"

I persisted, moving close to her, prick in hand. But she backed away. She put on a please-be-reasonable face and raised her hands, palms out.

"Please, Pedro Juan, calm down. I know you want me, but I don't want you. Calm down. Put that away, get out, and don't come back here again."

"Let's talk, Martica. We can work things out," I said, tucking my prick back in and zipping up my pants.

"No, we can't. Don't hassle me anymore. I don't like men, Pedro Juan! Do I have to spell it out for you? I-don't-like-men-damn-it-I-don't-like-men! So get the hell out of here and leave me alone. Pricks make me sick."

I was crushed. I knew it, but I have the bad habit of conveniently forgetting whatever I'd rather not remember. Until that whatever hits me on the head and knocks me cold. I still dared to ask, "Are you seeing someone?"

"Yes. A girl. And I like her a lot. All I have to do is kiss her and I come. I touch her thigh and I have three orgasms. I don't like pricks! When I fucked you, I always had to think about a woman. So will you please go away and leave me alone!"

"All right. I'll see you later."

"No. Not 'I'll see you later.' Goodbye. I never want to see you again."

I left her house and wandered around for a while. She had already told me her story. But similar things happen to a lot of women, and they don't end up dykes. She grew up in a little town in Villa Clara. Her stepfather was after her for years, always trying to rape her. Her mother didn't want to know anything and accused her of provoking him. It was hell for her at home. She got married when she was sixteen, to escape, but the cure was worse than the disease. On her wedding night she was a virgin, and the guy turned into a wild animal. He was a rough, macho type, twenty-six years old, who fucked her for hours without tenderness or love, taking her everywhere he could. When he saw that she was bleeding from the ass and cunt, it made him even wilder. She was crying with pain and humiliation, and he was drinking rum, his prick stiff, implacable. The shame was even worse because her mother had given her instructions on how to please her husband, and she had followed them to the letter. When they got to the hotel room, she shut herself in the bathroom, washed herself, and put on perfume and makeup and a little red negligee. When she came out, shy and embarrassed, the guy laughed his head off, "You look half-slutty and half-bashful! Why did you put on all that shit?" He was drunk. And he took advantage of his drunkenness to mock her. He ripped everything off her, laughing and cursing. And that was the beginning of the hellish orgy.

Her daughter was born nine months later, and her husband devoted himself to the conquest of all the women in the neighborhood, every single one. He liked married women best. He turned into a real Latin lover, with a gold chain around his neck, a silver bracelet, and white shirts, pants, and shoes. As dumb as an ox. Two neighborhood girls, head over heels in love, got pregnant, and he had two more children. Martica endured it for two years. Then she couldn't stand it anymore. She got a divorce, took her daughter, and went to Havana to live with a bitter, lonely old aunt. The aunt was full of bile, too corrosive to bear for very long. Martica was about to give in and go back to her terrible hometown when the old lady died of a massive heart attack. Hallelujah. When she died, Martica blossomed.

I went back to my room on the roof with its common bathroom, the most disgusting bathroom in the world, shared by fifty neighbors who multiply like rabbits, since most of them are from the east of the island. They come to Havana in clumps, fleeing poverty. In Guantánamo a person joins the police force and then arranges to be transferred to Havana (no Havana native wants to be a policeman in the city), dragging his whole family along. And somehow they all live in a twelve-foot-square room. I don't know how they manage it, but they do. And in the bathroom, shit is piled up to the ceiling. Each day no fewer than two hundred people shit, pee, and wash in that bathroom. There's always a line. Even if you're about to crap in your pants, you have to wait. Lots of people, and I'm one of them, never wait in line: I shit in a piece of paper and I toss the bundle onto the roof of the building next door, which isn't as high. Or into the street. Doesn't matter. Terrible, but that's how it goes. When you're at a low point, you've got to make do.

I sat on my bed, a little depressed. It was almost dark, and it was quiet. On a shelf, I had some mementos: stones, shells, ashtrays, coins, clay miniatures, and a slave's shackle. I found it half-buried in the red soil of a sugarcane plantation, in Matanzas. The wrought iron shackle once pinched the ankle of some black man brought over from Africa. A pathetic cane cutter. No one will ever know what kind of miserable, suffering life he lived under the whip in the vast cane fields of Matanzas. I felt a presence in the room. I had no interest in unwanted company. A shiver ran through me. To clear my senses, I patted a little alcohol on my head. I picked up the shackle, went out on the roof, and threw it far away. It was dark. I don't know where it fell. I patted on more alcohol to clear my head again.

Then I was really alone. The air around me thinned. It was a struggle for me to accept being alone. It was hard for me to learn to be self-sufficient. I still believed it was impossible, or that it was unnatural. "Man is a social being," I had repeated to myself many times. That, the tropical heat, my Latin blood, and my crazy mixed heritage all conspired, tightening around me like a net, to make me unfit for solitude. That was my problem, and my goal: to learn to live and enjoy life inside myself. And the issue isn't a simple one: the Hindus, the Chinese, the Japanese, any race with a thousand-year-old culture has dedicated a good portion of time to developing philosophies and methods governing the inner life. Even so, every year several thousand people kill themselves, crushed by the weight of their own solitude. And it's not as if a person chooses to be alone. Instead, little by little, you're left on your own. And there's no way around it. You have to learn to live with it. You come to an immense deserted plain, and you don't know what the fuck to do. Lots of times you think flight is the best idea. Flight to another country, another city, somewhere else. But still, you're trapped. Other times you believe the solution is not to think so much about yourself and your stupid loneliness, which is heightened when you're alone and silent. Well, then you've got to take action. And you go out and meet a friend, or a woman who'll have a little sex with you. I don't know. Anybody, just so you don't have to be alone. You know by now that rum and marijuana just depress you even more. A little bit of sex, maybe. And if not, then at least a friend.

I thought about all that, and then I jumped to my feet and laughed. Heartily. A good smile, unnecessary and absurd, is a tonic. It always works for me. And if I manage to hold it for a few minutes, and laugh inside and out, that's even better. "I'm going out," I thought. And I left to go and see a friend.

I went down the stairs. The building dates back to 1936, and in its heyday it mimicked the massive banks of Boston and Philadelphia, with their solid, sober façades. In fact, the façade is still in good shape, and tourists are always amazed by it and take pictures, and it even appears in magazines, especially as photographed on stormy days. I've seen impressive photos, with the wild sea crashing against the Malecón, in that gray-blue hurricane light, the building splashed with water but solid and august. A splendid, majestic castle in the middle of the hurricane. But inside it's falling to pieces, and it's an incredible labyrinth of stairs without banisters, darkness, foul smells, cockroaches, and fresh shit. And makeshift rooms crowding the hallways and black men's quarrels and brawls. I came out onto the sidewalk and there in front of me was the old sign, so old it was almost illegible: "A Revolution without danger is not a Revolution. And a revolutionary who risks nothing is a revolutionary without honor." The slogan wasn't signed. It sounded like Fidel or Raúl. On the corner there was a huge new billboard. In big, brightly colored letters, it read: "Cuba, land of men of stature." In one corner a black athlete leapt against a blue sky. I don't know. It was incomprehensible.

I wanted to visit Hugo. It had been a long time since I saw him. I walked for a while, caught a bus, and then another. At last I made it to Hugo's house in the Cerro. He lived an isolated life, retired from the world. Years ago he was a television technician, and a good friend. We were colleagues. Then I went away and I lost touch with him. When I met up with him again, he was crazy. He had been given electroshock treatment, and he was kept sedated by a whole arsenal of tranquilizers, dosed several times a day.

He was incredibly sharp, but obsessive. A deadly combination. His face and eyes were distorted by the shocks, and his eyelids drooped. He told me the story again of the workshop boss who made his life impossible when he found out that Hugo's whole family was in Miami. The man shadowed him, trying to catch him violating a regulation. Every so often, and with no apparent motive, he would say, "We're all revolutionaries here; this is no place for traitors." Hugo began to have nightmares about him, until one day he couldn't take the provocation anymore and he attacked the man with a screwdriver, blinding him in one eye and seriously wounding him. Shut up in a tiny cell with two black criminals, he fell apart. In the end, he went crazy. He screamed and foamed at the mouth for days, until he was taken to the insane asylum and given his first massive shock. For seven years he was locked up receiving electroshock treatment.

Anyway, Hugo couldn't have rum, and I needed a few drinks. And when he told me his story, he got upset. It was always like that, every time I visited him. He smoked twenty cigarettes in an hour. I left. What else could I do? Best to leave, and let him be. He had enough with his own problems. I promised myself I would never go back.

I was hungry and broke at midnight in Havana in 1994. There weren't many people around. I kept walking, slowly. I thought I might as well go to bed. I needed to sleep. One section of the Malecón was dark. The streetlights had been turned off. There, on the wall, two women were kissing frantically. Lips locked, nothing else mattered to them. I eyed them for a while from the shadows, but I didn't stop. Was it Gay Day? I kept on. Barely fifteen feet away, a black man was watching them and jerking off. The man faced the sea, with his back to the people walking by, but he was jerking himself off frantically with his left hand. And a few feet farther down, a pretty white woman, not bad-looking, was checking out the black man and burning with desire. From where she sat on the wall, she moved closer to him in little bounces. The two of them were going to get it on when she completed her maneuvers.

None of it aroused me. I was holding firm. I have to learn to survive. I have to take the blows and bounce back each time, or I'll be down for the count and that'll be the end of me. They'll pull me out of the fight.

1:15 / The Day I Was Exhausted

One morning in the street there was the body of a woman who had been stabbed. She was a tall, beautiful mulatta, dressed in a very short black skirt, a blouse, and a white bra, all drenched in blood. She was sprawled on the sidewalk and there was blood everywhere. People were saying that she had been cheating on her husband. It was so bad that the man couldn't take it anymore, and he stabbed her. You could tell by the rivers of blood that he had attacked her with true hatred. There was a terrible grimace of pain on her face, and her lips and nose were split, smashed, clotted with coagulated blood.

This was a simple crime of passion, the kind that is common everywhere. But here it wouldn't be written up in the papers because for thirty-five years nothing bad or disturbing has been acceptable news. Everything has to be fine. No criminals or unpleasantness can exist in a model society.

But the thing is, you've got to know. If you don't have all the information, you can't think or make decisions or hold opinions. You turn into an idiot, ready to believe anything.

That's why I was so disillusioned with journalism and why I started to write some very raw stories. In such heartbreaking times, you can't construct exquisite texts. I write to jar people a little and force others to wake up and smell the shit. You've got to get your snout to the ground and smell the shit. That's how I terrorize cowards and mess with the people who like to muzzle those of us who speak up.

I couldn't keep quiet any longer, writing stupid little things in exchange for a few words of praise. The rules of the game were too strict. You could only say "yes." And it wasn't worth it.

I said to hell with it all, and I wrote some naked stories. My stories could run bare-assed out into the middle of the street, shouting, "Freedom, freedom, freedom."

I was on the roof for an hour, watching the police and the people around the body. I live on a roof, 130 feet above the street, but a neighbor lady lent me a pair of binoculars, and there I was, in the first row, as morbid and bloodthirsty as everyone else, with the best view in the house. Many of those who watched played the lottery that night. They played 50, which stands for the police, according to the Chinese numbers. Or 67, a stabbing. Assassin is 63, blood is 84, and 12 is wicked woman.

Then I reread what Babel said to Konstantin Paustovsky about his writing methods. I don't read those testimonies of writers anymore. They do me more harm than good. They made me believe that methods and techniques really did exist. Nothing like that exists. Every writer creates himself as best he can, all by himself, following no one's advice. And that's excruciating, but there's no other way. Nevertheless, what Babel has to say is good.

Well, I was worn out from working so hard, and I needed to take a break. I went to spend a few days with my mother. She lives in a city near Havana. There, I could recharge my batteries a little and then come back to my roof. I'm a lucky guy, though it doesn't always seem that way.

By noon I was at my mother's house, but she was out. Selling things, working her little schemes to survive. Her retirement pay, sixty pesos for a sixty-eight-year-old woman, is a joke. Luckily, she's still strong (most of the time), and she can walk. She keeps her spirits up. I help her out a little, when I have any money. Anyway, I had something to eat, and I sat down in the smoking room. I like to visit my mother and do nothing. I just hang around and talk to friends, who say, "I don't see you on television or read you in the magazine anymore. What's up?"

And I answer, "Nothing's up." Which is true: nothing's up.

So that's where I was. Sitting there relaxing with a cup of coffee, smoking, when Estrella came in. That woman is like the ill wind that blows no one any good. She is the loudest, rudest, and most vulgar woman I've ever met. I've known some real bitches but even they had better taste. And that redeemed them. Estrella is off her rocker, half-crazy, half-hysterical, and practically a bitch herself. I don't know how she manages it, but she has no taste at all. She's married to an uncle of mine who lives in the country. She came in like a whirlwind, no hellos, not even a glance at me, dropped her bag on the dining room table, got herself a glass of water, and asked me where my mother was.

"She's not here."

"She's always out, working the streets. The woman never stops. The police are going to put her in jail for dealing on the black market. She'll sell anything."

"Any good news for me?"

"No good news. Everything's a disaster. What kind of good news do you expect, considering the misery we live in?"

"Then fuck off, Estrella."

"Ay, child, if you're in a bad mood, don't take it out on me."

"I'm not in bad mood, for God's sake."

But I was in a bad mood. That idiot woman irritated me, always complaining, saying stupid things, being such a drama queen.

"I'm just upset," Estrella said.

"You're always upset. Take a pill."

"The thing is, Luisito kicked his wife out of the house yesterday. I caught her fooling around with one of the neighbors, with Roque. Can you imagine how I felt? A man who's always been our neighbor. He snagged the girl by telling her he was going to set her up in her own house. You can't trust anybody these days. I cared about her. She's only fifteen, but she works hard. She helped me out a lot around the house, and she seemed like a good girl."

"Well, cheer up. This morning a black guy from my neighborhood stabbed his wife for the very same reason. His wife was screwing everybody, and the guy's already in jail. He'll get twenty years at least. So you can be glad all Luisito did was throw her out."

"Maybe. Do you think so? Yes, you're right. They had only been together for six months. But we had already gotten attached to her, and we miss her."

"How did it happen? Did Luisito keep watch and catch her with the guy?"

"Yes. Luisito already had an idea what was going on, and he told her he was going to town and after that he was going to the coast to fish for crabs, and that she shouldn't expect him until very late. But he came back that same afternoon and he caught them. One of Roque's sisters was lending them her house for their dirty business. But Luisito didn't hit her or anything. He grabbed her by the arm, brought her home, gave her her clothes bundled up in a towel, and said, 'Get out of here!' The girl was crying and telling him he was making a mistake, that it wasn't what he thought it was. All of this in front of me. I had no idea what was going on, and so I started screaming and getting in between them. Look, my arm is all bruised because Luisito kept pushing me away and I kept coming back. I didn't know what had happened. When he came back from showing her to the road, he explained. He handled himself well, Pedro Juan, he handled himself well, don't you think? If it had been me, I would have beaten them both to a pulp. Her and that man. They would have both gotten a taste of machete! But Luisito is a gentleman. I would have kicked her right out, no clothes, no nothing. After all, he bought her those clothes himself. When she came six months ago, all she had were the clothes on her back, some broken sandals, and the dirt on her feet. But I'm not worried. Luisito has rice and dollars, because he always harvests a big crop and he sells it all. So he has food and dollars and that's what women want. Their struggles are over! Food and dollars for shopping! In two days, he'll find himself another one."

"Well, Estrella, that's life. Don't get all worked up; calm down. I'm going to the bathroom. Sit down, and the old lady will be back any minute now."

I went to the bathroom. When I can, I like to shit in comfort, taking my time. I took a magazine in with me so I could shit and read, no hurry. But Estrella can't sit still, and she came after me. There I was shitting, and she was talking to me through the door.

"It's hot around here these days. Do you remember Tácito, who lived in the village, next door to your Aunt Siomara?"

"Yes, Estrella, I remember him."

"Well, he poisoned his mother."

"His mother?"

"His mother. She was an old lady, eighty-four years old, who spent all her time arguing and nagging everyone."

"How did he kill her?"

"He put some kind of acid in a glass of milk. They say that after just a drop the old lady started to scream that she had a burning feeling in her stomach and she died instantly, foaming at the mouth."

"And how did they catch him?"

"Things got ugly because someone gave the milk that was left over to a little pig that was on the patio, and it died the same way, squealing and foaming at the mouth. I don't know how the police found out. Some neighbor probably told. Two days after she was buried, they dug the old lady up, performed an autopsy, and found the same poison that killed the little pig. He used enough to kill a horse! And people are already saying he must have killed his father-in-law ten years ago to get the thirty-thousand-peso inheritance. That man will rot in jail. And he isn't young. Tácito is probably sixty years old, at least."

I wiped my ass and flushed the toilet. Then I came out of the bathroom and left the house. Estrella was irritating me, and I didn't want to hear nattering on and on in her screechy voice.

I needed to pick a little *escoba amarga* for a cleansing. I had to purge my room on the roof because twice in the last few days I had smelled the light fragrance of a woman. As if her spirit were floating around. And that does me no good. It's bad to have spirits roaming the place.

Well, I left. A black couple, friends of mine, live just outside the city. Raysa and Carlos. She and I had a long affair. We still pick it up again every once in a while. But since she got married, we've toned things down. She's a sweet, beautiful black woman. When I arrived, she had the radio on at full volume. The announcer was saying, "Freedom, love, hope. Three things can be said about Cuba: freedom, love, hope." The announcer had a smooth, pleasant voice.

Raysa was alone. She turned off the radio so we could talk.

"Make coffee. I'm going to pick a little bit of *escoba amarga*, and I'll be right back."

"Ay, Pedrito, I don't have coffee. The cupboard is bare. *Escoba amarga* I do have. Out back there. Take as much as you want."

I picked a bunch of the herb and put it in a corner.

"Are you going to purify your place?"

"Yes. One of my neighbors who's a *santera* will do it. She says she'll purge my room and hers together because they're right next to each other."

"Carlos and I need to go to a *santera*. But together. I'd like him to be told what he is, so that he'll leave; so he'll come to a decision once and for all and let me live my life."

"I don't understand what you mean."

"Pedrito, every day the man is more of a loser and every day he drinks more. Now he cries whenever he gets drunk. And he's so jealous I can't turn around without feeling his eyes on my back. I think he's a faggot. A few days ago I was visiting Caridad, an old friend of mine, and a neighbor came over. We kept talking, but after a while he said to Caridad, 'Leave me alone with this girl, because I have something I need to tell her.' I didn't know the man, and I thought he wanted . . . well . . . I thought he wanted to seduce me. But that wasn't it. He said, 'Don't say anything yet. I'm going to tell you what I've seen because you need to know it, and I've been brought here to tell you what I know. You live in a wretched, dark little house, a stifling place where blood will be shed. Your husband is a black man who barely talks and who likes to drink bad *aguardiente* and listen to loud music. But he's not the man for you. I see your husband sleeping with another man, in the man's arms, both of them naked and asleep. But that shouldn't bother you. Your man is white, gray-haired, with the same tastes as you. He's romantic and loving, and he likes to drink rum with wine and listen to soft music. This man went to a spiritist, and he's looking for you, because the spiritist described you to him. You two will find each other if you look. But it won't be easy. Each time he has an affair with a black woman he thinks he's found you, but he hasn't. And he keeps looking for you. Beware of your husband, because he doesn't want to leave you. He knows that his destiny is elsewhere but he doesn't want to accept it. You're going to leave him. I see you leaving with a suitcase and stepping in blood. There is blood all over the floor, but it isn't yours. Be careful. You must light a candle for Santa Bárbara every Saturday at dawn.' "

"My God, Raysa, that's enough to give a person the shakes!"

"I'm scared. Every time I think of it, I get goosebumps."

"Well, leave Carlos. Go now, before something bad happens."

"I'm going to. I can't take it anymore. I have a friend who's hustling in Varadero and living it up. Foreigners, clothes, perfume, everything. I don't even have soap."

"Every time I come here, you tell me the same thing, but then you don't do anything. You accuse him of being hopeless, but you're just like him. And the days go by one by one, and you're still hungry."

"Now I'm really going to go to Varadero. Even if it's only for fifteen days. All I want is to get myself some clothes and a few dollars and have a little bit of fun, try everything. I'm just as happy to play dyke as to fuck four men at a time and get drunk every night. I want to have fun!"

"How old are you, Raysa?"

"Thirty-six."

"And you're still waiting to have fun?"

"Still waiting. How much longer does it have to be?"

"So why don't you leave Carlos?"

"I don't have anywhere to go. Plus, he's incredible in bed. His prick is so big and long it reaches all the way down my throat. And that makes me crazy. Pedrito, he comes and his prick is still as stiff as a rod. I really turn him on!"

"It's not as good when it comes to your ass. You've always said that he's so big you can't get him in."

"No, I can. If he goes slow, he can do it. And with lubrication. He greases himself up and he gets all the way in. That's my problem. That I like it."

We kept talking about the same things. Each of us wanted to turn the other on. She was telling me how she did it with Carlos, and I had an enormous erection. When I couldn't stand it anymore, I took it out and started to give myself a slow hand job.

"Pedrito, are you crazy? What if Carlos comes home from work? He'll be back any time now."

"All for the best. Maybe he'll like my prick and he'll suck it for me, since you don't even want to touch it. Keep telling me about the mirror."

If Carlos came home and caught us, he'd bring Changó down on all three of us, and that would be hell. I came right away. I wanted her to catch it in her mouth, but there was no way. Well, I shot three long jets onto the table. I hate to waste come like that. She cleaned it up right away. And we sat down again. She tried to restart the conversation, but I couldn't pay attention. I just wanted to sleep with her, and if Carlos came home, get rid of him as best I could. But no. A forty-four-year-old man can't indulge in such madness. I picked up the bunch of *escoba amarga* and left. Really, all I wanted was to rest a little and stop making things so complicated for myself.

I was living a little more comfortably. I managed to get a room on a roof with just two neighbors. And I had to give up the beer-can business. There was lots of competition, and we were forced to scuffle like dogs in the dumpsters of Miramar. Sometimes I couldn't even come up with twenty empty cans in a morning. Now I had a new business, and I was doing better for myself.

The room was clean, with a kerosene stove, its own bathroom, and lots of fresh air. It was on the ninth floor of another building near the Malecón, with a view of the sea. The neighbors weren't bad: an old married couple, always screaming and fighting, and a bolero singer and his wife.

I had known the singer fifteen years ago. In those days, he had his own group and he was young. Armandito Villalón and The Comets. They played catchy little songs. Some were picked as "the neighborhood hit of the week" at the radio station where I worked. Then Armandito got desperate for money. He disbanded the group and started singing solo with cassette backup in three clubs every night. He made a lot of money singing the same boleros over and over, until his voice was ruined and his stomach ulcer turned into cancer from all his rum and cigarettes. He had a heart attack and he was skinny, starving, and wrinkled. The country was seized by the crisis of the nineties, and on top of everything else, he went looking for more trouble: he joined a group for the defense of human rights. He was up against the wall. Every so often, on the slightest of pretexts, he was locked up in jail for a few days, side by side with real criminals.

It was around that time we started to see each other again. I was his new neighbor and I said hello to him the way I used to, when I was working at the radio station and he was recording his little songs. But the man was bitter, irritable, obsessed with freedom and human rights. And hungry. He only had one gig, at the Salem Club, Fridays to Sundays. The Salem is a hellhole in downtown Havana. One night I went to have a few drinks and, while I was at it, listen to some of Armandito's boleros. I couldn't get in because the door was barred and there was a fat black man, as fierce as a gorilla, who was in charge of locking and unlocking it. I didn't like that scene. I can't be locked up like a prisoner in a disgusting club where they sell bad rum for a hundred bucks a glass. The man told me that's how they keep fights under control until the police arrive. "If there's a brawl, I lock the door and no one comes out until I let them out, ha, ha, ha," said the idiot, who had the face of a mental retard.

I mentioned it to Armandito the next day, and it became the theme of another speech on human rights: "Yes, we've lost all self-respect. This country is a prison, a repressive system lodged inside each person's head. The solution to any problem is to impose rules, bars, barriers, discipline, control. It's unbearable, Pedro Juan."

I just said, "You're going to drive yourself crazy, pal. I can barely deal with my own problems, so tell me why I should get myself mixed up with politicians, who are sons of bitches and in the end just do whatever their dicks tell them to do. It's the same no matter where you are. Politics is the art of the scam."

And he replied angrily, "That's exactly why we are the way we are. Because of pessimism and conformism. We've got to confront all of that and denounce it. We've got to fight and speak the truth." The man was a live wire. He always talked about the same thing. If he didn't stop, he'd be in electroshock treatment soon.

On the roof he kept a chicken coop and two pigs. They were obsessed with those animals, he and his wife. They spent hours sitting by the cage, staring at them, mesmerized, feeding them vegetable peelings. Ever since the crisis began, in 1990, lots of people had been raising chickens and pigs on their patios, on roofs, in the bathroom. That way they had something to eat. The wife worked in a worker's cafeteria and she brought home scraps for the animals. She was skinny and ravaged too. Around the same time he had cancer and his heart attack, Armandito got a divorce. He left his apartment to his first wife and their two children and he came to live in the room on the roof, with the mulatta. At the time, she was lovely, a tall, beautiful woman with the happy, mischievous grace of mulattas. Not anymore. Now she was withered, too skinny, though sometimes she still flashed sparks.

The old couple in the other room had a pigeon house too, and a chicken coop. They sold the pigeons for *santería*. The old man was a *santero*. And he never talked. He was the sullen type. Always squabbling with the old lady. I never found out anything about them. They barely said hello. That's how it is. They hate you because you're white. So, fine. I never got to know them, nor did I care to.

I had no problems when it was cold and there was a strong wind off the sea. But in April, when it started to be hot and it was dead calm, there was a stench of shit, and the gnats and mosquitoes moved in. It was unbearable. Neither the old couple nor Armandito washed out their coops. Well, all right. Sometimes they sprinkled a little bit of water around. We had water problems, and we had to carry buckets from the cistern in the basement of the building. Nine floors, no elevator. Every five or six days the water level rose a little higher in the cistern and then it was pumped out of the tank and we could get it from a faucet.

The roof turned into a stinking place, with gnats biting by day and mosquitoes by night. It was impossible to sleep.

In general, I'm not a lover of good smells. Right now I can't even remember any particular woman's perfume. I don't like smells like that. Either that, or they don't interest me. On the other hand, I'll never forget the smell of the fresh shit of a boy attacked by sharks in the Gulf of Mexico. He was a tuna fisherman. He was going about his business in the stern of the boat, pulling up the splendid silver fish one by one, when he fell overboard. Three enormous sharks were swimming with the tunas, and in two bites they shredded his guts and ripped off his leg. We hauled him up very quickly, still living, his eyes wide with horror; everything happened in less than a minute. And he died immediately, bled to death, without ever being able to speak or understand what had happened to him. For months we were together in that stern, but I can't remember his face or his name. All I can remember clearly is the terrible stink of the boy, with his abdomen slashed open and his guts spilling excrement onto the boat's deck.

There have been other terrible smells in my life, but I don't want to talk about them anymore. Enough of that.

The smell of the chicken and pig shit started to attract more cockroaches. There had always been cockroaches, but now there were more. And rats: huge animals that came up from the basement of the building, almost eighty feet below. They came up the drainpipes, ran to the cages to eat peelings and scraps, and then plunged down again to their dens.

We plugged up the drainpipes with stones. One day a rat jumped from the toilet bowl and ran through the room to the roof, faster than lightening. I couldn't believe it. It seemed impossible to me that the animal could climb up the sewer pipe and break the water seal of the toilet.

I was pissed. This was too much. I went to talk to Armandito and the old couple, which got me nowhere. They wouldn't move the animals off the roof, even if the rats took over everything and drove us out with their fangs snapping at our heels. On my piece of roof I could do whatever I wanted, but I had no right to ask them to do anything. And they showed me a newspaper clipping about roof laws. I tried not to raise my voice. But I couldn't help it. In the end, I told them they could all go to hell.

It was August, and it was too hot. I was fed up with arguing and I thought about poisoning all the animals. I found my two strychnine seeds in a tight twist of paper. I picked them up in the botanical garden at Cienfuegos, at the foot of a strychnine tree. Some latent criminal instinct made me keep them for so many years. I thought about how I might sneak up to the cages at night and give the animals the poison mixed with a little rice. But I would be found out. It was better to wait and kill them little by little. And what if the old people ate the dead animals and they died too? Shit, what do you know, a little detective novel was already taking shape. The heat, the humidity, the gnats biting, the stink of shit. And me with no idea how the hell to poison those animals. I needed a little fresh air. I took the four dollars I had left and I went to San Rafael Boulevard to try to sell them. Hopefully a peasant would come along and I could hit him up for sixty. The exchange had dropped from 120 pesos to 50 in a little less than a month. The government wanted to manage the crisis by sweeping up everything: pesos and dollars. It seemed to me that people were poorer and hungrier than ever, but at least, all of the money was safe in the king's coffers.

As I was walking along Galiano toward San Rafael, a light-skinned mulatto shot past me like an arrow, and behind him came a peasant with a knife in his hand, shouting, "Cut him off, cut him off!" I didn't cut anybody off. The peasant ran past me. It seemed he had been sold some counterfeit bills, and by the time he realized it the man was already far away.

Then I was told that the peasant caught up with the man and stabbed him in the shoulder, and a policeman punched him a few times too. It's a good trick, but people already know it and it's hard to get away with it: you paste a number five or twenty, cut from a photocopy of a bill of the appropriate denomination, over the one on each corner of a one-dollar bill. It works if you hand the money over quickly, in a dark place, and you cover up Washington with your thumb. You've got to find a guy who's in a hurry to trade and, above all, travel light and make a quick getaway.

I got to San Rafael and I was there for a few hours, but no buyers showed up. There were lots of people selling . . . And hardly any peasants. They're the ones with money. They make their fortunes out of people's hunger. It's a new era. All of a sudden, money is necessary. As always, money crushes everything in its path. Thirty-five years spent constructing the new man. And now it's all over. Now we've got to make ourselves into something different, and fast. It's no good to fall behind.

1·17 / Restoring the Faith

I lived without stopping, ever. I needed a break, needed to be alone, in a quiet place where I could think. What I'd think about I didn't know. But I sensed that I needed to stop and think a little. Maybe look deep inside myself. Backward, too. Even if afterward everything was the same. I envied Swami Nirmalananda, who sends me his books from India and does nothing. He just meditates and burns incense in the hills of Karnataka, among the trees and wild animals.

But it's hard to say, "Stop," if every day you face infinite temptations. An envelope arrived today from Paris. The painter Nato was inviting me to his series of happenings, *Art and absence of clothes*, next summer in Boissise Le Roi. That lunatic doesn't realize I don't even have the money to buy a jar of Nescafé. And I'm worried about my constant fatigue, which hasn't let up for months. I don't know if it's anemia or AIDS. Other times, depression and sadness overwhelm me. And I keep struggling against fear. Struggling is what I call it, at least. I can't struggle alone. But every night I pray and I always ask God to take away my fear and to clear up the confusion in my head. I'm paralyzed by fear and confusion. And God does what he can to help. He gives me signs that I'm on the right path.

For many years, I felt far from that invisible, parallel world.

When I was thirteen, I smashed a ball into the crucifix my mother had hanging on the wall over my bed. I struck at it with fury. In catechism, I was supposed to believe without the slightest doubt in the Holy Trinity and Adam and Eve. But no, I countered with Darwin. An earthquake started to rumble inside me. And right around that time, there was an influx of Russian manuals on Marxism and night school instruction in revolution. Then I was called into military service (in my case, four and a half years of it; I've always been the lucky guy wallowing in all the shit).

My military unit was stationed at Rancho Boyeros, and each year on the sixteenth of December, we recruits watched the pilgrimage to the temple at El Rincón. The pilgrims were on their way to make requests of San Lázaro or to thank him for something. All along their path, for many miles, thousands and thousands of people dragged chains, stones, rods, wooden crosses. They were dressed in sackcloth. Or they walked on their knees, shredding their skin. Others invented a variety of tortures. We enjoyed ourselves without understanding anything at all. We felt very superior to and distant from those mesmerized people and the paraphernalia of their obsession.

Many of us used to be like those people. We were true believers. Then we were told, "Oh, that's shit, and anyone who says otherwise will be shoved aside, and maybe he'll get a few knocks on the head, too." It was like that: either you're with us, or you're out on the street. And decide fast. It's always that way in life: if you decide fast, you win or you lose. If you won't decide, you're an idiot; you'll be pushed aside and spit at too, as a mediocrity and a little gray man. And no one wants to condemn themselves to being a little gray man.

So for years I was what I was supposed to be, and proudly too, with the truth in one hand and the red flag in the other. Then came the crash, and in a few years time, everything was ashes. But a person can't drift forever. Either you find something to grab on to, or you sink. And to top it all off, then we found out that even the head of the government had his *santería* gods and necklaces and ten *santería* elders ministering to him. Ah, fuck it all.

Well, around that time, everything started to go badly for me. I spent too much time unmoored, bracing against the gale. If you have nothing to hold on to, and the hurricane keeps blowing harder, it's certain you'll be picked up and tossed, torn apart. Then, out of simple curiosity, I went to see a spiritist with African ties. I expected nothing to come of it. But for forty-five minutes, the woman spoke one truth after another and described people, names and all. She told me what was wrong with me and what to do about it. And we put it into practice, and here I am. I'm not going to tell that story. It's no one's business but my own. But I began to regain my faith, and now sometimes I go to El Rincón.

Still, I don't much like being there with all the fetish salesmen and the believers swarming everywhere, and that man who guards the altar and orders the women to lower their arms when they get carried away (we men pray in silence, but the women are different, waving their arms and sighing and praying in a murmur). That man has no consideration for anyone. He wants to keep strict order. And I'm tired of always hearing about order and discipline and seriousness and sacrifice. That's all I've ever been in life: orderly, disciplined, serious, and self-sacrificing.

But sometimes I go and pray a little. And when I come out, there are all the patients from the leprosarium, and the AIDS sanitarium too, hiding behind the mango and avocado trees.

I don't even know why I'm telling all this. Maybe it's because I'm a little gloomy thinking about the fate of José Montalvo of San Antonio, Texas. His last letter came in 1991. He had cancer, and he was on a homeopathic treatment plan. Chemotherapy didn't work for him. His letter was full of affection; he kept his spirits up by providing social services to the homeless of Aztlán and by writing poems and struggling with the wreck of a house he had bought and his three-year-old son. "Every damn monkey has his hour; someday

you'll publish your stories. Keep up the good fight," he wrote then.
That was three years ago. I don't know if he's dead by now. I was
confused and scared, and I paid no attention to Montalvo and his
Chicano cancer. He was making his farewells, and I never said
goodbye.

Today I was rereading his letters and books. That's how it goes.
Like a pendulum. Back and forth. Sometimes I read papers from
years ago, and I feel that the past has come back to haunt me: I'm
lonelier now. Little by little, we all get lonelier. All the women I've
loved I've left behind. The places I was happy. Children move on.
All my friends. Everything I once had and is now lost. Things I
wanted to preserve but tossed overboard instead. And I catch myself
writing as if the end is near. And God won't help me cleanse my
soul and accept everything as it is.

1:18 / Me, Shitraker

"Gordon" was crossing the Caribbean, slowly, southeast to north-east. It was in no hurry. For four days, the hurricane had been drift-ing along, leaving two thousand dead in its wake in Haiti, three hundred in Santo Domingo. The furious sea leapt against the Malecón, and the wind pulverized the salt caked on the ruined old buildings. I had nothing to do. Nothing urgent, at least. In the long term, there are always prospects, hope, the future, everything soon to be better, God our savior. But that's all always in the long term. Just now, this minute, there's nothing.

A black man was in the pedestrian tunnel under Maceo Park, showing women his long prick, stroking it and pulling on it. He was very tense, and he pranced a little back and forth, glancing from side to side, tugging on his long black thing to make it stiff. When he saw me, his idiotic expression didn't change. He was definitely high on marijuana or cocaine or pills. People always get angry at id-iots like that. Not me. I don't care. The truth is, lots of women like to see pricks in places where no one usually shows them. And there are men who like to see them too, if only to envy them and think, "If only I had such a big, brawny cock." Though they'd never admit it, even if they were being burned at the stake. And if anyone points it out, they reply, offended, "You've got a dirty mind, Pedro Juan, and you think everyone else does too." So exhibitionists (and every day there are more of them, in parks, on buses, and in doorways) fulfill a beautiful social function: they sensualize the passerby, relieve them for a moment of their daily stress, and remind them that despite everything, they are creatures of instinct, simple and fragile. And dissatisfied, above all.

The best thing in the world is to stroll along the Malecón in the middle of a terrible storm. You walk along, and sometimes you think, sometimes you don't. It's best not to think, but that's almost impossible. Only with lots of practice is it possible. A Mexican tourist was walking toward me and all of a sudden he smiled and said, in a Michoacano twang, "Is it going to storm again? Oh, looks like it is." I didn't answer. I didn't know if it was starting again or if it was still far away, and I didn't care. The guy stopped smiling and walked on. It started to rain in sheets. There wasn't a soul on the whole Malecón. It was five in the afternoon, but with the sky overcast, it was already getting dark. The light was gray, cold, and wet. Which is rare on this island of stark, searing light. Light filtered through a fog of rain and salt air. I took shelter behind a column, waiting for the downpour to stop. It seems I'll have to learn to live with these intermittent attacks of melancholy and sadness. It's like living with an old bullet wound that aches whenever the weather's damp. I may have my reasons for grieving. But it shouldn't have to be that way. Life can be a party or a wake. You decide for yourself. Which is why this misery is a blight on my life. And I chase it away. That's what I'm always doing: chasing away the anguish, the grief, and all the rest of it.

When it cleared up a little, I walked up Campanario. On a corner across the street, a crowd was gathered around two policemen who had arrested a young mulatto, maybe sixteen years old. They had him handcuffed, with his back against the wall. Everyone was looking at him. They were waiting for a squad car to come and take him to the station. He had tried to steal a bicycle. The boy was ashamed, and he stared at the ground. His chin rested on his chest. I watched him for a while. Suddenly, his knees gave way. And he slipped down until he was on the ground. He was so scared, he couldn't stand. The murmur of the people around him was always the same, "Ah, so now you're sorry? Should've thought of that first, shouldn't you, you stupid shit?" I moved on.

I walked away from the Malecón and the wind for a few blocks. In the park at San Rafael and Galiano, it was almost dark, but all the usual fauna was in evidence. I sat down on a bench and a little farther along was a very skinny, very cheery woman, talking to another woman, "When I got a taste of him, I said, 'Ahh, I'm marrying a stud' . . . yes, yes, he put it in there just right; he gave me four children, one after the other; a perfect record! I was the one who made us stop; I got an IUD and told him that was it. If it was up to him, we would have had ten or twelve kids, ha ha ha . . . he was a real stallion." Then a boy came up to her, whispered something in her ear, and she got up and left in a hurry, very quickly. She didn't even say goodbye to her friend. Hustling on the boulevard. Either you move fast or somebody else takes your place.

Today I wasn't looking to make a buck. I had twenty dollars in my pocket, a fortune. I was thinking I might rework the story about Rogelio that began "No more shitting on the roof, *cojones!*" In Cádiz I couldn't get it published because it had *cojones* in the first line (I can't understand it—*Don Quixote* is a whole catalog of words like that. Well, maybe *Don Quixote* is a bad example. After all, Cervantes died in poverty). It's strong stuff, they told me. Ha. They don't know the meaning of strong. I had to rework it, but the *cojones* were staying right where they were. Those *cojones* were fixed in place.

A very old, dirty black man sat down next to me, wanting to talk. He said that he was a stunt skater and a sailor. He had traveled to every continent, going ashore at each port with his skates. Even in New York he put his show on three times. Lifting up his shirt, he showed me his chains. He had everything chained around his waist: his wallet, a giant knife, some nylon bags with papers inside, and an aluminum cigarette case. He had learned the trick from a Greek on board the *Caiman Island*. I listened to him for a while, but then I'd had enough. I said goodbye as nicely as I could and moved to another bench. By then it was very dark, and I didn't want anyone around me. If my twenty dollars were stolen, I'd be back at zero.

The old man had made me lose my train of thought. I wrote the story about Rogelio years ago. He had just died, and I made up a lot of things about his life. It's not a good story. Truth is best, the hard truth. You pick it up on the street, just as it is, you grab it with both hands, and if you're strong enough, you lift it up and let it fall on the blank page. And that's all. It's easy. No retouching. Sometimes the truth is so hard that people won't believe you. They read the story and they say, "No, no, Pedro Juan, there are things here that don't work. You made this up." But no. Nothing is made up. I was just strong enough to get hold of the whole mass of reality and let it fall all at once on the blank page.

Case in point: later I found out that when he was very young, Rogelio had to identify his mother in the morgue. A lover cut her into six pieces. Rogelio was eight years old. From then on, he was fucked. His mood changed twenty times a day: he'd swing from overwrought tears to the most hideous violence, from being soft and weak to being a fearless superman. He was full of contradictions, and he had no staying power. So needy for love and so cowardly and dependent that he tolerated with anguish all his wife's lovers, one after the other. There was always someone. At the age of forty-six, he couldn't stand it any longer and he died of a massive heart attack. Now, four years later, his wife is a walking skeleton with a serious bone disease. His youngest son is in prison half the time, and the rest of the time, he's crazy and desperate. His daughter is a mostly unsuccessful prostitute at the hotels for foreigners. The three are obsessed by the desire to emigrate. They think they'll find a solution in the United States. They're starving, penniless, and they've forgotten Rogelio ever existed.

So I need to rework the story. Now it'll be much stronger. Not a single lie. I only change the names. That's my profession: shitraker.

Nobody likes it. Don't you hold your nose when you pass the garbage truck? Don't you hide your trash cans out back? Don't you avoid street sweepers, grave diggers, sewer cleaners? Aren't you disgusted when you hear the word *carrion*? That's why no one smiles at me either and why they look the other way when they see me. I'm a shitraker. And it's not as if I'm searching for anything hidden in the shit. Usually I find nothing. I can't say, "Oh, look, I found a diamond in the shit, or I found a good idea in the shit, or I found something beautiful." That's not the way it is. I'm not looking for anything and I never find anything. As a result, I can't prove that I'm a pragmatic or socially useful kind of guy. I just do what children do: they shit and then they play with their shit, smelling it, eating it, and having fun until mom comes along, picks them up out of it, bathes them, powders them, and warns them that a person doesn't do things like that.

That's all. I'm not interested in the decorative, or the beautiful, or the sweet, or the delicious. That's why I always had my doubts about a sculptor I was married to for a while. There was too much peace in her sculptures for them to be any good. Art only matters if it's irreverent, tormented, full of nightmares and desperation. Only an angry, obscene, violent, offensive art can show us the other side of the world, the side we never see or try not to see so as to avoid troubling our consciences.

So. No peace or quiet. Whoever achieves perfect balance is too close to God to be an artist.

I put my hands in my pockets, and I felt the twenty-dollar bill. I would buy a bottle of rum and a box of cigarettes. In my room on the roof, the storm would still be raging. Best would be to bring a mulatta up with me too. Then a crazy black woman showed up out of nowhere. We know each other from the neighborhood. I never say hello to her, but she's pushy and she always tries to start conversations with me. She came hurrying toward me. For a few years, she was the poorest, filthiest, smelliest woman in the neighborhood. Then she became a high-class prostitute in shiny red and white dresses, reeking of perfume. Now she's a Jehovah's Witness. She gave up everything to preach. She goes around with a Bible, wearing glasses with thick lenses and modest clothes in muted colors. She saw me, and there was no time for me to do anything. Rushing up to me, she burst out, "Brother, do you know how to read the Bible? There's a Psalm I'd like to discuss with you. It's the fifty-first, which says: 'Have mercy on me, O God, according to your steadfast love . . . blot out my transgressions.' Do you know why David is praying for purification? Do you? I'm sure you've never even thought about it."

Ah, no. I didn't have the strength. Sometimes that's the way it is. A person gets bored and there's nothing to be done. I was off to pick up rum and cigarettes. Then I'd see about what to do next.

1.19 / Child of Chaos

Through the window I could see a gray-haired, slightly forlorn and dirty-looking old woman in the building next door. Sitting in a rocking chair, she rocked furiously, singing in a steady drone, mixing up lines from the International, the National Anthem, the March of July 26, the Anthem of the Literacy Workers, of the Militias, and of the new International, repeating everything. Sometimes she'd be quiet for a second, as if to catch her breath, and she'd ask, "Who's last? Isn't anybody last in this line? Who's last for bread? Well, if no one's last, then I'm number one; oh, I'm sorry; I asked but no one answered. Friends, who's last?" And then she'd start up again, "No savior from on high delivers, no faith have we in prince or peer."

I was waiting for my uncle to get home from work. I had been sitting there for an hour listening to the crazy woman. At first she got on my nerves. After a while, I didn't even hear her. I had adjusted to her paranoia.

There I was, slightly bored, when a kid, sixteen or a little bit older, came rocketing in. Barely acknowledging my existence with a little nod and a "hmm," he started pestering my uncle's wife, who was close to sixty.

"I need one of uncle's shirts and ties. Hurry."

"What for?"

"For passport and visa photos. Hurry, auntie."

"You've finally made up your mind?"

The boy wasn't listening. He went to the bedroom closet, opened the door, and started rummaging around for a white shirt.

"Look, this one. Iron it for me, auntie."

They came back into the living room.

"Carlitos, did you say hello to Pedro Juan yet?"

"I don't know who he is."

"You two do know each other. Pedro Juan is your uncle's nephew, but he lives in Havana, and it's been years since you've seen each other. This is Carlitos, my nephew."

I still didn't remember him. Then I thought I might have a vague recollection of him as a child. Hyperactive back then too.

"Is he your niece Odalys's son?" I asked her.

"Yes, he's Odalys's youngest boy."

"Oh yes, now I remember."

They're related to one of my brothers' wives. But this lady was my uncle's wife too. Sometimes even I can't keep track. Back home, no matter where you go, you run into cousins and nephews of your nieces and nephews. I think I have hundreds and hundreds of relatives. Though they're not really all family. Carlitos was still confused. Auntie gave him the definitive explanation.

"He's Zoila's son. Zoila's oldest."

"Ahh, of course. The thing is, you're balder and skinnier now."

He shook my hand happily. I smiled. Auntie started worrying about Carlitos again.

"You've finally decided?"

"I've always known I'd go."

"Carlitos, this is serious. It's a life decision."

"I know."

"And what are you going to do there? You don't have a job."

"Sure I do. Dad owns an electric company, and I'm going to work for him."

"He *works* at an electric company."

"He's the *owner*."

"Ay, Carlitos, he lives in New Jersey and you don't even speak English."

The kid turned away from his aunt and said to me, "Listen, Pedro Juan, Dad has been there for four years and he owns an electric company. Now he wants me to come live up there. Me and my brother. But my brother doesn't want to go. He's so wishy-washy and indecisive—that's no way to live. Me, I'm out of here."

"Carlitos, are you sure he's the owner? Most likely . . ."

"Damn it, Pedro Juan, he's the owner. I'm a little crazy today and I don't have much time, but some other day I'll explain it to you. My father is a tiger when it comes to business. He's already a millionaire. Knot my tie for me."

I picked it up and knotted it.

"So you'd go to New Jersey to be with your father?"

"That's right. That's where his company is."

"It's cold up there, and you'll be homesick."

"I won't be homesick at all. And I like the cold. Damn it, Pedro Juan, are you going to be just like auntie? Don't spoil it for me! Listen, man, think if you know anybody who wants to buy a Japanese watch or a motorcycle."

He showed me the watch on his wrist and pointed out into the street.

"That's the motorcycle, all chrome and in perfect condition. I'm cleaned out, man, and I have to make enough to get by on until I leave."

By then the shirt was ironed. Auntie just raised her eyebrows silently. Carlitos pulled on the shirt, still warm. He put on the tie.

"Fix the knot for me, will you please," he asked me.

Auntie made a last attempt at persuasion.

"What about your wife and the little girl?"

"They can stay here, auntie! Don't hassle me anymore. I can't hang around and starve to death in this shit hole. When I've been over there a year, I'll come back to visit you all in my luxury yacht, you'll see—because I'm not flying. The first thing I'm going to buy is a luxury yacht. Then a car, and then a house with a pool. I'll be a millionaire in a year! You'll see."

And to me, he said, "Well, man, I'll see you around. I have to have my photo taken today, so tomorrow I can go to Havana and get my papers in order. Once that's taken care of, I'll be halfway to paradise and halfway out of this hell."

1:20 / The Mysterious Life of Kate Smith

Kate Smith's life is a complete mystery now, I think. No one will ever find out how she really spent the eighty-nine years before she died, technically murdered. Technically. Legally, it wasn't murder.

I have two versions of Kate's story: one of them her own and the other that of a neighbor who hated her.

At one time, all the shacks on the roof were three luxury penthouses, rented by three single North Americans who could afford the rent, and who threw discreetly wild parties, inviting a mix of queers and courtesans of every color. They lived on ham, olives, and whisky, according to Abelardo, an old Asturian from Spain, the delivery boy for some warehouses of imported goods that used to be on the corner where another building like this one stands now.

When the Revolution triumphed in 1959, one of the Americans bowed out of the tropical party and went back to the United States. Another one, on a very unusual CIA mission, tried to assassinate Fidel: he made friends with the head of state, discovered his interest in scuba diving, and presented him with a beautiful isothermic cork wet suit, soaked in a poisonous substance. This same gentleman went on to enjoy the company of queers (coarser ones, maybe) for twenty years or so in a Havana prison.

Only Kate was left on the roof, locked up behind bars. The building's owners fled to Miami, the rents went down, and the building filled up with people. There are more of us on the island every day, and by now we don't know what to do with ourselves. The powers that be call it "housing redistribution." The redistributed call it "living like sardines." The powers that be can't even begin to imagine what it's like for six or seven people to live together in a single twelve-by-twelve-foot room, with a sliver of a bathroom to match. And if they can imagine it, they play dumb.

As I was saying, Kate kept her apartment and her piece of terrace with a view of sea right over the Malecón. The rest of the space filled up with shacks and common strangers. Very crude people. Most likely I'm just another piece-of-shit lowlife. I don't know. And I'd rather not know. It must be depressing to be sure about things like that. She put bars and locks on all her doors and windows, even inside the little house, cordoning off each room from the next. She gave English classes, mostly conversation classes. And that's how she supported herself.

When I got here, the old lady was already nearly eighty, but she was in good shape; she exercised and she had enough energy to go down to the Malecón some nights, offer good money to huge black guys and bring them back upstairs with her, get her kicks, pay them, and then ciao, hasta la vista. They say she never used the same ones twice. Well, I'm no dark-skinned black, more like a bleached-white mulatto, but the old lady latched on to me. She tried everything she could think of to snare me, offering me free English classes, ping-pong matches, and jujitsu practice sessions. When she found out that I was once a radio journalist, before my breakdown and before I moved into the building, she invited me over to listen to Wagner. I can't stand Wagner. He's as bad as Mozart. And she regaled me with stories of her Hungarian immigrant childhood in New York around the turn of the century. At the age of seven, she only spoke Hungarian. One day she was teased so mercilessly in a bar, where she had gone to sell tickets for a raffle, that she learned English in a month, and a short while later she had forgotten all of her Hungarian; she threw away her white collars with embroidered white lace borders and changed her name. Then, as a young woman, she was a member of a group that sympathized with the Bolsheviks. She was persecuted, and she escaped to Mexico, then moved on to Jamaica, where she settled for a while. Finally she came to Cuba, around 1950. That was her version.

She never told me her last name (I found it out much later, from the Ouija board). One day, I said to her, stupidly (every time I say something stupid I suffer the consequences, but inevitably I say stupid things, and I'm always suffering the consequences), that we could write a book about her life. It would be a bestseller. She kicked me out of her apartment, shouting all kinds of ridiculous things, "No, I must hide. They'll kill me, they'll kill me. I'll never be pardoned in my own country, you fool; you're just another idiot; get out of here. I don't want you around anymore."

Out of her head. Completely out of her head. I took my leave nicely. "Crawl up your mother's fucking cunt, you piece-of-shit old bitch. You're the idiot yourself. Old slut! Black dick fucker!" I left and that was the end of it. We never spoke again.

I got the other version little by little from a retired old woman who lived in a room next door until she died. This old lady had worked for the Secret Service for years, in Intelligence, I think; but she made some slip and she was discovered and booted out. She knew a lot of things no one else did. Sometimes she'd hint about the millions of dollars paid to one guerrilla or another, about the America Brigade, about Carlos the Venezuelan, and about various other things. I won't write about any of that now. I don't want more trouble.

According to this old lady, Kate was a Nazi and worked with women in a concentration camp in Germany, fleeing back to America in 1945. She knocked around for a while, and when she came to Cuba ten years later, the Bureau for the Repression of Communist Activities was at the height of its powers. Kate changed the dates to confuse me, but the old policewoman assured me that it had been

1955. So she was no Bolshevik; if she had been, the BRAC would have served her up to the FBI on a silver platter.

Kate was terrible. When she was very old, she started allying herself with young people to avail herself of their services. She'd bring them home to live with her, and right away she'd change her will and designate them her heirs, but nobody could stand her for more than a few weeks. They all gave up, saying they had to leave to keep themselves from throttling the old bitch. I never found out what kind of nasty tricks she pulled. And the ones who got kicked out wouldn't say much. Out of pride, I suppose. I had enough to worry about trying to keep my head above water, and I couldn't bother myself about one more old bitch.

At last she came up against a married couple determined at all costs to get themselves a home. They were pathetic young slobs from the asshole of the world, and they were starving, without a cent to their names. They had never set foot in a house with a telephone, stereo, gas stove, television, refrigerator, or ocean views. So, when that's where they found themselves, they thought they had it made, and they said to themselves, "We're not moving from here no matter what."

So when the old lady started acting up, asking to have her ass wiped every time she took a shit, or trying to lure the man into bed with her (she said she was afraid of sleeping alone), they went shopping for the strongest sedatives on the market. And then it was pill time for Kate. She snored like Sleeping Beauty of the Roof. They kept her drugged, but each time she woke up, she'd try to raise hell again. Until finally they made up their minds. They increased her dosage, and she went into a coma. For three days, she agonized, tossing about on the floor in the throes of death, locked in her room. Then they took her to the most horrendous hospital in Havana, saying they didn't know what was wrong with her. No doctor came to look at her. She was too repulsive, slimed with shit, urine, and vomit. In two hours, she was dead. To save themselves trouble, they donated the corpse to the medical school, and bye-bye. That was the end of Kate.

But as everybody knows, bad seeds are hard to root out. Kate Smith still roams the roof. Every chance she gets, she sticks her nose in where she's not wanted. Sometimes she haunts the Ouija board. She just gives her initials, K.S. Other times she calls herself K. Smith.

The murderers live behind bars now. They think what they've got is a real penthouse, and they won't talk to us, the lowlifes in the shacks out back. They want to build a wall and really separate themselves from us. They don't know that back here we've got a Ouija board and that it works. I don't know how it works, but it does. K.S. keeps coming back, night after night. She answers every question I ask her about her murderers. She's relentless. But she clams up and vanishes when I ask about her life. Even now she won't let anything slip. She's a demon-child of Satan, the bitch.

1·21 / Christmas of '94

Sunday, December 25, early in the morning, Angelito came up to the roof. He was sixty years old, and he lived on the fourth floor. Very nicely and politely, he asked permission to check the water tanks. Later I realized I had confused melancholy with politeness. He said that it had been days since he had had water at home. I let him climb up to the tanks, and a second later, he threw himself down into the street. One hundred and fifty feet of free-fall.

Two stray dogs were the first to come up to the body crumpled on the cement. They ate a good portion of the hot, bloody brain; a delicious breakfast treat.

The elderly and the aging took the matter seriously, showing real interest. It was the fifth death in the neighborhood in the space of a few days. Lily, the storekeeper, said to me, "Respectable people don't travel or do business or go to parties or get mixed up in crowds in the month of December. Believers know that whatever the year brings, it can take away too." None of the younger people were worried. Death has no meaning when you're young. It's too far away.

For years, Angelito was always drunk. His family was scattered: one daughter worked as a prostitute until she managed to get married, and then she moved to a town in Segovia and settled down happily as a housewife. A son left on a raft for Miami. The son's wife, when she found herself without a husband and with a teenage son, seized her chance and began to sing and dance in a salsa group, until by a stroke of luck, she suddenly found herself in Mexico, heading up a radio program as "Lady Salsa." Angelito was left with his wife—they fought and screamed constantly—and his grandson, the son of Lady Salsa and the raft man. Then his wife died of a heart attack, and the old man lived alone with his grandson, Eduardo, a friend of mine.

No one remembered that it was Christmas. The young people knew nothing about it. All they knew was what they had heard the old people say about Christmas Eve and Christmas Day. It was a cold, beautiful Sunday, the sun bright and the sea rough, foaming white on the Malecón, and behind it the deep, intensely blue sky. And in the sky, scraps of cloud scudded quickly, the cold wind blowing hard from the north. Not even such a vision of paradise could dissuade the old man. He threw himself into space anyway.

Eduardo went away with the police. They drew up a death certificate. He was back by noon, and he came up to the roof looking for me. I had a big stash of alcohol hidden in my room. And he was cheerful.

"Man, we're going to make lots of money tonight."

"How? Aren't you busy taking care of things with your grandfather?"

"No, no. That's finished. They say Forensics will be in touch with me later about something or other. Do you still have alcohol?"

"Yes. I've sold a few bottles, but not many."

"Look, I scored two hundred Meprobamato. Tonight a group of Goths are meeting in Colón cemetery. If you bring ten bottles, you'll be able to sell them all."

"Fantastic! How much should we say?"

"A buck for a bottle and a buck a pack for twenty pills."

"Sounds good, man."

"Listen, Pedro Juan, don't let me down. I'll come by for you around eleven and we'll head out."

"Have you been there before?"

"Don't worry about that. I've got a contact name, and there won't be any trouble."

I did good business that night. We went in by the street behind the cemetery. There was a blackout, and it was like walking into the mouth of a wolf. The Goths were gathering inside a big family vault of stone, bronze, and glass; it was neglected and dirty, and the stained glass windows were smashed. Steel letters set in the black marble portal read: Gómez-Mesa Family. In the center was a pink funerary statue of a seated figure, delicately carved.

Some people sitting on the statue lit candles and kissed a skull that was being passed ceaselessly from hand to hand, smoked marijuana, popped pills, and one sang some very slow rock music, accompanying himself on a guitar. Luckily, they bought my alcohol right away. In a corner, a black grave digger who helped them get in and watched out for them was fucking one of them in the ass. If the police showed up, I'd be in trouble, so I interrupted the black man, gave him a dollar, and kept nine for myself. The scene was heating up, and Eduardo didn't want to leave. He was already stoned, and he had a hard-on from watching the black man fucking the Goth in the ass with his huge stiff prick. I got the hell out of there. The truth is, I was scared.

1:22 / Oh, Art!

I put the coffeepot on the stove. Day was breaking, and I went to the window. It's beautiful to watch the sun rise over the sea from up here. Gazing into eternity is a good way to keep your nose out of too much damn squalor—though I'm almost used to the damn squalor. Besides the sea, the clouds, and infinite space, you can see the rooftops of other buildings. I'm at the highest point in the neighborhood. I almost couldn't believe my eyes, but there they were, 250 feet away, on another roof: two girls fucking a guy sitting on a carton of beer. They were wild. The way they were moving! One of them, the one straddling the guy, had beautiful tousled black hair and big, perfect breasts, a gorgeous white body. Rocking astride him, she thrilled to the feel. The other girl, thin and nicely shaped, teased both of them: she nipped at their backs and necks, thrust her tongue into their kisses, and with one hand, she did something between the other girl's buttocks. Then she lay down on the ground, spread her legs wide, and masturbated so that they could get a good look at her black, hairy sex. Oh. And there I was, watching from a distance.

I was careful they didn't see me. My prick was already as stiff as a poker, and I was stroking it. I could almost hear them. Luisa was waking up. I called her to come over and get off with me. But no. "Oh, I don't like that kind of thing." She went out to the sink on the roof to brush her teeth. I insisted, and then she watched for a while, but she *really* wasn't turned on. Very strange. Luisa is a wild woman, and when we fuck, she tells me the things she's done with everyone else. There are always more stories. We've been together for four months, and her repertoire seems limitless. When I'm inside her, the two of us swimming in each other's juices, then Luisa starts talking, and she'll say, "Ah, sweetie, I love pricks so much; I'm such a slut. Once . . ." Each time she tells a better story. She goes into full detail, gets a kick out of it. It's great. Much better than phone sex. Free and live. I hate technology. And with phone sex, technology gets in the way.

Now the guy was jerking himself off, still sitting down, and the two girls spread their legs in front of him and masturbated. They kept it up for a while. Finally, they got dressed, lit cigarettes, and sat on some beer cartons, ready to have a nice conversation. The guy showed every sign of being a European traveler, down to his olive-green backpack. He was an explorer braving the tropical jungle, broadening his horizons by conversing with the native whores. He was smiling and listening. The girls talked and gestured and smiled. They were trying to be agreeable to get more cash out of him, though whores here come very cheap. Oh, the magnificent tropics, humid and sensuous, the tropics within reach of any budget. They had finished just in time. On the neighboring roofs, men were already checking the water tanks, looking to see if the water levels were rising or if they'd be without water for days again.

As I poured the coffee, I heard the old lady downstairs shouting, "Pedro Juan, telephone!" She loves it that I'm always in my room, because she charges me a peso for each call. It was Carmita. Hassling me at seven in the morning, wanting me to come over. Great! A little early-morning business.

Luisa left for her job at the post office. She earns a pittance. I've told her twenty times to quit. As it is, any little thing she sells, she makes three times her salary. Since there's nothing (or rather, there is, in fact, everything, in the dollar stores, available at Tokyo prices) you sell pens, lighters, envelopes, any little thing you can pick up, and you're set. To hell with schedules, bosses, and power trips. Anybody with half a brain can make good money. You've got to take advantage of the crisis: make the best of things. It's too bad I'm not connected to the swindlers upstairs, who divide the spoils among themselves. Well, the little fish get their share in the end. Same as always.

I had more coffee, lit a cigarette, and went out. At eight o'clock in the morning, San Rafael Boulevard was already bustling. The police were there, keeping an eye on the street vendors. But despite the police, the vendors slip past you, whispering their calls, "pizza," "hamburgers and cold drinks," "dollars at fifty pesos, come on, I've only got two left," "coconut and peanut bars, coconut and peanut bars." And on and on, selling everything. It had been thirty-five years since vendors were heard in full cry in Cuba. Now they were starting up again, but fearfully, whispering in the customer's ear, sometimes so softly and rapidly they couldn't be understood. Once in a while a policeman would "confiscate" a bag full of pizzas or hamburgers and take all the vendor's money for good measure. The guy would hand everything over, terrified, because otherwise he'd be slapped with fines, a trial, and a criminal record. It's the police who have most in common with criminals. The meeting of extremes.

The crisis was severe, and it seeped into even the tiniest corner of each person's soul. Hunger and poverty are like an iceberg: the biggest parts can't be seen at first glance. "But one has to move cautiously, my friend and not spin out of control. Little by little, we'll become part of this complex world and market economy, but without abandoning our principles, et cetera." Fuck that! The ridiculous nineties! But I was already recovering from them. I was completely recovered. And I was sated with sex. With Luisa, I came two or three times a day, which is very good for the soul. Discharging semen as you produce it, you keep the storerooms open and lots of things just fall into place and you don't have to worry about them anymore. As I always say: a man without a woman is a complete mess.

I stopped to look at some little Christmas trees. Green pines, small ones. It had been years since I last saw anyone selling Christmas trees. Ever since Christmas, Christmas Eve, Epiphany, all those holidays, were outlawed. Lots of people were watching. Most of them had never seen a Christmas tree in their fucking lives. And behind me I heard a black man, "Let me suck on your titty just a tiny bit, sugar."

And the black woman, "Go on, mother fucker, get away, mother fucker."

And the guy, "Come on, sugar, just a little tiny suck. Come on, don't make a fuss; everybody's watching." And they kept joking back and forth. The woman was beautiful, and the man was big and strong. They were in good spirits.

I like the Boulevard. All the dealers are there, and sometimes something goes down. But just as I was hurrying to see Carmita, who should I run into but Panchito. Oh, hell. Panchito, who never shuts up. I tried to slip away. But no.

"Hey, Pedro Juan!"

"I'm in a hurry, man. I'll catch you later."

"No, wait a minute."

"Damn it, man, I've got people waiting for me."

"Ah, Pedro Juan, don't be such a big shot. Come over here. Do you know anyone who sells bicycle inner tubes?"

"No. I don't have anything to do with that."

"I'm broke. I can't live without my bicycle. The buses from here to Mantilla are out of whack, man."

"Well, Panchito, I've got to go."

"All right, brother, see you."

You've got to cut Panchito off, because otherwise he gets started on some harebrained topic, and next thing you know, it's the next morning and you're still standing there.

At last I made it to Zanja and Dragones. Carmita lives in a wide hallway, directly over the newspaper *Chung Wa*, at the entrance to Chinatown. It was a rat hole, but she had fixed it up a little and moved in with her invalid father, in his wheelchair. The place was hot and dark, the roof was very low, and it was full of dust. Ugh, it's disgusting to live cooped up that way. But what do I care. I've never asked her what happened to the family's ancestral home, in the city where we were both born. It was a turn-of-the-century mansion, surrounded by gardens. It's best not to ask. Now she calls me any time she has a little job for me. That day, I was supposed to wait there, and when I was notified, go somewhere else and pick up two paintings: one by Lam and another by Portocarrero. The same people had a little one by Picasso, too. But they wanted to keep it hidden a while longer. Everyone in Havana had heard how a Picasso got stolen from a rich guy in Miramar. It was a simple job: abracadabra, now you see it, now you don't. Easy, right?

Now, just for moving the Lam and Portocarrero from one place to another, I'd make a hundred bucks. Fine by me. I settled down to wait.

We spent all day drinking rum and eating french fries, sitting against a wall of glass panes, at the end of Carmita's hallway-house. She came up with the idea so all the light wouldn't be blocked. It was nice: a long wall of wood and glass, and farther in, a jumble of books, antique furniture, and porcelain, marble, jade, and bronze pieces. It looked like a museum. Like it cost a fortune.

But there was something oppressive and sad about that place. I didn't know what it was, but I could sense something. I felt strange all day, sad, heavy-hearted, wanting to cry. I thought it was the rum, but rum usually puts me in a good mood and makes me feel like kidding around. I couldn't understand what was happening to me. Carmita noticed.

"What's wrong? Why are you so quiet?"

"I don't know. I'm a little sad."

"Is something wrong?"

"Something's always wrong. I'm used to it."

"Do you know I'm almost convinced of something?"

"What?"

"That those glass panes come from coffins."

"Carmita, for God's sake! Did you get them from the cemetery?"

"I believe in God and the saints. *Santería* comes from the devil."

"That's wrong, Carmen, that's wrong. How could you put up that glass?"

"Because it's impossible to find window panes. You know how it is. They can't be bought at any price. A grave digger from Colón sold me these. And they fit the space well. But lots of people who sit here feel the same way you do. Some of them even cry."

"You're crazy, damn it. You can't do things like that. The dead are here. I can feel it. And that's why things never get better for you. You've got to get rid of them and purge this place."

"I'm not going to take them down or purge anything, and I don't believe in any of that shit! And you, with your *santería* necklaces and your *ildé* and your red handkerchief, excuse me, but all of that is shit!"

"Don't insult me, please. You can do what you want."

Just then Carmita's partner came in. They had been together for years. Carmita and I had known each other since we were children, growing up in the same neighborhood. We went to the same school, and I always liked her. She was pretty and sweet. Then I lost touch with her. I left town, and one day I ran into her in Havana. She was an architect, and definitely a dyke, a little emaciated and skinny, with a certain melancholy look in her eyes. She quit working as an architect and started dealing in art and antiques. She knew a lot about that kind of thing. Most importantly, she knew the value of each piece and what the asshole diplomats who bought from her could get for it in Europe. It's great to be a diplomat. You have immunity and you have your sealed briefcase, all very nice. It's as if you've been told: do whatever the fuck you want, because as far as you're concerned, there are no jails or policemen or treasury officials. Nothing like that. You're Superman.

Carmita and her girlfriend came into the room. I kept drinking rum in that gallery crammed with dusty knickknacks, sadder than a penguin in a cane field. Finally the call came for me. It was ten at night, on the eve of San Lázaro. Carmita kept a little altar to the saint, and she had decorated it with flowers. She wanted me to light a candle. She brought her father in too. We stood there for a while. Each person said a prayer, to consecrate their candle, I suppose. When we came out, the gallery was in flames. Everything was burning: the books, the furniture, the wood and tile ceiling. It was a raging fire.

"Carmita, by God, I warned you!"

"Screw you, Pedro Juan! Help me get these paintings out."

Between the three of us, we hauled out paintings by Amelia Peláez, Romañach, and Ponce, which had been hidden behind the bookshelves. Carmita saved a marble piece too. The flames were huge, and pieces of the roof were falling in. We ran downstairs and I was burned a little, but not badly. The police were already outside, but there was no sign of the firemen. The three of us stood there like statues watching the fire, which had engulfed the whole upper floor. It started in the gallery and demolished it in just a few minutes. I was transfixed by a blue grafitti scrawl on the wall: "Lilliam, I don't care who knows it—you're everything for me. Erick." It was lit in red and orange by the flames, and then it was dark again. A shout from a policeman ordering us to move back snapped me out of my trance and I moved to one side. Another policeman came over to us.

"No one was left inside? Is anyone hurt?"

Then we remembered Carmita's father. She screamed. Dropping the paintings and the marble piece, she went running toward the fire, shouting, "Daddy, daddy." I didn't see her come out again.

At last the firemen arrived and got the fire under control. The

Chinese from the newspaper were hopping nervously around howling that they'd lose their press. Carmita's girlfriend sat crying on the sidewalk. A policeman gathered up the paintings and the marble. He had no idea what they were, but any minute someone would show up who did know. It was best to move on. There was lots of confusion, and I was able to cross the police line. No one stopped me, and I went along Dragones toward Prado. It was almost midnight, the day of San Lázaro. I sat on a bench, said a prayer, and asked the saint to help me, and something echoed in my head. Something that kept repeating, *I'll help you, pilgrim, I'll help you, pilgrim.*

Sometimes, almost always, in fact, it's best to let yourself be guided by instinct and not think. Planning screws up a lot of things in life. Without thinking, I got up and went walking toward Casablanca. There was a four a.m. train for Matanzas, and I slipped down the darkest streets until I came to the docks. I didn't want to run into a policeman who might ask for my ID. I hid for an hour in a doorway. The launch arrived. I crossed the bay. In Casablanca I bought a ticket and got on the train. The locomotive was electric, one of the old ones from the Hersey factory, almost fifty years old. The cars were three tired freight carriers. They had holes knocked in them for windows, and seventy plastic seats, small and as hard as steel, had been installed in each one, as had a dim light bulb. A few fat spiders moved around the bulb weaving their webs and capturing dozens of small moths that flew desperately, blindly, around the light. The spiders had more than enough food. Maybe it was a monotonous diet. Probably they longed to suck the blood of a fly once in a while.

The train left at four o'clock sharp. A miracle! At least something was still running on time. It was almost empty. Of the passengers, a very young little hustler and his three companions stood out. They looked like Goths or something, maybe escapees from the AIDS sanitarium. Then there was a big, dirty black man, wearing pants made from a jute sack; he was traveling to fulfill a vow to San

Lázaro. And a fat, half-crazy old lady, who tried to talk to me a few times and put her hand on my thigh, until I changed seats and told her to go fuck herself in her mother's fucking cunt. The other passengers were a couple: the girl was white, with dyed blond hair, maybe fifteen years old, looking dirty and neglected. She lit one cigarette after another. With her left hand she held a handkerchief to her neck. I thought she might have had an operation until I got a better look. No. Her neck was covered with hickeys and bite marks. Next to her was a black man, an enormous orangutan, who had his arm around her and drooled just to look at her, smelling her, licking her. She got a kick out of it. Every once in a while she would take off her handkerchief, show off her bruised neck, and say loudly enough to let everyone know what savage lust she inspired, "See what you did? Don't do it again."

I couldn't sleep. It was impossible in those seats. I picked up a page from a magazine off the floor: fossil hunters on the Isle of Wight steal a 120-million-year-old dinosaur print. They have to sail from the mainland, use special saws, cut the stone and haul a 450-pound slab back to then sell it for four hundred dollars. I don't think anyone would work that hard and risk so much for so little money. People get bored. A dinosaur movie excites them, and off they go, like children. Everybody wants a giant footprint in their back yard. Well, I was having more luck with paintings and antiques. Too bad it all had to get fucked up.

The train moved slowly through the night. It couldn't go faster than ten or fifteen miles an hour, or the cars would go off the track. It arrived on time in Matanzas, at 8:10 in the morning. I was back in my hometown, burdened by all the memories of shit and happiness the place holds for me. Too many people still knew me there. And by eight in the morning, they were all out on the streets, running around, on the lookout, scraping for pesos. I had to hide. *I'll help you, pilgrim, I'll help you, pilgrim.* But I couldn't think of anything. All right. I left the station. I walked a little ways. From a distance, I saw the place where I lived for twenty-five years. I was happy there, but I never knew it. You only perceive happiness when it's past.

I had a cousin in Matanzas, and I managed to make it to her house, before I could think of what to say to her, but without running into old friends (or, even worse, old enemies). She was a good cousin, married to a gruff, hard-working man who rubbed her the right way with his sandpaper heart.

She brought me coffee, made some rice and beans; I ate lunch and took a long nap. I was feeling better, and thinking I should get going, when her husband came home. He has a farm on the outskirts of Matanzas. He's a strong man, sixty years old. We had some rum, bad, kerosene-stinking rum. But I praised it as if it were vintage brandy. I decided to tell him that my nerves were shot, that I was in psychiatric treatment, and unemployed. That I needed to get out of Havana for a while to recover.

"Up on the roof all I can think about is jumping and landing a hundred feet down."

"Oh, Pedrito, don't say such things! May God forgive you," said my cousin.

"I'm tired of all the poverty, all the hunger, all the people around me. Everybody's always trying to fuck you over, squeeze a few pesos out of you. Because that's what poverty is. Shit attracts shit."

Then her husband said to me, "Stay here with us and rest a while. And if you don't want to think about anything, and you want to stay away from people, you can live in the hut on the farm. And meanwhile you can help me out. Can you do farm work?"

"I can do anything. What do you grow?"

"Cassava, corn, beans, sweet potatoes, squash, peanuts. A little bit of everything. Thanks to the crop, we aren't starving to death. It's in a hard-to-reach spot, and the soil is rich. Big weeds, *aroma* and *marabú*, used to grow on the hill. Whatever you plant there does well."

"All right. I'll do it."

The next day, he woke me up at five in the morning and we

went up to the farm. We got there before dawn. It was paradise. It had been years since I walked in the forest, in the mist and the early-morning quiet, a few blurry cows standing in grass dripping with water. All those trees and that green-gray. The man had a guano hut and even a well. I set up camp there and sent a message back to my cousin: "This place is the cure for my nerves. If anyone asks for me, say you've heard nothing."

So here I am, a runaway slave. My cousin says I was always crazy. "Just leave him up there, and he'll get tired of being alone." But I won't. It's good to be up here by myself in this green and blue forest. Nothing to worry about, nothing to fear. Just land and sky and green. It's beautiful. Besides, if they catch me in Havana, they'll chop off my balls.

II / Nothing to Do

When it is said that a man is a tiger, that does not mean he has the claws and skin of a tiger. —Shri Ramakrishna

Cities, like dreams, are made of desires and fears, even if the thread of their discourse is secret, their rules are absurd, their perceptions deceitful, and everything conceals something else.
—Italo Calvino, *Invisible Cities*

Nothing to Do

2.1 / Nothing to Do

At noon I went to see my aunt in Old Havana. She has cancer of the intestines. The doctors have given up hope. They don't want her in the hospital because they don't know what to do for her. Doctors are good diplomats. They never reveal their ignorance or admit it when they make mistakes. At least, their mistakes they cover up, and ignorance can always be disguised. They told me, "Your aunt is in the final stages of her illness now. She should be kept at home. She has two more weeks left at most." The old lady had been at death's door, in excruciating pain, for two years, hemorrhaging and terrified of dying. She was always an evil bitch. But I don't believe God should punish anyone like that. Of course, God leaves no room for argument.

A neighbor woman takes care of her. I pay her a few pesos, and she tries to help, more or less. Now it doesn't even bother me to see my aunt in pain and all skin and bones. A person can get used to anything.

I started out walking slowly. On Saturdays there aren't many buses running in Havana, hardly any at all. It's best not to worry. So my aunt is dying of cancer, so there's practically no food, so the buses aren't running, so I don't have a job. Best not to worry. Today there was a front-page interview in the paper with an important minister, a show-off. He was fat and he had a big smile on his face, and he was saying, "Cuba is neither paradise nor hell."

My next question would have been, "So what is it, purgatory?" But no. The journalist just smiled contentedly and used the quote as the front-page headline.

I was relaxed, having lots of sex, feeling at peace with myself. Not worried at all. Well, there are always worries. But for now I was able to keep them at a distance. I pushed them a little way into the future. That's a good way to keep them blurry and out of earshot. A woman was living with me. I had gained back a few pounds. And I was alive, though I had nothing to do. Surviving, I think it's called. You let yourself glide along, and you don't expect anything else. It's as easy as that.

Two big, fat, flabby, ugly, white, red, peeling, slow, self-absorbed tourists were walking very slowly past the National Museum. Yes, that's exactly how they looked. The old man had a cane and an enormous heavy suitcase. I couldn't imagine what he was carrying in it. Apparently, they were out for a stroll on a calm, sunny Saturday afternoon. The woman was just as repugnant as the man. The two of them were dressed for fall in an icy fjord city. They were sweating, and they had a stunned look on their faces as they stared all around. They consulted a guidebook with great deliberation and gazed at the historic ship and historic airplanes under the historic trees. Nothing made sense to them. The man looked at me. His mouth was pushed in, as if someone had punched him hard. He was staring at me. Taking advantage of the situation, I brought out my shiny three-peso coins imprinted with Che's head.

"Good afternoon. How are you? Do you like a coin? Is a commemorative coin with Che Guevara image. Only one dollar every one."

"No, shit, youggrrrhttchchssyyye, out! out!"

I didn't understand what he was grunting. He threatened to hit me with his cane. Such hateful people should never leave home.

Their livers must be rotting away and their breath must stink of putrid flesh.

"Go crawl up your mother's stinking cunt, you old bastard!"

He didn't understand me either, but at least I had the satisfaction of answering back. Ugh, what monstrous people!

Luckily, not everything is shit. I kept walking along Trocadero toward home, and as I passed 162, I saw a young couple with a little girl. They were out for a walk too. She was an incredibly beautiful mulatta, with a white skirt and a firm ass, generous and high-set. A mulatta like that throws the landscape off kilter. It's not just her ass. It's all of her. Her warmth, her sensuality, that tight dress showing off her cinnamon skin. She was one of those mulattas with a swing in her step. They know they're in charge, and they carry themselves incredibly well. They move through life turning everything upside down, destruction in their wake. Next to her was her husband, a well-dressed little black man. Between the two of them was the girl, probably three years old. This is why it's so hard for Cubans to live anywhere else. Here you may starve and you may struggle. But the people are out of this world. Like that mulatta. She must have been twenty-three, but when she was forty or fifty, she'd still be just as beautiful. And you always know she's there and that someday you could love her and the two of you could be happy together. While it lasted.

Before going home, I walked to Manrique and Laguna. There was rum. I got in line to buy my monthly bottle. I had my ration book in my pocket, though by now, 1995, it was a joke. The line was moving slowly, and I had some time. I went to my building. On the first floor, one of the decrepit old ladies sold me an empty bottle. I got back in line, and there was Chachareo singing and fooling around, as always. He was a pitiful, ragged old man. He always managed to wheedle a bit of rum out of people, and he'd collect it in a beer can. He sang, told stories. The people in line would ignore him, but he kept shoving himself drunkenly at them. He'd search out your eyes, then caper around, and when you were buying your bottle of rum, he would ask for a little. It was always the same. He only needed a quarter of an inch every half hour to keep himself perennially tipsy.

Then he looked at a boy, part mulatto but mostly Indian, and just as he was about to dance around singing about beer and rum, the kid blew up and shouted, "Cool it. And stay away from me, or I'll put two bullets through your head, you drunken piece of shit. Don't mess with me!"

He pulled up his shirt and showed his pistol. Chachareo felt challenged.

"You're not man enough to draw that pistol!"

A guy behind me said to me, "That little prick is a policeman. And a nasty son of a bitch. Trust me, this is going to get ugly."

The policeman tightened his lips and looked away, putting on a tough-guy face. Chachareo went on, "Today's the day you die! Do you think you can scare a real man that way? If you draw that pistol, today's the day you die! I'm a real man!"

From the line, two women called, "Chachareo, keep singing. Come over here by us and keep singing."

The policeman tightened his lips. His eyes flashed lightning rays, but he didn't draw his pistol. Chachareo went to the end of the line. The women called him over again. From the line, someone shouted in falsetto, "Policeman, oh puleezeman." People laughed, and the policeman turned bright red.

He was at the boiling point. Near the back of the line, Chachareo was saying something about Easterners who come to Havana and act like big shots, and he started to sing a guarachita, rhyming marijuana with Havana.

No blood was shed, thank goodness.

At last it was my turn in front of the barrel. I got my little bottle filled, my ration book marked, and I paid. Then I went straight to my room on the roof. No one was there. The old man next door had killed himself. The old woman developed a horror of the room and of loneliness, and now she was with one of her daughters. Luisa wasn't home either. There was a strong smell of perfume in the air. She had doused herself with half a bottle. She likes those strong perfumes. Everything about her is outrageous. She must have been out on the Malecón, since it was dark now. Probably she was making lots of money. Fridays and Saturdays are good, though lately there's more and more competition.

I poured myself a glass of rum and sat down quietly outside. El Morro was golden and the sea calm. An enormous empty tanker moved out of the port. Three sailors were working in the prow. They picked something up. The machinery purred softly. The boat was so big and it came so close that I could almost feel the steel plates vibrating. It was green and red, and it steamed quickly away, fading into the evening fog. A solitary figure, dressed in white, leaned against the railing on the third deck. He watched the beautiful golden city in the dusk, and I watched the green and red ship lose itself in the fog as it slipped away.

2·2 / Stars and Losers

I like to smell my armpits while I masturbate. The smell of sweat turns me on. It's dependable, sweet-smelling sex. Especially when I'm horny at night and Luisa is out making money. Though it's not the same anymore. Now that I'm forty-five, my libido isn't what it used to be. I have less semen. Barely one little spurt a day. I'm getting old: slackening of desire, less semen, slower glands. Still, women keep fluttering around me. I guess I've got more soul now. Ha, a more soulful me. I won't say I'm closer to God. That's a silly thing to say, pedantic: "Oh, I'm closer to God." No. Not at all. He gives me a nod every once in a while. And I keep trying. That's all.

Well, it was time to get out. Solo masturbation is the same as solo dancing: at first you like it and it works, but then you realize you're an idiot. What was I doing standing there naked jerking off in front of a mirror? I got dressed and went out. I had put on dirty, sweaty clothes. Today I was definitely repulsive. Going down the stairs, I ran into the morons crying on the fifth floor. They're young, but they're morons, mongoloids, or crazy, loony, I don't know, some kind of retards, idiots. They've been together for years. They stink of filth. They shit in hidden places on the stairs. They pee everywhere. Sometimes they walk around their room naked and come right up to the door. They make a racket, they slobber. Now she was sitting on a stair step wailing at the top of her lungs. "I love you so much, but I can't. I love you so much, but I can't do it that way. I love you so much. Oh, darling! Ohhhh! I love you so much."

He lit a cigarette, moved to one side to let me by, and said, "I know you love me, sweetie, I know you love me, sweetie." And he started sobbing too.

At least today they hadn't crapped on the stairs. What they needed was a good grooming with a stiff brush, soap, and a cold shower. Coming out into the four o'clock light, I stopped: what to do? Should I go to the gym and box a little, or head for Paseo and Twenty-third? Last time I won twenty dollars at Russian roulette. It was the right time of day. Someone would surely be there. I went off to play Russian roulette.

I like to walk slowly, but I can't. I always walk fast. And it's silly. If I don't know where I'm going, what's the hurry? Well, that's probably exactly it: I'm so terrified, I can't stop running. I'm afraid to stop for even a second and find out I don't know where the fuck I am.

I stopped in at Las Vegas. Las Vegas is immortal. It will always be there, the place where she sang boleros, the piano in the dark, the bottles of rum, the ice. All of it just as it always has been. It's good to know some things don't change. I gulped down two shots of rum. It was very quiet and very cold and very dark. So much heat and humidity and light outside, and so much noise. And all of a sudden, everything is different when you come into the cabaret. It's really a tomb, where time has stopped forever. Just sitting there for a minute, it made me think.

Soul and flesh. That was it. One glass of rum and already the two were in painful confrontation, the soul on one side, flesh on the other. And me torn in between, chopped into bits. I was trying to understand. But it was difficult. Almost impossible to comprehend anything at all. And the fear. Ever since I was a child, there was always the fear. Now I had given myself the task of conquering it. I was going to a gym to box and I was toughening up. I'd box anyone, though I was always trembling inside. I tried to hit hard. I tried to let myself be swept away, but it was impossible. The fear was always there, going about its own business. And I'd say to myself, "Oh, don't worry, everybody's afraid. Fear springs up before anything else. You've just got to forget it. Forget your fear. Pretend it doesn't exist, and live your life."

I downed two more shots of rum. Delicious. I was in a delicious state, I mean. The rum wasn't so delicious. It tasted like diesel fuel. And I went off to play Russian roulette. I had seven dollars and twenty-two pesos left. Not bad. Things had been much worse and I had always managed to stay afloat.

There were people at Paseo and Twenty-third. And Formula One was there, with his bicycle. It was the right time of day. Almost five o'clock. There's lots of traffic at that intersection. Traffic in all directions. We settled our bets. I played my seven dollars at five to one. If I won, I'd have thirty-five. I always bet that the kid will make it across. A black man, wearing silver and gold chains everywhere, even on his ankles, went by. That asshole always bets he won't make it. "I bet on blood, man. Always blood. That's all you need to know." Whenever we ran into each other he'd take my bet at five to one. Even so, I never made much money.

A month ago, I set a record: I won thirty-five dollars in one shot. I was lucky. Delfina was with me. I cashed in, showed her the money, and she went crazy. I call her Delfi because she has the most half-assed name in Havana. We went to the beach, and we rented a room there and partied for two days, with all the food, rum, and marijuana we wanted. Delfi is a beautiful, sexy black woman, but I found out I couldn't handle orgies like that anymore. All Delfi wanted was prick, rum, and marijuana. In that order. But I couldn't always be fucking. When I couldn't get it up, insatiable Delfi tried to see what she could do by sticking her finger up my ass. I slapped her a few times and said, "Get your finger out of my ass, you black bitch." But still, we kept fucking and fucking. Maybe out of inertia. When the rum and the marijuana and the dollars ran out, I came back to my senses. I ached everywhere: my head, my ass, my throat, my prick, my pockets, my liver, my stomach. Not Delfi. She was twenty-eight years old, and she was a black powerhouse, muscular and tough. She was ready to keep going for two or three more days without stopping. Tireless, that woman. Amazing. She's a marvel of nature.

The kid who was going to play Russian roulette picked up his bicycle. He had a red handkerchief tied around his head. He was just a kid, mulatto, fifteen or sixteen years old, and never separated from his bicycle. He wouldn't even let go of it to take a shit. It was a small, sturdy bike, shiny chrome with fat tires. He earned his living from it. He got twenty dollars straight up each time he made it across. He was good. Other times, he performed stunts, and he charged for them, too: he'd make ten children lie down in a row in the middle of the street, then he'd back up several feet, cross himself, take off like a shot, and sail over the kids. He'd do that on any street, wherever he was called. People bet on him, but he wouldn't bet. He'd take his twenty dollars and get out. He was vain, and he'd say to people, "Formula One, that's me."

Now Formula One was riding up Paseo. He did a few jumps on his bicycle between cars. He looped, leapt into the air, twirled a few times, and landed on one wheel. He was a master. People watched him, but they didn't know what the kid was up to. There were seven of us, and we played it cool on the corner by the convent under the trees. There wasn't even one policeman around. Formula had to wait for an order from one of us. Just as the light turned green on Twenty-third, a guy next to me dropped his arm and Formula took off like lightning down Paseo. On Twenty-third, heading toward La Rampa, thirty cars accelerated when the light turned green, rush hour traffic raring to go. And heading in the opposite direction, up the street toward Almendares, came thirty or forty more, growling and desperate. In total, Formula had seventy chances to be crushed to death and just one to live. My seven dollars were in the balance. If the kid was killed, I'd have nothing. I needed Formula to cross safely and earn his twenty dollars. And he made it! He was a flash of light. I don't know how the fuck he did it. Just like a bird. All of a sudden, he was sparkling on the other side of Paseo, twisting in the air and laughing.

He came toward us laughing as hard as he could. "I'm Formula One!" I collected my thirty-five dollars. I gave five to Formula and called him aside. I shook his hands. They were dry and steady.

I looked him in the eye and asked him, "Don't you get scared?"

He shrugged his shoulders. "Oh, whitey, don't make me laugh. I'm Formula One, man! Formula One!"

Before his time, four boys were killed in the same spot. I don't want to think about it. Two others didn't have the guts to go for it. That's life. Only a very few survive: the biggest stars and the biggest losers.

2:3 / Breaking Out

I was buying food outside the city and bringing it back and selling it in Havana. Anything would sell, from heads of garlic to lemons, even ox meat, whatever could be found. I came to a farmer's house and the guy had a dead horse on the patio. Its belly was already half-swollen. The farmer could barely hold the men off, a crowd with machetes, knives, and sacks. They wanted to cut the animal up and take it away in pieces. They were like a pack of dogs. I counted them: eight skinny, starving, dirty, wild-eyed black men, dressed in rags. The farmer explained that the animal was sick when it died and that it was rotting quickly. They weren't arguing. All they were asking was to be allowed to take a piece of it, and they would bury the head and the hooves themselves, and whatever else was left of the mangy, skeletal beast, covered in green flies. Worms and pus oozed from its rear end.

"Why don't you just let them eat it and to hell with it?" I asked.

"No. I'm waiting for the police to come. If they don't confirm that it died sick, then I'll be taken to court."

"And after that?"

"After that they can eat it. What do I care?"

I asked him if he had chickens, eggs, anything. But all the guy wanted to do was wait for the police to come so he could wash his hands of the whole business. He said, "Do you see what I'm seeing,

Havana man? We thought the Angolans were savages because they ate fried rats. And the Ethiopians, with their rotten cow intestines. Now it's our turn. There aren't even any cats left. They've been eaten. Find me a cat and I'll buy it from you. I'm overrun by rats."

It seemed he had had a good scare. The men were desperate.

I knew one of them. In the past, he had helped me find farmers with food to sell. He and his family had changed their last name three times in just a few years, and they still didn't think they had it right. A hundred years ago, slaves took the same last name as their masters. They were baptized with a random first name and the master's last name. But these people weren't sure which family their great-grandparents and grandparents had belonged to. They had even less of an idea where Nigeria or Guinea were. In just a hundred years, they had forgotten everything. Now all they wanted was to mix with whites. They said it was for the "advancement of the race." And they knew what they were talking about. People of mixed blood are far superior to pure blacks or pure whites. Crossbreeding is a good thing.

He was nice, that black guy. Always laughing.

"What's up, Gener-Iglesias-Pimienta?"

"Fighting the good fight, Havana man."

"I can see that. This horse is rotting. Leave it alone."

"No. When it's cooked over a good fire, the rot won't matter."

"Do you know if anyone's got food?"

He thought for a minute and said, "Oh, yes, Carmelo, the old man across the way. Yesterday he had farmer's cheese. Maybe there's still some left."

I went off in search of Carmelo. He had nothing left. Two cows don't make for much. People had already snatched up what he did have.

The train was about to come. There was no time left to keep walking the fields. It was incredible, but true: I was returning empty-handed. It was a little after six in the evening when the train arrived. I spent the whole night famished and nodding off in a dark car stinking of filth and urine, crammed with hundreds of people returning to Havana with chickens, pigs, sheep, sacks of rice and foodstuffs. The only idiot coming back empty-handed was me. Fuck, shit, each time I thought about it, it made me want to beat my head against the wall of the car. I hadn't looked hard enough. I could have found something, lemons, oranges, enough at least to pay for my train ticket. We were entering the jungle, being dragged in kicking and squealing.

All of us were creeping out of our cages and beginning to struggle in the jungle. That's what it was. We were stiff coming out of our cages, sluggish and fearful. We had no idea what it was like to fight for our lives. But we had to try. We had been locked up in a zoo for thirty-five years. We had been given a little food and medicine, but we had no idea what it was like out there beyond the bars. And all of a sudden came the switch to the jungle. Our brains were sleepy and our muscles soft and weak. Only the fittest could hope to survive. I was trying, hard. Very hard.

The train got in at dawn. I live close to the station. I climbed up the eight flights to my room as best I could, and I lay down to sleep. I had a nightmare: a guy who was really me came up to me with a knife and cut some steaks out of my belly. The guy kept talking and talking, but I wasn't listening. I don't know what he was saying. At the same time, I was screaming in pain each time he cut a piece out of me. There was no blood. Just a few fine, red, fresh sirloins, and me screaming. Then I woke up. Someone was banging on the door and shouting, "Pedro Juan, Pedro Juan!"

It was Caridad, hysterical, dragging her little boy by the hand. It had been five years since we broke up, and we had this six-year-old boy. Lazarito came out mulatto, but luscious. At the age of six, he looks like he's ten. He inherited the best of both of us. Which is, by the way, just what I was saying before.

Caridad came in like a whirlwind and wouldn't let me say a word. She's been living with a little white playboy pimp for a year now. She doesn't like black men.

"I caught Roberto sucking Lazarito's prick! He was sucking his prick and playing with him, the bastard! You've got to kill him, Pedro Juan! You've got to kill him, goddamnit! He's a faggot, the bastard, and he wants my son to be one too!"

"Hold on, calm down. Sit down for a minute and tell me what happened."

"Are you just going to stand there like nothing happened? Man, don't you have blood in your veins?"

"Sure I do. But how did it happen?"

"Never mind. Never mind. I'm not telling you shit. I left early and I came right back. He was expecting me later. And I took him by surprise. I threw a kitchen knife at him, but I missed. Oh, I should have stabbed him! The boy was still half-asleep, in bed, and Roberto was sucking his prick and masturbating him."

Lazarito looked scared, and he was crying.

"Now I'm going to the police to accuse him of child abuse! The bastard. I won't rest until I see him in jail!"

And turning to the child, she shook him by the arm.

"And you have to grow up to be a man, damn it, you have to be a man! Why did you let him do that to you? Come on now, tell me. Why did you let him?"

Tears were rolling down Lazarito's cheeks.

"Don't cry, damn it, men don't cry! You're a man, so stop crying!"

And she went out, dragging the boy after her.

"You find him and beat him up, Pedro Juan! You find him and kill him, I'm going to the police!"

I didn't go looking for him and I didn't kill him either. I slept until late in the afternoon. When I got up, I was hungry as a wolf. I wanted to wash and go out for something to eat. But then Caridad came back, just as upset as before. She hadn't calmed down, and she was still dragging Lazarito by the arm.

"You're a fucking loser! Starting today, Lazarito is no son of yours. You don't know how to stand up for him. Why didn't you smash that fucker's face in? Don't tell me you're scared of him. You're a gutless son of a bitch. Don't ever speak to me again and don't ever come visit the boy. I never want to see you again. That bastard is behind bars and he's going to be tried. But I'll be the one bringing charges against him, because you're a pathetic excuse for a man. From now on I'm Lazarito's mother and his father too, because you're a good-for-nothing and a piece-of-shit coward."

And she left without giving me a chance to open my mouth. I stood there in the doorway. Thinking. No. There was nothing to think about. My mind was blank. And there wasn't even any rum to be had.

2:4 / My Ass in Danger

Luckily, I was only locked up for seven days. A huge brute was determined to fuck me in the ass, and I was running out of ways to stop him. The only thing I hadn't tried was stabbing him in the heart with a homemade blade. I always kept a poker face, I didn't talk to anyone, I kept everyone at arm's length, but he tormented me so much that one day I went for his neck. The guy was a hulk, like a retarded orangutan. I couldn't beat him in a fistfight; he knocked me out. So I couldn't even prove I was a man that way. Well, he didn't care what anyone was. One of the other inmates told me that he would latch on to someone and watch him and work him over and then force himself into his ass no matter what. His last victim was a young black man, and he had to be taken straight to the hospital, hemorrhaging.

I made it out with my ass intact, and I tried to keep cool for a while. At the trial, they gave me a ten-thousand-peso fine just for being caught with twenty lobsters. If they had caught me with the beef a day earlier, I would have gotten three or four years. That really would have been the end of my ass, and maybe my eardrums too.

I found myself a disgusting job in the slaughterhouse, working with ground soy meat. All day hauling boxes of half-rotten skins, cow muzzles, intestines, fat, eyes, ears, all the stinking shit no one ever thinks about, the most repulsive stuff. Between the two of us, a black man and I set the boxes down near the mill. Boxes of soy came in from the other side. And two other guys measured the ingredients for the ground meat. "Protein. Lots of protein for the people, my friend," the measuring man shouted at me over the noise of the mill. And he laughed, with his fat, lazy face. I never knew if he was joking or not. That was all the conversation we had. He talked. I didn't want any more trouble and I refused to open my mouth, because even talking about protein was political. Like whether the government was mixing in poison to kill everyone and blame it on the Yankees. What the fuck did I care. I was cool.

But trouble has a way of finding me. Leaving the slaughterhouse one afternoon at four, I didn't even wait for the bus. I was walking. I crossed Carlos III. As I went along Espada toward San Lázaro, there was a bar that had a special rum from Santiago, *paticruzao*. Goddamn, it was good. You can never find it anywhere. It was an airy bar, in the neighborhood of Cayo Hueso, but very quiet at that time of day. A bar with benches. They sell soup and broth to the poorest of the poor. Sitting down in a corner, I ordered a double and felt much calmer. Rum smooths over my tiredness. It numbs me. I was sitting on a bench right next to the sidewalk. The doors were wide, the kind that slide up. I like to sit next to the door. That way if there's a fight, you can get out right away.

The guy drinking next to me started telling me his story. He was a soldier and a week ago he was hired for a special little job. For a few days, he worked from eight in the morning till ten at night, and at the end of it, his eyes would sting, but he made six dollars. His wife took the money, bought a pair of tennis shoes for their son, who had no shoes, and four days later, the kid had ruined them. "We can't keep on like this, pal. The people getting out of here have the right idea." And he went on telling the tale of his woes.

I was listening to his story, but I had my eye on a mulatta who was drinking rum and having a fine time talking to a very fat woman and a black man with six chains around his neck. The black man kept paying for drinks with twenty-dollar bills. The mulatta was watching me out of the corner of her eye too, and I wanted to go up to her the first chance I got. I focused too intently on her mouth and her breasts and on the fun she was having, and I got a hard-on, a serious one. It had been days since I had sex, and I wasn't about to let that mulatta get away from me.

The bartender was a big black guy with the face of a killer, who every two minutes kept saying, "I've got crab enchiladas. Special. With a little bit of hot pepper, too. Make you a ladies' man tonight . . . They're extraspicy, extrasexy."

I was about to finish my second double, when all of sudden, there were two guys in the door behind me, two guys covered in blood and stabbing each other, staggering, half-dead already. Everyone saw them except me, because they were behind me, and I didn't react in time. They fell right on me. Besides being half-dead, they must have been drunk or stoned too. I tried to get off the bench, but the two of them collapsed on top of me. One of them sliced me with his knife, slashing me in the arm and on my right side. Everything happened so fast I couldn't figure out what was going on. I didn't know where they had come from. It all happened in silence. There were no shouts, or even groans. Both of them were dead on top of me, swimming in blood. The place had emptied in a second. The bartender was all alone at the other end of the bar. Even the poor left their plates of soup half-finished and ran out.

A woman came in shouting something and crying, "He killed him, he killed him." Screaming, she threw her arms around one of the corpses.

I tried to get away, but I was up against the bar, and the two dead bodies and the woman were blocking my path. I tried to move anyway. I really had to get out of there. But no. A policeman had come already. He grabbed my arm and asked for my identification.

I tried to explain, "I was having a few drinks here." But it was as if my voice were muted. I could barely hear myself speak. Or it was like I was hearing myself from a distance. I felt for my identification in the back pocket of my pants, and when I held it out to the policeman, I saw that I was covered in fresh blood. My own and that of the men who had just died. I was drenched in blood, too much blood for me to seem innocent. I definitely looked guilty.

Then followed a whole chain of events: patrol car—police station—statements—no one understands why so many cuts and so much blood if I don't know anything—searching for my only witness, the bartender—the guy doesn't show up—held seventy-two hours until things are cleared up—there are other cases—they forget about me—I spend ten days locked up—luckily, it's somewhere else—the guy who's after my ass isn't there—at last they let me go—I lose my job in the slaughterhouse—it looks like I'm back to selling black-market lobsters and beef.

2·5 / Cheerful, Free-Spirited, Noisy

Sometimes you need very little: sex, rum, and a woman who'll murmur sweet nothings in your ear. Nothing clever. I'm tired of sharp, clever people. Then she's gone, and you lie there alone and peaceful. You drink more rum. Or you shower and go to sleep. The next day, you wake up fresh and rested, ready to smile and tell everyone you're fine and life is great. And people say to you, "Oh, how nice. At last, someone who's happy to be alive."

But it's not always like that. Not everything is so easy or goes so smoothly. Sometimes I run into women who are too disconcerting. Like Carmen. She's one of those people who answer life's questions in the simplest of fashions: either you have money or you don't. Nothing else matters. I keep meeting more and more women like her. Maybe they've always been around, but I'm just now starting to notice them. Anyway, I don't want to talk about Carmen. She's too cynical. A practical cynic, I mean. Or maybe not even that. Practical cynics are more productive. No. She's too spiritually poor. Lacking enough spirituality to take advantage of the kind of pathetic gorilla-man who gives her money. She hates him, but she puts on a good show and she charges for it. She's not worth remembering.

Then came María. The complete opposite. Incandescent. A tempestuous poet from Guanabacoa. She'd write poems to me on green paper in her big, round handwriting and shower me with them: "I swoon in the voracious cataclysm of the impossible." "Your breath, a volcano in my body. My mirrors howl."

I couldn't take quite so much ardor, withstand the insatiable voracity of a frenzied mulatta. My skin and my heart were burned up in a flash. Then I was reborn from the ashes. And I was still alone.

So there I was, with nothing to do. Peaceful on my roof, drinking rum in the twilight. I wasn't interested in having a serious relationship with anyone anymore. I had been wounded so deeply that I couldn't bear the thought of going through the same thing again. And I decided to live in solitude. My usual life, but alone. It makes sense: every once in a while someone fascinates me. Someone manages to shine. I like it that way. No pledges of eternal loyalty.

But man can't live on love and loneliness alone. He has to do something to make money, so he can eat, and drink a few beers every afternoon. I had lost my ground-soy-meat job in the slaughterhouse, and I couldn't find other work. The crisis was at its height in 1995. Everything was in crisis: ideas, bank accounts, the present. Never mind the future.

One afternoon I was having a beer sitting next to some of the old regulars. Just to get a rise out of them I asked, "How's it going, Old Regulars?" They didn't catch my tone, and we chatted for a while. One asked me what I did. I told him nothing, I didn't have a job.

And another, who had been quiet up until then, asked me, stumbling over his words, "Do you want to work at the Municipal Hospital? It's a good job. The work isn't hard. I was there today, and there's a vacancy."

"If it was so great, why did you leave? What did you do there?" I asked him.

"I was in the potato room. You go there, talk to Doctor Simon, and tell him I sent you, that Rafael sent you. You'll like it. Everybody likes it there."

The next day I went to the Municipal Hospital and asked for Doctor Simon. I imagined I would have to peel potatoes all day. I was steered down some dark corridors, I waited for quite a while, and finally there I was in front of Doctor Simon.

"Rafael told me to come see you. He said there was a vacancy."

"Right, we had to fire him."

"Oh, he didn't tell me he was fired."

"He was lucky we just fired him and we didn't take him to court."

"What was he accused of?"

"Of raping cadavers."

"What? But didn't he work in the potato room?"

"The potato room is what people call the morgue. And it's against the rules to call it that. Are you a friend of Rafael's?"

"No. I just happened to meet him."

"He's an imbecile. We caught him raping a woman's corpse. I myself tried to pull him off, but he's such a moron, he ignored me until he had his orgasm. He came inside a corpse! And then he tried to appeal to the union and make a fuss because I fired him on the spot."

"Is he retarded?"

"He must be. I don't know. He confessed that he used to do it all the time. And he worked here for three years."

"It takes all kinds."

"The opening is for an assistant. You'd have to assist the doctors in the morgue."

"Oh, doctor, I don't think I'd be able to. The coroners? No. I couldn't."

"You've got to be mentally prepared. Most people can't take it."

"Human beings are mentally prepared for life, not death."

"If you want a hospital job, you'll have to stop philosophizing."

"Of course, of course. No more philosophy."

"I think the autoclave people need an assistant."

I went to the autoclave room. The autoclave is a caldron-sized pressure cooker. It's where all the instruments go. They're disinfected and reused. My job was to retrieve them from all over the hospital. I went around the wards with a little cart and I was given tweezers, syringes, things like that. Eight hours pushing a little cart, making 120 pesos a month. A miserable existence. At least it was entertaining. A person could do the work for a few months, waiting for something better to turn up. Whole lifetimes go by like that, while you wait for something better. And then there were the nurses. The cheerful nurses. I liked some of them, and some of them liked me. I went out with two or three of them. Nurses are very good people. They're cheerful, simple, easygoing. No brain-teasing tangles or anything like that. Nothing complicated. And they make a person feel good. The only problem is that they want to marry doctors so they can come and go from the hospital in a car, and put on serious faces, as if they're very worried, and not look at anyone. Then they'll wear lots of makeup and necklaces and beautiful white bathrobes sent to them from Miami as gifts from the doctor's relatives. Some of them have already managed to lure doctors into their snares. Into their cunts, I mean. But that's all right. The rest are still cheerful, noisy, free-spirited. And best of all, simple. They'll stay that way until they snag a doctor at last.

Then I got involved with one of them. Very cheerful, noisy, free-spirited. She was a big mulatta, still somewhat pretty, but beginning to lose ground. Her name was Rosaura. She had a child with a doctor, a white one, of course, but she didn't end up marrying him or riding in his car. She still took the bus. When she turned forty, she gave up. There was a lot of competition from pretty young nurses. We went out, and it was very nice. I don't know why it is, but nurses are especially uninhibited. They're comfortable giving you blow-jobs, they strip in front of you, they drink rum, they masturbate, they whisper X-rated stories in your ear. Autobiographical stories, I mean. They put on a sex show for you, and they know how to do it right. Maybe I was lucky and landed some of the hottest ones. But I like that. I can't resist playing games. And prudish people usually play their games when they're fully dressed. I've had plenty of chances to find that out for myself.

Everything was going fine. She wasn't bothered by my lowly job or my token salary. I was white, the sex was good, and we played by the rules. That was all that mattered. Mulattas are racists. Much more so than whites or blacks. I don't know why it is, but they can't stand blacks. Rosaura used to say to me, "I've never had a black boyfriend. Sleep with a black man? Me? No way. The minute they start sweating, they stink. Besides, they're crude." Well, there was no mystery in it. One day I went to her house, and her mother was very black. She says her father was just as white. They talk about all that out loud. And that's it. No mystery. It's more like a crazy comedy.

Rosaura had two brothers. They didn't work. They were home and we drank a little rum. We chatted. All well and good. Then the old lady told me I should come back another day to consult the *santos*. She brought me into the *santos'* room. It was properly furnished, an impressive place. The old woman was showing me the room to warn me, as if to say, "Look what I have here. If you treat Rosaura like shit, you'll be sorry." That old *santera* was tough. She took good care of her family. Her children and grandchildren were all she had.

Well, things were going fine with Rosaura. Everything very loose, very happy, oh so nice. But one morning a doctor came into the ward, thirsty and sweating, opened the refrigerator, took out Rosaura's glass of ice water, and drank from it. Rosaura, who saw him do it, got angry. "Listen, you pig, why are you drinking out of my glass? Give it to me!" And she tried to take it away from him. The doctor, thinking he was being funny, spit some water at her, straight out of his mouth into her face. Bad move. Rosaura got even angrier and smacked the guy. The doctor thought she was playing, but Rosaura was mad. The doctor was a karate champ. He dropped the glass and put her in a headlock. There was a struggle. Rosaura fell squarely on her buttocks and fractured her spinal cord. Afterwards, it was discovered that she had osteoporosis. She had an operation, and she was put in a cast from her neck to her coccyx.

When her brothers heard the story, they grabbed two big

butcher knives and went looking for the doctor all over the hospital. The guy managed to escape in time, then went into hiding, and called the police. The two black men were thrown in jail. Rosaura pressed charges against the doctor and against another man for covering up for him. They had to give up their jobs and they were forbidden to practice ever again. "Now I'm on the donkey's back, and I'm going to beat him all the way to the finish line," Rosaura told me. Her legs were paralyzed. A splinter of bone had pierced her medulla. She would probably be in a wheelchair forever.

The old woman wanted to do her part. "My prettiest daughter crippled, and my two sons in jail. That son of a bitch will pay. He'll pay for everything he's done. Pedro Juan, you have to bring me something of his. A shirt, a handkerchief, anything. I'll make him a cripple. I'll curse his bones! He's going to wish he was never born. I won't stop until I see him in a wheelchair. You bring me something of his, my child, whatever you can find, steal something with his sweat on it, and bring it here, because I'm going to finish him off for good. Go on, you're the man of the house now."

Damn it, just when things were going so well. Why the fuck did I ever start things with that mulatta in the first place?

2·6 / Doubts, Many Doubts

Extreme poverty was wreaking havoc. Things just kept getting worse, and everyone was trying to get out however they could, go somewhere else. It was a stampede. Carlitos, born and raised in the midst of chaos, called his mother and brother every day, crying. He was miserable in Miami, and he couldn't sleep. He wasn't enjoying his *American dream*. He was spending a fortune on phone calls and he wasn't concentrating his interests or energy on anything concrete. He couldn't. Inside of him was the desperation of chaos. His heart still beat behind bars.

At the time, I was sleeping with his sister. She was a doctor, and she read Bécquer and loved Mexican soap operas and the poems of spiritual counsel by Benedetti, which she'd copy for me on prescription slips, flooding me with them so that I would learn a little poetry. She planned to give me an education in aesthetics. She was convinced of my bad taste when she discovered *Poetry Against Hairloss*, by Nicanor Parra, in a corner of my apartment.

She used phrases like "making love," "we could be happy," "I never tell lies." She was a confused person. It's often that way. It's confusing to be surrounded by too many people. And then comes the tug-of-war between what you should do, what you can do, and what you want to do, and what you shouldn't do, can't do, and don't want to do.

She was always having dizzy spells because she took too many sedatives; she had tried to commit suicide three times and the suicidal impulse still lingered, coiled and suppressed. She spent lots of time with a psychologist who was trying to help her come to terms with her life as it was.

Anyway, she wasn't trustworthy, and my sex and her love didn't last long. "An abyss of misunderstanding separated the beautiful young lady and the distinguished older gentleman," as they say in the romance novels.

By the way, I counted, and in the last five years I've had sex with twenty-two women. Hardly ideal for a forty-five-year-old man. Not that I regret anything, but I was worried. Not on account of my inner self, but because of AIDS. I'd hate to die before my time because I stuck my prick in the wrong hole.

Well, promiscuous or not, I had to keep going. Keep toughening myself up, of course. People thought I was starting to act my age. But it wasn't that. I was just trying to make myself tougher and tougher so no one would be able to jerk me around. It was every man for himself. I had to carefully ration the little love I had left inside so the level in the tank wouldn't drop to zero and the engine wouldn't fail. I hadn't given up hope of refueling somewhere, idiot utopian thinker that I was, screwed but dreaming of finding something beautiful inside myself that would fill me up so that once again I could be the generous good lover I used to be. How stupid can you get? I'd ask myself sometimes. Other times, when I was calmer, I'd tell myself it was still possible.

So that's how it was. I worried about getting older and about the way old people are fated to be lonely, things like that. But there were always more women, and they'd tell me, "Oh, I love older men! It would be so nice to live here with you, and we could do this, we could do that." And I would think: right, I'm a respectable older man. If they knew the truth, they'd run away screaming and never come back again.

So there I was, forty-five years old, still alone. And each day things got better for me, and easier. "It hurts most the first time you're burned, then you develop a thick skin," as my friend Hank says. Once you turn forty, everything is simpler. Or at least you see things more clearly.

I had come to some conclusions. Ha ha. "Some conclusions." Ridiculous! Is anyone in the world really qualified to claim that? Well, what I mean is, I finally understood a truth as old as man himself, but I had to keep relearning it: the guiding principle of the poor is to love and admire whoever has money and tosses them a crumb. The guiding principle of the slave is to love and admire the master. It's as simple as that. The poor man, or slave, it makes no difference what you call him, can't afford to have a complex ethical code or demand much from his pride, since he's always in danger of starving to death. "If the master gives me a little, that's enough, and I love him"; that's all. Women generally understand that and accept it from a very young age. But we men make things a little more complicated, wanting to rebel, take stands, and all that. In the end, we come to understand it too, just a little bit later.

So, one face of poverty is the well-developed instinct for self-preservation. But poverty has many faces. Maybe the most distinct is the one that strips you of all nobility, or at least of generosity of spirit, turning you into a mean, wretched, calculating kind of person. Survival is all that matters, and to hell with solidarity, kindness, or peaceful living.

While I was in the midst of so many doubts, my old friend Alejandro came to visit, a little bit drunk, and happy. He had just found out he had won a U.S. residency visa in the lottery. He was ecstatic. All his female friends wanted to marry him. They were offering him money to tie the knot and take them with him. But he refused them all. He only wanted to take his mother. "She's the only burden I'll shoulder, so long as the bastards at the embassy let me have a visa for her. I can't leave the old lady here alone."

I brought out a bottle of rum, and we drank. We drank a lot that night, Alejandro planning what he would and wouldn't do in Miami. We talked so much that now I can't remember anything we said. I told him, "I'm going to send a letter in for the next drawing. Maybe I'll get lucky."

Today I'm hung over. The rum was disgustingly bad, and I have a headache. But even so, I'm still trying to put my inner life in order. From the outside, it looks as if I have no problems. Everybody thinks there's just one Pedro Juan, very dependable, very capable, very happy. They don't realize that on the inside all the little Pedros are rolling around punching each other, tripping each other up. They're all trying to show their faces at the same time.

2:7 / Hanging Out in Havana

I was out in the country for a few days, and I came back loaded down: lobsters, beef, and twelve liters of rum. The police searched the bus twice, and both times I was practically choking on my balls. But I look respectable, and that always saves me. At the bus station I had to hire a car to get home, I had so much to carry. The pirates were charging sixty pesos for the short trip to Central Havana. If I tried asking them to give me a better deal, they'd always come back with the same song and dance: "I have to make at least enough to pay for the gas. And gas is high . . . gas is high."

At last a very timid man came up to me and offered me his rickshaw, a bicycle with a little cart attached. He seemed almost embarrassed.

"I weigh 176 pounds and these boxes weigh 110 pounds more. Will you be able to do it?"

"Sure, why not."

"What will you charge to take me to San Lázaro and Perseverancia?"

"Twenty-five pesos."

We went along Ayestarán, Carlos III, Zanja, Belascoaín, San Lázaro. Each time a little down slope gave him a breather, the guy told me a piece of his life story. He was a metals technician at a foundry. When the crisis began, he lost his job. "I've been scrambling to make a living on the street for five years now. It isn't easy. My wife, a kid, and me. And now she's pregnant again. But she's keeping it. After all, four mouths are as easy to feed as three."

The guy was pedaling hard, sweating. Eleven o'clock on a May morning, and the sun was already beating down hard.

"You must lose three or four pounds a day working this little gig."

"No, not anymore. At first I got skinny. But no more. At least now the cart is paying its keep. It brings in a few pesos. Even if it's just enough so that we can eat, we scrape by."

"Right, and anyway, brother, we're all skinny."

"True. And who knows how much longer this misery will last."

The man was skin and bones. He couldn't possibly have been any skinnier. We arrived. I paid him and thought about giving him a five-peso tip. But no. No one tips me. On the contrary, everyone haggles over the price of the meat, the rum, the lobsters. So I wished him luck, and it was on to the next thing.

A black luxury-model Havanautos was parked outside the building.

I went straight to my room. I put the lobsters and the meat in the fridge. Then I made coffee, and I sat down to rest. The old lady next door started screaming. It seemed she was having a nervous breakdown because there hadn't been any water for four days, not in this building or anywhere nearby. There was nowhere to get even a bucket of water. And the old lady was shouting. All of a sudden she came out on the patio, hysterical, tearing at her hair. "Get me some water, damn it all, get me water from somewhere! A curse on that fucking son of a bitch."

A son and a daughter were taking the brunt of it. "Shut up, mother, shut up, can't you!"

Everyone came out of their rooms to watch Prudencia have her attack. It was an old black man who finally calmed her down, coming up to her and whacking her with a branch of *paraíso*, mumbling something that no one understood. Prudencia collapsed and I thought she had passed out. The old man kept passing the *paraíso* over her. He revived her. People sat her in a chair. I thought about bringing her some coffee, but I held myself back. No one eats at anyone else's place here. They're terrified of witchcraft, as well they should be. I'm new in the building, and people don't trust me. I don't trust them either.

The stench of shit and piss wafting from the bathrooms was unbearable. Four days without water in this heat, in a building where almost two hundred people live, is enough to drive anyone crazy, just like that fat old lady. I closed the door and went out to sit on the corner for a while.

Right away, a guy I know came up to me.

"Hey, man, Formula One is coming this afternoon to jump over ten kids."

"Great! One hundred pesos says he makes it."

"No, I'm betting he'll make it too. I know he will."

"So much for that, then. Do you know anyone who might want to buy beef or lobster?"

"Fuck, Perucho, don't you know Robertico?"

"No."

"Robertico has been living in Germany forever, man, and he's back home visiting. Go talk to him."

"Where does this Robertico live?"

"In the building. The last room at the back. Look at the Havanauto the guy rented. He's rolling in dough. And he's here with his German wife and their two kids."

"And he has everybody staying in the room?"

"Right. There are probably nine of them, plus Robertico, his wife, and the two kids. So that makes thirteen people all in one room. He's so rich I don't know why he doesn't go to a hotel."

"How long has he been in Germany?"

"Eleven years, man. He left here in '84. On one of those work-study contracts, remember? You really aren't from around here, are you? Go see him. He'll probably take the stuff off your hands."

Robertico had three solid gold chains hanging around his neck, with huge dangling medallions of Santa Bárbara, San Lázaro, and La Caridad del Cobre. Plus the white and red necklaces of Obatalá and Changó. The room was full of suitcases, packages and boxes of clothes, fans, electric cooking pots, a new TV. Robertico was like a beautiful black maharajah, half-naked, sweating, maybe thirty-five years old. By his side was a sturdy German woman, slightly taller than he was, and their two little mulattos, the luckiest mestizos in the world: their parents were perfect. The mix seemed unreal, but it made a kind of sense: a blond woman, blacks, mulattos, bright and shiny objects in that dark, stifling, filthy room in a crumbling building.

Most interesting was the German woman. She didn't understand any Spanish. She just smiled and said, "Hello." I would have given anything to know what she thought of the place, with its stink of shit and no water in the heat and asphyxiating humidity. Despite it all, she was laughing and seemed very cheerful and relaxed.

Robertico was a hard sell. At last he managed to bargain me down a little, and he took the whole shipment. Beef, lobster, rum. He had even brought a new freezer back with him, and now he used it for the very first time. When he paid me, I told him I had been in Germany years ago. He opened a bottle of rum and raised his glass to me.

"Yes? When?"

"In 1982. Thirteen years ago."

"In Berlin?"

"I was there for a year, working in Berlin. I got to know the whole socialist side. In those days I was a journalist and I was in Europe a lot."

"And now you live in the building?"

"Yes."

"Fuck, man, you've really had shitty luck. You'd never lived in a place like this before?"

"No, but it's all right. I'm scraping by."

"Nobody will ever know how much I miss this island. For eleven years, I've been working like a dog. Ingrid and the kids are my only joys."

"But you're doing well for yourself."

"Yes, I do well, but it isn't easy. I can't have two drinks without wanting to cry. I can't even speak Spanish with my children. They don't like it. I try to teach them, but they don't like it."

"But now you'll have to stay there till you die. If you're used to the good life, you won't be able to live here."

"I can't leave Germany now. Things are going downhill here. I come back every two or three years, and each year it's worse."

"Now we don't even have water."

"If the building doesn't get water soon, I'll have to go to a hotel. And I don't want to. I like to hang out here at home, with my people."

"Well, Robertico, I've got to go. Thanks a lot for the drink, pal."

"What are you doing tonight?"

"Nothing."

"Don't go too far. We're going to drive around and see if we can pick up a couple of whores and take them to the beach. I don't like to go out with the black guys from around here anymore because they get drunk right away and start a fight, and we end up at the police station."

"We whites get drunk too."

"It's different. I don't know you, but I can tell you're a responsible guy."

"And the German lets you out by yourself?"

"Oh, I do whatever I want with her. You don't want to miss the action tonight; I'm paying. And we're going to live it up, man.

We'll pick up two chicks and we'll screw them till dawn. I have to relax. When I go back, all I have to look forward to is an electric screwdriver and a shipment of tiny screws. Eight hours, Monday to Friday, tightening screws."

"All right. I'll be around, in my room."

2:8 / What Remains

Last night, in the middle of the music, the drunken uproar, and the usual Saturday racket, Carmencita cut off her husband's penis. I don't know how it happened because I try to steer clear of the people here. The truth is, I'm terrified of them, but I can never let them know. If they sense they bother me or they scare me, I'm dead.

I was sitting in my doorway, leaning up against the wall, breathing a little fresh air and wondering where the fuck I could go until the building calmed down enough so I could go to bed. I couldn't get used to sleeping where it was so noisy. So there I was in the doorway, and all of sudden this black man comes running out of his room shouting, covered in blood, and clutching his balls. Behind him came Carmencita, shrieking too, with a knife in her right hand. Throwing the piece of penis she had in her left hand on the floor, she shouted something like, "Now let's see you screw everyone you feel like screwing, you son of a bitch."

The man was screaming in terror, and right away two or three people picked him up between them and took him to the hospital. They left the scrap of penis on the floor, but an old lady picked it up, put it in a little plastic bag, and ran after them, shouting, "Take this so they can stick it back on! May God protect him!"

Carmencita shut herself up in her room. I thought she was probably trembling in fear of the vendetta to come, whether it would be her husband's brothers with their machetes after her, or the police, or the man himself, who would be ready to eat her alive when they let him out of the hospital.

Last week, Lily set fire to her husband. He was still in the hospital, but he didn't want to press charges. Some said he was in love, and others said he was in critical condition and practically unconscious. Whatever. These black women are dangerous, always ready to explode. Sometimes I think they pass death powders to each other, and that's why they go so crazy over a man who is definitely nothing special, just one out of the dozens each woman will possess and pine away for in her life.

Everything was calm today. Sundays are boring. The building is still, silent, even. It's like a huge, clumsy monster that wallows around, breathes fire, and triggers earthquakes for six days and on the seventh day rests, gathering its energies.

I wanted to take advantage of the calm to write a story about two transvestites who live in the building. They're friends of mine. They're everybody's friends. They're sweet guys, friendly, always happy. Everybody seems to love them. One of them dreams of becoming a famous singer and cultivates a Marilyn Monroe-like persona called Samantha. The transformation is so successful he could win acting prizes no matter where he went and make a good living. Here he's a poor pathetic slob, people make his life impossible, and he supports himself doing a little hairdressing at home. After the show they put on at the America Theater, the witch-hunt began. No one went after the faggots. That would have been too crude. They were after the managers and businessmen who made it possible for the transvestites to appear on stage. It terrifies the Old Man to think that any small space set aside for personal freedom might become a space where free ideas were exchanged.

But I'm not making much sense to myself today. I can't write. All I do is repeat one sentence: I love scars, not wounds. Why do I keep repeating that like a paranoid freak? I love scars, not wounds.

Every day I'm more like the blacks who live in the building: they sit on the sidewalk with nothing to do, trying to make ends meet by selling a few rolls of bread, a bar of soap, a few tomatoes, whatever turns up, day after day, never thinking what will we do tomorrow, what will happen next. They sit on the sidewalk with a bar of soap in one hand, or two packs of cigarettes, letting the day slip by, and they just keep living. And time passes.

I was thinking about that, being bored, loving the scars, when Luisa came in. She was dead tired and sleepy, but she had made her daily bread: she had brought back a small fortune. Forty dollars, two cans of beer, and half a bottle of whiskey. It could have been better on a Saturday night, but it was all right. She washed up and took an aspirin, then we put on the fan and went to bed naked. She didn't want anything else to drink. I poured myself a glass of whisky with ice. She told me about the guy she had picked up the night before on the Malecón. She likes to give me the details, every little detail. Last night's guy wanted to have sex on the beach, on the sand. And that's what he got. Full moon, palm trees, and a gorgeous mulatta. It doesn't get any more tropical than that. The guy, a typical European, had his own condoms in his pocket. Everything was straightforward. He didn't want anything strange.

"He had a very skinny prick, but it was bent to the left and it hurt me. No, it's all right. I'll tell you the whole story later, but let me sleep now, big boy. I'm exhausted."

And in an instant, she was asleep. I finished my whisky and poured myself another. During the day I don't get tired and I can't sleep. I like to look at that naked mulatta. She's beautiful. So skinny, lovely. So long as this lasts, it's bliss. You can't ask for more. This is the best it gets around here.

Then I remembered that morning. Once, years ago, I was living in a beautiful place with a big terrace overlooking the Caribbean. I woke up very early and went out on the terrace, and there was Venus, shining fervently in the shadowy dawn. I went to the children's room and I woke up Anneloren, who would have been five or six then, and I brought her out on the terrace. I showed her where

Venus was, and I said to her, "That's what happens every single day, first Venus comes out and then the sun. For all eternity. Everything important, all the most important things in life, last forever. And we know they're there, and we can give thanks to them."

And then I don't know what else. I think I kept drinking whisky, until the bottle was empty.

2·9 / Stormy Weather

For days I had been letting loose some foul-smelling farts. All I had
to eat were black beans, and they were rapidly transformed into
noxious fumes. Even I was revolted by the smell of rotting shit.
Luckily, I was alone in the room. Luisa was spending the week with
a rich Spaniard and she was at a hotel. If Luisa had been home, I
would have been embarrassed. Really. One fart is funny, but more
than two is disgusting. And if they stink like that, it's even worse.
Maybe Luisa would bring some money home with her. It would
make our lives a little easier. Things would be better, if only for a
few days. I hoped the bitch hadn't spent it all shopping, on clothes
and perfume. We needed something to eat.

I had been out of money for three days, and the black asshole
next door kept hammering tin, making buckets.

Luisa probably wouldn't come back until she had seen the
Spaniard off at the airport, and meanwhile there I sat, starving to
death. No. I'd sell some buckets. I went and talked to the guy. He
gave me a bucket on loan. If I could sell it, I'd make twenty pesos. It
was shit, but it was better than nothing. It would have to do. I took
the bucket and went outside. It was raining. There was a storm on
its way in from Tampa. I didn't know why it was raining so hard if it
was still so far away.

Anyway, I thought I'd rather get wet than be stuck in that building. I was going deaf listening to the bucket guy banging tin all day. Then there was somebody else delousing her little black kids, all ten of them, and another woman hysterical because every time it rained, chunks of the roof and wall would fall down and she kept praying to all the *santos* to keep the building from collapsing.

Almost without realizing it, I was heading toward Arturo's house with my bucket. Arturo's an old mystic, a Rosicrucian, a yogi, a primitive painter, who feeds himself on fruit and honey, and absorbs cosmic energy. "Karma is all we need. Your confusion begins and ends in itself. You need to clean house, meditate, balance your karma." He always gives me the same advice, but I don't have time for such foolishness. I've got to be out looking for food. If I tried to digest that karma shit, I'd starve to death. Besides, any second that slut might board a plane, and then so much for me. She'd be landing in Europe by the time I found out. So I just had to keep putting one foot in front of the other. One foot in front of the other or I'd starve to death. The alignment of my karma and all that shit could wait until later.

Arturo, who must have been close to sixty-five, was having an affair with a twenty-year-old actress. I liked the girl. But it was hopeless. She was hypnotized by the old man. I don't know how he did it, but he had her mesmerized. He painted nude pictures of her. Arturo has a tiny house close to my building, and he makes good money, the old crocodile, because he sells his paintings to tourists for dollars. He barely peeked around the half-open door. It looked like he was naked. He didn't want the bucket.

"I can leave it for you, and you can pay me tomorrow, Arturo."

"No, I don't need it. Thanks."

"Would any of the neighbors be interested, do you think?"

"I don't know; I don't know."

"Well, take care of yourself, old man."

"Sure thing, see you."

The shepherd never lets the wolf near his sheep. I moved on, walking slowly from door to door with the bucket in my hand. Every once in a while, I'd hold it up. "Look here, special deal, this is the real thing. It'll last forever. Special deal. They don't make them like this anymore. This is real iron; it'll last a lifetime." Every once in a while, someone would ask me how much it cost, just to mess with me. Barely listening to my reply, they'd keep on walking.

I headed down Galiano, toward the Malecón. The sea was getting rough, and the wind was blowing hard. Was the storm on its way back? I walked to where I used to live years ago, going up to the roof and ringing the bell. Maybe old Hortensia would buy the bucket. I was soaked by the rain, but I didn't care. I felt good wet, in the middle of the storm and the wind.

Hortensia had always been a policewoman. She was captain of the State Security Unit. She retired years ago. She had recently been widowed, and now she lived in fear.

Since her husband died, she was a filthy mess. She didn't have money, or food, or water, or soap. Her family couldn't stand her. She lived alone and she was half-crazy. She always used to think everyone was plotting against her. Even squashed flatter than a cockroach, she was still as bossy and dictatorial as ever, which is why even her daughter avoided her. Once—when I was Hortensia's neighbor—her daughter said to me, "I can't stand her, let me know when she dies." I thought she was a real bitch. But then later I didn't. Later I understood.

"Since you left, there's no living on this roof. It's a nightmare."

"Why do you say that, Hortensia? You've got to find the strength to go on. It doesn't matter whether Lucio's dead or not."

"Oh, child, it does. He was all I had. And look at the way I argued with him and how I wanted a divorce. Now everyone has turned their backs on me."

"No, no. Don't say that. You'll always have God." (I say that to get her goat. She doesn't even believe in her own mother.)

"God is a crock! I never have any money. A person can't get by without dollars in this country. The hell with counting on God to help! Come in, sit down, let's talk awhile."

"No, Hortensia, no. I have to go. I'm trying to sell this bucket."

"The moneybags next door will buy it from you."

"Do you think so?"

"Yes. They're filthy rich. He works in a dollar store and he robs the place blind. The son of a bitch. Stealing from the government and Fidel!"

"Never mind that, Hortensia. Forget about politics for a while. Try to enjoy the years you have left as best you can."

"Oh, child, I'm near the end. And look what the Revolution has become."

"Yes, the Chinese say life goes in cycles. You always end up back at the beginning."

"I can't understand you. What are you talking about?"

"Nothing, don't be sad. Call those people for me and see if they want the bucket."

And they did. They bought the bucket from me. And then I left. I wasn't in the mood for Hortensia's tirades. When I was at the door, she said, "The people can't be neglected this way. This building is falling to pieces, there's never any water, or gas, or food. Nothing, child, nothing. What is this? How long will it last? The government has to take care of us. Aren't you a journalist? Why don't you write something about this building? See if you can reach someone, touch their hearts . . . There are lots of us old people here and we're being ignored, because . . ."

"Hortensia, haven't you noticed me selling buckets? I'm not even a street sweeper anymore. One of these days I'll come by when I have more time and we'll talk. I'll see you later."

I went down the stairs. The elevator had been broken for years. Twelve floors down. On the second floor it occurred to me to knock on Flavia's door. We once had a lovely two-year affair. We made a pact to live together and love each other forever, she with her sculptures and me with my novels. In those days, she called me daddy and she was very loving and she'd say, "I really need you, daddy." But she went away to Spain, and then to New York. She took perfectly good care of herself, and she forgot our pact. She didn't need daddy anymore. Then she came back. We saw each other for an hour. It was a sad day for me when we said our good-byes. A happy day for her. Lots of time had gone by since then. She'd traveled to New York again. She'd had solo shows, been toasted with California wine, and sold her drawings for a thousand dollars each. She was showing me the photos now. And she pointed out the gallery owner and a little fag who helped her hang the show, and her cousin and the neighbors, who were there too. So, she seemed much more relaxed. After all, she had dollars, and dollars are a good sedative. She made me coffee, and she said, "Oh, it's such a struggle to be famous in New York. It's better to make money and have fun, don't you think?"

"I don't know. I've never gone looking for fame in New York."

"Oh, don't be that way. Are you still bitter?"

"I was never bitter. I just got very sad."

"Well, let's not talk about that anymore."

"All right. I just came by to say hello and see how things were going."

"Don't lose any more weight. You've gotten very skinny. Why is that?"

"I'm taking ballet classes."

"Oh, you're a pain."

"Well, see you."

And I left. She doesn't realize what a trail of sad poems, what grief and tears she left in her wake. She doesn't know. And she'll never know, because I won't give her that satisfaction.

Now it's raining hard, and the wind is coming in gusts. I don't like days like this. They make me even hungrier.

Luisa was still running around with her twenty-four-karat-gold Spaniard. She came by the room for barely a minute, gave me ten dollars, and said, "Everything's going fine. He's Spanish, from Asturias. A rube, but rolling in money."

"What's a rube? You pick up these strange little words so quickly."

"Sure, a person's got to learn. And what do you have to say for yourself, bumming around and not even trying to get yourself a Spanish girl?"

"Don't hassle me, Luisa! The hell with Spanish girls! What is a rube?"

"A hick, my man, a hick. A country boy. A peasant. A farmer."

"Ahhh . . ."

"And he wants to take me home with him."

"Sure. They all want to take you home with them. But the minute they're on the plane . . ."

"Oh, don't be so negative. You'll jinx me. I'm going. When I'm finished with him, I'll come back here . . . Oh, honey, I miss you."

"You're a crazy cunt. You wouldn't miss your own mother."

"Don't talk to me that way, baby."

"If you missed me that much, you'd give me more than just ten dollars. I'm about to starve to death."

"Sweetie, the thing is, he hasn't given me any money. He pays for everything. I swiped these ten measly bucks yesterday so I could bring them to you. Don't be ungrateful, darling."

She kissed me and kissed me, and she left. That mulatta is incredible. She's turned my brain to mush. When I was alone, I hid the ten dollars in the crack of the door hinge, carefully folding it in between the wobbly, rusted screws, and I went to sit on the eaves.

I was living on the roof of a building on the Malecón, on the twelfth floor, maybe two hundred feet up. And I had gotten in the habit of sitting on the raised edge of the roof with my feet dangling in empty space. It was easy. I just pulled myself up. Beautiful eaves, supported by gargoyles carved in stone. There were sculptures of griffons and birds of paradise too. It was an old building, very solid, Boston style, but it was slowly tumbling down with all the people trying to live crammed inside.

Anyway, it was simple. I felt like a bird and I remembered the times I used to fly a glider off a hill in the valley of Viñales, back when I had real balls, and I'd squeeze my butt cheeks together for fear of crashing. But that flimsy thing never failed me. Now, at night, I'd jump up to the eaves and sit there in the cool night air, and I'd see everything below me, shadowy in the dark. I was always tempted to slip off and go flying away, feeling like the freest guy in the world.

That night Carmita came over. She's a player. She was seeing three men at once: a sailor, a mechanic, and a customs official. Carmita is something. She's forty-one years old, but she acts like a girl of eleven. She has a passion for sex, money, and games of chance, but not in that order. I think it goes money, sex, money, betting, and more money. And cheating and winning no matter what. She lives on the fifth floor with her children and her lovers. I still don't know how she manages to alternate them so they never meet. That night I got the feeling she was planning to add a fourth victim to her collection of useful men. All of a sudden, there she was, shouting behind me. I was like a bat in the moonlight, under a beautiful full moon, the night sky clear and blue. The sea was barely moving, and the Malecón was quiet, almost empty. I was in ecstasy, suspended in space, thinking of nothing. It's glorious to hover in the air, by the sea, a cool June breeze blowing, silence all around. It's then a person thinks of nothing. I was able to think of nothing because I was floating, retreating inside myself, not searching for anything. Me and myself, united. It was like a miracle in the middle of storms and shipwrecks. A miracle inside of me. And then suddenly Carmita was screaming, "You're going to fall, Pedro Juan! What are you doing there? Mother of God!"

"Hey, be cool. Why are you screaming like that?"

The woman was talking to me like she was my mother or something. And it was the first time she had come up to the roof. If we had been living together, she would've knocked me off the eaves with a few good slaps.

So, I don't know how it happened, but a few minutes later I was downstairs, buying some cheap kerosene-tasting rum. It's much better with ice and lemon. We drank two or three glasses and we talked for a long time about the millions of people who've lost their jobs. All selling whatever they can on the street, trying to make ends meet.

"They don't interest me, Pedro Juan. They can die for all I care."

"Girl, I feel sorry for them."

"Well, I don't. Who's giving you a helping hand? As far as I can tell, you're pretty fucked, and if you weren't pimping, you'd starve to death."

"That's true, but . . ."

"And who feels sorry for me? Those people who sell lemons and pizzas drag their problems out into the street for everyone to see. I had to hump that fat, drunk, stupid mechanic for two years so he would give me sixty pesos each week. That was my problem. All behind closed doors. Nobody needed to know about it. That's how I made a living until the sailor came back and I kicked the fat slob out."

"But you're a cynic."

"Speaking of cynics, what are you, taking advantage of that whore? Because everybody in the building knows it. And I'm not a cynic. Ever since I was little, I was taught that you don't marry a man for his looks or because you like him or to be a house pet. He's there to work and to support me. If he doesn't put out, he can get out. I teach my children the same thing. I don't want bums or losers in my house. And especially not pimps like you."

"Leave me out of it. What do you get from your sailor?"

"He came home loaded down with presents. All kinds of things. Clothes, shoes, perfume, everything. He brought me two gorgeous pieces of Chinese silk. He was in China."

"Like Marco Polo."

"Who's Marco Polo?"

"A friend of mine."

"Oh, well, I don't know if Marco Polo has good taste, but Yeyo certainly does. Everything he brought fits us perfectly. Even the shoes. He came back with all kinds of things for me and the kids. That's what I call a husband, boy, and not a pathetic loser!"

And we kept on like that. Three or four drinks later, I had the urge to touch her, who knows why. Well, I do know why: I had tuned out while she was talking about meals and kitchens and how her apartment shines because she's constantly scrubbing with a little rag that she always carries around with her, and that my room was a filthy pit. "A woman's touch is what you need here. I'll make it so you could eat off the floor, with some nice little curtains." As she chattered away, I was checking her out. She's forty-one, but she's fine. When I couldn't stand it any longer, I got up from my chair and I patted her head and stuck my pelvis in her face. Then she unbuckled my belt and unzipped my pants, gradually revealing my pubes and my prick, which stiffened slowly, anxiously, looking up as if to ask whether someone had called.

"Oh, Pedro Juan, what a beautiful prick. It's precious!"

She said that caressingly, like it was as sweet as candy. And she took it in her mouth gently, tongue, lips, teeth, everything. Her mouth was warm and wet. She nibbled a little on the head, doing everything as if she were in a trance, her eyes closed. She persisted, rapturously, until she had swallowed all my come. All of it. She licked up the last drop.

"Let's get in bed, sweetie."

"Ugh, no, wait. Let me rest a minute."

She had sucked me dry and she wanted me to keep going like a fifteen-year-old boy.

"No waiting. You've got a tongue and fingers. After choking me to death, you can't leave me hanging. Let's go!"

She was already taking her clothes off. An incredible body! Forty-one, a diet of rice and beans, three children, and knowing nothing about creams or gyms or saunas. She was perfect.

Well, that's how it was. I poured myself another drink, and I spent a long time doing everything I could with my tongue and fingers, she panting from one orgasm to the next. At some point I recovered a little and I stuck it in her, but it wasn't very hard. I gave her a little brushwork with my prick, just like that, half-soft, on her clitoris. She panted a lot, had two more orgasms, and that was it.

"All right! Let's get some fresh air."

It was almost midnight. The roof was silent and deserted. I had managed to satisfy her. My tongue was tired, but I felt full of energy. Streaking naked like a comet from the bed to the door, I went out on the roof and there were two guys in the blue light of the full moon. They had been watching it all through a half-drawn blind, and they were tucking their pricks back in. I scared them, really startled them. They had been watching and jerking off at our expense. In a blind rage, I threw myself at them bare-fisted. They didn't have much time to react, and they were pretty scared. They were kids, and I landed a whole slew of punches, but one of them took a few steps back, pulled out a pistol, and pointed it at me.

Then I understood. They were in uniform.

"You're policemen! You fuckers, watching me and jerking off!"

The other one drew his pistol too, but my shouts had woken the neighbors and drawn them up to the roof. Naked, I kept shouting at them, but there was nothing I could do while they were pointing their pistols at me. All of a sudden one of them brought out some handcuffs. He tried to handcuff me. No one understood what was going on.

"I'll be damned if you handcuff me! They were watching us and jerking off, there through the blinds! Carmita, come out here! Carmita!"

I went into my room to put on a pair of pants. Carmita had gone. She ran downstairs as soon as she saw there was a mess with the police. That bitch! She left me high and dry!

"Citizen, you're making a public nuisance of yourself. Besides, you're exposing yourself in a public place. Come with us and let us put the cuffs on."

The neighbors jumped in.

"This isn't a public place. Who do you two think you are? And what were you doing up here at this time of night? Looking through gaps in the blinds? You've got a lot of nerve!"

In a second, more than twenty neighbors had gathered and were harassing them. The officers tried to regain control of the situation, playing tough.

"Get your identification, citizen, and come with us."

"The fuck I will! I'm not going anywhere with you! Get out of here. Get out and go to hell."

The neighbors tried to calm me down. Meanwhile, the policemen opted to disappear down the stairs, because there were too many people harassing them and asking them what they were doing on the roof so late at night. They retreated, almost running, and threatening:

"We'll be back right away. You haven't seen the last of us."

They were gone and everything calmed down. The neighbors went back to their rooms and went to bed. I grabbed what was left of my ten dollars and I went down to have a beer and something to eat. In the end, things hadn't gone so badly. I got in a few punches before they drew their pistols. That was nice.

2:11 / The Doors of Heaven

For Salvador Rodríguez del Pino

The Chicano and I drank a lot of beers sitting at a table in the lobby of the Hotel Deauville. On a Sunday night in Central Havana it's dangerous to sit down to drink with a fat, rosy-cheeked white guy. A sixty-year-old man like him must have lots of money. The hordes get a whiff of dollars and circle around, ready to sink in their fangs. Everybody was getting the whiff, and we began to be besieged. Children begging for coins, whores making advances, guys offering rum, tobacco, aphrodisiacs, everything on the black market, at very low prices. Each person with his or her own story. Poverty was destroying everything and everybody, inside and out. After socialism and don't bite the hand that feeds you, it was every man for himself. To hell with compassion and all the rest of it. We were having a good time. The Chicano was telling me stories of his gay childhood in Acapulco. He was gay, a flaming queen since before he could remember. And that's why he was so much fun. He told his family history all backward. And it was fabulous to hear about the tribulations of the wealthy in the middle of the Mexican Revolution, and about the nightly wanderings of the ghosts of Scottish great-grandfathers and great-grandmothers and maiden aunts. There's a reason the fucking Mexicans write so well: they've got lots of great raw material and they've always been the underdogs.

At midnight the Chicano went to the hotel bathroom, and

three whores went in after him and tried to rape him or something. He got scared and hurried back in search of my protection. A gang of kids, black and white, surrounded us just then, begging for something, anything. They made hungry faces and put out their hands, pleading, "Sir, please, give us something to eat, give us something to eat, give us something to eat." I tried to shoo them away.

"All right, that's enough! We don't have anything to give you."

Then one of them took charge, gracefully leading the group away.

"Excuse us, sir. The way things are, it makes us crazy. Don't mind us. Let's go, let's go!"

They went running off, but the leader came back and, smiling, he said to me, "Did you see how I got rid of those crazy kids for you? Why don't you give me a little something? Even just money for a hamburger."

"Forget it, kid! We don't have anything for you. Go to hell."

I noticed the Chicano was a little nervous.

"What's wrong, Enrique?"

"Nothing, just that one of those girls tried to stick her hand down my pants. And that's serious business. You know? She tried to rape me. It's all too much for me. I'm a little shaken up. Let's get out of here and go find somewhere to eat."

We had already downed eight or nine beers, on empty stomachs. They were having their effect. We were a little tipsy, but not very. The Chicano paid and we headed toward the Malecón. There were thousands and thousands of people out. In the heat and the humidity of July, they were all creeping out of their lairs to get a little fresh air and listen to some music. It was beginning to be dark on the Malecón, and the music was loud. In fact, different kinds of loud music were blaring from all sides. The sea was still. There wasn't even a light breeze. Nothing at all. Just sticky heat, thousands of people, darkness, and the smell of overflowing sewers.

Two of the whores who had followed the Chicano into the bathroom caught up with us. They grabbed his arm. They were two pretty, sweaty young mulattas. Too thin, maybe, and with dark circles under their eyes.

"If you don't want to sleep with us, at least give us a dollar for a hot dog."

"No! I don't have anything to give you. Nothing. Thank you, please."

"Oh, you're a faggot! That's what's wrong with you. Look how hot he thinks he is. Go screw your friend, go on! Fuck him in the ass, hustler boy, fuck him in the ass, since that's what he likes!"

Oh, hell. I didn't even bother to reply. It wasn't worth the effort. We kept walking. People were looking at us and we looked back at them. Everybody was sweating.

"I haven't been dry since I came to Cuba," Enrique said to me, laughing and drying his sweat with a red handkerchief. In the snowy mountains of Colorado, maybe he wore it around his neck to protect himself from the cold. I amused myself for a while with images of cowboys on horseback in those mountains, wearing leather jackets.

"We have to have some dinner, Pedro Juan. Aren't you hungry?"

"Yes. There's a stand on that corner."

We went up to the stand. There were lots of little tables all around it. All taken. And lots of people standing up, and lots of noise. Where had so many people come from? Making our way to the stand past sweaty, screaming, dancing, laughing bodies, we ordered two servings of chicken with french fries and two beers. I really wanted to get drunk that night. But when I'm in the mood to drink, I can have one beer after another, up to twenty or thirty of them, lose track, keep going, and still I'll only be half-gone.

A mulatto, just a kid, pushed his way in between the two of us. He shoved and didn't excuse himself. He just pushed us, crowded up to the counter, pulled out a ten-dollar bill, and ordered something from the counterman. Another mulatto, maybe almost all black, a kid too, came up behind the first kid's back and grabbed his shoulder. He jerked him sharply around so the first kid's back was to the counter, and with an expression of hatred and ferocious rage on his face, he stabbed him twice in the chest, barely an inch from me. Everything happened so fast that I didn't realize the flash of shiny steel was a knife, stabbing and sliding out cleanly twice, not one drop of blood, from the chest of the mulatto with the ten-dollar bill.

Without thinking, I gave Enrique a push to get him out of the way. And I pressed myself as tightly against the counter as I could. The stabbed boy went off at a near run and the other kid ran after him, stabbing him wherever he could catch him. There were screams. People moved back. A policeman shot his .45 into the air three times. It was strange. There was a plainclothes policeman in the shadows, far from the white and well-lit counter, but I saw him clearly. He looked scared and trapped. He scanned the crowd for Enrique with his eyes, with the intention of getting him out of there. Enrique had fallen to the wet and dirty ground, and he was struggling with four guys who were holding him down and rifling through his pockets. With my push I had only managed to shove him down. I went quickly to his rescue, shouting to scare the predators off, "Hey, what the fuck is going on?"

They scattered, then disappeared. I helped him up.

"Let's get out of here, Enrique!"

We made our way as best we could through the crush of screaming people. Crossing the Malecón, we headed for the wide sidewalk that runs beside the sea. Then I realized we were the only whites around. In Maceo Park a salsa orchestra was playing: *It's the way you look, you're a naughty girl. I want to have fun with you tonight, pretty baby. We're gonna have a ball.* And everybody was dancing madly.

"Did they get anything? Check."

Enrique checked his pockets. He was missing the sixty dollars he had had in his shirt pocket, a pair of glasses, and his driver's license. He still had the little bit of money he was carrying in his pants pocket. His right shoulder hurt, the one he hit when he fell. His back and backside were muddy.

We walked quickly away. The stretch of the Malecón after

Maceo Park is the exclusive territory of faggots and dykes. The gay hundred meters. Free love, as the Americans say. If a person keeps walking toward Vedado everything changes. The gays are a buffer between the agitation of the black power types and the relative calm of Vedado. Vedado seems more sedate. But it isn't. Everything is tainted. The truth is, we're all mestizos. The unrest here is underground. You just have to scratch the surface and it explodes with the same ferocity. We came to a pizzeria next door to the Hotel Saint John; a clean, well-lit pizzeria, not crowded, air conditioned. Oh, what peace! You pay in dollars here, and it's a cheap place, but inaccessible to the rabble stabbing each other for ten dollars outside.

We ordered pizzas with ham and beers. We breathed deeply, we smiled. I like to breathe fresh, sweet-smelling, dry air. It gives me a feeling of luxury, comfort, and well-being. You inhale in an air-conditioned place and only lightweight and efficient neutrons are drawn into your lungs. The protons stay outside, out where it's humid, hot, noisy, crowded. No mobs in here. The few people inside were well-dressed, well-fed, and made quiet conversation.

At the next table three sturdy young Mexicans wearing thick gold chains and bracelets chatted contentedly. Enrique smiled at them and asked them—in his best Mexican accent—if they were from Guadalajara. No, they were from Monterrey. They were preaching the word of God. They had arrived this morning and they'd already held a service.

"How did you arrange it? Did you have contacts?"

"No, sir. Before we came we fasted for three days and prayed we would find brothers and sisters here hungry for the word of God."

"We prayed that many would follow us into the house of God. And in fewer than twenty-four hours, we were successful. This morning a boy tried to sell us something on the street. And we told him no. We told him we were preaching the word of God. And somebody else came over and invited us to their church. Well, it wasn't really a church. It was a family home where services were held. And right there, before our very eyes, two people broke their *santería* necklaces and told us the devil had led them astray, and they repented of worshipping graven images. Right there, in front of everybody, they got down on their knees. It was very moving, sir."

"So you've accomplished something," Enrique said.

"Yes, sir, thanks be to God. We'll preach every day. We'll visit many houses of worship in the next few days. We're needed here. The devil has a hold on this land, and the people need God. We've got to show them the way."

We had nothing to say to that. The conversation languished. We finished the pizza. Enrique got in a taxi and left for his hotel. He was smiling. He seemed happy to have had such an entertaining evening.

I had to walk back along the Malecón. It was already two in the morning. I crossed the gay buffer zone, and I remembered the preachers' story. Everyone here was sinning, sinning frenetically. A black man and a black woman were fucking sitting facing each other on the wall of the Malecón. Maceo watched them from above, astride his bronze horse. They had their eyes closed, and they were moaning and panting. I couldn't resist the temptation, and I watched. I sat down forty feet away and listened. The guy pulled out and masturbated, and he masturbated her too. And I saw it all. Then it was too much for me. Pulling my prick out of my pants, I masturbated too. A mulatto, sitting on the other side of the couple, was doing the same thing. Farther down there was a woman slumped against the wall of the Malecón. Half-drunk, maybe. I didn't want to come by myself. Sidling up next to her, I showed her my prick, nice and hard in my pants. She had seen everything. She knew what was going on a few feet to her right. She reached her hand out, took hold of my prick, and squeezed it hard, then she took her hand away and made signs to me that her stomach was empty and she wanted something to eat. She took my prick again and squeezed it hard, looking me in the eyes. She was dumb, and she wanted to eat.

"Do you want a hot dog?"

She growled in her throat to say yes, "hrrgh, hrrgh," while at the same time nodding her head.

I checked my pockets. I had ten pesos and two dollars. Jack shit. I couldn't pay the woman a dollar hot dog for giving me a hand job. And it would probably be with a dry prick because most likely she wouldn't want to wet it with her saliva. I shook my finger no at her, and I looked at the blacks. They were still fucking with their eyes closed. I moved closer until I could hear them. Sitting down facing the sea, with my back to the city, I scrubbed away. A few minutes later, I ejaculated, shooting a good jet of come into the dark, calm water. The Caribbean received my semen. There was lots of it. Too many days without a woman, letting time slip away.

2·12 / The Snake, the Apple, and Me

That woman seduced me the same way the snake hypnotized Adam with its gaze and tempted him to taste the apple. I was bored, and it suited me fine to be around a woman who could give me a little loving. I was under contract with an operation drilling oil wells, and twenty-five days a month I was living in a trailer parked on the outskirts of a town near Havana, working on the coastal reefs a few feet from the Caribbean. Ten hours a day lugging things like pipes, pieces of iron, mud bricks, drills. It was hard work. You were always covered in grease and mud and stinking of sulphur. I'd get very tired. At night I'd swallow down the stew they made there and fall onto my cot like a beaten dog, until I had to get up at five the next morning. Sometimes I thought the routine was better than being back in Havana, in absolute poverty with my brawling black neighbors. Other times I wanted to say screw the oil and go back to the building. Eternally indecisive, that's me, utterly confused and with as much back and forth as a pendulum. When it comes down to it, I prefer suffering to squalor.

I didn't have the time or the strength to think. And that was a good thing. My reckless, risk-filled life had always led me to dead ends. All my wild, ridiculous affairs, for example. I was always tormented, running, speeding in and out of different places. The way a person does who only searches and never finds.

At the same time I was getting older. And I found I wasn't able to be as cynical anymore. I was losing my energy, my good cheer, and my virility. I couldn't manipulate people cynically the way I could when I was young and determined to come out on top no matter what.

The woman had set her sights on me from the beginning. She was the nurse at the town clinic, a pretty, sturdy brunette. She might have been thirty-five, ten years younger than me. We ran into each other a few times. I had to go have an infected wound looked at, and there she was with eyes just like Libertad Lamarque and rosebud lips like Sarita Montiel. She seemed a little stuck up to me, but she had a solid body. A nice ass, nice breasts. So I didn't care if she had putty for a brain. I made my move. We talked, and she said she would go out with me, but only if I would come to her.

"This town is full of terrible gossips. Come over to my house tonight instead. I live alone. Do you like to play dominoes?"

"Yes, but . . ."

"But what?"

"No woman's ever asked me to play."

We saw each other that very night. I scrubbed myself, trying to wash away the stink of sulphur and mud. Her little house was in a dark, isolated spot, half-overgrown by grasses and bushes that didn't exactly make a yard.

The whole thing unfolded slowly and painfully. The little house was dark, built of unpainted boards, with very little furniture, almost empty. The windows and doors were tightly closed, and the heat was stifling. There wasn't a single feminine touch: a curtain, flowers, something pretty set somewhere. Nothing. Nevertheless, I let myself be drawn toward the apple. I let myself be drawn despite the woman's awkwardness. She led me into the kitchen, and we sat down at a table. We played dominoes and drank warm rum, the cheapest and most disgusting kind, the kind you only find in the sleaziest bars. She brought out a pack of unfiltered cigarettes and smoked.

Half an hour later I managed to escape playing dominoes. It was pure torture. I was almost ready to give up and get the hell out of there. I tried to make conversation for a while. In spite of everything, what I really wanted was to take a bite out of the apple. Fat chance. She was mostly talking about baseball. I don't have anything to say about baseball. Nothing pro and nothing con. Then she wanted to talk about karate. She showed me her rough, callused hands.

"I practice every day. I can break a board with a single chop."

"And don't those calluses bother you at work?"

"No. On the contrary."

"What do you mean?"

"Don't be so nosy."

"I don't want to know. I don't care."

She got up and went into the bedroom, coming back with an envelope in her hand. Inside were photos of her in a bikini. A prudish bikini. In various positions. They looked like anatomical illustrations from a medical book. Very stiff poses, the photographer planted right in front of her. I'd never seen anything more ridiculous. She thought she'd turn me on showing me that shit. Maybe she thought it was hot pornography. Hate began to boil up inside me.

"And what is all this?"

"Me."

"Who took these? Where was it?"

"Don't ask so many questions, sweetie. It's not good to know too much."

She moved closer. Maybe she was waiting for me to kiss her or grab a breast. But there was no way. I was about as attracted to her as I might have been to one of the guys who worked with me, hairy as bears and always sweating and stinking to high heaven. I asked myself how the fuck I could get out of there gracefully, without having to tell her to go screw herself. I don't like to be rude to a lady.

"Why don't you put on some music?"

"I don't have a radio."

"This house is only half-furnished."

"Yes. The thing is . . . well, I'll tell you . . . I've been away from Cuba for a long time. I just came back."

"Ah, a mystery woman."

"I can't tell you everything. You'll find out eventually. Bit by bit."

"You're State Security."

She made a vain gesture, as if to say "maybe." I pointed to the closet where she had gotten the photos, and I said, "And you've got a gun in there, and you were in the America Brigade, running around in the jungle with the monkeys and the snakes."

"Hey! Who the fuck are you? Do you know who I am? What do you know about the America Brigade?"

Panicking, she got up. I was terrified. She was a karate champ, and I had barely even boxed. I still don't know what the fuck made me say all that to her. Was it telepathy? Whatever it was, telepathy, chance, or something else, I'll never know. Now I had to calm her down.

"No, girl. Never mind me. I was teasing you. You're tense. Relax, relax."

"Don't ever tease me like that! Don't you ever!"

"Listen, it's very late and my wake-up call tomorrow is at five in the morning. I'm going."

"It's not late. It's not even ten yet. Do you want more rum?"

"No."

"When will we see each other? Will you come over tomorrow?"

"Maybe I will. In the evening."

"Come by the clinic and let me know."

"Can't I just come by?"

"No. Let me know first."

"They trained you well, my friend. Always on the alert."

"I told you not to tease me like that. Tell me right now how you know who I am."

"No, no. I'll let you guess. See you tomorrow. Goodbye."

And I managed to slip away, coming out into the fresh night air and breathing deeply. Then I realized something important: that woman didn't smell like a woman. That's why my testicles hadn't responded. Nothing responded.

I worked for a year on the oil wells, but I never saw her again. All I did was work hard and not think. I got a little rougher. I developed wrinkles, I aged, and my skin was tanned by the sun and the salt and the sulphur.

2:13 / In a Loud Place

We met sitting side by side on a bus for an hour and a half, both of us exuding sex from all our pores, sniffing each other out. Anisia was nineteen and I was forty-five. She was a thin, wiry mulatta, well-proportioned, lovely, with merry, sparkling eyes. Something was in the air. A strong current flowed between us. We exchanged telephone numbers, and then goodbye, this is where I get off. Are you staying on? Yes, I'm staying on. Well, see you later. I'll call.

Now, after many phone calls, she was here. I'm never home. Finally we spoke, and she came to visit me on the roof, arriving sweaty and panting. Those stairs, nine flights of them, are an ordeal. I got another phone call. The old lady on the eighth floor was shouting for me. She charges me a peso per call. I have to cut back, because by now I could buy the phone company. I went downstairs. It was Zulema. She was upset. Her nephew had just come back from Sweden and meantime she'd kicked out her sailor man in the middle of a drunken fit. Why the fuck does everybody come to me with their problems?

Eight years ago, Zulema's nephew went to work in Varadero, to get away from his communist father. Then he found himself a rich Canadian woman to marry, left the island with the ugly old rich Canadian, found work, perfected his English, became a Canadian citizen, struggled fiercely for a divorce because the old lady didn't want to let him go, and married a girl who had less money but who was young and pretty. Now—who knows exactly how he ended up there—he lives in Sweden. After he had been there for five years, he came to visit for a week, very proud of himself because he weighs three hundred pounds, travels to a different country each year on his vacation, has a pretty little house with an exhaust fan in the kitchen, and works at a factory that manufactures war planes and rockets. Being here made him nervous and depressed. He was always drinking chamomile tea because everything was in ruins and dirty and poor, and he was used to things being pretty and clean and bright.

Zulema told me all of that in a rush. She was proud of her factory worker–nephew's success, the three hundred pounds he weighed, his exhaust fan.

"Things have gone so well for him, Pedro Juan."

"Right, right. And does he still remember his Spanish, or does he speak Swedish or what?"

"I don't know, I don't know. That's not the point. He's so fat! He says he eats meat every day. Oh, I'm so happy! What does it matter if he speaks Spanish or Chinese! Or whether he can speak at all. At least he's getting enough to eat and he owns his little house. Here he was nothing but skin and bones."

"Hmmm."

"I'm sad because he lived with me for a long time. He's the nephew I loved most. He would come stay with me while he was working in Varadero, because his fights with his father were terrible. He was always wild. You should have seen the way he made faces behind the old Canadian lady's back. I couldn't understand anything because they spoke English to each other, but he would make faces and laugh at her behind her back, and the old lady wouldn't know what I was laughing about. The first time he brought her here and introduced her to me, he said, 'Aunt, this fossil is an old witch, but she has money and I'm going away with her.' He was speaking in Spanish, and the old lady couldn't understand him. He's very clever. Before that, he went out with a Peruvian, a Mexican, who knows who else. Lots of women. But he would say to me, 'Aunt, they're worse off than I am. They can all go to hell, because I'm not interested in romance. I just want to find someone with money.' And so he spent three years in Varadero until he ended up with someone worthwhile. He knew what he wanted. He has backbone; he's not a pushover."

"Well, now all you need is your visa."

"Yes. God willing, he'll still be homesick, and he'll take me away with him this year. You have no idea how strong my little cupcake is. He can pull more weight than a tractor."

"Well, I have to go. I'm busy."

"You, busy? Don't kid me, old man. You've got all the time in the world. Come over later. I have news for you: I had to kick out the sailor, that drunk. The bastard, he was always drinking and he smoked two packs of cigarettes a day. Imagine, never giving me a cent for milk for the kid. He fucks like a dream, I like him and all, but it doesn't matter, because when I go to the store, I can't ask them to give me my groceries for free because my husband is hot and we make love four times a day, but he's a loser and a drunk. No. Because what they'll say is, 'Fine, you can fuck four times a day, but you're not going anywhere with your groceries until you pay for them!' No way! A girl's got to be firm. I kicked him out. I'll tell you all about it later. I think when he left, he was crying. I don't know. I couldn't look at him. Come over later to talk, sweetie. If you want, you can stay here."

"Won't he be back?"

"No. I took his key. If he comes back, he's got some nerve, and I'll kick him out again. Come tonight."

"All right, okay, don't call me. I'll come later. Goodbye."

"Bye-bye, darling."

I wasn't planning to go over until the alcohol and tobacco smell of the sailor had faded away. If a person has to make do with other people's half-eaten leftovers, he should at least make sure they're not covered in saliva.

I went upstairs and there was Anisia, sitting on the floor, looking through a porn magazine she found among my papers. I sat down next to her.

"Hey, were you going through my things?"

"I didn't touch your papers. The magazine was sticking out and I picked it up. Oh, baby, my mouth is watering. Look at this."

She was leafing through the full-page color photos: blacks with big pricks fucking huge, heavy-set women like Rubens's odalisques.

"Which do you like better, the blond women or the black men?"

"The blacks. They're incredible."

"Why?"

"I like those big, long pricks."

"But you must be small."

"I am, but I like it when it hurts. It's a sweet little pain."

"Hm. Do you want a drink?"

"Sure, why not?"

I poured a little rum into two glasses, thinking that no one needs pornography. All we need is true love, and a little soul and religion and philosophy. But that requires time and silence and reflection. Which means we lose ourselves moving too fast, surrounded by too much noise. The noise gets inside us and we act impulsively, without stopping to think.

"Have you ever been in love, Anisia?"

"No, never. I don't want to complicate things for myself. I have to get off this island, Pedro Juan."

"You too?"

"What do you mean, me too? Who else has left?"

"No, never mind. So where will you go?"

"Miami! Where do you think? I've got an uncle there, and I want him to bring me over."

"You're at the right age to do it. If you have children here and get mixed up in things, it will be harder."

"Yes, but first I have to smooth the way for myself. A little while ago I went to a black magic *palero*, and he told me to buy a white Obatalá necklace to prepare myself."

"And why haven't you bought it?"

"Because it costs fifty pesos."

"I'll give you the money."

"No, don't give me anything. I do people's nails and their hair, and I make my own living, and with what my husband gives me, that's enough."

"Well, I can still give you a present, can't I?"

"Give me flowers, write me a poem."

"Do you like that?"

She made the face of a naughty child.

"Of course. Sometimes I copy a poem and I give it to myself."

"Really! I wouldn't have guessed you were a romantic."

"Oh yes, my dream is to be the wife of a poet, and for him to spend his life writing me poems and bringing me flowers and perfume."

"Your husband isn't like that."

"No way! The man is always covered in grease, he's a mechanic. He's cruder and dumber than a yucca log."

"Leave him."

"No. He's the man for me. I'm like a jealous dog with him."

"Then teach him to bring you flowers and poems."

"Everyone's different. The last poem I copied I learned by heart, and it says something about that. Do you know how it starts?"

"I can't imagine. Who wrote it?"

"I can't remember. I think it's by Benedetti. It goes: "Don't blame anyone, don't ever complain about anyone or anything, because essentially you've lived your life as you pleased."

The naughty face she was making was driving me wild. Reaching out my hand, I unbuttoned her blouse. She wasn't wearing a bra, and drops of sweat were still running down her chest. Her breasts were beautiful, small, dark, and firm, with round, adolescent nipples. I kissed them, sucked them. She let herself be fondled contentedly. I had a nice erection. She squeezed me hard. We got a little hot. She told me about the good times she had had with black men. Only once did she let a black man take her from behind.

"It was a little while ago, with my husband. I smeared him with honey and I said, 'Nice and slow, don't you go crazy.' Even so, I had to be like a mule to take it. Oh, Pedro Juan, my eyes were popping out! I thought I was going to die. I couldn't breathe, but deep down I like the pain. I haven't dared try it again, but any day now we will. I have to get used to it. What he's got isn't a prick, it's an arm. It isn't easy, old man, it isn't easy!"

"How many men have you been with, Anisia?"

For a minute, she considered whether she should tell me or not. At last she said, "Once I counted and it was fifty-eight."

"So now it must be close to seventy?"

"More or less. Maybe a little more."

"Do you like them that much?"

"What?"

"Pricks. You're addicted to pricks, girl."

"Yes, addicted, sick, whatever you want to call it, but it's the first time I've had two at once. I've always had them one at a time."

"Sure, one at a time. One today, another one tomorrow, another one the next day. And no condoms."

"That's true. Condoms weren't made for me. I like flesh against flesh."

As she spoke, she unzipped my fly, pulled out my prick, and

rubbed it slowly. Eyeing it as if it were a treat, she slipped it in her mouth and sucked, sliding up and down until there was a great jet of come and she swallowed it all, licking her lips. The come ran out of her mouth, and she licked it up with her tongue. She didn't want to lose even a drop. I shout a lot when I come. I can't help it. As the come spurts, I scream, moan, bite. It's because the head of my prick is very sensitive. That's what makes me lose control. When I started to moan and shout like a lunatic, she got scared. In her eyes, I was an old man, twenty-six years older than she was. And that's a lot. Or isn't it? She let my prick fall out of her mouth. It was still dribbling come. I exhaled loudly, my eyes rolled back in my head. It's a strange, sweet ecstasy. I let myself go and savor the feeling. It always happens this way. Especially when I get a blowjob. If I have my prick in a cunt, it's a little more controllable. Everyone is startled the first time and thinks I'm about to die from too much loving. Anisia was really scared. At last I was able to get hold of myself. There was another little spurt of come. With my hand I milked my prick thoroughly, from the base, and I shook the last few drops out on the floor.

"Did you swallow it all? Was it good?"

"Yes, yes. Are you done now? Are you all right?"

"Don't pay any attention to me. It's always this way."

"I thought something was wrong with you. I almost ran away."

I fell into a chair. Exhausted. Panting. I had loosed all my life into her mouth, and she had swallowed it. I needed time to recover.

"So you were going to leave. If I had had a heart attack or something, you would've just left me here on the floor."

"Of course. I can't get mixed up in anything like that. You don't understand, if my husband found out, he would beat me to death."

"Well, never mind, Anisia. It's all right. Do you want a drink?"

"No, I can't. I have to go."

"Listen, don't worry. Nothing's wrong with me. This is normal. Pour yourself a drink."

"I'm not scared, but I've never seen a man like that."

"Like what?"

"Your reaction. You scared me. I have to go. I'll call you."

She got up, gave me a kiss, and she was gone. I haven't heard from her since.

2:14 / Taking the Bull by the Horns

I woke up from a drunken sleep on the wall of the Malecón just as the sun was rising, with a terrible headache. I had no idea how many hours I had been there. I sat up and tried to think. Then I realized my shoes and my shirt were gone, and my pockets were empty. Even the key to my room had been stolen. Now I'd have to force the lock. My head was pounding, but I tried to gather my thoughts. I had been drinking late into the night with a fifty-year-old woman: fat, stocky, but with good tits and a nice ass. All right to fool around with for a while. She's one of my neighbors, and she spends all her time raising chickens and stinking pigs on the roof. I don't know what her name is. Everybody calls her Cusa. She's always flirting with me. She comes out in the morning to feed the chickens dressed in a nightgown: it's white, see-through, and so worn out that it's even more transparent, with no bra, big, dark nipples, and the tiniest panties, lost between her enormous buttocks. Out of the corner of her eye, she glances toward my room to see if I'm checking her out or paying no attention. She knows a man without a woman will snack on anything—whatever wanders between his jaws.

The woman's a fighter. She has two teenage sons to support. She's the kind of person who works and works and works like a mule and is very serious and responsible, never laughing or having a drink and taking everything seriously. But she likes me. Even women as unbearable as she is get stirred up sometimes, and their glands work overtime, secreting fluids. Then they get as frisky as cows in heat and they go after someone who can get those juices flowing. That's what would happen to Cusa. I didn't pay much attention to her until her glandular overdrive happened to coincide with mine. Then, instead of fucking her like an animal in my room and sending her back to her own, I wanted to do things right. Sometimes I remember what a nice, polite guy I used to be. I asked her to come walking with me on the Malecón. I had three dollars. It was enough to impress her. First I bought two cans of beer. Quite a luxury. And then a bottle of rotgut rum. When I asked her out, she hesitated. She would have preferred a secret fuck in my room to parading along the Malecón next to me, though I don't have a bad reputation in the neighborhood: I'm not a druggie, or a flasher, or a troublemaker, or someone who's always mixed up with the police. It doesn't matter if every once in a while you smoke a joint or jerk off or get plastered, that doesn't give you a bad reputation. Moderation in all things. It's the guy who's always high and always showing his prick to the neighbors who's really screwed up. He's the kind who'll come to a bad end.

Well, at last she decided she could leave the chickens and pigs alone on the roof for a few hours and go out for a stroll down below, though she made me keep promising we'd keep it secret from her children. Ugh, these serious types are a drag. There was another hitch: responsible women like that always expect too much from a man. I realized she was hoping for more than a good fuck every once in a while. She wanted to snag me. Roast a chicken every Sunday, invite me over for lunch. And try her luck with me. If I wasn't careful, I'd end up being sucked in, and I'd be stuck raising chickens side by side with her and being bored all day, not to mention helping her raise her kids. That's not the life for me. Anyway, I don't like old women. I'm old enough as it is. At forty-five, I might as well be eighty.

Cusa's good for a roll in the hay every once in a while. And that's it. She goes her way and I go mine. It's been a long time since I stopped writing poems to women about how I was leaving them free to return to me of their own accord or to sail new seas. No. That's all finished now. It's been years since I expected anything, anything at all, of women, or of friends, or even of myself, of anyone.

Even so, if she wants to make me fried chicken and french fries for lunch every once in a while, I won't say no.

So I guess I overdid it drinking that rotgut on an empty stomach. I'm not sure what happened. What I am sure of is that I didn't screw Cusa and I didn't do anything too crazy. If there had been a scene, I would remember. I guess I just drank too much, and the old bag got scared. She ran off and left me half-unconscious on the Malecón, the bitch.

I'd barely pulled myself into a sitting position, and I hadn't even had a chance to think when a patrol car stopped right in front of me.

"Over here, please, citizen."

I dragged my aching self over to the car. I felt as if I'd been beaten all over, and my head was pounding. Had somebody sold me rat poison instead of rotgut? That alcohol was mixed with something lethal. I thought I was going to burst.

"Your identification."

"Man, I guess I got robbed last night because . . ."

The policeman wouldn't let me finish. He got out of the car. The other guy stayed behind the wheel. I already knew the drill. "Put your hands on the roof of the car, spread your legs, put your head between your arms, no talking." He frisked me. He didn't find a cent. He told me to get in the back seat. There were no more questions, and they took me straight to the station. For two hours, I sat waiting on a bench. At last they called me in. They pressed charges. I protested I had been robbed. I kept insisting, but they still wouldn't let me go. I went back to the wooden bench. It was a good thing I was weak and felt like fainting this time. Other times, when I had more energy, I'd invoke my civil rights and who knows what else, which was when they'd realize they were policemen and get nasty and drag me into a cell. Finally, a few days later, they'd remember me and let me go, but not before threatening me a dozen times. This time, I was more diplomatic, and they left me sitting on the bench until the shift change at six in the afternoon. No one explained anything to me. The new officer came in. He went through the papers piled up on the desk. He called my name.

"Pedro Juan?"

"Yes!"

"You can go."

I got the hell out of there. Outside, I stood for a minute on the corner by the precinct house. At Zanja and Lealtad. My stomach was churning, as if four dogs were fighting inside me. I was on my last legs. I had to do something, or I was going to faint from hunger. I walked a few blocks, and then I sat down on the curb. I tried to sort out my thoughts, but I couldn't. I was still drunk. It must have been forty-eight hours since I'd eaten anything. All I'd had were liquids. Was it possible I still had traces of alcohol in my bloodstream? The Gregorian chants of the monks of Silos sounded in my head. I used to hear them all the time, so often that I learned them by heart. I couldn't remember where it was that I had heard them. They played on in my head like a refrain. I slapped my face to wake myself up. Pulling myself together, I started walking. I didn't know where I was going. Automatic pilot took over, I guess, and made me keep moving.

I felt very empty inside, as if I had no guts or shit or heart or anything. I was empty, light. I walked on automatically and my thoughts were clear: you've got to take the bull by the horns, Pedro Juan. You have to stop pussyfooting around and be tough. You steel yourself up, you step in front of the bull, you grab him by the horns, and you can't let him throw you. No way. You wrestle him down, and then you go happily along your way. Until the next bull comes along and tries to gore you, and you steel yourself up again and demolish him. That's the way it is—one bull after the next. There's always another bull to fight.

I walked up Zanja to Reina, and I kept going straight, walking slowly, dragging myself along. I was heading away from home, but I didn't realize what I was doing. Why didn't I go toward the Malecón? Why didn't I drag myself toward the Malecón? I wasn't thinking. My automatic pilot seemed to be malfunctioning. The gothic church at Reina and Belascoaín was open. I went in. Sitting on a bench, I looked at the stained glass windows, and of course, the Gregorian chants swelled so strongly that I couldn't understand why no one else heard them. They boomed so loudly inside me that I was sure everyone must be able to hear. But no. No one did. Nothing else happened. I was too giddy to pray. Either I had nothing to wish for or I couldn't pray and give thanks. I never ask God for anything. I just thank him. I usually have a lot to be thankful for, but this time I didn't. I was transparent, light as air. I got up and walked along Carlos III, *Unter der Linden*. It was a nice time of day. Late afternoon. The twilight and the trees. Happy hour, as the most beautiful woman I ever knew used to say. Her husband would be out drinking from late afternoon until ten at night. And I'd take advantage of his absence to spend two or three hours with her, and afterward we'd all end up drinking together, after ten, as if the three of us were good friends. I think he suspected something, but that's another story. Ever since those days, the twilight really gets to me.

No drinking, Pedro Juan, I told myself. You've got to find food. It was then that I realized I was a piece-of-shit bum. A disgusting beggar. Dirty, with a two-day beard. I had no shoes or shirt; I was still half-drunk and practically unconscious. I could beg and then buy something to eat. Later I could figure out how to get back to my room and get my hands on Cusa and wring her fucking neck. "How could you leave me there, you bitch from hell?" I'd ask, whacking her as hard as I could. When a woman deserves it, I like to slap her around. And I'd fuck Cusa like that too, slapping her in the face. I wanted her to be really hurting, her face really stinging, while I got it up and stuck it in her. That would be sweet.

And the bitch would say, "Stop hitting me—just give it to me. Stick it in all the way, really give it to me, baby. Stop hitting me, damn it, that's enough!" And right then she'd come and scream and pant at each spasm. I'd have a ball with that busty old broad.

I stuck out my hand and started to ask everyone who passed by for money, muttering something indecipherable. When you're begging, you can't speak clearly, or try to make sense, or anything like that. You're pathetic vermin, a germ begging for a few coins for the love of God. Scum of the earth. That's the way it's always been done, since the beginning of time. Begging is an art, and you have to be good to fake being a moron, a raving idiot, a hopeless drunk, a brainless lump. Only an idiot can beg. If you're a little bit smarter, you've got to do something else. That's the way it goes. To be convincing, you've got to look like a moron. But even that didn't work. No one gave me anything! I walked a long way down Carlos III, slowly, raggedly, aimlessly. Staring like a moron, or an idiot, shoving my upturned palm in people's faces and babbling gibberish. No one gave me even a penny! Terrible! Nothing. I could have starved to death that night. I walked the full length of Carlos III. Two or three hours I was walking. I don't know how long it was. Begging, for the love of God. And everyone turned aside, looking away from me, or looking through me as if I were a ghost. I had never begged before. It's terrible to beg when everyone is so poor. They're all scraping bottom themselves, and they hate anyone who comes complaining to them. Lots of people would say, "You must be kidding, man. I should be the one begging."

So, not a cent. At least I did finally come to my senses. I needed to get home. Why had I been avoiding going home? The truth is, I didn't want to show up looking like such a wreck, and practically at death's door. The neighbors gossip. Now I understood myself. That was the reason. With my head a little clearer, I said to myself, "Go home, Pedro Juan. Try to make it. It's dark now, and nobody will see you." I guess I turned off the automatic pilot and put myself back in charge.

Then I saw I was in front of Zulema's house. She would help me, for sure. I crossed the street, went up the stairs. At least she'd give me something to eat, and I could get a shirt and a pair of shoes. Zulema lives in a twelve-foot-square room, a shitty dump just like my place. My room is where we've had the best times, because between rounds there's the ocean to watch. Her room only has one crappy window looking out onto a hallway full of dog shit, where the neighbors shout and fight. That's it. All she could hope for now was that Carlos Manuel would bring her to Miami. Carlos Manuel was the love of her life. They got married, they had a son, and Carlos Manuel tried to leave the country illegally. The border patrol caught him. At the trial, he was sentenced to two or three years in jail, but the guy was a loudmouth, and he said a few stupid things about the government and communism. It wasn't much. Compared to what he was really thinking, he barely said anything. But it didn't go over well. His lawyer didn't even try to defend him. He was sentenced to ten years in jail. He served his term, and when he got out, he put his papers in order and he got the hell out of here. He couldn't live in Cuba. Zulema's family wouldn't let her go. Her mother was in bed for a year with the shock. Now the man is in love with Zulema again and he's trying to get her out of the country legally, along with his son, who's twenty now, and a daughter Zulema had later with one of her other husbands.

I struggled up to the third floor and knocked on her door. She opened the door, and when she saw me, her eyes bulged out as if she had spotted a ghost. She tried to shut the door in my face. I stopped her.

"Zulema, wait! Please, for God's sake, it's me, and I'm dying."

She kept trying to push the door closed. She hadn't said anything, hadn't even opened her mouth. She just kept trying to close the door. There was a terrified look on her face.

All of a sudden, the door was wrenched out of her hand, and a huge guy appeared. He looked like a gorilla. He was a massive mulatto, with a big black mustache. The man was furious.

"What the hell is going on?! What the hell is going on?! Who is this disgusting piece of shit, girl?"

"I don't know! I don't know him!" said Zulema.

"Zulema, how can you say you don't know me?"

"Do you know him or don't you?" the gorilla asked her.

"God, no, Pipo. He's a thief! I don't know him! I have no idea who he is!"

"Listen, you bitch, why are you . . ."

The guy didn't let me finish.

"How dare you call my wife a bitch? Are you crazy?"

He grabbed me and hit me like I was a punching bag. I can't describe how it felt, because when I try, I vomit. His fists weren't flesh and blood. They were lead, solid lead. Balls of steel. He shattered my bones, kicked me down the stairs, and closed the door.

The Gregorian chants started to echo in my head again. Ave Maria. Hallelujah. I don't know how long I was out cold.

I woke up in a bed at the hospital. My jaw, my left arm, my collar bone, and several ribs were broken. The nurse said they operated on my spleen. It seems my liver and kidneys are ruined too, and there's nothing to be done about it. The doctors all asked me if I had drunk grain alcohol or sulfuric acid.

Well, I don't know. It could have been worse. I can't move, and there are two or three tubes dripping fluids into my veins. I like one of the nurses, but with my gray beard, I look like an ugly old man, a godforsaken old bum. And the nurse talks baby talk to me. They like to do that. Nurses are all the same. They love to treat their patients like idiots or retards or sickly little children. It makes me mad. Well, at least I'll have time to think while I'm here. Zulema told me once that her life had been hell. I guess it still is. I'll have time to think about that: how a nice, pretty woman gets herself into such shitty situations and can't get out, even though she knows she's wallowing in filth and shit. Poverty warps people.

Most importantly, though, I've got to get better and take that bull by the horns. Then I'll give old man Pipo the thrashing of his life. I'll wait for him on the stairs and beat him to a pulp. After I pulverize his balls, he'll never get it up again.

2:15 / The Moron at the Factory

After the Trotskyites left, Luisa and I didn't talk about them anymore. One afternoon we fucked for hours. It's like that sometimes: all day or all night, nonstop fucking. There's nothing else to think about. Luisa came back from the factory at noon, and we were carried away on a wave of languid, effervescent delight. We couldn't stop. We'd fuck for hours, every which way, in bed, on the chair, tongues, fingers, everything, in every orifice. We'd liven things up with half a bottle of cheap rum.

It was great fucking like that. Luisa would tell me X-rated stories about her husbands, and I would tell stories too. We'd whisper them into each other's ears in lavish detail, and we'd come and keep going on and on. A psychologist would've had a field day listening to us making love, with Luisa pressing her heels on my buttocks and lifting her knees trying to get me all the way inside. "Come on, make me scream, make it hurt!" she'd say over and over again. A psychiatrist would've eaten it up. But psychiatrists are always middle class, and the middle class never knows what's what. That's why they're always scared and want to be told what's right and what's wrong and how to fix what's wrong. They think everything's deviant behavior. It must be terrible to be middle class and judge everything from a distance like that, never trying anything out for yourself.

While we were taking a break, we drank some rum. Luisa was

quiet, thinking for a while, staring into space. Next to the bed were stacks of the pamphlets the Trotskyites had left. She stared at them thoughtfully, and asked, "Do you think Trotskyites fuck like us?"

"I don't know. Well . . . sure. Why not?"

"They're revolutionaries."

"That has nothing to do with it."

"It can't be the same, Pedro Juan. They don't spend much time doing what we do. Maybe on Sunday afternoons, or something. But not like us."

The Trotskyite woman—they were a husband and wife, Canadian, though you never know, maybe they weren't husband and wife or Canadian—left Luisa a pamphlet in Spanish titled "Female liberation through socialist revolution!" The title, in bold type, was printed over a young Soviet woman dressed in black and wearing an overcoat, gloves, and a scarf, a serious expression on her face, with the saddest and most beautiful eyes in the world and an AK rifle slung across her chest. There was nothing fierce about that sad-faced, serious woman dressed all in black. I was sure she was a sweet, warm Russian girl. In one corner, it said, "Soviet honor guard." Luisa tried to read the pamphlet, but it made no sense and little by little, we used it up as toilet paper.

Luisa was always nagging me about being a bum. Back in those days, she wasn't hustling yet. She worked in a factory that made orthopedic shoes and she wanted me to work in the warehouse. "You can steal a pair of shoes a day from the warehouse," she'd say.

"Who're you kidding, Luisa? They'll catch me and I'll be the one stuck behind bars. You'll be as free as a bird, without a care in the world."

"Don't be ridiculous. Everyone steals right and left, from the bosses on down to Juan the moron."

I let myself be convinced. I started work as a stockman. The first few days, I almost died. One pair of shoes weighs nothing, but hauling cartons packed with twenty-four pairs each for eight hours is a whole different story. I almost got a hernia on my balls, for God's sake!

At night, Luisa would massage my back. She has the hands of a boxer, hard and strong. She'd give me great massages with hot lard until my muscles were toned.

Every day I stole a pair of shoes. Luisa would sell them, and we got by a little better. She was an accounting assistant in the company's offices, and she had good business sense. She knew how to make money, anyway. She always got what she was due, and she always knew what she was doing.

There was a moron working at the factory. He was a big, burly, young black man. People said he was the manager's nephew, Juan the moron. He swept the floors in the morning and in the afternoon he wandered around. He did whatever the fuck he felt like doing. Being a moron does have its benefits.

He'd always hang around the women in the offices, and they'd tease him. The joke was to tell him he had a dick the size of a baby's and he had never had a hard-on.

The moron would ignore them, but they teased him until finally he pulled out the colossal thing and showed it to them. That was no prick. It was a big, fat, black beast, twelve inches long. The guy was all puffed up with pride, showing off his already half-erect monster, basking in the attention. The women screamed and threw staplers and paperweights at him, but it was really all a game. They liked seeing that throbbing piece of black flesh. Who knows how many of them fantasized about it at night, while their husbands were fucking them with their God-given pricks, which were surely much smaller. Morons always turn out that way. What they lack in the head, they gain in the prick.

So far, okay. Except the Moron Show wasn't just an occasional entertainment. No—it went on every afternoon. Always in the offices, for the women. Luisa kept me informed. Every night she'd have something new to tell. Who egged him on. Who said what.

And on and on. One afternoon, three of the biggest troublemakers took him into the bathroom and tried to jerk him off, but his prick was filthy, and none of them wanted to touch it with their bare hands. One of them had the idea of using a jam jar so they wouldn't have to touch him. Who knows how long it had been since the moron washed. His prick wouldn't fit in the jam jar. One of the women went to find a bigger jar. The prick just barely fit. They jerked him off. They wanted to see him come. They told Luisa he filled the whole jar up with semen, and a little bit even spilled out. I found that hard to believe. Afterward, they measured the jars. The first one was two inches in diameter. It was a Cuban jam jar. The other jar was Russian and three inches around. Luisa, who was obsessed with figures, measured some similar jars for me, to back up her story.

After that, Juan the moron realized he had become the office superstar. And he got a little more daring. He wouldn't just parade his giant cock around like a model on a runway anymore. Now he was up to something new. The moron mumbled things, very quietly. No one could hear what he was saying. And he'd masturbate a little. But that was as far as it went. Luisa told me that as he masturbated and mumbled under his breath, he'd go up to one or another of them and they'd laugh and scream, "Don't spray me, moron, don't spray me!" It was a hypnotic phallus. What they really meant was "Spray me, moron, spray me!"

One afternoon I saw him. I came up from the warehouse to the offices to tell Luisa something. Bad timing. There was the moron, in the middle of his show. He had been masturbating, parading around so everyone could see him, for a while already. He was breathing hard and swaying from one desk to the next as the women shrieked. When they saw me come in, they froze. Luisa, who was having a good time and laughing her head off, went deathly still when she saw me.

"All right now, what is this? You, moron, put that thing back in your pants. What's going on in here?" I shouted.

But the moron was in his own world. He didn't hear me. I went over to slap him a few times and make him pay attention. I pulled him up close. It pissed me off to see my woman getting such a kick out of the moron's prick. I stepped forward and hit him hard in the face, smacking him twice with my palm. And just as I did, the moron's eyes widened in fear and he started to come in long jets of jism, and it got on me. I jumped back, but the stuff shot six feet out, like jets from a hose. I still can't understand how that moron managed to produce so much come and keep it saved up. He turned around and kept spurting jism all over the desks. I saw it happen! I'm not kidding! If I'd heard the story from someone else, I never would have believed it. That black moron had at least a quart of sperm on tap. I was about to jump him and beat his ass, but I stopped myself. He was just a fucking moron. I can't stand abusive behavior. I stood there, not knowing what to do.

But it was over in a second. Luisa came running up to me, bringing a piece of paper to clean me off with. I blew up at her. I shoved her and told her to go crawl up her mother's fucking cunt.

I left, and I never went back. Luisa and I didn't speak for days. She kept working at the factory for a few more months, until they closed it down for lack of raw materials and electricity. The crisis was ravaging everything. For a while we were hungry and we suffered, until I got tired of being so poor and I came to a decision. One afternoon I grabbed Luisa and got right down to business. "All right, enough of this sitting around and being hungry. You're going to the Malecón to hustle!" I made the right decision. For a while now, that mulatta's been bringing home up to three hundred dollars a week. At last. To hell with poverty!

2:16 / Escaping Hell

I came out of a tiny theater on Industria, behind the capitol, where they show old movies like *The Bridge on the River Kwai*. I whistled the marching tune for a long time, walking and whistling. When that movie came out, I was seven years old. Forty years have gone by, and I'm still whistling the same thing. Cuba may be the only place in the world where you can be yourself and more than yourself at the same time. But it's hard. You try to cling to a small, manageable space. It's dizzying to think how huge the world is, or to realize how tiny you are.

It was almost dark. I picked my way across Central Havana the way a person might cross a war zone, until I came to the market at Laguna and Perseverancia.

"How's it going, Lily? What's up?"

"What's up? Take a look at that. God have mercy, may his soul rest in peace."

A corpse was being carried out of the house next door on a stretcher covered with a sheet. They put it in an ambulance. I thought I caught a whiff of rotting flesh.

"Who is it?"

Lily paid no attention to me. She was staring at the ambulance in the shadows on the street. She crossed herself twice, repeating "God have mercy." I stood there silently for a while, leaning on the counter. Two black men came into the market. Lily had a bottle of rum, and they started drinking. The dead man was a forty-three-year-old sailor. He had been their neighbor for years. Six months ago he came back from a trip with a sore on his tongue. Cancer. He got worse very quickly. He was vomiting blood and he stank. For a few days, he was unconscious, and then he died. He had been a cheerful man who wanted to get better fast so he could go back on board ship soon. He left three children behind. The world's full of bastards, and this poor saint had to be taken, when he and his wife and his children were the best people in the neighborhood, et cetera. I waited to hear the whole story, and then I left. Lately I've heard about a lot of similar cases. Everybody dies of cancer. I kept whistling the River Kwai marching song and thinking how I had nothing to eat at home. I had seven pesos. A guy came by selling pizzas. I bought one. It was pizza in name only, because if an Italian saw it, he'd faint from the shock. Disgusting, cold, and as stiff as cardboard. I gagged it down. There were two pesos left in my pocket. "God will provide," as one of my mothers-in-law used to say, when I still had mothers-in-law. Well, I'd trust in fate. Tomorrow would be another day, and I'd think of something.

That's the way you live: bit by bit, matching up each little piece hour by hour, day by day, era by era, matching up people from all over inside yourself. You assemble life like a jigsaw puzzle.

I don't like to talk about the different stages of my life because it stirs up painful memories. But that's the way it is. A person lives in chapters. And you've got to accept it. I've been poisoned with resentment and hatred by a lot of the people around me. It was easy to see where things would end up: I'd become part of the chaos and keep sliding down that slippery slope until I ended up in hell. By the time I was roasting in hot oil and flaming sulphur, there'd be nothing to be done.

My hide was already smoldering and stinking of sulphur when I managed to catch myself. And I started to recover some of my better qualities. But it was hard work. I was never the same again. Life can't be lived over, thank God. Best of all, I stopped slipping so fast toward hell. All these hurdles life puts in your way. If you don't know how to clear them, or you can't, you're stuck. And you might not even be given the chance to say goodbye.

The elevator was broken again and the stairs were dark, the light bulb missing. With the bulbs stolen, the elevator trashed, and more and more illegal loft rooms built for more and more people, any minute now, the building will collapse. I've had it up to here with this destitution. The morons took a crap again on the stairs. The stink of fresh shit is unbearable. The neighbors' association keeps trying to get the lock on the front door fixed to keep it closed, especially at night. After midnight, people come in and do all kinds of things on the stairs: fuck, smoke grass, shit, piss. But it's impossible to keep the door locked and make sure everybody has a key. It's a pipe dream. For years the old building's looked like a down-at-the-heels aristocrat.

The only people who live here are blacks, old hags, a few young whores and some older women who used to be high-class call girls when they were young, old drunks, and dozens of immigrants from Guantánamo who come in waves and somehow manage to live twenty to a room.

Even so, the dreamers of the neighbors' association hope to keep the door locked and make the stairs safe and quiet again. The building is falling to pieces. Literally, not figuratively. It's on the ocean. And all the wind and the salt in the air make it crumble, and no one knows who to go to for repairs.

Anyway, I don't know why I'm talking about it when I don't care what happens. I could've left on a raft. I had lots of chances to leave on rafts my friends built. But I never did. I've been sailing on the gulf, and I know what the Caribbean is like. Rafts scare me. Sometimes I wish I didn't know so much. Ignorant people are happier. People think they're brave because they paddle off to Miami on truck tires. But they aren't brave—they're kamikazes.

It was quiet on the roof for once. There's usually some commotion. The heat was terrible. Not even a whisper of a breeze, the sea like glass. There would be a full moon, and it would be a beautiful night. From the eighth floor, you could see for miles. I couldn't be in my room. It was like an oven inside. We needed a storm to cool things down a little. I stripped and went out on the roof. There was still water in the tanks. I took a bath. And then I stood around, letting myself air dry. There are seven rooms on the roof. I'm the only one living alone. People don't like to live on their own. But I do. That way I don't have to feel responsible for anyone, not even for myself. I was always too responsible. I've had enough of that. Sometimes one of my neighbors comes and spends the night with me. She's thirty-two, black, and very thin and wiry. We like each other, and we have fun in bed together. She's very dark, and her armpits and her sex have a strong smell to them. That turns me on so much that we must look like two lunatics rolling around. But that's as far as it goes. Luisa skipped out one night after she made three hundred dollars off a guy. The mulatta thought she'd come into a fortune, and she didn't want to share it with anyone. It's been two months since I've seen her. One of these days she'll come back with some story and without a cent in her purse.

I could hear drums beating everywhere. It was the seventh of September, the eve of the festival of La Caridad del Cobre. The drums sounded from all directions and I remembered those movies about explorers on the Congo. "Oh no, we're surrounded by cannibals." But it was nothing like that, just blacks honoring the Virgin. That was all. Blacks on holiday. Nothing to be scared of.

From up here, the whole city was dark. The thermoelectric plant in Tallapiedra was belching out solid clouds of black smoke. There was no breeze, and the smoke hung in the air. A smell like ammonium choked the city. Through the thick fog of gas and smoke, the moon cast a silvery light on everything. There were hardly any cars out, only one or two on the Malecón. Everything was quiet and still, as if nothing was happening. There were only the drums, muffled in the distance. This was a good place for me. All the way to the horizon, the sea was silver. When I couldn't stand the smoke and the gas anymore, I went into my room and closed the door. It was still hot. It would cool off later. The only window I left open was the little one facing south. Through it I could see the city, silvery in the smoke; the dark, silent, smothered city. It looked bombed out and deserted, and it was tumbling down, but it was beautiful, this city where I'd done so much loving and hating. I went to bed alone and in peace. No sex. I'd had too much sex the last few days, and I needed a break. I'd take a break and give thanks to God, ask him for strength and health, nothing else. I didn't need anything else. I've had to conquer my demons and be strong. There's no getting around it. Without faith, no matter where you are, it's just another hell.

Everything was going wrong for me. Things had been going wrong for a long time, and there was no sign of a lull in the storm. The storm was inside me. I was directionless, adrift, sailing as fast as I could toward nowhere at all. And there's nothing worse.

Sometimes I'd be in a good mood for a few days and I could hide my rage. On one of those days, I had a nice conversation with Margarita, a skinny, wiry little black woman with big breasts. She lives downstairs, on the second floor. Ever since I first saw her, I liked her, but you can't go around seducing every single woman you happen to like.

I asked her out for a beer on the Malecón, then up to the roof for a little rum, until finally she flopped down on the bed in my room. We fucked frantically. It was great, and we were at it all night. Afterward, though, everything was the same. Nothing had changed. I was just as disillusioned and full of rage as before. Especially on days when there was a full moon. I don't know why the full moon makes me so angry. It throws me completely off kilter and I turn into a rabid dog. I've tried to fight the idea, but it always proves true. It's not so crazy. So in the end all I can do is come to terms with it and stop struggling in vain.

It was Margarita who bore the brunt of my rage. Our sex life was amazing. But I couldn't stand her. I was broke, eating badly or even worse than that, and seriously considering trying to get a job as a street sweeper. The first day would be the worst, then I'd get used to it and to hell with it. At least I'd be guaranteed a little bit of money each month.

She was always praising me. There I'd be, a wreck, and she'd tell me, "You're an incredible man, you're all I need, I love you." I couldn't stand that ridiculousness. It was too much for me, but still, I couldn't do without her. She trapped me with the color of her skin, the smell of her armpits and her sex, with the feel of her hair and the taste of her breasts. I liked her, but she was constantly saying silly things, and she had a sign taped to her door that read: "Caution. Children running wild."

Sometimes I thought it was all a farce. She was always smiling, with a look on her face that said, "I make you feel good, and you pay the bills." The mercenary spirit of the age, goddamn it. She didn't have a job. She had lost her last one three years ago, and she was the kind of helpless person who little by little lets herself starve to death and has no idea what to do about it. The only money we had was what I was able to earn, fighting for it tooth and claw.

A salsa band had a hit song out back then:

> Get yourself a lover to pay the rent
> He'll make you feel fine
> He'll keep you in the money
> Make sure he's over thirty, make sure he's under fifty
> Get yourself a lover to pay the rent.

It had already happened to me before, with another beautiful black woman. She was a college professor, very elegant, very refined. It was a long, drawn-out romance. We had secretly wanted each other for years, but we were never together in the right place at the right time.

Until she spent a few years on her own, completely alone the entire time. Then we finally connected, and it was the real thing. I was having a fantastic time, because her lust for me turned her into one of the biggest sinners in the history of mankind. The minute she felt my prick grazing the lips of her cunt, she'd lose control. All her intellectual baggage would go out the window, and she'd become a triple-X wild woman, Mrs. Jekyll and Mrs. Hyde. All without a drop of rum or one puff on a joint, nothing. She didn't need anything. It was an a cappella performance. She'd talk and talk, and in the throes of one orgasm after another, she'd talk some more. She was a mulatta on fire. And all of her paraphernalia turned me on. I can't pretend now that I was a saint and say her twisted ideas disgusted me. No, no. The truth is, it all made me extremely horny.

"I want to your slave, darling; you can tie me up and whip me. Here's a rope and here's a leather belt. I want you to beat me and make me fuck four men at once, right in front of you. I'll be a whore; oh, take me. Look at my ass, see how firm it is. It's all yours, all yours. And I'm going to be a dyke for you too. Find me a pretty little white girl, and I'll make her go crazy for you, you'll see. I want to be your slave, baby. Hit me. Whip me, darling. Bite me and leave a mark. Put your finger up my ass."

She had a collection of porn magazines, and she liked to make herself come by looking at the blond, green-eyed girls. I had a fantastic time, and I never tried too hard to understand. It's impossible to understand everything. Life isn't long enough to enjoy and understand all at the same time. You have to decide which is most important. In the end, I left her. Not because of all her crazy games but because it became clear to me she was giving me the evil eye, and I would get hurt. When my little slave saw I liked her tricks, and they worked, she started asking for things: clothes, shoes, expensive meals, perfume. Her greed was unleashed. At the time, I could give her what she wanted, but one day she sat staring at me. We were sitting across from each other, and when she opened her mouth, she said a terrible thing: "Pedrito, you have so many clothes, you won't live long enough to wear them all."

Heaven forbid! I had a lot of clothes then, and I dressed well, but

I wanted to live a long life too. No doubt about it, that black bitch was giving me the evil eye. I never went back to her house again.

Another time, things happened the other way around. It was with a Spanish woman, a Catalan. She thought of herself as the all-powerful mistress. I was a cockroach waiting to be crushed. In bed, we were equals, but when we got dressed, she called the shots. I almost killed her. But I stopped myself. I turned my back on her and left. It's always the same: I leave, and the women stay behind.

I don't want to talk about that yet because I'm not ready to tell my audience, scalpel in hand, "Pay close attention and cover your noses. I'm going to shred some guts. A caveat: shit will come out, and it will stink. In case nobody's told you, shit stinks."

No, I can't do it yet. I've got my scalpel ready, but I still can't bring myself to slice deep and get to the bottom of all the shit.

That's how miserable life is. If you've got character, then you're rigid and contemptuous. Strict regimens and discipline turn you into an implacable kind of person. Only the weak are submissive parasites. And they need the strong. They'll sacrifice everything for the chance of a crumb. They give up their pride. I know it sounds bad when you say it out loud, but the truth is, some people are leaders and others are followers. I can't obey anyone, not even myself. And it costs me. It really costs me.

Then you're filled with fury and rage, and you've got to decompress. We all know how: alcohol, sex, drugs. Well, maybe some people gorge themselves on chocolate or binge, I don't know. In my neighborhood, it's lots of sex and some alcohol and marijuana. There are a few mystics, too, and they're the ones who really know how to live. But that's another story. Forget the mystics and the believers. There aren't many of those, in any case. They don't count.

Margarita withstood my rages for a long time. She learned how to ignore them. She could get by on very little. She just wanted to be loved. That's what she always asked from me. Everybody in the neighborhood was after her; they all wanted to subjugate her to the phallus. This neighborhood is full of blacks and mulattos and whites with little to do and nothing to occupy their minds. There's a kind of meshing of gears: if they get her to try the phallus and she likes it, she falls in the trap. It's simple and primitive, but it works.

It's nothing new. The woman who inherited Vargas Vila's money would smile and say, "Seduce them, corrupt them, get them hooked. They're weak." I never believed it, but she kept repeating it until one day, she told me Vargas Vila had hated women. "He was a misogynist," she told me.

"A faggot?" I asked.

"I don't know about that. But he was a misogynist."

Anyway, there was Margarita, everybody after her. And there I was, wild and out of my head with rage, but at least I didn't have the slightest interest in seducing or corrupting her. She could do what she wanted with her life, so long as she left me alone.

Sometimes I'd even buy her gladiolis and white jasmine and give them to her at night. And all I asked was that she accept them silently and keep her mouth shut. But the bitch would always sniff at them dreamily and close her eyes and thank me and tell me how wonderful I was and how much she loved me. And that would infuriate me. Why couldn't she just take her flowers and shut up?

And why can't I control my arrogance? Why do I let it swell up and shame me? Nothing can reach me when that happens. It destroys me.

Then I realized it's when I'm near a slave that my rage flares up. I'm transformed into a proud, cruel master, an angry master. So I have to stay away from slaves, leave them alone. The contagion is terrible.

2:18 / Every Man for Himself

Last night we were drinking until dawn, Haydée telling me stories about her out-of-body experiences and how she's always afraid and doesn't dare try to do anything. Jorge was listening. He always listens and never says anything. We went to bed half-drunk at four in the morning. They have just one small room, with a bathroom and a kerosene stove. Haydée spread a blanket on the floor, and I dropped down like a ton of bricks. Even through the fog of sleep, I thought I heard them grunting and panting. Those randy blacks just can't get enough.

I got up at nine in the morning, washed my face, and walked to the train station with my twenty frozen lobsters. The train for Havana leaves at noon. It's always packed, which is a good thing, because the police don't bother doing searches.

A funeral procession was moving down one of the main streets. Everyone was on foot, walking in silence. There were too many people, and the silence was deafening. I had my box of lobsters with me, so I had to keep a low profile, but I tried to find out what was going on. Nobody could tell me anything.

The people on the streets were dirty, dressed in rags, starving, and nobody was talking. They were all worrying about the same things: money, food, and survival.

Then I spent the whole afternoon rattling around in the train, which left three hours late and took its sweet time getting back, stopping every five minutes.

I finally got to Havana at ten that night, the whole day wasted in that stinking train. But I was happy to be back in my rat hole of a room. It's nice to be happy, to be in a good mood. If you let yourself get discouraged, you might as well be dead. I put the lobsters in the freezer, drank a glass of sugar water, and went to bed. I was beat.

I fell asleep as soon as my head hit the pillow, and at seven in the morning, there was a knock at the door. Margarita's wake-up call. She must have a sixth sense. How did she know I was back? She made me coffee. With the excuse that it was hot and she was going to sweep and clean, as if the room were a palace, she took her dress off, seducing me with her naked body. We fucked a little. I hadn't seen her for three days. I like that woman. Especially when she manages to keep quiet for a while. Most of the time she won't shut up, and she tries so hard to make you like her that it drives you crazy. Anyway, my attraction to her is purely sexual. That's all it is, and it's enough. My heart is hard now, and the only feeling I have for women is in my erections.

These fleeting affairs are sweet, free of expectations. There is no future and no past. So many things are ruined when you expect too much of them. To learn not to expect anything is an art.

Margarita did want to clean after all, and then she wanted to make us lunch. But I wouldn't let her. I don't ever want to play house again. Enough already. I went out to sell four of my lobsters, and I sent Margarita back to her room. So long, see you later.

A hick from Guantánamo who lives in the building across the street rents out his car, and he has money. The car is a '54 Plymouth, a big, red beast with huge mudguards, extrawide. It's a monster, all red metal and little windows. In my opinion, it has a sinister look, but the tourists call it a "classic car" and they like to rent it and drive around Old Havana or pick up whores in it and take them to the beach. As I was admiring the condition of the old heap, he said, "Man, this car is a gold mine; it's a porn gold mine."

"What do you mean a porn gold mine? Are you crazy?"

"You have no idea, man. Lots of foreigners like to pose with whores inside there or on the roof or on the hood. Crazy business, crazy! And then they ask me to take photos or film them with a video camera. And that all costs extra! You don't know how much money I make out of this piece of junk."

The Guantánamo hick bought two lobsters. Not bad. He paid me a dollar each, no haggling. I made a good profit. I get them from the fishermen three for a dollar. What pisses me off is that I can't buy two hundred at once. I went on my way, stopping at Urbano's little restaurant. Yes, he'd take ten. That was it. I had made my money for the day! I brought them to him, got paid, and went to buy some rum. A little work goes a long way. Life is short.

At the rum dispensary, the line was around the block, but I sidled up, gave the worker a look, and handed him my bottle. He filled it up, and I gave him his thirty pesos. Right there in plain sight, in front of everyone waiting in line. If you've got money, there's no reason to stand clutching your ration book and cooling your heels for two hours just to buy a bottle of rum. Fuck that. I pay double and I'm out of there in a flash. The complaints started up right away. There were the old folks with their whine, "Not fair, you have to get in line like everybody else, you have to have a ration book." It pisses them off when someone with money comes along and screws them.

I walked a little ways away and shouted, "Who cares about fair, you toothless old bastards? Go to hell."

As I was shouting, old Martín came up to me, tipsy as always.

"Come on, Pedro Juan, leave them alone. Forget about those losers. I want to go up on the roof with you. I've been saving a little bottle for the two of us to share."

"Fine, Martín, you say the word."

"No, no, I can't. You have to tell me when to come."

He's been saying the same thing for months. I'm sick of hearing it.

"Martín, I'm up there every single night. I never go out."

"All right. I have a few little stories to tell you, things you can write down later."

"I don't write anymore, Martín. Haven't you seen me out trying to make a living on the street?"

"Aren't you a reporter, boy?"

"I used to be. Used to be. I'm nothing anymore."

"What? Don't kid me. I'm serious."

"Never mind, Martín. Come on up whenever you want. Bring the bottle and we'll talk about women and baseball."

"No, listen. I'm serious. When I was a kid, I lived next door to that guy, you know who I mean . . ."

"Who?"

"Who do you think?"

"Shhh, Martín, just forget it. I don't write anymore, Martín. Take care."

I turned and left.

Back in my room on the roof with my bottle, I would boil a lobster and drink my rum. Rum and lobster don't go well together, but that's what I had, so it would have to do.

That's what I was thinking when I ran into Tony, a guy I used to work with. We said hello and stood there talking for a while. Mostly he talked, because he had just been in Matanzas investigating a UFO that landed there a few days ago. And yes, it sounded like it was a true story. It was especially convincing because the witness was a farmer, too stupid and ignorant to tell a lie. The UFO was the size of a small car. "Just like a turtle, like a turtle shell." It came down silently, a man got out, picked some grass, went back into the machine, and took off without making any noise at all. The marks were still there, and they had been photographed.

"All right, Tony, fine. I've always thought there must be life on lots of other planets. The thing that bothers me is that they don't want to communicate with us."

"Maybe they think we're still savages?"

"Sure. That's it—savages. Predators. Brutes."

"All right, Pedro Juan, don't get worked up."

"See, you show up and get me started and then you tell me not to get all worked up."

"Well, I've got to go."

"See you later."

Just what we needed, real extraterrestrials on the loose. I went upstairs and put the lobster on to boil. I sat there in silence. Each day I'm happier being quiet and alone, and I don't expect much. I can't explain exactly what I mean. When I'm surrounded by silence, I am who I am. And that's enough for me.

My life is always escaping its bounds, like a river that overflows its banks and floods the land. When that happens, I have to give up as much as I can, make decisions about what's useful and what's good. It's the only way I know to control the flood and turn the waters back between banks. Back and forth, like a pendulum. It's always been that way. I've learned to live with the floods, the way they sweep everything away, and with the calm that comes afterward, the new restraint, the loneliness, the silence. It's been a long apprenticeship, infinitely long. I suspect it will never end.

The lobster was boiling, and I was making inroads on the rum, when María came by. She's an old neighbor lady who has premonitions and sees things sometimes, and I help her interpret what she sees. She was widowed a year ago. She had her husband under her thumb when he was alive, and she used to brag to me that he was afraid of her.

"I'm going to tell you something that happened to me yesterday afternoon, and see what you think, because you've got a feeling for these things."

"Me? No, María. You're the one with the feeling. If you gave consultations, you could make a good living."

"I'm too old to start now. I didn't try it when I still could have, and now it's too late."

"Well, what happened to you?"

"Child, I was reading a magazine, and I leaned back and closed my eyes to rest for a minute. I didn't fall asleep. I just closed my eyes, and there was Manuel, calm as can be, not angry at all, and he said, 'I'm going to kill you.' Then he disappeared."

"And what did you do?"

"I opened my eyes, and I wasn't afraid, but I can't get it out of my head. The things I see always come true! What should I do, Pedro Juan?"

"I think you are afraid."

"I'm not, I'm not."

"María, set out a glass of scented water with perfume in it, and go see a *santera*, someone who can give you a really good service. That spirit needs to rise up. Your husband died in an accident. His death was unexpected, and he's still grieving. If you don't do something soon to give him solace, he'll take you with him. You've got to hold a service for him, or two or three, as many as it takes, so that he knows he belongs in the cemetery and not here. It's time for him to be gone."

"Oh, child, I don't believe in any of that."

"Then you couldn't have seen anything."

"But I did. How can you doubt me?"

"María, you can't have things both ways. Do you believe or don't you? If you don't believe, then nothing happened, and you can forget about it. If you believe, then you have to hold a service and help him rise up."

María left, indecisive as always. Ever since the very beginning of the Revolution, she was a Party member and an army officer. Always the same, giving orders and taking charge. The neighbors were careful around her and called her "La Capitana." Now she's lonely and old and poor and dirty. She doesn't even have the heart to wash herself.

Silence once again. I concentrated on the rum and the lobster boiling. But almost immediately I heard the tap of my next-door-neighbor's heels. She's a beautiful mulatta, maybe twenty years old. She's got style. She's a whore, but she could be a model. A beauty. She lives in a rat hole, just like mine, but she's unyielding: if you don't have money, she won't even give you the time of day. Sometimes she says hello but not very warmly.

"Good morning, neighbor."

"Good morning yourself. You're back late from work. It's almost noon."

"And who told you I only work at night? You're a little out of line."

"Hey, I can smell that perfume all the way over here."

"Well, too bad. You'll just have to suffer, sweetie."

"So cruel."

"That's a song, 'so cruel.' See you later. I'm going to take a nap."

"Listen, sugar, when are you going to give me a chance? You're making me crazy."

"When you're a rich daddy with big bucks. But so long as you're broke, you're not getting near me. Shoo, shoo! Bad luck is contagious."

"All right, baby, be mean. Sleep well."

"Bye, sweetie."

"Bye, sugar."

She went inside and closed the door, and I went back to my little feast. That's the way it goes. If you've got money, the world is yours, and if you don't, you can go to hell. Just like in a shipwreck: every man for himself.

I like that woman. She came from the country a year ago, with calluses on her hands and her toenails stained red from the soil. She says she's from Palma Clara. Who knows where the fuck that is!

She doesn't trust anyone, and she thinks everyone is out to get her, but once she told me a few things: she left school in the fifth grade, when she was twelve, and started picking coffee beans so she could make her own money, because her father drank and smoked away everything he earned, "and there were seven of us kids at home eating cornmeal and yams. I don't know how we managed to grow up strong and healthy," she said. When she was sixteen, she realized that picking coffee was work for brutes and pathetic slobs. One afternoon she showered, put on clean clothes, walked off down the highway without saying goodbye, and came to Havana. Just like that, with no idea what Havana would be like. She'd heard you could make a living in Havana because there was money here, so she came. When she told me her story, you could see the determination in her eyes. "I'm pretty, sweetie, do you think I don't know it? Fuck picking coffee and being hungry! I've had enough of that. I'll never go back to Palma Clara again . . . may God forgive me . . . though when my mother dies, I'll have to go back, because she's a saint."

So that's how she arrived, empty-handed. The first few days, she lived with a truck driver who had picked her up hitchhiking. But she left him before the week was out: the man wanted a little slave, someone he could fuck whenever he wanted and keep shut up at home, where she was bored to death. The hell with him. She went to live with a neighbor. Then she started whoring on the Malecón, and in less than a year, the country girl was a new person. Now she even talks differently, and she knows how to walk. Any minute now she'll leave this shit hole of a roof and move to a decent apartment. I like people like that, strong people. Soft people are always whining and crying. It's the weaklings who think each day is their last.

Really, it's the opposite that's true: every day is a new beginning.

III / Essence of Me

I was hanging around the restaurant Floridita, spending time in the red light district, roulette in all the hotels, slot machines spilling rivers of silver dollars, the Shanghai Theater, where for a dollar twenty-five you could take in an extremely filthy stripshow, and in the intermission see the most pornographic x-rated films in the world. And suddenly it occurred to me that this extraordinary city, where all vices were tolerated and all deals were possible, was the real backdrop for my novel.

—Graham Greene on *Our Man in Havana*

Man is not made for defeat . . . A man can be destroyed but not de-
feated.   —Ernest Hemingway, *The Old Man and the Sea*

3:1 / Sharing a Cell with Basilio

Basilio is sitting on his bunk, scratching between his toes. His feet stink. Every once in a while, he smells his hand. He scratches, and then he smells his hand again. He likes the smell, and he does the same thing every afternoon, before he takes a shower. When there's water, that is, and we can wash. Time passes quickly when there's no way to keep track of it. We don't have a clock or a calendar. All we know is that Sundays are for resting and being bored here inside. We've been sharing the same cell for a year, at night. During the day, I work in the mattress workshop, and he works on the little farm. He's a dumb hick; he likes the outdoors.

I had a bad time here at first. I got claustrophobic and I went berserk. When I realized I was locked up, rage built up inside of me, and I started to shout and foam at the mouth. I hit two guards who were trying to restrain me, and they beat me right there until I passed out. When I woke up, it was worse: I was in a cage, a small box with bars on all six sides, in which it was impossible to stand up or stretch out full length. You always had to be curled in a ball. The cages were on the roof of the building. And I was left there for days, out in the open, in the sun. How many days went by, I don't know. They brought me out limp, half-dead. I'm making a short story of it, because I don't want to remember the details. It's frightening to understand we're no better than beasts and that we hate whoever tells us so out loud.

"Basilio, man, stop scratching your feet; you're making it stink in here."

"Aren't you the gentleman? Where do you think you are, sweetheart?"

"Listen, sweetheart and sugar may be what you call those faggots you fuck on the farm, but when you're talking to me, show some respect."

"Playing tough, are you, friend?"

"You better believe I'm tough. This is no game. You treat me with respect, is that clear?"

We aren't friends. There is no such thing in jail. You've got to keep people at arm's length. You can't let anyone get close, because when you least expect it, they'll go for your ass. Anyway, Basilio can't keep his mouth shut. You've got to watch out for the talkers. They'll fall into anyone's clutches; they're spineless. I don't talk. Better safe than sorry. Basilio doesn't know much about me, except that we happen to be from the same neighborhood, El Palenque. I left that place years ago. It's a shantytown, shacks built of tin and rotting wood and strips of nylon, on the banks of the Quibú, which has stunk of shit since the first day of creation. As a kid, I thought all rivers flowed with shit. When I first saw real water, I couldn't believe it and I wanted to know how it could be so clean, what had happened to all the shit and mud.

One time when I was down on my luck . . . ha, as if I were ever up on it. But otherwise it doesn't sound so dramatic. One time when I was down on my luck, I went to see my old buddies in El Palenque and got work at Dinorah's sugarcane-juice stand, grating cane and hauling ice. I'd get up at night to grate husks, and at six in the morning, I'd go for ice with my wheelbarrow. Then I crushed it with a mallet. Dinorah called what we made "frappé." I've never forgotten that little word. By eight she was grinding cane in the mill and selling the juice with ice. It was a fine job. But then one day . . .

It was almost dark, and Dinorah and I were hot for each other. She was in her fifties, but still in good shape, with firm breasts and a nice ass. She knew how to take care of herself too. She was scrappy, streetwise, a fighter. There's no other way to be in El Palenque. Either you're tough or you're tougher. When you start getting weak, you've got to get out of there.

I like women like that. They have sturdy backs and strong backbones, and it turns me on to take them from behind. They turn into coconut treats dripping sugar syrup when you show them who's boss.

A man and a woman know when they want each other. They don't have to say anything. That afternoon, I hid a bottle of rum. When the ice ran out and we were about to close, I offered her the bottle, saying, "Dinorah, take a swig."

"And who told you I drink?"

"I can see it in your face. Don't pretend you're the Virgin Mary."

She laughed. I liked her laugh. It was a hearty, generous, confident laugh. It was Ochún and Yemayá. Life's force. She poured a little rum on the ground for the *santos*, then took a drink and passed me the bottle. We closed the stand, and we sat there inside, dirty and sweaty, reeking after a long day's work in the sun. But I like that. I hate perfume and makeup. I don't want to figure out why that is. I try not to let people know; I don't know why I hide how I feel. But I don't like women who are pretty or clean or sweet-smelling. I don't like them polite or refined, either. I like the dirty, sweaty ones, with unshaven armpits and lots of hair all over.

There was nothing else to say. We passed the bottle a few more times. I closed the little back door to the stand and threw myself at her, kissing her and squeezing her buttocks. She was ready for me, and she asked, "Oh, sweetie, how much longer were you planning to torture me?"

I pulled down my pants and stripped off her shirt and pants. We pawed each other a little, and she took me in her mouth, saying, "Oh, dirty prick, look how filthy and smelly it is. But see how hard it is too and what a big head it has!"

And she sucked expertly.

Then I thought I'd try what I always like: entering her from behind while she's standing up, making her bend over forward. That drives me wild. But when she bent over, her buttocks parted and a terrible stench of fresh shit rose from her ass. She had shit herself. Now, I may be a pig, but that was too much even for me. My prick drooped, and I was seized with a terrible fury. A wave of hate swept through me.

"You're covered in shit, you've got crap all over your ass!"

"Me?!"

"You shit yourself; you filthy pig!"

"Filthy pig yourself! Your prick was disgusting, and I sucked it anyway."

"It's not the same."

"It is the same!"

"You're a filthy pig with shit all over your ass!"

"And you're a real gentleman. You even lost your hard-on. You were born in the shit of the Quibú, so don't put on airs."

"At least I don't have shit all over my ass."

The rum went to our heads, and we insulted each other some more. Much more. Finally she kicked me out and told me she never wanted to see me again.

I went away. I left El Palenque because Dinorah was a *santera* and I didn't want her to put a curse on me.

Then I turned to easier, better-paying work. I became a hustler. But I only went with old lady tourists. I don't have the stomach for faggots, I really don't. I get violent and I want to beat them up. It's different with the old ladies. Sometimes they're even interesting. It's easy money. You put on a sleeveless shirt to show off your muscles, you lean against a wall near a hotel, and you're all set. The old ladies with money flock to you, like bees to honey. Some of them like blacks, but they're scared of them too. They think they're thieves and murderers. And I play on their fears so I get more clients, "Oh, yes, they're terrible murderers and real animals. They're bastards, and they like to hit women. No, you should never go with them; they could kill you. With those huge pricks they've got, they'll tear you up inside. They leave you bleeding on the bed, and they run off with everything you've got. It's happened to lots of women I know." They look at me in horror and they believe every word of it, and then they ask me for my phone number, so they can give it to their friends who are coming soon for the summer. They live in a dream world. They think everybody has a telephone and a car and eats steak for lunch. Idiots. Naïve, maybe. But I was having fun and making good money, and that was all I cared about.

Sometimes they were wrecks, their bodies ravaged by time and hard use. When it was like that, I had to be a magician, a real magician. Lights off, curtains closed, music on, a shot of rum, eyes closed; I'd think of another woman, psych myself up, and go for it. It's easy to drink cold beer, nothing to it. But when the women were ravaged and ruined, it was like drinking warm beer, much more difficult. Oh, life, how cruel you are to old women, wearing them down and pounding them into third-class ground meat!

But I had a few good ones, too. Dina Peralto was one of them. She wanted me to learn Italian and come live in Florence. She was crazy about me. Her face was covered in thousands of wrinkles. She traveled with ten pots of creams, and she ate only carrots and whole-wheat bread. I'd eat two good steaks at each meal. She'd watch me happily and pay the bill. She had no experience at all, and everything I did for her was a thrill. Incredibly, her vagina was tight, pink, narrow, moist, and adolescent, with a mild and pleasing smell. With good reason: her husband had only recently died, at the age of ninety-three. She was seventy-one. She told me stories about all her trips around the world and how sweet the old man had been, how he would always say, "Leave everything to me. All you have to do is play bridge and golf." She called me her "Machiavellian gigolo," but she never explained what she meant by that. We spent a nice month together, and then it was goodbye. That's business. And it's all for the best. I can stand my old ladies for a few days, but after a month I'm ready to slit my wrists.

It was a time of plenty. Lots of food, drinks every day, money in my pocket, good cigars. And lots of stories taking shape in my head. All I had to worry about was the police. One day I went a little crazy. There were twelve or thirteen of us, hanging out on the street behind the Noiba Hotel. Then Chiquitico pulled up in his taxi. He was a friend of ours, and he would give twenty dollars to the hustler who came out on top. The woman was elegant. She was even wearing a pearl necklace. You could see she had the face of someone used to giving orders. And she took her time looking us over, so she'd be sure she was making the right choice. Our general practice is to show the merchandise, so the customer can see what she's getting; that way, when she's back home, she won't complain because it's too little or too big, too skinny or too fat. So that's what we all did: we pulled out the merchandise and shook it a little to plump it up.

The police were on the prowl, dressed in plain clothes. There were a few of them planted nearby. They blocked off the street, and we were all arrested.

They wanted to sentence me to five years for exhibitionism, public indecency, and assault of a tourist. Ugh. Luckily, I had a few dollars saved up, and I hired myself a good lawyer. I got off with two years.

And here I am. Transformed into a good little sheep, working hard in the mattress workshop, so that any minute I might be released for good conduct. The only problem is I won't be able to go back to the same business. No more old lady meat market, because if I'm caught again, that's a repeat offense. The best Cuban souvenir will no longer be available to the ladies. There's no way around it. That's life. I'm too old to be caught again and spend ten years in jail. I'll see what I can find to do. I like this mattress business. You make good money, and you don't have to work too hard. I'm learning to give tattoos too, and that's another way to make pesos. My tattoos are popular. People like them.

For now, I'm locked up here, with Basilio scratching at the crud on his feet, the filthy bastard, and waiting for word that the water truck is here and we can wash up, or that we'll have to go straight to the cafeteria, stinking of old sweat. We all have rashes and scabies. Well, not all of us, because I make my few pesos giving tattoos, and I always have soap. That's life in jail for you. Days go by, and the smallest things take on significance.

At least Basilio is a talker, and he entertains me. He's been in jail all his life, for stealing horses. The first time he was caught he was sixteen and he got four years in a reformatory. When he came out, he was caught again and got two more years. Then it was the same thing again, and he got three. He's serving six now, and he has two left to go. He always complains that he doesn't have a wife or children, that women always cheat on him, and that his mother is all he's got. It seems to me he must have a screw loose, because stealing horses like that for fun isn't something a normal person would do. I could understand it if he sold them, or killed them for food, but he just steals them to run them in races and bet on them. His brain must be fried.

"Maybe they'll let me out next month, when four years are up."

"And what will you do, Basilio? Don't get stuck in that same shit with the horses."

"No. I already told my mother I want to buy a horse and cart and be a delivery man."

"But a horse and cart will cost a fortune. Your mother must be dirt poor, living in El Palenque."

"My mother runs her own business and she has pesos."

"What does she do? Sell water from the Quibú?"

"No, man, she has a sugarcane-juice stand."

"Oh, then she does make good money."

"Yes."

We were quiet for a while. Basilio kept scratching his repugnant feet. All of a sudden, something clicked in my head, and without thinking, I asked, "Dinorah's stand?"

"Yes. Have you been there?"

"I've walked past it a few times."

"That's my old lady, man. When you get out, you'll have to stop by and meet her."

"Oh, right."

3:2 / Stab Her, Man

Two men came to the door. They knocked. Betty opened the door, but she left the metal grille locked.

"What do you want?"

"Are you Betty?"

"Yes."

"We're carpenters. Luis told us there were some repairs you wanted done."

"Oh, yes, but . . ."

"We came to take a look. If we can agree on a price, we'll start work tomorrow."

"All right."

Betty unlocked the grille. The men came in, one big and black with a scar on his face that looked like a knife wound. He had been sliced from behind his ear to his mouth. The other one was a skinny, unshaven white guy, dirty and smelling like he hadn't washed for days. Both of them had vacant, bloodshot eyes, but Betty's a respectable woman and she doesn't know anything about anything.

They came in. The white one closed the grille and the door. The black one pulled a bayonet from under his shirt. It was polished and shining like silver. They moved quickly, launching themselves at Betty and getting her in an arm lock. They almost broke her right arm. Ripping her clothes off, they pushed her onto a small sofa. Betty is very white and a little fat, her flesh flabby. She's forty-one, but she looks ten years older. She was so scared she couldn't say a word. The white man held her down while the black man took a piece of rope out of his pocket and tied her hands behind her back. Then he pulled down his pants and pushed his prick at her mouth. She closed her mouth hard, but he hit her in the face with his palm.

"Come on, slut, open up and swallow."

The struggle turned him on. His prick stiffened, and he forced her to open her mouth and take the length of him down her throat. Tracing the point of the bayonet blade back and forth over her stomach, he raised fine lines of blood. His prick got even harder and bigger, and Betty vomited a little. He liked that. With his prick, he smeared the vomit on her face and in her hair.

"Spread your legs, bitch. You're going to love this."

Climbing on top of her, he forced himself inside her. She screamed in pain, but he slapped her and made her be quiet. She endured the rest in silence. Suddenly, she felt something warm and thick fall on her face. The white man was masturbating and splattering her with come. There was a lot of it, and he rubbed it on her face and in her hair. When the black man saw that, he came inside of her, panting and biting her breasts.

It seemed to Betty that her heart would stop, but it didn't. She was trembling with fear and pain. She hurt as if someone had hammered a rod into her. The black man got up, leaving his pants undone and his monstrous prick hanging loose. He grabbed the bayonet and started to prick at Betty's sex. She screamed again.

"Don't scream, damn it, or I'll really stab. I already feel like burying this in to the hilt . . . I'm going to bury it in your fat belly . . . tell me where the money is."

"I don't have any money!"

The white man shoved all his fingers and his hand into her vagina, viciously. He closed his fist inside of her and punched her hard in the ovaries.

"Tell him where the money is, you fat old bitch! Tell him or I'll kill you!"

She was bleeding heavily now. He had torn her apart. She didn't know anymore if it was the black man or the white one who kept hitting her inside, laughing at the flow of blood. She was writhing in pain.

"Tell me where the money is, bitch. Tell me where it is."

"It's in the kitchen. In the blender jar."

The black man went into the kitchen. He came back leafing through a wad of fifty- and twenty-dollar bills. There were lots of them. He put them in his pocket. By now there was a puddle of blood on the sofa. Blood flowed from the woman's vagina, and she was trembling.

"Stab her and let's go!" said the white man.

"Don't be in such a hurry, you animal! Remember there's jewelry too. Come on, fatty, tell us where you keep your jewelry. And don't tell me you don't have any, old bitch, or I'll cut off your nipples."

And he started to prick her with the blade again. Now he was jabbing at her nipples, her breasts, her face, breaking the skin and making small cuts, bloody and painful.

"I don't have any jewelry. Who told you I did? All I have is money. That's all I have."

Betty's voice trembled. Her whole body was trembling. She curled up. Hot blood bubbled out of her and onto the sofa. There was no more pain; it was numbed by fear. Her brain was floating on a thick liquid and without thinking she mumbled something, babbling, "If my husband comes back, he'll kill you. He's a policeman. He went out to get cigarettes, but he'll come back and shoot you,"

"A policeman?" the black man asked.

"Yes. He'll kill you if he catches you here. Go!"

They started to shake, suddenly seized with fear.

"Stab her, man, and let's go," said the white man.

"No, you idiot, my fingerprints are all over the place."

The black man picked Betty's blouse up off the floor and went into the kitchen to wipe off the blender and the back of a chair. He was shivering as he came back, his legs shaking with fear.

"Stab her, man, stab her, the bitch knows us now."

The black man put the blade to her throat. His hand was shaking:

"Listen, fat bitch, you keep your mouth shut because I'll get in here and cut you to pieces. Go crazy, do whatever you want, but forget you ever saw my face. Forget all about us."

"Stab her, man, don't preach her a sermon, stab her!"

The black man's hand was shaking.

"No, you stab her! Why do I have to do all the killing? Take it, you stab her, and we'll go."

"No, I won't. I won't do it! Come on, enough, let's go. This is getting too messy."

The black man put the blade away. He opened the door and the grille with Betty's blouse wrapped around his hand, and they were gone.

Betty lay on the sofa, terrified and bleeding. In the nursing home next door, a senile old man was shouting, "Rosa, Rosa, Rosa, Rosa." Betty could hear him now, through the half-opened door. The old man's sad story drifted through her head as her mind wandered, his nightly lament slowly fading into silence.

When she came to again, it was the middle of the night. Everything was quiet. Feebly, she tried to get to her feet, but she couldn't. Her hands were still tied behind her back. She let herself roll gently to the floor, then wrestled herself into a standing position. Everything was spinning around her. She leaned against the wall and was overcome again by panic, shaking with fear. What if they came back? They might come back and stab her to keep her from talking. It was very quiet. Choking back her fear and nausea, she moved outside, propped herself up against her neighbor's door, and kicked it. She was barefoot, completely naked, and she was at the end of her strength. She kept kicking. Her neighbor was an old man who lived alone, just as she did. Minutes went by. He was probably asleep. At last the old man came, asked who was there, and very cautiously opened the door a crack. Betty told him what had happened. It was three in the morning. She had been unconscious for nine hours. Now she thought she was going to faint again.

The old man untied her hands, helped her back onto the sofa and into the puddle of blood, and told her he would go find a doctor. He was so scared he was practically shitting his pants, but he pulled himself together. Very cautiously, he left the building and went to stand on the corner, waiting there until a police car drove by. A few minutes later, the neighborhood was roused by the howl of sirens, announcing the arrival of the detectives. Betty was taken to the hospital, where she was treated and given several blood transfusions. She described the two men, and an expert prepared computer portraits. A week later, she was able to go home. Now she can't sleep at night, and she's sure the men are coming back. A woman has approached her twice on the street, whispering in her ear, "They told you not to talk. Now they're going to cut out your tongue." Then she turns and walks quickly away. Betty can't stop worrying, and she doesn't know what to do.

3·3 / The Apprentice

A terrible wind, hot and damp, was blowing from the south, raising clouds of dust and making everything dirtier than it already was. At home, the heat was suffocating, and Luisito couldn't stand it or the stupid way his mother only talked about the church and God and sinners. And his father was always going out onto the roof, checking on his pigeons and chickens so he wouldn't have to listen to her. His mother was sleeping now. It was quiet, but the heat was stifling and he was on edge. He went down the stairs and out onto the Malecón, where he sat looking out to sea. Full moon, blue night. Dark clouds shot through with silent lightning in the distance, to the north. The sharp rays of light could only be seen against the roiling clouds. Whenever he sat here at night, he thought about his three brothers, and a wave of sadness washed over him.

All of a sudden, he felt someone grab the back of his neck, pull him down, and start hitting him. There was no one else around. Luisito shouted, but they kept hitting him, punching him in the face, beating him. They were hitting hard.

"Stop, stop, don't hit me. You've got the wrong guy; it wasn't me; it wasn't me!"

"No, asshole, you're the one we want. You've got some money owing."

Then, pushing him and ripping his shirt, they let him go. Felipito and El Papo. Two losers just like Luisito, old childhood friends of his from the neighborhood.

"Hey, I know you two, damn it! What's going on? Papo, we've been friends since we were kids."

"I need you for a friend like I need a hole in the head. I'm Chivo's man. I can't be hanging around a shit-ass loser like you."

"All right, Papo, stop acting like a gangster. You're a nobody just like me."

"I used to be a nobody. Now I've got a shitload of cash and I'm working for El Chivo. So you better show me some respect."

Felipito was holding Luisito's arms behind his back, and El Papo drove his right fist hard into Luisito's belly. It hurt. Luisito doubled over. Felipito straightened him up with a jerk.

"Luisito, I'm going to keep this short. You owe Chivo seven dollars and forty cents. Tomorrow you better come find me and hand it over, because Chivo doesn't want to see your ugly face."

"If I can't tomorrow, I'll have it for you the day after."

"Don't give me that. Either I get it tomorrow or I'll beat your brains out. I'm not going to go easy on you like today. You'll get the full treatment."

"All right, man, I'll try . . ."

"Trying isn't good enough. You better move heaven and earth. Oh, and Chivo said to tell you your credit is no good with him anymore. If you want more weed or coke, it'll be cash down. Adios, Luisito, and try to take better care of yourself, cause you're not doing so hot."

They walked away. Luisito's whole body ached. He felt his face and his head. There was no blood, but he hurt like hell all over. He sat back down on the wall and thought, "It's true. Things haven't been good for me for three years. That's the way it goes. If you have money, you have friends, and if not, you get fucked."

A few tears welled up in his eyes as he thought about how unlucky he was, and he said to himself, "Luisito, be strong and find that money somehow, because if you don't, those assholes will beat you to death, and you're too young to die. You can't die yet."

Far away, lightning kept flashing in the clouds over the sea. He wished the rain would fall and cool him off a little, the way cold water is squeezed out of a sponge over boxers who are down for the count. He couldn't even have that. The wind from the south was hot and sticky. He went walking toward Old Havana, thinking how he'd have to sleep with the old faggot to make a few bucks that night, and how on the way there, he'd have a few shots of rum to cheer himself up.

The sea was calm, very clear and blue. Under the full moon, everything looked beautiful. Seven men were fishing along the shore, floating in inner tubes. You could make good money that way, but being out in the cold night air with your butt in the water was bad for your bones. Those guys were fools, he thought.

Walking slowly along the Malecón, he looked at the fishermen again and thought about the raft he built with his brother and five other people in August of '94. It was right around here that they launched it, at two in the morning. They even had a compass so they could keep heading north. After half an hour on that piece of junk, it was sinking under their weight, and his own brother ordered him to swim back to land because there were too many of them. It had to be him who got screwed. He always had to be the one, the youngest of four brothers. Three years had gone by since then. Now they all lived in Nevada, and Luisito was still poor as dirt. And cursed with bad luck. Any little scam, he was always the victim. It was as if someone had put a spell on him. He closed his eyes and felt sick just thinking about sticking his prick in that fat old man. It wouldn't be easy. He'd have to get paid first. He crossed the Malecón and walked up Galiano to Trocadero. Turning left, he walked a few more blocks, and he was at the old man's house.

There was no one on the street. At least he wouldn't be shamed.

He knocked on the door. After a while, the old man looked out through the peephole and asked who was there.

"It's me, don't be scared. Open up."

"You made up your mind at last, child!" And he opened the door happily.

He was a fat, saggy old man. Three hundred pounds of lard. Ever since his parents had died, he lived in constant fear, and he never went out. He would only walk the ninety feet around his house. He was pathetic, that fat old man, sixty years old and grinning and twirling like an ancient whore.

Luisito knew his way around the house. He went straight to the back and looked in the cupboard for a bottle of rum. Finding it, he poured some into a glass. The old man followed him.

"Child, what happened to you? Take off your shirt and let me clean you up. You've got bruises all over."

"Don't touch me, you old faggot, or I'll whip your ass! Here, suck on me and try to get me hard so I can fuck you."

"Oh, that's what I like about you. You're such a brute."

Luisito couldn't get hard. He was disgusted, furious at himself, and he ached from the beating. What he wanted was to drink all the rum, smoke a joint, and beat the old man up. He was seething with rage. He wanted to beat the stupid old man to death and take all his money.

"Give me ten dollars. I'm leaving."

"But you haven't done anything. You didn't even get a hard-on. Anyway, I don't have ten dollars. Or even one dollar. Who do you think you are? Earn your pay."

That was the last straw. Luisito slapped him twice in the face, and the old man started to squeal, dropping his pants. He had a tiny penis, almost like a child's, buried under his enormous belly. Stroking it, he started to masturbate.

"Oh, that's what I like. Slap me in the face. Hit me, fuck me!"

Luisito felt even sicker and angrier. He hit him some more and got a slight erection; the old man took it eagerly in his mouth, still jerking himself off. Luisito pulled away. He went into the bathroom, rinsed his prick, and tucked it back in his pants. The old man was still masturbating like mad in the kitchen, and he called, "Come back, sugar, come back!"

Luisito went into the kitchen and got the bottle of rum. The old man tried to grab him with his left hand while he masturbated with his right. Luisito swerved away and walked back through the house again to the front door. In the front room, there was a beautiful porcelain carriage with four horses sitting on an antique table. It had to be worth a lot of money. He slid the bottle into the back pocket of his pants, picked up the carriage in both hands, and went out. The old man ran panting to the door, trembling in fear, but he didn't dare say anything, let alone shout at Luisito.

"Come back whenever you want; come back again some time," he said, in a voice barely louder than a whisper.

He closed the door and went over to a beautiful cigar box covered in embossed leather. He took a cigar. His hands were shaking. He sank down into a chair, struggling for breath. Lighting his cigar, he inhaled, and sat there smoking voluptuously in the quiet before dawn, still petrified. Picking up a piece of paper and a pencil, he started to write automatically, to calm his nerves.

Villainous swordsman the feeling
The pheasant scratches
Lamenting in judgment or jest

3·4 / Sick, Very Sick

I had nothing to do that afternoon. In fact, it was the same every day. There was never anything to do. I had five pesos left in my pocket and I sat down on the floor, leaning against the doorjamb. It had been days since my last drink, and I had no money. I was waiting. Waiting for what? For nothing. Just waiting. Everybody's always waiting, day after day. Nobody knows what they're waiting for. Time passes, and your brain goes numb, which is a good thing. When you don't want to think, it helps if your brain is numb. Sometimes I think too much, and then I panic. I used to study, work hard, set goals for myself, and try to make my way in the world. Then everything fell apart, and I ended up in this pigsty. Some people have scabies, others have lice or crabs. There's no food or money or work, and every day there are more people. Where so many ragged people come from, I don't know.

So it's best not to think too much and instead just concentrate on having fun. Rum, women, marijuana, a little rumba whenever possible. Everything else is shit, and it's better not to poke around in it if you don't want to raise a stink.

That's where I was, more or less, skin and bones and ravenously hungry, but thinking about buying myself a two-peso cigar so I could smoke away my troubles, when Monino showed up.

"What's up, man?"

"Not much. You're seeing it."

"Hey, I'm doing pretty well for myself. Let's go have something to drink."

I took off with Monino. I know what his deal is. He deals marijuana and coke for Chivo. The people who buy the coke are from Vedado and New Vedado, artists, musicians, the sons of factory bosses and cops, big shots. A little packet of cocaine costs six or seven dollars. Who can afford it? You can buy a joint for ten pesos. If you sell two or three of them, then you cover your costs and the one you keep for yourself is free. The things a person has to come up with in this life to get along.

We went to a cafe on Galiano. Monino bought a bottle of rum. We sat on the Malecón and passed it back and forth. I bought myself a cigar. Beautiful: rum and a cigar, sitting out in the fresh air on the Malecón, with the sea before us. A huge white three-masted luxury yacht—*Le Posant*—was drifting in the gold and orange afternoon light, waiting for the pilot boat to usher it into port. There must have been at least fifty hotshots on board. I guess it is worth having money, and not just the bare minimum. You need enough left over so you can step on board a yacht like that and sail around the Caribbean, swigging the best bourbon, chomping on almonds, a skinny chick with big tits by your side. Beautiful. That way you never have to know the people on shore are living like cockroaches. From a yacht, all you can see are palm trees, golden sunsets, and beautiful beaches lapped by turquoise-blue waves. Once you and your money are on board, you forget about all the dirty tricks you've had to play and the people you've had to crush and bully to keep your pockets full. That's the way it is. The more money you have, the more you make, and the poorer you are, the poorer you get.

I was hungry, but when you've had enough rum to drink, you forget. When we finished the bottle, we were nice and high. Not too drunk, just pleasantly loaded. Monino is my friend. He's helped me out a lot. I started trying to convince him to set up a mattress-making shop. I learned the trade in jail. After two years in the workshop there, I was good at it. It's easy work, but it was a lost cause. Monino has no interest in any kind of work. All he's interested in is weed and coke.

"Drop it, man. I'm not going to bust my balls. Let's go have a smoke. I've got two little joints."

"Two? Damn, man, I love you! Let's go up on the roof."

By then it was dark. We went back to the building and made it up the stairs without anybody seeing us. But once we were on the roof, there was Jorgito, jerking off and watching a couple through a window as they fucked in the dark. It was hard to see exactly what was going on. Jorgito was guessing at their shapes. We looked too, but it was hard to see anything.

"Come on, hurry up and finish. We want to sit in that corner," I told him.

We just lit one joint at first, savoring it and sucking in the smoke. It was good weed. I had had enough, but Monino wanted to smoke the other one. It knocked me out. Skinny as I was, with my stomach empty, the combination of rum and tobacco and weed was deadly. I dozed off. Monino shook me a little.

"Hey, are you staying here? Get up, go down to your room."

"No, I'll go later. I feel sick."

"All right. I'm leaving. I'll see you tomorrow. If you want to set up that mattress shop, I'll lend you the funds. We'll talk tomorrow."

After lying there half-asleep for a while, I woke up. Or maybe it was hours later. I don't know. My prick was as stiff as a rod. It had been days since I had a woman, and every time I fell asleep I'd get hard. My brain relaxes, and I'm off like a rocket. I was alone on the roof. I went over to where Jorge had been standing. The window was closed. I was still high. I came down off the roof. The building was quiet. It was late. And there was Esther, sitting on the floor in her doorway.

She's over fifty, maybe even sixty, and incredibly fat, with huge, flabby tits and a huge, flabby ass. She's a cheerful, loud-mouthed black woman, and she has ten or twelve children, of every color of the rainbow and every age. I had never even considered fucking her. I wasn't attracted to her; I can't imagine anyone would be attracted to her. It would be like fucking a turtle. I've always liked skinny, happy whores, with firm muscle. But I was horny and half-loaded, and the old whale was horny too, and she'd had some rum.

"Tell me, white boy, what are you doing awake and on the roof at this time of night? What are you up to?"

"Nothing. I went up to have a few drinks with a friend and I fell asleep."

"It's two in the morning, sweetie. That's why you boys get in so much trouble with the police. Who's going to believe you?"

"Oh, grannie, don't hassle me."

"Who are you calling grannie? Do I look like your grandmother? Come on, have a drink to clear your head a little."

I drank a few shots with her, got plastered again, and lost control. My prick stiffened, and I rubbed it through my pants. I like to give women thrills that way. They all like it, even if they pretend to be disgusted. They like to see a man getting hot sitting next to them.

It was what the old woman was waiting for.

"You're plastered, sweetie."

She put her hand on my prick and squeezed.

"Feel that beast! He wants woman's flesh."

And just like that she pulled me out of my pants and took me in her mouth. She was a pro, naturally. We went into her room, and I spent an hour riding that huge bulk of warm, sweaty flesh. The two of us were sweating, sweltering. It was nice. It really was nice. She came five hundred times, and she kept saying, "That's what I like, white boy, I like to come like a bitch in heat."

When I finally came, I fell asleep right there in her bed, and I said, "Smother me with those breasts . . . oh yes, I love fat."

She laughed and pushed her enormous breasts into my face, rubbing me with the damp, flabby mass of her belly. I wallowed in her flesh like a pig until I fell asleep. I was exhausted.

3·5 / Impossible Nights

All afternoon, Clotilde sat outside her building, but she wasn't sell-ing anything. On the ground beside her, she had two cartons of cig-arettes, some cigars, three sealed packets of instant raspberry drink, four toothbrushes in their plastic packaging, and two bundles of white onions, all cheaper than in the stores.

It was almost dark. When she couldn't sell anything, she got de-pressed, even more depressed than usual. She had been depressed for years. Everything started to fall apart in April of 1980, when her husband went to the port at Mariel to watch the flotillas of yachts coming and going. He got excited and boarded a yacht, forgetting everything he was leaving behind. Six hours later he was in Miami, and she never heard from him again. She's been told he lives in New Jersey, and he's doing well for himself.

Their son was five, and Clotilde focused her energies on him and waited for news from her husband. But Central Havana isn't a good place to raise a child. He dropped out of school, working at odd jobs every once in a while or not bothering to work at all. One day he came home with a wooden suitcase full of the paraphernalia of magic tricks: hollow dice, double funnels, trick bottles, a hat with a hiding place in its crown. The suitcase had silver stars painted on it, and in big letters it said, "Cherry the Magician." He wanted to be a circus magician, and he practiced every day; he was quick and clever with his hands. But he never got the chance. One afternoon at the beginning of August in 1994, a huge antigovernment demonstration passed along the Malecón in front of the building. After two days of unrest, people built rafts out of anything that might float, and they left the island. One morning the boy left too. By that time he was nineteen, and he told his friends, "My father has a huge business in the U.S., man. It'll be great."

He didn't say goodbye, sneaking behind his mother's back as he had always done. Clotilde found out from someone who saw him on a raft paddling out to sea. She never heard from him again. She doesn't even know if he made it alive or if a shark ate him up. Still, she's been keeping track. Three years have gone by, and the boy will be twenty-two in June.

Sometimes Clotilde wants to kill herself. She's thought about doing it with pills, dousing herself with alcohol and lighting a match, or hanging herself, but she doesn't dare. She's afraid. But she knows it's only a question of time until the fear passes. She's tried everything. She's gone to church. She's prayed. She's tried to find a job but had no luck; it didn't help that she was a skinny, filthy old woman, dressed in rags, her breath stinking of the rotting liver inside her.

Every day she gets drunk. Food doesn't interest her; only alcohol. Now it was dark, and she made up her mind. Gathering her wares, she climbed the dirty staircase, with its stench of urine and old shit, and went to her room. Picking up a bottle of homemade rum, she took a long swallow.

It was dark and quiet. In the corner was the stupid Cherry the Magician suitcase. And Clotilde cried. She felt sorry for herself, and she was full of rage and hatred. She cried some more.

The building was on the corner of Malecón and Campanario, ravaged by the wind, salt air, time, and neglect. There were gaping holes in the brick, cracks in the roof and walls. A few days of rain and a strong wind from the north and it might easily collapse. But it was full of people, no one knew exactly how many. They'd come and go. A few light bulbs glowed faintly yellow. Shadows and silence. Everyone was living here illegally, scurrying around like mice, ducking into corners. The police might come by any day, evict them, and send them back to their home provinces in the east, or steer them toward shelters on the outskirts of Havana, two rows of cots, one for men and the other for women. And back in the country, what was there for them to do? What could they sell? They were better off here, even though they knew any night the building might collapse and crush them.

In the room next door lived an old man, also alone. He liked rum too, and sometimes they drank together. He was black, dirty, and unshaven; he couldn't remember the last time he had a bath. Clotilde would go over and knock on his door, and they'd drink together. She was always the one who talked, telling her story over and over again. He wouldn't talk. He had never told her anything. But he was lonely, hungry, filthy. He'd listen in silence and drink. Clotilde didn't even know his name. Now the old man finally spoke, "For years, I've been waiting for Robespierre, but I'm not waiting anymore. It's all over."

"Who is Robespierre? Your son?"

"Oh, drink your rum and leave me alone."

"Life has crushed me."

"That's the way it is. Either life crushes you, or you crush it."

"There's no way out for me, old man."

"It's your pride that's been crushed. Forget your pride and give up your expectations."

"So what am I supposed to do? Should I start picking things out of the garbage, like you? Should I pick shit out of the garbage?"

"Why not? You can't be proud. Pride will kill you."

"You're an old pig. A black one, too."

"And you're an old white pig. That's why you don't know anything."

"Oh really? So blacks know more than whites?"

"Sure we know more. We know everything."

"Go to hell."

Clotilde picked up her bottle. There was still a little rum left in it. She went out, but she didn't want to be alone, closed up in her room. She sat on the floor of the hallway, across from an enormous crack in the wall. Through it she could see the dark sea, the silent night. There weren't many people out on the Malecón. Waves crashed on the reefs, spraying salt into the air over the city. She drank, thinking of nothing. Over the years, she had learned to drink without thinking, her mind wiped clean.

3·6 / Sewer Rats

My job was disgusting, but it was going all right. I had to make the rounds of Central Havana with a wrench, unclogging gas pipes.

Early one morning I went down into a filthy basement, just like all the other basements in the neighborhood, full of rotting boards, puddles of stinking water, and a foul smell. A dirty old man told me he was the one "in charge" of the building. We didn't have flashlights, and there were no light bulbs. The old man stood next to me lighting matches.

"We have to go find a light bulb, because if you keep lighting matches, we're going to be blown to smithereens."

"No, no. We'll be fine."

"What do you mean we'll be fine? This is my job. I know what I'm talking about."

"No, son, go on, all you've got to do is clean out the pipes."

"You're an old fool. I'm getting the hell out of here."

We were at the back of the basement. Turning to feel my way toward the door, I stepped on some half-rotten boards, and out came the rat. Feeling itself being crushed, it attacked me rapidly and viciously. I felt its claws sink into my flesh. It bit me in the belly and the chest, clawed me in the face, and then disappeared.

There was no time to react. I had never felt anything so disgusting on my skin. The bites and the scratches hurt, and I panicked, running to the door in the dark. The old man didn't realize what had happened, and he didn't follow me.

I made it to the door, went up a few stairs, and at last came out into the light. The rat had bitten me in the left arm too, and the bite was bleeding and it hurt. I was covered in stinking sewer mud.

My day was shot. I went to the clinic. It was full of gloomy old men and women sitting and waiting on benches. I made a fuss. I explained to the old people that I couldn't wait in such a long line. My case was urgent. The old people's mood turned from gloomy to angry. They refused. They said their cases were urgent too and that I had to wait my turn. There was only one nurse, working slowly and halfheartedly, and I didn't like the look of her. She had a beautiful, slender, young body and a nice ass, but her face was grotesque: she looked like a man, with her greasy, pockmarked skin, a beaky nose, pus-filled pimples, and thin, dirty, tangled hair. To see the head of a hideous man on that perfect, beautiful body made me shudder. She bandaged me up and gave me a tetanus shot, moving unenthusiastically. She complained that she was hungry and that she hadn't had breakfast. I asked, "Don't I get a rabies shot?"

"There isn't anything."

"What if the rat had rabies and gave it to me?"

"Bring it in to be tested. But even if it's infected, we don't have the vaccine." She turned away from me brusquely and shouted toward the door, "Next."

Shit. I left the surgery, but after taking a few steps, I came back. Sticking my head in the door, I asked again, "Do they have it at any of the hospitals?"

"What?"

"The rabies vaccine, sweetie."

"I already told you no."

An old lady pushed me out of her way, muttering about people who don't wait in line. The nurse blew up.

"Ma'am, you wait outside until I call you. Don't get pushy, or I'll close up and you can all go to hell."

And she slammed the door.

I wasn't happy with the way things were going. There had to be a stock of rabies vaccines somewhere. I stood in the clinic doorway, trying to figure out what to do. Some guy came up to me and asked, "How much do you want for that?"

"For what?"

"For the monkey wrench, brother."

I had forgotten all about the wrench. In a matter of seconds, I decided I was never going back into a stinking Havana basement to chip cement and crusted shit out of those pipes again.

"One hundred pesos, man."

"That's a lot of money."

"The hell it is. This is an English monkey wrench, the real thing. It's been years since you could find a wrench like this."

"Give it to me for eighty."

"No. One hundred, take it or leave it. I'm not in a hurry to get rid of it."

The guy pulled out a hundred pesos, gave them to me, and went off with his wrench.

Just then, the ugly nurse came out. She saw me counting the money, and her face lit up.

"You're loaded, big boy!"

I looked hard at her. She was ugly as a dog. But I had a problem and she could help me solve it.

"Do you want to get a pizza?"

"Why not, sweetie? I'd love to."

We went to a stand nearby and had a snack: pizza and mamey fruit shakes. When I paid, she stared at the bills, and just like that, a light bulb came on over my head. I'm lucky that way—I never have to think. Changó and Babalú Ayé show me the way when I least expect it.

"Want a shot of rum, baby?"

"I'm working, sweetie, I can't."

"Listen, I'm just dying to spend money on you."

"Come on, pal. What about your rabies vaccine? If you're going to get it, you can't drink."

"Maybe I can't, but you can. What's the story with that vaccine anyway?"

"The director of the clinic has a secret supply for emergencies."

"How much does it cost?"

"Oh, I don't know. Do you want me to find out for you?"

"Sure."

We went back to the clinic, and she found the vaccine. Forty pesos. I got the shot. She scowled at all the old, gloomy, angry people, telling them that she was going to close and she wouldn't see anyone until one o'clock. We left the clinic.

And now what was I supposed to do with Ugly Face? That vaccine was really going to cost me.

"Sweetie, there's no place to get rum anywhere near here. Let's go to Pompilio's."

The man had a vat of rum, and he was selling bottles of it for thirty pesos.

"Give me one bottle," I said.

"Buy two. We're in no hurry."

I bought two bottles.

"Let's go to my place so I can change out of my uniform."

She lived nearby, in a crumbling building at Campanario and Malecón. An old woman was sitting in the doorway, selling cigarettes, toothbrushes, and other trinkets.

"Clotilde, give me a whole carton."

"A carton? You're doing well for yourself today. I hope your good luck lasts."

I paid, but I don't like cigarettes.

"Do you have any cigars?"

"No, not today."

We went up to the second floor. She lived in a room reinforced by wooden struts. The whole building was collapsing and propped up with struts. If even one piece of wood was removed, the place would fall apart. Cockroaches swarmed over the damp walls. We went into her room. The first shot of rum she tossed on the floor, for the *santos*. She took a long swig, and said, "Sit down."

There weren't any chairs. I sat on a broken-down cot.

"I woke up today feeling like shit and I didn't want to work, so you really saved my life."

I didn't say anything. I needed a drink to get me through the time I was going to have to spend with Ugly Face. But I couldn't give in to temptation. Taking another swallow, she turned on the radio. Salsa. She opened the window, and light from the Malecón penetrated the damp shadows, bringing with it the smell of salt and a breeze off the sea.

"This is for you, sweetie, my savior."

Dancing sensuously, she started to take her clothes off in a slow striptease. She put her dress on a hanger and hooked the hanger over a strut. Then she hid her face in the dress and danced.

"Oh, baby, look what you're doing to me."

And I showed her my prick, eight inches of steel, thick and veined and angled to the left.

"Oh, I love to see it like that; but don't take your pants off, sugar. Leave it just like that, sticking out. Do you want a smoke?"

"You have weed?"

"The best. It's from Baracoa. I sell each joint for twenty pesos. But this time it's on me. Smoke as much as you want."

She opened a drawer in a little bedside table. Inside was a huge bundle. It had to weigh two pounds at least. Happiness at last!

We had a great time. She was crazy for dick. She told me she'd been drinking and smoking since she was twelve. She was from the east, from a village in the hills, and she'd been living in this dump for two years. She'd only been working at the clinic for a little while.

"But I'm about to quit. I make more on the side."

"Doing what?"

"Whatever I can, sweetie. Selling penicillin or marijuana or rum, anything. Or I give hand jobs to old men on the Malecón."

We kept fucking, and she kept drinking. By now, I liked her. At first I avoided looking her in the face or I kept my eyes closed. But after two joints, I decided I liked her beat-up boxer look.

Just as it was getting dark, we had to stop. We were hungry. She was wasted, and she was already getting started on the second bottle. I sat down by the window, looking out at the sea. I had forgotten about my rat bites. They must've been healing.

"Hey, let's go out and get something to eat."

"But we have to come back up again, sweetie. My pussy's already sore, but I don't want to stop until tomorrow."

"Fine, get dressed and let's go."

Just then, someone knocked at the door. It was a skinny, dirty old man, underfed and unshaven. They whispered together in the doorway, then she came over to me.

"Sweetie, go outside and wait for me downstairs for a minute. But don't leave."

"What's going on?"

"This old guy comes over every once in a while and brings me detergent, oil, soap . . . well, he helps me out, you know what I mean . . . go wait for me downstairs."

"No. I'm getting the hell out of here."

"Sugar, it will be quick. He can't even get it up."

"Oh, no. I don't like the sound of this."

"Well, get used to it, because I've got three or four old men just like him, and they're the ones who pay my rent. My salary at the clinic doesn't even last a week."

I looked her straight in the face. It was a nice contrast. Half man, half woman. I went downstairs and sat for a while on the Malecón. I was tired, squeezed dry, high, and hungry. And now the slut was giving some old pig a hand job. I liked that bitch, but she was worse than the sewer rat that bit me. I was sitting there thinking when I heard her shouting to me from her window, "Come up, sweetie, come up! Hurry!"

She sounded drunk, but scared too. I went running up the stairs. The old man was stretched out on his back on the floor, naked.

"Is he dead?"

"I don't know!"

"What did you do to the bastard?"

"Nothing, nothing. I got him a little hot, sweetie. He likes to lick my ass and things like that. Everything was fine, but then all of a sudden, he passed out and fell off the bed."

I tried to lift him up and put him back on the bed. But then I realized. "Aren't you a nurse?"

"Yes. Well, no. I'm just an aide."

"Same thing. Check and see if he has a pulse, if he's breathing."

She knelt down and tried his wrist and his neck.

"Nothing. He doesn't have a pulse. My God, he's dead!"

And she started to cry as if the dead man were her grandfather.

"Shut up, don't cry! The old bastard isn't worth your tears."

"I just feel so sorry for him."

"Sorry? The hell with him. Anyway, he died happy. What more could he ask for?"

"What'll we do now?"

"We'll put his clothes back on, drag him into the hallway, and get out of here."

As we were dressing him, we found eighty pesos in his pockets. Leaving him sprawled in the hallway, we went down the stairs and went out to get something to eat.

"Oh, sweetie, you're so smart. A dead old man? My God! Leave him for someone else to find!"

3:7 / Crazies and Panhandlers

A decision was made to clear all the crazies and panhandlers off the streets. Some important event was coming up, maybe the anniversary of some historic occasion or the fall tourist season. I don't know. Something important. I never know what's important. Once I used to classify everything like that. Some things were important and others weren't; some things were good and some were bad. Not anymore. Now everything seems the same to me.

So, that was the plan. Crazies and panhandlers off the streets. And they chose me and a few others to get the job done. After the gas-pipe unclogging, I spent a while doing nothing. Not so very long, though, because that cunt Ugly Face never paid my way, the bitch. When she realized I was broke, she kicked me out, and that was the end of that.

First I became a garbage collector. I worked from midnight to eight in the morning. They were paying me for the danger, the night hours, and the abnormal working conditions, by which they meant that a person might have an accident and be killed on the job. Well, all in all, I made close to three hundred pesos, the same as an engineer. Plus a hearty breakfast at the end of the shift. But I had to rub myself raw jerking off, because no woman would come near me. I made them sick. They said I stank of mold and shit. I don't believe it. I washed every day. Maybe it was a psychological stink. As soon as they heard what I did for a living, they started whining about how I smelled like shit and rotting garbage, and saying my fingernails and my ears were caked with crap. They kicked me out. And so it was back to jerking off for Pedro Juan. It's not that I'm so much hornier than everybody else. I'm normal. But after three or four days without fucking, I'm desperate enough to lose control and kill myself jerking off.

Well, the bosses chose four of us. They gave us gray uniforms, tennis shoes, and gray caps with the insignia of the Department of Public Health. We garbagemen dress in rags: cut-off shorts, no shirts, and beat-up shoes. What with the sweat, the grime, and the mold, a person can't wear real clothes.

Our task was simple. We had to circle slowly around the city and trick the crazies and the bums into getting into the truck without making a fuss or creating a disturbance. The truck was big, white, soundproof, and windowless, with signs on it advertising an electronics retailer. We were informed that the job would only last two or three weeks and that we shouldn't tell anyone about it. "It's not that it's secret, but it's got to be done discreetly. When it's over, you'll get little baskets full of soap and cooking oil and detergent and other things. It's a good deal for you," one of the bosses told us.

At least it was a cleaner job, and we'd get something out of it. There was something a little exciting about it too, because they never let us get in the back of the truck, and we were never told where the people were being taken. Men dressed in white, like nurses, ushered them into the truck, and then there was silence. The crazies never even screamed. Maybe they were given a shot. I don't know. It's better not to know too much. "Hold your tongue or it'll be cut out," as my father used to say. That's why I kept my mouth closed. Anyway, that's what happens if you let yourself be knocked around: you go crazy or you end up begging on the street. It's their tough luck if they let it happen to them. So: into the truck they went. And who knew if they would ever see daylight again.

I wasn't keeping count, but I think we picked up several hundred people. There might have been another truck doing the same thing. Three weeks passed, and nothing strange happened. The last night was the most complicated. In the early hours of the morning, we tried to pick up a dirty old man. He was stretched out asleep on the doorstep of a hospital. When I moved him so two of us could lift him and carry him to the truck, we saw he was lying in a puddle of blood. He vomited up some black blood; at the same time he clutched a sack of mangoes. The sack was heavy, but he dragged it with him, vomiting black blood on the mangoes. It was foul-smelling blood. The old man was all ripped up inside. We dropped him back down on the ground.

"What should we do with this piece of shit, brother?" I asked my partner.

"If we leave him here, we'll have to come back for him later," Cheo said.

"Yes, but he's just going to get crap all over the truck and then die. Let's drag him over to the guardhouse."

We picked him up again. The old bastard wouldn't let go of the sack of mangoes for a second. There was no one at the guardhouse, just an old black woman with a broom and a bucket. She got very angry when we dragged the man in, all covered in blood.

"What is this?! No, no, no! Not here."

"What do you mean not here, ma'am? Where else is there?"

"No, no. Leave him outside."

"Don't you work here? Go find a doctor. Come on, Cheo."

We turned to go, but a policeman stepped out from a dark corner.

"Hold on now, just a minute. Where are you going?"

"Look, this guy was vomiting up blood in the doorway of the hospital, and we picked him up and brought him over here."

"At this hour? It's 4:30 in the morning. Papers, both of you. Where do you work?"

"We don't."

"You don't work?"

"Yes . . . well . . . we're garbagemen."

"In those uniforms? Are you garbagemen from Switzerland or the U.S. or what?"

I didn't know what to say. And Cheo was a moron; he never opened his mouth. The old man started to vomit even harder on his sack of mangoes. The old sweeper woman went crazy because she was going to have to clean it up. Bringing up all the filth he had left inside him, the old man started to shake and then he died, stinking much worse than a garbage truck. It even made me sick, which is saying a lot.

In the middle of the whole mess, two huge black men drove up in a taxi. One was a lighter-skinned mulatto, with a gold chain around his neck. He was too beautiful to be a man. He looked like a movie star. He was crying in pain. His pants were around his ankles, and he was bleeding, with a stick up his ass. He couldn't walk. The other man was helping him. You could see he was scared, but he held him up anyway. The policeman went to see what was happening.

"It was my husband; he put the stick in! I can't get it out; I'm going to faint, officer, ayyy . . . don't let my husband go, don't let him leave me alone . . ."

And he fell to the ground unconscious. The big, strong black man, even more frightened now, shouted at him, "You faggot, what husband are you talking about? I'm a man, officer. I don't know this person."

While the policeman was trying to unfasten his handcuffs from his belt, the black man escaped. He was running fast, and the policeman couldn't catch up. The taxi driver got out of his car and went through the unconscious man's pockets, trying to find something to pay his fare.

In the middle of everything, the old woman dragged the sack of mangoes covered in bloody vomit into a corner, picking out the cleanest ones and eating them. Cheo and I got out of there. We needed some *aguardiente*, but at that time of night, all the bars were closed. Cheo, hurrying along beside me, kept saying, "Man, picking up garbage is easier. This is too weird for me."

And in fact, the next day we went back to being garbagemen. And it seems like all the work we did was for nothing, because now I see even more crazies and bums on the street. They multiply like rabbits. Everywhere you look you see them, filthy, drunk, talking to themselves. Every day, Cheo says the same thing, "Man, any minute now maybe they'll make us stop being garbagemen and start picking up crazies and bums again. Will you do it? I won't. It's too confusing for me."

3·8 / The Return of the Sailor

After two years without a word from her sailor, Carmita received a telegram from him, postmarked Maracaibo, saying he was on his way back and sending her lots of love. Carmita didn't know what to think.

"I had forgotten all about him. Do you think he's gone crazy?"

Another cable arrived a week later. "I've been delayed for a few days in Puerto Cabello. I can't wait to see you. All my love."

This time, Carmita ran out onto the roof with the news, sharing it happily with all the neighbors. Over the course of the week, she had had time to think better.

"Oh, I'm dying to see him. He's the man of my dreams!"

And right away she began planning for his arrival. She went to the Merchant Marine office, passed herself off as his wife, and got them to send him a radiogram. "I received your telegrams. I'm waiting for you with open arms. Kisses."

That same afternoon she started being very sarcastic with Miguelito. The man had been supporting her and her two children for a year. He was fat and crude, and he had a huge mustache and outdated sideburns; he was as hairy as a bear too and always sweaty and smelly. He visited Carmita's room three or four times a week, whenever he felt like it. Then Carmita would have to get rid of the kids, close the door, and do whatever he wanted her to do. If she had her period, they'd have anal sex. He always left her forty or fifty pesos, plus a piece of meat, a little rice, or some other kind of food. He really wasn't much trouble, and he didn't ask for much. But she couldn't do without him. Sometimes he'd miss a week, and then Carmita would go looking for him at his workshop. He was a lathe operator, and he made good money, enough to support his wife and three children and Carmita and her two. There was just one problem: Carmita couldn't stand him. Sometimes, sitting on the edge of her bed, she'd cross herself and pray to the *santo* standing on the bedside table.

"San Lázaro, help me through this dark valley."

Miguelito would crush her to him like a gorilla, squeezing tight, and say, "Stop talking nonsense and come here."

That almost always happened after he had been stretched out for a while, stroking his stallion-sized prick, watching her as she paced the room and stripped her clothes off piece by piece, delaying the moment she'd have to get in bed. That ritual turned him on even more. At least the "dark valley" only lasted five minutes, because she had learned how to move her pelvis and squeeze his prick inside her so he could never last more than five minutes without coming, grunting and panting. Then he'd be sleepy and contented, and he'd always say the same thing, "You're a wild thing, the way you squeeze every drop out of me. You've got a velvet fist between those legs."

And that was it. A little while later, he'd leave, after a bracing cup of coffee and a cigarette.

Two days after the second telegram arrived, Carmita picked a fight with Miguelito, knocking over his coffee cup and accusing him of being stingy and taking advantage of her, and kicked him out without a qualm.

"Don't you ever show your face here again, no matter what! If I need to get in touch with you, I'll call you at work. Get out of my sight, and don't ever let me see you here again."

Miguelito was a man of few words or no words at all. In any case, he knew she'd come looking for him when she needed twenty pesos. So he didn't even respond but just shrugged his shoulders and left.

Carmen informed her two children of Luisito's imminent arrival. They didn't remember him.

"Don't you dare be rude to him when he comes. I want you to give him a hug, say hello, and then get out of here. I can't have you getting in our way."

Then she cleaned her fourteen-by-sixteen-foot room thoroughly, including the loft. Down below was the main room, with its stove, sink, small cupboard, and shower. Up above, on the loft, was Carmita's bed and a bed the children shared. A piece of mirror hung on the wall, and worn, stained clothes dangled from three hangers on a length of wire stretched in one corner. She scoured everything, until there wasn't a speck of dust anywhere. Even if the heat and humidity made her stink, she often went for days without showering; she didn't like soap or water. But she was obsessive about keeping the apartment clean.

To cover up a few gray hairs on her temples, she dyed her hair jet black. Carmita was forty-four, but she looked ten years younger. She shaved her legs and armpits carefully and painted her fingernails and toenails a pale pink color that contrasted nicely with her dark skin. By pretending to have a migraine, she got rid of the nosy neighbor ladies, and she sent the children outside.

"Don't come back here except to sleep. The rest of the time, you have to stay away. You're big boys now. Big boys can take care of themselves."

Her sons were ten and twelve, but they were old hands at the disappearing game. Carmen had always had men around, and ever since the boys were five or six, they'd spend hours roaming around, with nowhere to go. "Stay out of the way," she'd tell them each morning.

When everything was ready, she sat down to wait, listening to light music on Radio Enciclopedia and reading old romance novels, published forty years before in serial in *Vanidades*. Two days later, when Luisito showed up, Carmen was cool as a cucumber, relaxed, smiling, and smelling of cologne.

It was late at night when he got in, carrying six enormous suitcases, each weighing a ton. He had been to Japan, China, and Vietnam, and his ship made stops in every port. Then, on the way home, they passed through the Panama Canal and sailed on to Argentina, Brazil, Venezuela, and Colombia. Total travel time was twenty-eight months. He brought back everything from pieces of Chinese silk and Vietnamese fans to giant terracotta elephants, Colombian marijuana stashed in shampoo bottles, Japanese watches, and masses of cheap jewelry bought in Hong Kong. He also had fifteen hundred dollars, and once back on land, he was paid ten thousand pesos in back wages.

It was like Christmas and Epiphany rolled into one, and the partying started immediately. Luisito's stored-up sperm was about to flood his brain, and his circuits were threatening to blow after so much time without a woman. Carmita deployed all her wiles. She was determined to win a gold medal and while she was at it, break a few world records; she wouldn't settle for anything less. In forty-eight hours, black circles spread under her eyes, wrinkles formed on her face, she lost ten pounds, and her neck was marked with hickeys and purple bruises, which she displayed proudly to prove to the neighbor ladies that her macho was literally devouring her, and that she was still a desirable woman who could drive any man mad.

In the brief periods when he let her out of bed, she snuck things out of his suitcases and sold them around the building. Handkerchiefs, embroidered blouses, shoes, combs, incense, ginseng extract, Buddhas, elephants, sunglasses, plastic toys. All at bargain-basement prices.

The party was never-ending: rum, beer, cigarettes, good food, wild antics, and sex. At a seedy brothel in Osaka, Luisito had had a pearl inserted under the skin near the tip of his penis, and the novelty had both of them in ecstasies. They fucked themselves silly, the pearl rubbed in between.

On the third day, Luisito escaped Carmita's clutches for a while and went to his *santería* godmother's house. He gave her a packet of incense, a Buddha, an embroidered handkerchief, and five dollars, and asked her to call his brothers in Santiago.

Two days later, his four brothers arrived in Havana, hairy, dark-skinned, and cheerful, laughing constantly. They had already gotten drunk on the train, and they wanted to pick fights on every corner, to prove they were better and more macho than any other man. That was what they were like: young, lively, larger than life. Luisito was the oldest. He was thirty-three. The youngest was twenty-seven. Somehow they all managed to fit into Carmen's room, camping out on the floor. The party took a new turn. Going shopping with their brother, those voracious mulattos, bursting with muscle and party spirit, bought brightly colored new clothes, cologne, and even thick gold chains. They were in paradise, and they were the kings. Non-stop music, rum, and food. It was a blowout, Santiago Carnival style: full-on partying, never mind tomorrow. The fun was for the men; the women had to stay in the kitchen, working until they were called to bed. Carmita was stuck in the thick of it. The five brothers more than proved their masculine ability to consume limitless quantities of food and drink. They found four cheap whores and took turns fucking them standing up in the shower, behind the curtain.

Carmita stood it for three days, then four days. On the fifth day, in a rare moment of sobriety, she hid all the rest of the booty from the suitcases in a neighbor's apartment. Going through Luisito's pockets as he slept, she discovered he had only three hundred dollars and seven hundred pesos left. She got angry. How could that drunken piece of shit and his stupid brothers have blown so much money in so few days? Tears of rage came to her eyes, but just as she was about to slap him awake, she stopped herself. Money she could have lived on for two years, squandered in five days. She thought for a minute and then came to a decision: she took the three hundred dollars and the seven hundred pesos and hid them under the mattress. Then she woke up Luisito, jerking at one of his feet.

"You, wise guy, come on, up. I've had enough! You can go sleep off your hangover in hell!"

It was two in the morning, and the commotion could be heard all over the roof. All the neighbors had been waiting for it; they knew Carmita would explode sooner or later.

"What's wrong with you, woman? Let me sleep."

Luisito was so macho that the idea that his woman might rebel never crossed his mind. As far as he was concerned, the partying was normal, almost traditional, and would go on until all his money was used up. It had always been that way. His brothers woke up and realized Carmen was trying to kick them out.

"Luisito, the woman's out of her head. Slap her around a little, you're the man of the house."

But Carmita had a machete in her hand.

"Raise your hand and I'll cut it off!"

A machete whistling through the air, in the grip of a furious, determined woman, discourages even the most macho of men.

"The woman's crazy, man! Let's get out of here before she hurts somebody."

"Ungrateful bitch! We throw her a party, and now she's kicking us out."

Luisito tried to regain control of the situation.

"Go out on the roof for a minute while I try to talk to her."

"You'll be the first out the door, you drunken piece of shit."

"But darling, how can you give up everything we had like this? I want to marry you and . . ."

"Fuck you all! Get out and take your brothers with you. I never want to see you again."

As a last resort, Luisito tried to seduce her: he pulled out his big, beautiful prick and plump balls and stroked them.

"This is all yours, Carmen. Are you sure you want to give it up? If you say the word, I'll send the boys home, and you and I can be alone together again."

"No, no, forget it. Nothing's going to change my mind. Put your prick back in your pants or I'll chop it off with the machete, you bastard! You're an obnoxious bully, and your brothers have some nerve. I want you all out of here."

"But Carmita, what about all the wonderful days we spent together? Don't let yourself get carried away just because you're upset now. I want to have a child with you, darling."

"A child? What for? So it can turn out to be a drunken beast like you?"

"Darling, I dreamed about you for two years on that boat. Don't do this to me."

"You dreamed about me? Go trick someone else into bed with that song and dance. For two years, not a card or four pesos do I get, and now you show up thinking you'll get laid. Get out!"

"Oh darling, you're so wild. I love you very much."

They kept on like that for a while. Carmita never put down the machete or let Luisito get near her with his sweet talk. At last the sailor gave up. He got dressed and, crying, went out onto the roof. His brothers were disgusted.

"How can you, Luisito? For shame. Real men don't cry. Are you a man or a faggot?"

"That woman's not worth it. Cheer up. We'll go to Santiago and start the party again."

Carmita threw an empty suitcase after them.

"Go or I'll scream for the policeman on the corner and I'll make sure you all end up in jail. Get out!"

And she slammed the door in their faces. Luisito picked up the empty suitcase, and they left.

The next day, Carmita went out to sell an elephant made of fake porcelain. It was big, sixteen inches tall. She wanted five dollars for it. A neighbor bought it for three. Carmita took the money, happily.

"There, that's the last thing I had from the sailor."

Then she went outside to the telephone on the corner to call Miguelito.

3·9 / Essence of Me

With her beautiful round breasts and firm, erect nipples, the mulatta was an early morning vision of sin and desire: her yellow cot-
ton blouse, cut short and tight, baring her stomach and belly
button; her narrow waist; the twin globes of her ass encased in
skintight red Lycra. Still half-asleep, like a cat licking itself and
purring, she came out of her house, her rubber sandals squeaking,
her black hair stiff and tangled, and the sweet dreaminess of sleep in
her eyes. Giving me a sidelong glance, she walked on. So many
Cuban women—most of them, probably—are descendants of
Ochún, the black Virgen de la Caridad del Cobre. They're good-
natured, pretty, sweet, and loyal as long as they want to be, but they
can be cruelly unfaithful, too. Sensual, lascivious. In time, you begin to recognize them.

A big, brawny black man was trying to draw water from the well.
But there wasn't much water left in it, and he was having a hard
time getting even a bucketful. The well was the one in the middle
of the street, at the intersection of San Lázaro and Perseverancia.
Nobody knows why it's there; it may date back to colonial times. Its
cover is iron, just like its base. Nobody remembers the last time this
neighborhood had running water. People haul it home late at night,
from pipes half-hidden in broken pavement, at the base of walls. A

little bit of water trickles from them sometimes, mysteriously, at three or four in the morning.

The mulatta was looking at me more directly now, her eyes half-closed, her hair snarled from bed and a night of passion. She still looked sleepy, a hint of sex and wildness and rum about her. At the well, she tried to help her husband. He was in a bad mood and pushed her away. She straightened up, and with injured, sarcastic pride, in a loud, cold voice, she said, "All right, sweetie, I'll be waiting for you."

And she walked back to her doorway, swinging her hips and ass and almost staring at me. Her husband was watching, and he shouted, "Go wait inside!"

It was as if she hadn't heard his threatening command. She kept waltzing along in her sandals, that luscious walk, staring at me with desire thinly disguised as sleepiness. Then she went back inside.

I didn't have anything to do. What's more, I had no idea what to do the next day, next month, next year, or next century. Maybe not knowing is the best way to keep from worrying or sinking into despair. You don't know how you'll survive, but it doesn't matter. You live like a kite blowing in the wind, and you feel all right. But then sometimes there isn't even any wind.

I had to make a few pesos. After a year as a garbageman, I left the job. It was too much work. Night work too. The money was good, but it wasn't worth it. I could make just as much or more in a day, selling any old thing. Anyway, the stink of rotting garbage was driving women away. They'd run from me in disgust.

Now I used the perfume a *santera* had prepared for me: violet water with honey, infused with the scents from a stick of tobacco and two sticks of incense, "For me" and "I'm the boss." Every morning I'd sprinkle myself with one of those and I'd be off to a good start. Women would flock to me and doors would open for me.

Just as I was leaning against the wall to wait and see what might happen with that mulatta, the butcher from the corner store called to me. I went over. Almost whispering, he said, "Pedro Juan, I've got some beef. I need to get rid of it today."

"How much do you want for it?"

"I'll let you have it for a dollar and a half a pound."

"How many pounds do you have?"

"Eighty."

"Shit, that's a lot!"

"Well, come on. See what you can do."

"I'll find you a buyer, man."

I'd have to go to Vedado. The people of Central Havana live on pure air. Nobody has dollars, and everybody's used to making do with sugar water, rum, and tobacco, and lots of beating on drums. That's the way it is. So long as we're still alive, we'll keep on putting one foot in front of the other no matter what. You've got to struggle to survive. The only sure thing in life is death.

Just then the mulatta came out onto a balcony and saw me. We looked at each other. But I had to go. Pesos first and fun later, because if she wanted to go out that night and I was broke, not a penny to treat her, then she'd say, "Oh, what good are you? Go on, I'm not the girl for you."

A news show was playing on some radio, and the announcer kept repeating "this triumph," "results," "the nation's excitement," "with great rejoicing." I didn't know what he was talking about. He kept repeating the same things.

I waved to the mulatta, signaling that we'd see each other later. She smiled, satisfied. Her husband was still at the well with his buckets. Just then I had an idea, and I turned to the butcher.

"Man, I'm going to see some contacts, but give me five pounds to speed things up."

"Do you have any money?"

"No, pal, you know I'm broke."

"So then?"

"Man, you know I won't make any trouble for you. When have I ever fucked you over?"

"I know you're a good guy, but first things first."

"Let me have five pounds. I'm not going to disappear . . ."

"Oh, Pedro Juan . . ."

"Come on, come on. You'll see, I'm going to sell a ton of that meat, and it'll be off your hands."

He gave me the five pounds. It was good stuff, very little skin. But selling it was like playing with fire. With the stiff new penalties, you could get up to ten years behind bars. All for nothing. Selling at $2.00 a pound, my total profit would be $2.50.

Luckily, I sold it right away. I have a few contacts who always have dollars. I show up with food, and they buy whatever it is: chicken, red meat, cheese, eggs, lobster. Anything. They must eat like kings, the bastards.

I made four trips and sold twenty pounds. I made ten bucks, without having to slave as hard as I did on the garbage truck.

I'm lucky. Changó and Oggún show me the way. But I couldn't get that mulatta out of my head. I settled up with the butcher, who told me there was a little meat left to sell the next day, and I went to stand on the opposite corner, by the grocery stand. You can't stay frozen in the same spot forever.

As usual, the grocery lady was sitting on a box by the door of her empty stall, picking her nose. She's fat, in her fifties, her legs covered with cellulite and big, ugly, purple varicose veins. But she doesn't care: she always wears shorts and tiny shirts, exposing broad expanses of belly and breasts. Glancing at me, she raised her eyebrows in greeting, and kept digging in her nose, absorbed in her boogers. Then we talked for a while, going over the same old stories: her son is in jail, and his sentence was just increased to twenty years; he got himself in more trouble. Thank goodness her daughter's a little sex kitten and can take care of herself. She's got herself an Italian now. Ancient, ugly, and pot-bellied he may be, but he doles out dollars like there's no tomorrow. He takes her out and shows her a good time too. She says they'll get married soon, and he'll take her away with him. The other daughter, the youngest one, is ten, and practically white, "with nice hair and everything. She turned out to be good at school, and she wants to be a television reporter."

And she started telling me the saga of the son in prison again, ". . . he was a bad one from the day he was born. When he was ten, they locked him up for splitting some other little boy's head open, right there on the corner. And from then on, he couldn't stay out of jail. He's a no-good bastard, he is, a son of Oggún."

Then the mulatta came out on her balcony. She looked at me, but I pretended not to see her. A minute later she was clopping across the street. She passed in front of me, holding herself tall, chest out and butt cocked. Mother of God, what a sight! Just seeing her walking like that, so sexy, made my prick spring to life, swelling and stretching. Ahhhh.

She turned the corner and kept walking. I fell in behind her and caught up.

"Where are you taking me, sugar?"

"Me? I've got things to do. I don't know about you."

"We're going the same way."

"Oh, and how do you know that?"

"Listen, is your husband as fierce as he acts?"

"His bark can be worse than his bite, but sometimes he bites hard . . ."

"I don't want trouble."

"Are you scared of him? He won't eat you."

"No. I'm scared of what I might do."

"Oh, you're a show-off just like him."

"Well, think what you want, but he's got you under his thumb."

"No. It's all a show. I have to go along with it because he supports me. And he loves to play husband."

"Is he your husband or not?"

"He is, but it isn't such a big deal. Black guys just like to put on an act in front of people."

"Some kind of complex, huh?"

"Sure, it's the macho thing."

"All right, enough. I don't care about your husband. What about you?"

"What about me?"

"You and me, babe. What's up with us?"

"Oh, I don't know."

"Look how I am just from walking next to you."

You could see the outline of my swollen prick through the cloth of my pants. She looked and burst out laughing.

"Damn, sugar, you're out of control! And you haven't even seen anything yet. The minute you touch me you're going to come."

"I can't get you out of my head. I like you."

"But we've never even talked. How can you just like me like that?"

"You know how. Don't play dumb. I'm dying to fuck you."

"Oh really. That's very nice!"

"Do you like me?"

"I can like fifty men a day. But that doesn't mean I'm going to fuck them all. It doesn't work that way."

"Don't be a snob."

"I'm not being a snob. It's just that you white boys are all the same. You think all you have to do is ask and you'll get some."

"All right, fine, fine. First you lead me on, and now you tell me to forget it."

"See what I mean?"

"Honey, it's dangerous to play games like that with a man."

"Oh really? You're the one who started things."

"What do you want? Pesos?"

"No. What kind of joke is that? Do I look like a slut?"

"Anybody might be in a position where they need to make a few pesos."

"I've got my husband, sweetie. And he's got a knack for making money; it's like it just falls into his lap."

"All right, this conversation has gone on long enough. I'm going."

"It's your loss."

"And what loss would that be? Do you have anywhere for us to go?"

"Right around the corner, my godmother's house. Keep moving. I'll go in first, and you follow. Wait for a minute, though."

Nothing happened at her godmother's house. She introduced me as a friend. I sat in the living room, and she went into the kitchen with the old lady. A little while later, she came out with a cup of coffee. She looked at me and smiled her slutty little smile, then went back into the kitchen. Ten minutes later, she came out with her godmother, and they sat down. They had some new Lycra bodysuits in a bag.

"He wants four dollars each, and there are seven of them," the godmother said.

"I'll sell all of them tomorrow, for five dollars each."

"He says he didn't leave you many, but he has two hundred."

"He made a good haul."

"Looks like it."

They examined each one.

"Oh, godmother, they're all red and blue. He knows the white and yellow and red ones are easier to sell."

"Well, child, do your best."

We said our goodbyes and left together.

"Hey, whitey, don't walk next to me. Don't get me in trouble with my man."

"What's going on? When are you going to make up your mind about what you want? Why did you want me to come with you to your godmother's house?"

"So she could check you out, sweetie."

"Oh really? And what did she have to say?"

"You have to know everything, don't you?"

"All right, I'm leaving. You don't put out, and you don't make any promises, either."

"Listen, tomorrow morning around ten I'm going to Ultra to sell the bodysuits. I'll be there, by the entrance."

"I can't make it."

"You're busy?"

"Yes. I've got some business to take care of too."

"Oh, sugar, don't be that way. You show up, and we'll have a nice little chat."

"We'll see."

"If you come, I'll tell you what my godmother told me. Not what she said, but what the *santos* told her—they know. About you and me."

"Was it good?"

"Meet me tomorrow. I have to go."

"All right. As my father used to say, 'after her, shark, she's bleeding'."

"I'm not bleeding, and you're not a shark. So don't be an idiot."

And with that, we parted. Tomorrow would be another day. I was in no hurry.

I woke up with a hangover from the rum I had drunk the night before. It had to be nine or ten o'clock already. Looking out the little window, I saw a tourist snapping photos of crumbling buildings on the Malecón. Her husband was videotaping the same scene. Tourists love the sight of decay. From a distance, it makes a wonderful picture.

I went out on the roof. There was water in a can, and I washed my face and rinsed out my mouth while watching Isabelita out of the corner of my eye. She was sitting in a corner in the shade, resting and smoking a cigarette. Already that morning she had washed a ton of clothes.

"Isa, what time is it?"

"No idea."

"You're up early."

"Yes, it was still dark when I started. But now I'm all done."

"When I've got nice clothes, I'm going to give them to you to wash."

"For you, I'd do it for free."

"You'd do what for free?"

"Ha ha ha . . . anything. Whatever you wanted."

"Have you had coffee yet?"

"I've got a little left. Come on over."

Isabel is tall and thin, with light cinnamon-colored skin and long, black ringlets. We've been neighbors for years. I like her and she likes me; I don't know why we've never gotten together and made sparks fly. She lives with her ex-husband. They're always fighting, but nothing will ever make that black man move his lazy ass out of there. He says he has nowhere to go. The only way to budge him would be to light a fire under him.

There are six rooms on the roof and only one filthy toilet. Water has to be hauled up in buckets. People come and go. Sometimes there are forty people living here. Then some of them go back to their villages and things get better. Back and forth, like the tide.

Isabel has lost too much weight. Her cupboards are empty, just like everybody else's. But she's still cheerful and friendly, washing clothes for a few pesos, going hungry, dealing with the creep who lives with her, and trying to raise her eleven-year-old daughter. Maybe some days she gets a cigarette, a shot of rum, a little coffee, a fling with some guy she likes. Sometimes she might even have all of that at once. And music. Lots of music. There's got to be music. Then she tries not to think too much.

She noticed I was quiet as I drank my coffee.

"What's wrong, Pedro Juan? Did you wake up in a bad mood, or were you fucking all night and now you're exhausted?"

"No. It's been days since I've slept with anyone. I'm fine."

"If you haven't, you know it's because you don't want to, sweetie. All you have to do is ask."

"Don't tease me, Isabel. I'm worried. I'm out of work and things are tough on the street."

"Go back to being a garbageman."

"Never!"

"Listen, don't think too hard or you'll explode. Keep it cool."

"You're right. Anyway, thinking's not going to solve any of my problems. I'm going to take a walk."

"Later tonight, or whenever you want, call me and I'll make an offering to Santa Clara and one to the Virgen del Camino. You can put them in your room."

"You're so good to me."

"If you only knew . . ."

"Cut it out. No more mushy stuff—you keep flirting with me, and I can't start anything new right now. A romance with a slut is the last thing I need."

"What else is there for you? Your face gives you away. You're a cynical son of Changó and you like sluts; don't pretend you don't. Or are you planning to bypass women entirely and become a cocksucker?"

"Oh, don't be so dramatic. I'm out of here. I'll see you later."

I went walking slowly toward Ultra, up Galiano. At a government-run stand, I had a sandwich and a watery soda. It was said there were epidemics of conjunctivitis, hepatitis, and who knows what else, and the private stands were closed. It had been a terrible summer: blistering sun and humidity, bacteria scampering around happily and procreating, everybody with diarrhea, amoebic dysentery, giardiasis. The tropics, what bliss! How lovely it must be to come visit for a week and admire the sunsets from a far-off, quiet place without getting too involved.

She hadn't lied to me. There she was, so beautiful she stood out in the crowd, selling Lycra bodysuits at the entrance to Ultra. A real woman. She was wearing a skintight black bodysuit that left her back bare. Smooth, loose hair, stylish high-heeled platform shoes, and firm, perfect legs. A sturdy, goddesslike body. She was almost naked. You could see everything, nipples, belly button, the soft curve of her belly down to the small lips of her vagina. You could almost smell her armpits, the intimate, erotic scent of the sweat of black women. What a beauty, damn it! Women were all over the place, selling everything from dollars to Chiclets. They kept moving, scanning the crowd, keeping an eye on the policemen in the distance who pretended not to notice what was going on, though they had the hard look on their faces of men who know what's what. All the women were ready to stuff their merchandise into their bags and take to their heels. Poised, tense, not an ounce of relaxation.

I stood behind her for a second, smelling her. It was very hot. She was sweating, and she smelled faintly of sweat. My prick started to swell right away, all by itself. The minute I smelled her, I was turned on. I whispered in her ear, "I'll buy everything you've got left."

She swung around, startled. When she saw me, she burst out laughing.

"I knew you'd come, you bad boy!"

"Have you sold anything yet?"

"Nothing! I just got here. And look, four other people with bodysuits."

Part of a bolero from my childhood sounded in my head, and I sang it to her very quietly, almost murmuring,

> If I were no longer
> A part of your life,
> A word or an embrace
> Would be enough
> So much of me is part of you
> The taste on your skin must be
> Essence of me

"Oh, sweetie, that's so nice. Are you excited to see me?"

"I'm always excited when I see you."

"Oh, don't be silly."

"Don't you believe me? Fine, then."

We didn't talk for a while. She stood there with a bodysuit in her hand, hawking it in a low voice to the men passing by, "Hey, you, look here. A bodysuit for your girlfriend. Get one now before they're gone."

If it was a woman, she'd say, "This one's for you, look how pretty it is, so flattering. Get one now, they're going fast."

I watched her for a while from a distance. Then I came up to her again.

"Didn't you ask me to come here? What did you want to tell me?"

"Ha ha ha. Not right now. There's a time and a place for everything."

I had seven dollars in my pocket.

"Do you want a beer?"

"So early, on an empty stomach?"

"Let's go over there across the street. I'll buy you a soda."

"All right, let's go."

We crossed Reina. A sidewalk stand. A soda and a hot dog. A beer for me.

"All right, talk to me."

"There's not much to say, sugar. My godmother tells me we daughters of Ochún can't let ourselves be carried away by desire because afterward we regret it, but never mind that. You can't take religion literally if you want to enjoy life."

"You're right about that. So do you want me?"

"Of course. If I didn't, I wouldn't be here talking to you."

The men passing by were devouring her with their eyes. She was talking to me, but she was looking toward the stand. She was sexy in that bodysuit. Too sexy. A tall, fat, young foreigner, pasty white, was buying a soda. She was boring holes in him with her eyes.

"Hey, pay attention to me and look at me while I'm talking."

"Oh, old man, don't be such a drag. Live and let live."

She smiled at the guy. The guy smiled back. She detached herself from me. Her eyes shone just at the thought of dollars. She went up to him.

"Do you have a cigarette?"

And he said, "I don't smoke. But if you want, I'll buy you a pack."

He was a Spaniard. He lisped his *z*s.

"Oh yes, thank you. I'm dying for a smoke!"

I got the hell out of there. Let her make a buck. Maybe in a few days she'd have had enough of the Spaniard and she'd come back.

I walked down Galiano, singing the bolero softly,

> *Of my life, I give the very best*
> *I'm so poor what more is there to give?*

Back to the butcher shop. At least I could make a few more dollars selling beef.

"At this time of day, man? Why didn't you come earlier?" the butcher asked me.

"What time is it?"

"A quarter after twelve."

"Everything's gone already?"

"Since early this morning. I could have let you have ten or fifteen pounds."

"Too bad."

"Keep in touch, because I might be getting in another shipment."

"When?"

"Oh, I don't know. You know these things can turn up any time. Stick around."

I went up to the roof. Isabel was washing some pots and plates, squatting on the floor by a drain. From her room came the sounds of salsa on the radio:

Take me while I'm loaded
Who knows how long it will last

I leaned against the wall so I could check her out better. At that time of day, there was no one around. She has a nice ass. Not big, but firm and well-shaped. Coming up quietly behind her, I tousled her hair. She looked at me.

"Hmm? Back already?"

I was still horny from the other mulatta. And I felt a little sad, cheated. I crouched down behind her and kissed her on the cheek.

"Hey, what bug bit you? Did somebody get you hot and now you want to blow off steam with me?"

"No, no. What gives you that idea?"

"I've been after you for years. And now you want to do it with me right here in public, in front of everyone?"

"There's no one on the roof."

"That's what you think."

"Well, what do you care?"

She stood up, leaving her pots and plates scattered on the floor. Throwing her arms around my neck, she kissed me, sticking her tongue all the way down my throat.

"You're right, sweetie, if it's with you, I don't care about anything."

"Let's go to my room."

"Let's."

We fucked passionately. I didn't think it would be that way. We were like two wild things. I liked her a lot. Maybe because she wasn't cynical like that show-off of a mulatta, who liked her men down on their knees.

But I was still a little sad. There I was, single, no job, living in a dump, no children, no steady girlfriend. Looking at things that way, it was hard to see much reason to be happy.

We were sweating, naked on the bed, and I was stretched out on top of her, recuperating from an earth-shattering orgasm. I don't know where all that jism came from. Caressing her and kissing her very tenderly, I sang under my breath,

> A thousand years may pass
> Or more
> I don't know if there'll be love
> Where we'll be then
> But in heaven as on earth
> On your tongue you'll taste
> Essence of me.

"Don't be so sweet, Pedro Juan, don't be that way."

"Can't you use a little loving?"

"I've been needing loving for years."

"So have I."

"I don't want to suffer again, sweetie. I fall in love and then it's always a mess."

"You're right."

I rolled off to one side.

"Shit, look at the way I'm sweating."

She got up and started getting dressed.

"Open the door. We're roasting in here. And give me those sheets and that towel, and I'll wash them. You're turning into a real slob."

I opened the door. Isabel went out on the roof and back to her cauldrons.

I put on a pair of shorts and sat in the doorway. There was a cool breeze. Something was beginning, but I was afraid of that mulatta: a slut and a romantic, and she liked me. It was too perfect. And neither one of us wanted to make things more complicated for ourselves. Why go looking for trouble when there's already plenty to go around?

3·10 / Salvation and Damnation

On the corner of Infanta and Jovellar, a television reporter, microphone in hand, was accosting passersby with two questions, spitting them out like bullets, "What is happiness? Have you ever been happy?" A question like that, or, rather, two questions like that, require a moment of thought, but the reporter had no patience for ditherers. When the cameraman focused on the interviewee's face, lots of people had no idea what to say. Others refused to answer. Some tried to say something intelligent to flatter their egos but ended up babbling incoherently.

Coming out of his room and rounding the corner, the plumber ran smack into the camera, microphone, and reporter. When the question was fired at him, he wasn't flustered at all, and with resignation and bitterness, he said, "Happiness? Don't make me laugh, man, there's no such thing." He was about to go on his way, but the reporter persisted, "Have you ever been happy?" The plumber stopped for a second and answered, in an access of sincerity, "I was happy the day I got married. That was the last happy day of my life. It's all been downhill since then." And he kept walking calmly along, not hurrying at all. He was a big, brawny white guy, with lots of black hair on his head and all over his body. There was no gray in it yet, and though he was fifty-two, he still had the strength and stamina of an ox. He was born in the country, in a tobacco shed. His father was an immigrant, his mother Cuban. It had been forty years since he'd heard from either of them or from any of his eleven brothers and sisters.

In one hand he was carrying a heavy canvas bag full of tools and sections of pipe. Three blocks down the street he was finishing up a job he had started the day before, in a building honeycombed with rooms. Fifteen, sixteen, twenty rooms. Nobody really knew how many there were. Each time a census was taken, rooms appeared or disappeared and nobody could figure out why. The same thing happened with the people who lived in the building. There might be 100 or 150 or 200. They'd come and go, and nobody could count how many there were. As a last resort, the officials at the Housing Ministry would turn a blind eye.

The plumber was installing two steel tanks in one of the rooms. He'd done a good job. Now, when water came in from the aqueduct, which is to say, every few days, the people would be able to fill both tanks. A pipe connected the tanks to a faucet on a sink he'd also installed in a corner of the room next to the little kerosene stove. It wasn't much, but it was more than the neighbors had. The bathrooms were communal: one each for men and women.

There were also two laundry rooms, in a big roofless courtyard. The place was an early nineteenth-century colonial mansion, half-collapsed and overrun with rats and cockroaches, but it was still good for something, and it would be as long as it was still standing.

The plumber's name was Pancracio, which didn't bother him. Well, it wasn't that it didn't bother him but that he didn't even realize how ridiculous his name was. Notions of beauty or ugliness had no meaning for him. He lived alone in a single room with a door opening onto an alley between the university and the Las Vegas cabaret. He had a nice place. It was the best place he'd ever lived, really. He'd tried his hand at everything, from street sweeping and selling mangoes and avocados to laying brick for luxury houses. But he liked plumbing best. He didn't know why and didn't care why. He just liked it.

It had taken him thirteen hours to install the tanks, the pipes, and the sink. It was noon. The room's owner was a beautiful black woman in her forties. She had a husband, children, and grandchildren. Yesterday there were swarms of people coming in and out, but today she had arranged things so that she was alone with the plumber. Picking up his tools, he looked at her and said, "Well, ma'am. Now you've got water in your room. Happy?"

"Yes, Pancracio, it's perfect. Did we say two hundred pesos?"

"Yes, ma'am. Two hundred pesos."

"Now . . . Pancracio, I have a little problem."

"Oh, no. No little problems, or I'll rip everything out in ten minutes and take it away with me."

"Wait, don't get violent."

"I'm not getting violent. I am violent. I've been working here for two days, and if you don't pay me, I'll tear everything out and take it away. And if you send some black strongman after me, I'll eat him alive."

"Listen, sugar. Let's talk. We can make a deal."

"No deals. The deal was two hundred pesos."

"Pancracio, how long has it been since you've slept with a woman?"

"What does that matter to you?"

"It matters."

It was very hot in the room, no windows and no fan. The damp of the walls and the ceiling seeped into everything. It smelled of damp too, mixed with dust, sweat, urine, filth, cockroaches, rotting herbs. They were both sweating, but Santa went to the door, closed it, bolted it, and turned on a single dim light bulb hanging from the ceiling. Moving to face the plumber, she opened her blouse. She wasn't wearing a bra. Her breasts were big, strong, and beautiful, sagging only a bit, and her nipples were very black. Her skin shone with sweat. Smiling, she walked toward Pancracio and took her blouse all the way off. She had a slight belly and a gorgeous belly button where a trail of curly black hairs began and led provocatively

down to her sex. Untying her skirt, she revealed her mound of
Venus. Secure in her perfect African goddess beauty, she exhibited
her body casually, knowing all she had to do was uncover it and
even the coldest and most unresponsive man would turn into a hot-
blooded, seductive predator. Pancracio didn't know what to say.
He'd never had much interest in sex, and every day it interested
him less. It had been three years, or even longer, since he'd slept
with anyone. But the sight of that fabulous black woman approaching him, offering herself to him, was making him nervous.

"Ma'am, for the love of God!"

"Call me Santa. Don't call me ma'am anymore."

"Santa, put your clothes back on. Your children might come in
any minute. Your husband . . ."

"Nobody's coming, sugar. Don't you worry. We have the whole
afternoon to ourselves."

"No, no. Give me my money and I'll go. I . . ."

"Forget about your money, sweetie, and let's have some fun. I
promise you'll like it. Pretty soon you'll be asking for more."

Santa took off her skirt and panties and pushed Pancracio back
onto the bed, squatting over his face. When he smelled her strong,
acrid scent and poked his tongue up into her, Santa moaned as if
she were a tender adolescent giving herself to a man for the very
first time. And the game was on. Santa was a master, an expert's expert. Rotating her hips and her pelvis as no one else could, she had
Pancracio erupting like a volcano in less than four minutes. When
the come came trickling out of her vagina, Santa was swept away.

"What is this?! You're a wild man! Oh, it's gorgeous!"

With Santa convulsing under him, Pancracio lost control too
and started hitting her. Santa loved her men to slap her in the face,
making her skin tingle. It turned her on even more, and she came.
As she climaxed, Pancracio was still inside her, his prick still very
hard. And he kept hitting her. Now it hurt, and she tried to stop
him, but he was out of control. He tried to get even deeper inside
her, thrusting hard, and all the while he wouldn't stop hitting her.

He pummeled her face, hurting her. She tried to grab his hands, but he was too strong. As he was about to come for the second time, he grabbed her by the neck with his left hand and kept hitting her with his right. Practically strangling her, he repeated in a paroxysm of mad lust, "Swallow, cunt, swallow! Suck me, bitch!"

Santa was terrified. Almost choked to death, she managed to escape Pancracio's viselike grip as he collapsed face down on the bed, limp after his second orgasm. Once she was standing up, she began pounding on his back.

"You bastard, you almost killed me! Are you crazy? What the fuck is wrong with you?"

When Pancracio felt the blows, he stood up in one swift movement and punched her in the face. One single punch and Santa dropped to the floor, unconscious. Then Pancracio reacted. He tried to revive her, fetching a jar of water and tossing it in her face, then shaking her. At last she came to her senses. She opened her eyes and started to scream for the neighbors, "Help, there's a man trying to kill me! Get away from me, you bastard! Get away!"

Blood was flowing from Santa's nose and mouth. Pancracio dressed quickly and gathered his tools. Santa hadn't stopped screaming for a second. He opened the door and breathed in the fresh air. A little old lady and some children were standing there, frightened, staring at him. He didn't even see them. He left quickly, and as he went, he could still hear that woman screaming. Nobody tried to stop him. Going out of the building and onto the street, he walked the few blocks to his room. He wasn't afraid. He didn't know what fear was. He was just upset.

His room was a chaos of rusty old tools, pipes, hand dryers, soap dispensers, urinals. Over the years, he'd accumulated a flea market's worth of secondhand plumbing supplies. Everything was covered in dust, rust, and cobwebs. In one corner was his bed, neatly made and perfectly clean. Fixed on the wall was a small altar to the Virgen de la Caridad del Cobre. At the back, there was a tiny bathroom. That was all. Pancracio dropped his canvas bag on the floor and went over to a small kerosene grill next to the bathroom. He made coffee. He didn't want to think about what he had done. It was always the same. Every time he was in trouble, he'd flash back on the same scenes: his father hitting him in the head with a hoe, in the middle of a freshly plowed field. He was twelve years old. That night, his wounds still fresh, he ran away from home and away from his eleven brothers and sisters. He never went back. He kept moving, working at odd jobs, until he came to Havana. The other key moment in his life was when he was married. It was a happy day, but by the next morning, he and his wife were fighting, and a week later, they were separated. Since then he'd had no interest in anything. That was why even sex didn't appeal to him anymore. And when he did have sex, the same thing always happened: he'd lose his head and hit the woman he was with, and he wouldn't be able to stop himself. That's what the fights with his wife were about. No woman could take it.

And he couldn't control himself. He liked to hit women and call them whores; it was impossible to resist. Luckily, he never thought, or talked, or worried, or was afraid. He just got by as best he could, expecting nothing and desiring nothing. His life was simple: a frugal meal, cooked haphazardly on the kerosene grill, a cigar, and lots of work. He buried himself in work. No alcohol, or women, or gambling, or friends. No expensive vices. He already spent too much on coffee and cigars. Under a floor tile, in a corner under a pile of dusty junk, was a hole he had dug and lined carefully with cement, and in it he'd hidden thousands of pesos. It was his only passion. Moving the rusty pipe lengths and all the other junk, he lifted the tile, took the money out, counted it, and added more. He never spent any of it, even if he was hungry. All he craved was the feel of the bills in his hands. Three things made him happy: money, coffee, and cigars. He didn't even know why he put the Virgen on that altar. He never asked her for anything, and he didn't know how to pray. Several times he'd thought about taking her down and tossing her in the trash. But he didn't dare.

By now his coffee was ready. He poured it into a glass and lit a good cigar. Opening the door, he sat out on the doorstep smoking, watching the people and the odd truck or bicycle go by. He watched them and smoked, finally calm, his mind wiped clean. All he was doing was watching the people go by, and smoking. Nothing had happened. Nothing was wrong. Nothing was beautiful. Sometimes he just got angry, and the flames shot up, out of his control. But then they always died down. Rage was the downfall of many a man, but it wouldn't be his. Nothing could save him, and nothing could defeat him anymore.

3:11 / Casino Esperanza

A green jeep came speeding down San Lázaro, mounted with two loudspeakers and two red flags. It was broadcasting a protest speech, but it was moving so quickly the speech was impossible to understand. Only fragments of sentences could be caught: "We're making history," "on the university steps," "a historic uprising."

It flashed past, and the street was calm and quiet again, baking under the noonday sun, not a cloud in the sky.

Boys from the neighborhood were swimming off the Malecón, plunging into the dirty water tainted with gasoline and oil from the ships in the harbor and all the city's shit and piss. Everything runs off into the ocean, but the kids, and some adults too, come anyway. They spend hours in the sun, drinking rum and eating ices, ignoring the sewer smell and enjoying themselves. The tourists take pictures of them, and they stand stock still, laughing or making faces for the camera. After each photo, they drop their poses, and the children run to beg for coins.

I watched them for a while, but nobody caught my attention. The only women were skinny and dirty, surrounded by kids. I hung around a little longer, looking for trouble. Every once in a while you run into somebody appealing. When you're single in the jungle, you've got to be constantly on the prowl, every single day. A man doesn't need much: a little money, food, some rum, a few cigars, a woman. Being without a woman was making me neurotic, but having one of them, awkward and stupid, always by my side, gets on my nerves. And they all want the same thing: at first they're happy just fucking and drinking rum, and they laugh at all your jokes, sweet as can be. Later they still want all that, but they also want you to wear yourself out every day so you can bring home money and food for them and their three or four kids, the children of three or four fly-by-night husbands.

I can't take it. That's not the life for me. Let them support themselves as best they can and wring their children's necks. There are too many of us already. But no. They start fucking when they're twelve; by the time they're fourteen, they've given birth for the first time, and when they're twenty-five, they already have four or five whining brats, begging and screaming all over the neighborhood. Sometimes I think I'm poor in spite of myself. Poor people can't analyze their circumstances because if they do, they'll go crazy or hang themselves. But, like an idiot, I spend my life contemplating the grim landscape and thinking. A bad habit, possibly fatal.

Then a light bulb came on over my head: Shit, I'd go play dominoes at old Esperanza's place. The stakes were five pesos. If I was lucky, I'd dig myself a little way out of my hole. There was no reason to think I'd lose. And it's bad luck to worry about losing, anyway. I had twenty pesos in my pocket.

The old lady lives on the second floor of my building. She's a *santera*. Just stepping inside, I could already sense something strange in the air. She connects with a lot of dead people. That kind of thing doesn't scare me, because I'm immune to the effects. But even so, it's oppressive to feel so many dead souls floating around you.

Esperanza is ancient, and people say she's lost her touch as a *santera*, which means she's lost clients. She had to make money somehow, so a year ago she set up a table for domino games and another one for dice. She charges two pesos at the door, and those of us who play settle the rest ourselves. Sometimes there's cold beer. There's always rum and cigarettes. And of course, Esperanza takes numbers for the Venezuelan lottery, which comes in loud and clear at night on Radio Margarita. All things considered, the joint was a good idea. The neighborhood jokers call it "Casino Esperanza."

Both tables were filled, and eight men were waiting their turns. I staked a place in the line for dice, because the domino games take longer. Esperanza was in the kitchen. I went in and paid her the two-peso entrance fee, then I bought a double shot of rum, and we talked for a while. She'd been trying to convince me to have a session with her, and whenever she could, she would try to scare me.

"You need a good overhaul, Pedro Juan. I see a huge black man beside you, but his back is turned. And sometimes an Indian, but his back is turned too. You need to buy yourself a figure of an Indian and bring him to me to treat and then put it in your room. First I'll give you a session and then we'll cast those spells."

She always gives me the same advice. I never respond; I'm not interested in her sessions. I've already got my own, with my *santería* godmother. Esperanza knows perfectly well that you can't mix things up like that and that she shouldn't meddle. But to make a few dollars, she'd give Mohammed himself a session, and she'd be capable of convincing him to pay for the holy necklace she'd make for him, claiming he was a son of Changó.

What I was interested in was doing business in her little gambling den. I'd been trying to convince her for days, but she wouldn't give me a straight answer. I wanted to set up another dice table, a real one. And I'd be the dealer. I was practicing every day, and every day I got faster and better at it.

"Esperanza, listen to me. I can get a table with a green-felt top and a set of Chinese marble dice. Everything new and professional looking. Really elegant. It'd give this shabby joint some class."

"Please, Pedro Juan. You usually have better manners. What do you call that game?"

"Monte. You must remember it. They played it in every Havana casino until 1959."

"Sure, but I forget what it was called. Anyway, I never went to the casinos."

"No, you had other vices."

"You're not old enough to remember anything, Pedro Juan. What do you know?"

"Esperanza, you're getting senile."

"None of that, you hear? We're having a civilized conversation."

"I've told you twenty times that one of my uncles was a dealer at the Montmartre, and the dice and the table belong to him. He's training me, and I'd be your dealer. But I'll tell you something else that'll make your mouth water: my uncle's got a box of one hundred decks of cards, all sealed. So next I'll start a blackjack table and then a poker table."

"You're trying to drag me in too deep."

"I won't drag you in too deep. What I will do is make you piles of money."

"Get your head out of the clouds, boy. The way this country is run, you can't do anything like that on a big scale. Keep that in mind so you don't get in trouble. I do like the idea of the monte, because you could take personal charge of it."

"Tomorrow I'll bring the table over, and we'll break it in."

"How will we split things?"

"Let's wait and see how much I make, and then I'll be able to tell you what the daily take will be."

"All right, set it up. But I'm warning you, and make sure it's crystal clear: I won't have any arguments or fights in here, or any weapons. Some of these blacks like to carry knives around with them. Everything has to stay as it is. Loud music on the radio or the tape player, and everybody coming and going discreetly. No drunkenness or fresh talk. If anybody talks fresh, it'll be me, and if anybody raises their voice when they're talking to me, they're never coming back. And I don't want whores in here either, because women complicate things and cause fights. Everything's got to stay quiet and orderly, the way it's been up till now."

"Is the lecture over, ma'am, or is there more?"

"That's the lecture. And don't you break any of the rules because the minute you do, you're out on the street with your table and your dice and a kick in the pants. I won't give you a second chance."

"Very good, ma'am. We'll start tomorrow."

"What about the table?"

"I'll bring it over tonight. Don't worry about me. I know how to do things right. I've already been in jail for two years. I don't plan to go back."

"I know, you're as sharp as they come. The white man's natural talent."

"Ha ha ha. Pour me another double, and let's celebrate."

"Fine, but you can get drunk elsewhere."

"You never let down your guard, do you? Don't you ever laugh?"

"I've already laughed enough in my life."

"Is it true you used to work in the red-light district?"

"If you already know it, why bother to ask?"

"Esperanza, when they closed the bars, you must have been close to forty."

"That's right, but I was hot stuff. I was forty-two, but if you could've seen me, you would've fallen head over heels in love with me. At the time, I was seeing a twenty-six-year-old dandy, a pretty white boy who looked like an actor. I kept him dressed in white from head to toe, and he had so much gold on him even his fillings were gold."

"I can still tell you're beautiful."

"Don't make fun of me. There's nothing left to look at. I'll be seventy-six in September."

"But you're still going strong. You look sixty."

"I look it. You said it, not me."

"My uncle owned a bar there. At Consulado and Virtudes."

"That was a respectable place. It's still there."

"Which bar did you work at?"

"I worked at all of them, child. I started in the business when I was fourteen. I even worked at Marina's for four years."

"Marina's was famous."

"Yes, and high class too. There were no rowdies there, only men in suits and ties who brought us perfume and sent flowers the next day. Gentlemen, and stylish. We girls were quality too. Those were the best years of my life."

"Why did you leave?"

"Enough, enough. You know how to charm a woman, and you make me talk more than I should. I'm taking my secrets to the grave."

Katia, Esperanza's daughter, interrupted us, "Excuse me, please, you two may be having fun, but I have to feed my children."

"All of a sudden you're so polite."

"Same as always. I may be black, but I've got manners. Not like that prissy little bitch of yours who acts like she's white but who's really trash."

Katia has been under house arrest for a year. She was caught stealing at a dollar store, and she was sentenced to two years in prison, but she has a six-year-old son and a baby girl. At her trial, she was pregnant and showing, and that saved her from a jail term. She can't leave the house. A policeman might come knocking on the door any time to check up on her. She can't even be at a neighbor's house. If they catch her away from the apartment, she'll be locked up.

"Being stuck at home has suited you."

"You think?"

"Do I? Girl, let me tell you."

Katia was always skinny. Now she's gained at least thirty pounds, but no flab: it's all gone to her ass, her tits, and her thighs. The perfect distribution. She's firm, sturdy. The father of her children is a real hoodlum. He lives in the building across the street, and he's bad news. Esperanza won't let him in her apartment. He and Katia used to fuck on the stairs late at night, or wherever they could find a place. Now I don't know what they do because he can't come in and she can't go out. Sometimes I tease Katia to see if she'll take the bait. She flirts a little with me, wiggling her butt in my face, but it doesn't go any further than that. She likes to play, but she's tight with her husband, and she knows he's no softie. If he ever caught her screwing someone else, he'd kick her ass from here to the next life.

I leaned against the table. I was checking Katia out. Maybe I could get her without really chasing her, just staring at her. Just then, Isabel came in.

"Hey, what're you doing here?"

"I know which way the wind blows, sweetie. I'm just keeping an eye on my property."

Sneering, Katia attacked, "No one owns anything in this life, Isabel. Just when you think you've got it made, somebody steals your husband and you're stuck."

"Especially if you can't leave your apartment to keep an eye on him."

"What are you trying to say, girl? What was that supposed to mean?"

I stepped in to break things up before they got ugly.

"All right, all right. Stop it, both of you. Isabel, did you come down here to pick a fight? Go back upstairs and cool it."

"I won't go. Aren't you having a drink? What about me? Does it look like my mouth is sewn shut?"

"I'm waiting to play dice."

"Dice? In the kitchen, with Katia? That's a strange fucking game!"

"All right, calm down! Stop making a scene."

"Fine, I'll go in the other room with you and be your good-luck charm. I'm not budging without you. I know you like black sluts with big asses, but I'm not going to make it easy for you, sweetie."

"Oh, hell."

She followed me over to the gaming tables, and we watched for a while. Women are difficult. You fuck them a few times, and they think they're married. And if you don't show them who's boss, they get you wrapped around their little finger.

Isabel leaned against the wall by the window, looking out at the street. I picked up the dice barrel and started playing with three others. The place was heating up. Twelve neighborhood guys were pacing around waiting their turns. Starting the next day, I'd be amazing everybody with my monte table.

I had barely taken three turns when there was a terrible racket in the next room. First we heard a neighbor screaming, "Scoundrel, dirty bastard! I'm going to tell my son, and he'll beat your brains out, you son of a bitch!"

And then Esperanza and Katia started shouting. Then came the sound of slaps and Katia's children wailing. Esperanza came running hysterically out of the room, screaming, beating Katia with a belt. In the middle of the hallway, she gasped and went into convulsions, turning from black to ashy gray. She collapsed, and her head sounded like a stone hitting the floor. Stretched out full length, her body shuddered and stiffened. Katia threw herself down too, crying and screaming, "Mother, what's wrong? Mother, don't die! Help me, help!"

Taking advantage of the confusion, I pocketed the dice and dice barrel. Nobody saw me. Everybody was getting the hell out of there. The next minute, Isabel had me by the hand. We went out onto the stairs and then up to the roof to our rooms.

We ran up all eight flights of stairs, and when we got to the top, we could hardly breathe.

"I think Esperanza kicked the bucket," I said.

"You think? I know she did."

"Did you see what happened?"

"Katia's black stud was on the roof across the street and he was getting ready to take a shower."

"And you, like the slut you are, were watching him."

"You know how you like to check out big-assed black women? Well, I like to check out big-dicked black men."

"So why are you with me, then?"

"Enough, sugar, enough. He couldn't see me. I was standing at the edge of the window."

"Peeping Tom!"

"You're a Peeping Tom and a pervert too, so don't pretend to be shocked."

"All right, keep going."

"Katia came to the other window and she started getting him hot, sticking out her tongue and showing her tits."

"And the guy shot his wad."

"In an instant. He was in a tiny pair of briefs, and he stripped and jerked off on the spot. I've never seen so much come. His prick is the size of a small child. I don't know how Katia does it. He had both hands wrapped around it and there was still prick left over."

"And what was all the screaming?"

"Ofelia, the old lady on the third floor, came to her window and saw him jerking off, and started shouting that he was a dirty bastard and who knows what else. But he was already coming, his eyes popping out of their sockets. He turns into one ugly motherfucker when he comes! Then Esperanza heard Ofelia screaming and went to see what was going on, and that's how the fight started, with her beating Katia."

"Esperanza can't stand the man."

"Couldn't stand him. Now that Esperanza's out of the way, he'll come live with Katia and her children. He'll leave his building and that filthy pit of a room and take over Esperanza's apartment, because he's got Katia in the palm of his hand."

"Well, so much for my deal."

"What deal?"

"A deal I just made with Esperanza."

"There must be a curse on you, sweetie. You can't win no matter what."

"At least I swiped the dice and barrel in the middle of the scuffle."

"Well, that's something, at least."

"Sure. I can make something out of this. You'll see. I'm going to fix the dice so they fall my way every time."

The amazing thing about jail is that you learn to be at peace with yourself, alone in a small space; all your needs vanish. At the same time, you use all your lone-wolf wiles to keep the other ravenous animals from swallowing you up and invading your space. You learn to lie low, without moving or expecting anything, and you forget to think about time passing or what's happening outside. Lots of animals do the same thing: they lapse into lethargy; they hibernate.

Unconsciously, you create a protective shell, a tough hide that you learn to live in very effectively. Then, all of a sudden one day, they call you into an office, fill out a form, ask you stupid questions, and then they say, "Your sentence has been cut to five years and six months. Gather up your belongings. You'll be released this afternoon."

They don't do it out of the goodness of their hearts. They're forced to poke around and choose a few of their best inmates to let out because the prison is already holding twice as many prisoners as it should, and they don't have enough food, clothes, shoes, or work to go around.

So, that afternoon I was released, and I walked straight out and went back to the same shitty old room. I'd been gone for two and a half years. Silently, I stopped in the doorway and looked into the dark interior. Some things had changed. Isabel had another lover, and they were living in both rooms: hers and mine. She hadn't wasted any time. They were scared. I must still have had the same somber, menacing, calculating expression on my face I developed in jail as part of my shell. They were babbling incoherently, and I couldn't understand what they were saying. Isabel stopped visiting me in prison after three months, which meant we hadn't seen or had news of each other in two years and three months. I couldn't even remember exactly what she looked like. Now she didn't know what to do, and she was apologizing. I had no interest in her. We were only together for a few months, maybe a year. I can't remember. I really had nothing to do with Isabel. She just liked to play the role of wife. When she visited me in jail, she would say things like "when we used to make love," "I'll wait for you forever." I laughed in her face and said, "Since when have you been such a fancy talker? You sound like a society lady. You must be sleeping with some educated guy who talks like that, and you imitate him like a fucking parrot." She turned red, lowered her eyes, and denied it. But that was the last I saw of her. Until now, when she was falling all over herself trying to explain.

"Enough, Isabel. You have nothing to explain to me. I'm not asking any fucking questions. Get out of here now. I'm going to take a walk, and I'll be back in an hour."

"Don't go, Pedro Juan. We'll be right out."

"I'm going. I want to give you time to clean this place up and wash away the faggoty stink of perfume."

The guy didn't even let on that he'd heard. I like to act belligerent, like a good son of Oggún. It's when I'm at peace that I'm at my worst.

I went downstairs and sat on the wall by the Malecón. I had become too much of a loner to stay on the roof and deal with all the fuss the neighbors would make when they saw me. "Oh, Pedro Juan, you're back at last." Then out would come the bottles of rum and the drums, and it would be party time. I wasn't in the mood for parties or for rum. It had been exactly two and a half years since I last

touched a drop of rum, played the drums, or tasted marijuana or coffee, two and a half years without a woman. Taking some faggot in
the ass or jerking myself off didn't count. The truth is, I was bitter. I
was better off out here by myself, because the least little thing would
set me off. And I couldn't afford to get into any kind of trouble.

It was almost dark, and it was the last day of August. The heat
and the humidity were stifling. All of a sudden, the weather
changed. Heavy masses of black clouds covered the sky, and a cool
north wind sprang up, bringing with it a light fragrance. A strange
silvery light bathed the sea and the buildings. I hadn't seen anything like it in the forty years I'd lived here, ever since I was born.
Up above, everything was black and ominous, leaden, and down
here, everything was glowing silvery and ethereal. It was a beautiful
tribute to Oggún. A shiver ran up my spine. Oggún wanted rum and
tobacco. Now I could get them for him. Somehow I had to find a
glass of *aguardiente* and a good cigar to share with him in my room.
If Isabel had touched Oggún's cauldron or his irons, I'd kill her.

All of a sudden, it started to rain, and the wind blew in gusts. It
was pouring, and I was soaked in a second. It was refreshing, so I
stayed sitting on the wall. The sea was as smooth as glass; the silvery
light was vanishing little by little. The rain fell even harder. I closed
my eyes and all I could feel and hear was the water falling. Freedom.
At that very moment, I realized I was free again and I could do
whatever I wanted. I could walk away, take off running. I could flirt
with a woman, follow her, seduce her, and sleep with her that very
night.

I felt free and lighthearted, and I was flooded with happiness.
And it was still pouring. The rain kept falling more and more heavily, and it was getting darker.

After a while, the rain lessened a little. It was night. I went back
to the building, and climbed to the roof. The room was empty now.
Isabel gave me the key and tried to talk to me again. She was afraid
of me.

"Why did you let yourself get so wet?"

"What do you care!"

"Let me find you a towel."

"No. Leave me alone."

"But . . ."

I went into the room. There was nothing there. Just the same ripped mattress I had left behind, on a cot. In a wooden box in the corner were Oggún's irons. I went over to them and knocked three times on the box, greeted him, and asked his forgiveness for not going out to find rum or tobacco. I told him to wait until the next day. Turning off the light, I dropped onto the mattress and closed my eyes, and there was Isabel again, calling my name and knocking on the door. I opened up. She held out a glass of *aguardiente* and a cigar. She didn't dare come in. She stood there in the doorway.

"What's this for?"

"I haven't forgotten your habits."

I tried to reject the offering, but she had already gone back to her room. The bitch knew me. Feeling around in the dark, I turned on the light again and went over to Oggún's box. The irons were covered in dust and cobwebs. I sprayed them with a mouthful of *aguardiente* and bowed to them. I'd get back in Oggún's good graces. Isabel appeared in the doorway again.

"Do you have matches?"

"No."

"Here."

She handed them to me and kept standing there. She loves to play mommy, the cunt.

I lit my cigar and blew smoke on the irons. The rest was for me. Isabel was standing there, watching.

"I like to see you like that. Drinking rum and smoking your cigar."

I looked at her and didn't answer.

"That guy left. We're not really together."

"I don't care about your life. I don't want to hear any more stories."

"I saved you a plate of food. For later."

"Do you have more *aguardiente*?"

She went into her room and came back with half a bottle, pouring me some.

"Do you have honey?"

"For the irons?"

"Yes. They've been wanting it since I came in."

"I don't have any. But I'll go out early tomorrow and get you some."

I was quiet, enjoying being in my room, with Oggún's cauldron, drinking *aguardiente*, smoking, a good woman nearby dying to be fucked. It started to thunder. I went to the door. My room and Isabel's are the only ones on the roof with a view of the Caribbean. The rest is a labyrinth of rotting boards and pieces of brick, where people stifle in the heat, hungry and wallowing in shit.

There was an electrical storm in the distance, over the sea. All that could be seen were the flashes of light. The downpour had turned into a heavy drizzle, and the wind had died down. The rain was pattering on the tiles of my roof, an imperturbable music. It was as if my soul had fled my body years ago and was just now coming back. I could feel it filtering into all the tiny corners of my being.

Isabel was sitting on the bed, waiting for me. Just looking at her, I got an instant erection. I still liked that mulatta. After all, what right did I have to demand loyalty? I'm the least faithful of human beings.

I closed the door. We undressed each other slowly. Holding each other tight, we kissed. My heart was beating faster, and a tear almost came to my eye, but I held it back. I couldn't cry in front of her, the bitch. Caressing her, I pushed very slowly inside her, and she was already wet and luscious. It was like entering paradise. But I wouldn't tell her that either. It's best for me just to love her in my own way, silently, without letting her know.

Berta was seventy-six. She lived alone on the eighth floor, second from the top, of a building on San Lázaro, in Central Havana. It depressed her to go out on the balcony and look down on what resembled the aftermath of a bombing. Too much rubble. The ruined city murmured, rumbled. For a long time now, she hadn't even opened the balcony doors.

More and more often she took refuge in the memories stored in her wardrobe and dresser drawers. Dresses, gloves, hats with flowers, invitations to dances, empty bottles of French perfume, underthings made of Dutch lace, high-heeled shoes, jewelry boxes full of pearl necklaces, bracelets, chokers, earrings, pendants. Everything smelled of cedar and mothballs, and it was all threadbare, yellowed, aged. Nothing had been worn for thirty or forty years. When her husband died, Berta was sixty-three, and he was ninety-four. He was a well-known doctor in Havana. She had never loved him and had never been attracted to him. When they met, she was a lovely eighteen-year-old girl, and he was a man of forty-nine, a widower, polished and paternal. He promised her the world. She was dazzled by the glamor of it all, and five days later they were married. From that day on, Berta's life was a succession of parties and trips, the good life: Mexico, Puerto Rico, Miami, Caracas, New York.

But everything faded slowly away. The neighborhood was no

longer what it used to be. It filled up with common people from the provinces, uncouth blacks, ragged, dirty, rude people. The buildings crumbled since no one took care of them, and little by little, they became dormitories, thousands of people crowded into them like roaches, skinny, underfed, dirty, unemployed people, drinking rum at all hours, smoking marijuana, beating on drums, and multiplying like rabbits, people without perspective, with limited horizons. Everything made them laugh. What were they laughing at—everything. Nobody was sad or wanted to kill themselves or was terrified for fear the ruins would collapse and bury them alive. Not at all. In the middle of the debacle, they laughed, lived their lives, tried to enjoy themselves as best they could. Their senses were sharpened. They were like the weakest and smallest of animals, learning to conserve their strength and develop lots of different skills because they knew they'd never be big or strong, never be predators. Born in the ruins, they just kept trying not to give up or let themselves be beaten so severely that at last they were forced to surrender. Anything was possible, everything allowed, except defeat.

Berta had been living alone for years. She had never had children. She had only known the worshipful love of one man, a man she had always thought of as a father, a sweet, good man with whom she rarely had sex. Even when she did, it was brief and she kept her eyes closed, almost ashamed, willing him to finish as quickly as possible and roll off her. Nevertheless, she was a sensual, romantic woman who liked to read and reread *La Dame aux Camellias*, *Anna Karenina*, and *Wuthering Heights*.

It had been years since she'd been able to see well enough to read or knit or embroider. Even so, every afternoon she'd sit down to look at the pictures in old issues of *La Familia* magazine. She had a collection spanning several years, and she'd look at the pages of knitting projects, crochet patterns, wool socks. She liked to look slowly through her wedding pictures too, and photos of her travels. She lived in silence, absorbed in her memories. And she was always hungry. Her widow's pension didn't stretch far enough, and the little bit of food she could buy wasn't enough. Often she'd think, "These are times for young people, strong people. It's too much. We old ones won't survive." But her thinking didn't go any farther than that. Her analytic skills never got much practice. She had never needed to use them.

Little by little, Berta had become a prisoner of her apartment. She was afraid to go downstairs or leave the building, and it exhausted her to climb the stairs when she came back. The elevator hadn't worked for years. Once a month she managed to walk to the bank to collect her pension. A boy would bring her three or four small bags of food on one of the first days of each month. And that was all. She prayed a lot to the Virgen de las Mercedes, and she had gotten used to the silence and the hunger, to being so thin and almost penniless, confined to her apartment, which kept getting dirtier and dirtier, for two reasons: she didn't have dollars to buy soap or detergent, and she didn't have the strength to clean. Besides, she didn't care. It was all the same to her. She couldn't brush her hair anymore because tufts came out, and she was afraid of going bald. She still had most of her teeth; she'd only lost three molars. And she never got sick. At the height of the crisis, her neighborhood never had blackouts. For some technical reason, the supply couldn't be cut to save fuel. And that was a blessing because Berta was terrified of the dark. She slept with the lights on.

Down below, on the seventh floor, there were new neighbors. The old ones went away to Miami. The apartment was sealed for a few months, and then finally another family moved in. There were lots of them, and they made a racket, talking in loud voices, fighting, screaming, arguing, shouting to each other on the stairs, listening to very loud music, and laughing, drinking, and dancing until dawn. They made their presence felt. Now they were knocking down walls and building new dividers in their apartment, making small rooms. There were lots of them, and there wasn't enough space. The apartment was big, but there were always more of them. Each year more children were born.

At first Berta was afraid of them and avoided them, trying not to run into them. They seemed like a tribe of gypsies the way they clamored, demolishing everything in their path. But as the months went by, little by little, the old lady of the family made friends with Berta. She'd wave hello, remark on something, run to buy Berta bread, wash her clothes one day, and the next bring her a dish of rice pudding. One of the girls would clean her apartment, and the old lady would present her with a bar of soap. Berta didn't notice what was going on; it was slow, smooth. "They're good people," she said to herself. The wariness and mistrust she felt before, when she lived absolutely alone, were gradually diminishing. Now there was almost always someone keeping her company. One of the girls might be washing her hair with shampoo, painting her nails, running her a warm bath, bringing her a bit of cologne. And in her apartment, they kept it down. They didn't scream or shout or argue among themselves, they didn't play loud music on the radio, and they tried not to bother her. Now Berta wasn't as hungry as she used to be, and she wasn't dirty; she never went for weeks without a bath. And she'd gotten used to talking to people again too. Now she dared to open her balcony doors. The rubble was still there, but her new friends didn't see it. They noticed the people: a handsome man walking by, a whore coming home dressed in nightclub clothes at ten in the morning, a nice modern car, a bride and groom on parade in a '57 Chevy convertible covered in colored balloons, the old drunks on the corner. She was filled with the simple joy of youth, and her days were more amusing.

One morning Omar showed up. He was one of them, the brother of somebody, cousin of somebody else, nephew of the old lady. Where was he from? Did he live on the seventh floor now? Yes, but he'd been in another city, and he'd just come back. His explanations were brief and vague and difficult to understand. The old lady introduced him as her nephew. Omar was twenty-three, and he was a pretty boy, dark, with beautiful black hair combed straight back and wide shoulders, though he was slim. And he knew how to talk, knew how to seduce.

"You must have been beautiful when you were young. It still shows."

"Yes, I was pretty. Can you really tell?"

"Of course. Your skin is so smooth, so fine."

She took out pictures of herself as a baby, as a girl, of her wedding. She wanted him to see her as pretty. He was a charming boy, surrounded by so much vulgarity. And he was flattering her.

"If I had been around back then, we would have gotten married. I like elegant, ladylike women."

"You wouldn't have paid any attention to me. You would have been a dandy."

"What's that?"

"A dandy, a snob, a smooth talker, a ladies' man."

"Well, we would have had an unforgettable romance."

Berta didn't know what to say, she was so flattered. After all her quiet years alone, she was thrilled by the compliments that this Prince Charming was paying her.

"Oh, child, you could be my grandson."

"I could be, but I'm not, Berta. So never mind that. Think nice thoughts."

Omar didn't work, and he wasn't in school. He didn't do anything. All he had to wear was one pair of shorts and one shirt, both old and stained, and a worn-out pair of rubber sandals. He was poverty personified. His dream was to go to the United States and live in one of those cities where it snowed and it was cold, where a person could really bundle up. He would've liked to work as a truck driver or a bus driver, marry a blond, blue-eyed American woman, drive around in his supermodern truck and have three or four very light-skinned children, though it was possible they might turn out like their grandparents, in which case they'd be even blacker than he was. Omar was very racist. He was mestizo. His hair was kinky and he had a big mouth and dark skin, but he didn't quite look black. He was a mix, like everybody in the family. Ever since he was a kid people called him "The Moor," because he looked Arab. He knew he was handsome, but he wanted to be white, suave, well-dressed, and have lots of money and a car and a nice house. Like everyone else, he longed for what he didn't have. As soon as he saw Berta's apartment, crowded with antique furniture, rugs, china and bronze ornaments, drapes, he said to himself, "This is what I want." Omar was a professional playboy. It was the only thing he was good at; it was how he made a living. He liked to be kept by women, or by men—it made no difference. Older men and women were nice, because they were like mothers or fathers as well as lovers, and he never had to worry about money. He spent hours talking to Berta, listening to her stories, looking at her pictures with her over and over again, while the old lady and the girls busied themselves cleaning the house, doing the washing, bringing in food. Omar's and Berta's conversations grew longer and longer. They had a good time keeping each other company.

One afternoon Omar knocked on the door. He had been drinking. In one hand he was carrying a plate of food, and in the other a glass filled to the brim with rum.

"Berta, this is from my aunt."

"Oh, spaghetti, how delicious."

"Don't eat it yet. Have a drink."

"Oh no, child. It's been years since I've tasted rum."

"Just sip a little. Try it."

"I always drank cocktails. But maybe a taste."

Berta barely wet her lips. She was nervous. For a while, she'd been yearning to be alone with Omar. Her heart beat faster when she saw him, and she got upset when the hours passed and he didn't stop by.

Omar turned on the radio. He found a station playing light music, and he came up behind Berta, who was sitting in an armchair. He put his hands on her shoulders. Berta jumped, and her heart skipped a beat. Gently, with expert hands, Omar gave her a massage.

"You're making me nervous, Omar. What are you doing?"

"I like you."

"I'm an old lady."

"You aren't old. And I like you."

"God will punish you for lying to me."

"I'm not lying. I like you."

Very slowly, he pushed her dress off her shoulders, all the while kneading them and kissing her. Unfastening her bra, he caressed her breasts, sagging and wrinkled but still with large, luscious pink nipples.

"Mmm, these nipples are amazing."

"Oh, Omar, I'm ashamed. Let me get dressed."

"Drink some more."

And, putting his lips to Berta's, he passed a little rum from his mouth to hers. Biting and sucking on her nipples, he was slowly arousing her, savoring her as if she were a nubile, smooth-skinned woman, not a wrinkled and flaccid old lady of seventy-six.

He pulled down his shorts a little—he wasn't wearing anything underneath—and showed her everything, his pubes lush and black. Though she kept getting more and more nervous, she couldn't help staring, hypnotized by that glorious thing, so big and dark. Her husband's equipment was half the size and pale and soft, never so big and stiff.

Omar knew he had her entranced. Lifting her off the chair, he kissed her, taking the opportunity to pass a little more rum into her mouth. On the way to her room, he stripped her entirely of her dress. Omar was astonished. The old lady's vulva was pink, its lips pomegranate red, surrounded by white hairs. All the hair was white, no black in it at all, but it was luxuriant. Her mound of Venus was pristine, and her vagina seemed untouched, virginal. What Omar thought would be a sacrifice had become a pleasant and appealing task. Kissing that vulva, he sucked at it, then penetrated her carefully. She was narrow and moist, and she smelled good. He was enjoying himself, and he satisfied Berta, who was quietly feeling things she had never imagined were possible. Using all the tricks he knew, finally, an hour and a half later, he came. He wanted to give the old lady a little something extra, and so he came on her breasts, covering her nipples with come and then sucking it off.

Incredibly, Berta survived. She felt happy and satisfied. She was exhausted, and Omar was too. Not bad. The fun was repeated the next afternoon, and the next, for a whole week. Berta was learning to do things she had never considered trying before, and each day she enjoyed herself more. One night, after making love as voluptuously as usual, Berta said, "Why don't you move in here with me?"

"That would be nice. But I can't."

"Why not?"

"I'm a man, Berta. I don't like to live off women."

"But . . ."

"No, no. I appreciate the offer, but I'll stay where I am, sleeping on the floor in my aunt's apartment."

"You sleep on the floor?"

"Yes. I put a blanket down and that's where I sleep. I'm used to it, don't worry."

Berta was quiet for a while. At last she said, "Look, Omar, by the laws of nature, I don't have many years left to live."

"Oh, don't talk that way."

"Tomorrow we can go see a notary, and I'll make a will in your name. I'll leave you everything I own. This apartment, the furniture, everything."

"All right, Berta. You're everything to me. I'll move in with you."

The next day, Omar took her to see a notary, and they drew up a will. Then he brought her home and left her there alone for two days. He had another lover, a beautiful forty-eight-year-old mulatta who was supporting him. Omar already had clothes and shoes, and the woman had promised him a gold chain.

Berta was very upset. For a week, she had been enjoying his company every night, and sometimes they even made love twice. At two in the morning, she couldn't stand it anymore, and she called Omar's aunt. The aunt brought her a sleeping pill, soothed her, and sat next to her until she fell asleep.

The next day it was worse. Omar didn't show up. That night, there was a blackout that lasted several hours. It was a breakdown in the network, an almost unheard-of occurrence in that neighborhood. Terrified, Berta called for Omar's aunt, and the woman came running upstairs. Berta was trembling in fear in the dark. No one had flashlights or kerosene lamps. One of Omar's cousins brought up a scrap of candle she had been burning for her *santos*, but not even that little light could comfort Berta.

"I've been scared of the dark ever since I was little. Where is Omar? If only he were here."

"We sent someone to get him. He's on his way."

"Where is he?"

"He went to run an errand for me. He's coming. Don't worry."

"I know there's someone else. A girl."

"No, Berta, you can't think that."

"I do, I know there's someone else. And I'm here all alone."

"He really loves you, he does."

"No, no. I'm getting dressed. Call the chauffeur—I want to go dancing tonight. Where can I go dancing?"

"What?"

"Bring me my taffeta dress, the bright pink one. I'm not going to sit here in the dark while he's with another woman."

"Berta, what's wrong?"

"Nothing's wrong. Put on some music, and run me a bath with bath salts. I want to wear Chanel. I want to smell good when Omar comes."

"All right, all right."

"Go on, woman. And get me my dress. I'll go by myself in the car if he doesn't come in time."

Berta got up out of her armchair, but she was dizzy and she collapsed, unconscious but still alive. Her breath was coming in gasps. She died at three in the morning in the hospital, without ever recovering consciousness. The doctor asked if she had had a shock. Omar's aunt was the only one still keeping vigil by the corpse. The young people were too noisy, and she had asked to be left alone. Her voice when she answered the doctor was gentle and sorrowful.

"Certainly not, doctor! We took good care of her. I loved her like a mother."

"I ask because she died of a cerebral hemorrhage."

"No, doctor. She lived very quietly. She had everything she wanted."

"Would you like us to perform an autopsy? That way we can find out more exactly what caused her death."

"Yes, doctor. I'd appreciate it. You know how people gossip, and it wouldn't even surprise me if someone accused us of poisoning her."

3:14 / My Dear Drum's Master

I had a pigeon trap on the roof. Two boxes, really, with a decoy pigeon to lure unsuspecting birds. On the nearby roofs, there were lots of messenger pigeon houses.

I wasn't interested in breeding. My thing was simpler. Each day I'd catch one or two pigeons and sell them for twenty pesos to a guy who, it was said, resold them for use in *santería* ceremonies. I don't know. For all I cared, he could have been frying them and selling them as chicken. I was just trying to make a living. It was impossible to find work and even harder if you had a prison record.

That's how I spent my days, tinkering with the traps and sending the decoy out every so often. He was a strong male, but I'd worked him so hard he was exhausted and half-silly and he didn't want to fly anymore. Or maybe what was wrong was that he was tired and he couldn't understand why he had such bad luck: he'd find a female he liked, bring her back to the cage to woo her, and then she'd disappear and he'd be left wondering what had happened. The first few times he got upset, fretting in anguish and desperation, and I thought he might go crazy. Not anymore. Now he gets sad, but I don't give him time to get worked up; and I make him go up again, find another female, and bring her back. You can't let the decoy get attached to the female, because he'll fall in love in a matter of hours, and he's likely to pine away for her, with no thought for himself. That's love—which is why I'll have none of it in here. I have no time to waste on that kind of foolishness.

That's what I was doing one morning, working the traps and tormenting the decoy, when Isabel showed up with two blond, blue-eyed Europeans, white as paper. The woman was sturdy and healthy looking, but the man looked like a corpse. He gave me the creeps. The two of them were smiling and looking all around. They seemed surprised to find themselves on a roof overlooking the sea.

"Pedro Juan, let me introduce you to some friends. We met on the Malecón."

"When? Just now?"

"Yes, a little while ago."

The woman spoke some Spanish, the man none at all. She said, "Good morning."

"Good morning, *How are you?*"

"*Do you speak English?*"

"*Very bad. Do you speak Spanish?*"

"Just a little."

"*A lot of English and a lot of Spanish is so much.*"

"Ha ha ha. That's a good story."

"*Yeah. Do you need room or anything?*"

"No . . . well . . . maybe. *Maybe.*"

"*Ahhh. He is your husband, your partner?*"

"*He is my friend.* Friend, friend. He's a musician. I'm an anthropologist."

We stumbled along like that a little longer, the man looking back and forth from one of us to the other. Isabel interrupted, "On the Malecón they told me he wants to learn to play the drums, and I told them you were a music teacher."

"Me?"

"Yes, you. They want to pay for classes, damn it, and *you're* a teacher."

"Right, drums . . . I can teach drums . . . of course, of course, why not."

"You're the slowest gun in the West, sweetie."

"Fuck, then—like pennies from heaven."

"What are you talking about?" asked Angela. "I can't understand when you talk fast. Go slow, please."

"We were saying yes, you can take drum lessons. Cuban drum. *Cuban drum.*"

"Oh yes. He wants. Are you a teacher?"

"Yes, I'm a teacher. You want to learn too?"

"No. I not folklore."

"Oh . . . *and* . . . *What about you?*"

"What is your name?"

"I'm Pedro Juan and she's Isabel."

"We're Angela *and* Peter."

"We have the same name."

"*Pardon?*"

"We have the same name. Him and me."

"I don't understand."

"*Pedro is similar to Peter. Are the same names.*"

"Ohhh."

"All right, all right. Never mind. So—he wants to learn to play drums, and I'll teach him. We'll discuss the fee later. And what about you? You're just a tourist?"

"No, no. I'll be here for a year, studying. He's only here for fifteen days. He doesn't have much time left."

"So you're studying. What are you studying?"

She rummaged in her backpack and pulled out a Cuban magazine from two years ago. Leafing through it, she found an article titled "Love in black and white," on racism in mixed relationships in Cuba. It was a survey, and it only dealt with couples where one partner was black and the other white. They all complained that their family and friends made things difficult for them.

"What is this, Angela?"

"Racism. I'll be here for a year studying it. And then I'll write my thesis. Do you know what that is? A thesis?"

"Yes. And what is it you're trying for? A doctorate?"

"Oh, *you know*. Yes, yes. I do doctorate here in Cuba, but exam in Europe."

From that moment on, Angela fired questions at Isabel and me. Isabel is a mulatta, and I look one hundred percent white.

Meanwhile, Peter picked up the drum, which was in a corner, and banged on it violently, as if he wanted to punish it. It's a crime to hit a poor defenseless drum like that. I tried to show him how to do it right, but it was hopeless. He'd listen carefully, watch intently, and then bang again. Angela told us that he was a musical genius. He could play the piano, violin, saxophone, guitar, oboe, and all the traditional instruments of his country perfectly. Well, I didn't think he was so hot. After the second day, I decided he was a lost cause, and I'd collect my fee, teach him something new, and go off somewhere far away, leaving him alone hammering the skins. At least I spared myself the agony of listening to that rhythmless din.

The guy only ate vegetables and drank herbal tea; he wrote in a fat notebook and stared out to sea. He didn't smoke or drink alcohol or coffee. The entire time he was here, we couldn't say one word to each other. We just looked at each other and smiled. Sometimes he brought out a camera and took pictures.

After staying with us for a few days, Angela was bored and silent.

"Finally you've run out of questions."

"What? Talk slowly, please."

"Don't you have any more questions for Isabel and me?"

"Oh, no. No more."

"What are you going to do?"

"Reflect."

"Everything's theory with you."

"Theory's necessary."

"Sure, but practice is more fun."

"*Pardon?*"

"Go find a black man you like and live with him."

A big smile lighted her half-bored, half-sad face.

"Oh, yes. Is that possible?"

"Of course!"

"What do I have to do?"

"Nothing. Find a black man you like, go live with him, and then write."

"Yes. Participatory fieldwork. Yes, yes."

"Don't go without paying me for the nights you stayed here."

"Yes. I'll pay my share and tomorrow I'll go somewhere else."

"So quickly? You already have some black stud in mind? You're kidding me."

"I can't understand. Talk slowly, please."

"I said you're doing the right thing. Study, study those black men hard."

The next day, Angela picked up her backpack, paid, and left. We'd never had so much money at once. I set the decoy free so he could fly away with some little female. But he wouldn't. He had lost the will to live; and he stayed on the roof, sad and lonely. And he died, because I forgot he was there, and I never brought him food or water. That's the way it goes. He had become an idiot, and that's what happens to idiots.

Peter kept thumping on the drum, drinking herbal tea, gazing out to sea, and reading a little book called *John Cage*. We always thought there was something wrong with him, but we couldn't ask him about it. All we could do was smile. I'd show him a drum roll, and serious as could be, he'd give it some Celtic or Viking twist. The guy was a fuck-up, beyond help. He'd look at me for approval, and I'd smile and say, "Oh, *good, good!*"

The girls from the building pestered him. They all tried to seduce him, swarming around him. He would just smile, look out to sea, and ignore them.

"Do you think he's gay?" Isabel asked me.

"He doesn't look it."

"You don't look it either, and you like it when I stick my finger up your ass."

"Okay, you'll be sorry you said that."

"But it's true."

"All right, all right. You think you're funny, don't you?"

When he left, he bought my drum and took it with him. Then, for six months, we received postcards from his city. They always began, "My dear drum's master." And then there'd be some words in his language.

I kept all six postcards, one for each month. A few months later, I ran into Angela. She was on a bicycle, sweating. Her Spanish was excellent. We embraced joyfully in the middle of the street, and it seemed to me she had mellowed a little. She was cheerful, full of smiles, and more open.

"Peter was sending me postcards, but I haven't heard from him in a while."

"Pedro Juan, now I can tell you. Peter was very sick when he came to Cuba. He's probably dead now."

"Of what?"

"AIDS."

"Oh. Why did he want to learn to play the drum when he had so little time left?"

"I don't know. He was my friend. He asked me to come with him to see you, and I did. That was all I needed to know."

"Sure. Me too, I guess. Well, let's move on to happier topics. What happened with your black man?"

"My black man?"

"Didn't you hook up with a black man? For your thesis."

"Not just one. With lots."

"You enjoyed yourself, even though you're an anthropologist."

"Right, right. But it was because I'm an anthropologist. I've been with thirty-two black men. I have an index card and a photograph of each one. It was good fieldwork."

"And now what? Aren't you taking one of them back with you? Didn't you fall in love?"

"No, no. It was just an experiment. The men were all about love, lots of sex, pure passion. But I wasn't. It was just an experiment."

"I thought you'd fall in love in Cuba. I thought you liked black men."

"Oh, yes. I like them. But love is out of the question. I don't have time. It would be a big problem for me to have a boyfriend in Cuba."

"So you're still single."

"Yes, yes. Sometime soon I'll come back, I'll see one of them again, we'll make love, but that's all."

"Oh. Well. Then that's all right."

"Yes, everything's fine."

"When you come back, come see us on the roof."

"For sure. I'll be there."

"Bye, Angela. Have a good trip."

"Bye, Pedro Juan. Good luck."

We hugged each other and went our separate ways. That money had run out a long time ago, and no other foreigners turned up wanting to learn to play drums. It was a good little business, but students were scarce. So now I'm selling some strong, sweet-smelling, high-quality stuff, and I manage to scrape by, though music classes weren't as dangerous and I made more money. That's my real calling, no doubt about it: *drum's master*.

3:15 / A Good Whipping

Roberto's apartment is protected by heavy grilles with massive locks. It's like living in prison. People didn't used to be so rude. But for the last few years, even those with nothing really to steal haven't thought twice about locking themselves up behind bars.

Roberto has hundreds of porcelain figurines from Europe and China, ornaments of jade and colored marble, and pieces of bronze—everything antique, authentic, and beautifully crafted. He's a connoisseur. His whole life he's been acquiring things bit by bit, seizing chances to buy cheaply, especially from down-on-their-luck old ladies. Up to a certain point, the women proudly refuse, but finally they get tired of being hungry, and they start selling things, cheap. A pearl necklace, a gold brooch, a table lamp, a porcelain doll, the oak dining room set, a rug. Everything, at rock-bottom prices, so they'll be able to eat and keep themselves alive a while longer. Roberto pursues them for years, calling, visiting, bringing little gifts: half a kilo of powdered milk, a bar of soap, a little bag of black tea, a jar of tomato sauce, all sweetened with gossip, jokes, and stories. It's hard to say exactly how old Roberto is, but he's somewhere over sixty, shameless, perverted, cynical, and queer, a flaming queen. Some of the down-on-their-luck old ladies are shameless too. Some of them used to be "lady companions," as they like to call themselves, of the most elegant gentlemen of Havana.

Sometimes Roberto calls them courtesans, and they laugh and reminisce about the old days. He brings them porn magazines and lets them borrow them for a few days. The women are dazzled and excited by the color photographs of beautiful bodies copulating.

Which is to say, Roberto will try anything. Anything goes when it comes to getting what he wants. He's earned the trust and friendship of dozens of lonely old ladies, mostly in Central Havana and El Vedado. There are no members of the species left in Old Havana, where they've been completely wiped out. Roberto has always been capable, cheerful, gossipy, self-confident, a talker. He has a passion for green rugs, red velvet curtains, mirrors in gold frames, dim lights, strong perfume, and zarzuela: El Pichi and Las Leandras make him swoon. The sequins, the lace, the tapping of heels, the swishing, flowing gowns. He stores his Spanish dance costumes, castanets, and lacy undergarments in a wardrobe, protecting them with mothballs. It's been a long time since he's worn the clothes at the fabulous parties he used to throw in his apartment. He'd imitate Lola Flores—he knew her repertoire by heart—and everyone had a good time. Later he'd discover people had stolen ashtrays, glasses, silver cutlery, pitchers, little bronze figurines, and he'd get angry, until one day he said to himself, "Everyone who was anyone, all the best people, have left Cuba. The only people left are trash, scum, vermin. They're shit! So I won't throw any more parties. It's all over!"

By chance, a popular salsa song was playing on the radio:

> *We're what's available*
> *What's selling like hotcakes*
> *What the people like . . .*
> *We're the best.*

"The best?" asked Roberto. "The best?"

He turned the radio off, and from that moment on, he devoted himself to his painting and his collection of antiques. In garish oils and with wobbly brush strokes, he painted Chinese women in

kimonos crossing bridges, rustic couples in the moonlight under coconut palms, copies of the Naked Maja, and many other such hor-
rors. Nevertheless, he sold them, in bulk. He could churn out six
shoddy pieces a day. He had an assembly line set up, with three can-
vases in a row. First he'd apply blue paint for water, blue for water,
blue for water. Then bridge, bridge, bridge. Then Chinese woman in
kimono, Chinese woman in kimono, Chinese woman in kimono.
Then, to the right, he'd fill up the space with a weeping willow,
weeping willow, weeping willow. Other times, for weeks on end,
he'd paint dozens of African queens being carried through the jungle in Chinese litters by slender black pages dressed as ancient Egyp-
tians, with anacondas dangling from branches and lions popping up
between bushes. In the distance, he'd add elephants and giraffes. He
had customers. His work was easy to sell, so long as the buyer had
never seen a painting before. He was happy, and he considered himself a successful artist, convinced that the members of the National
Association of Visual Arts were endlessly and mortally envious of
him.

"I've been applying for admittance for years, but they're so envious they won't accept me. They know I overshadow them."

He liked to repeat that ringing declaration, feeling very satisfied
with himself.

So every day Roberto concentrated harder on his painting and
on his greedy, gaudy collection of antiques. No sex, no parties, no
outings or entertainments. He'd never had a steady lover. He liked
black men. More than liking them, he was obsessed with them. But
ever since the assault, he'd been afraid of them. It happened on a
Saturday night, a few years ago. Three huge black men showed up at
the door looking for trouble. It might have seemed normal, since it
was known that Roberto paid well. But he thought it was strange
that there were three of them. Macho men don't like having witnesses when they deal with faggots. Luckily, he realized that in time,
and he didn't open the grille, only the door. When they saw he
didn't want to let them in, they dropped their pants and showed off

their artillery. At the sight of all that muscle and sinew, Roberto got nervous. He was like a hypnotized fawn faced down by starving wolves, paralyzed. Going up to the grille, he put out his hand to touch those incredible pricks. He never planned to unlock the grille, because the men looked like hooligans and assassins. They weren't the regular neighborhood types who came to see him every once in a while, sneaking in so no one would know they were giving the old faggot dick for fifty pesos. No. These were real tough guys, huge and strong, with gold chains around their necks and shaved heads.

"Oh, gorgeous, let me touch!" Roberto said to one of them.

And he came close to the grille. Just then the man grabbed his arm, and with his other hand, he got Roberto by the throat and crushed him viciously against the bars.

"Come on, you piece-of-shit faggot, let's see the keys. Where are the keys, faggot?"

Roberto couldn't even squeak. He blacked out and fell to the floor, and that was what saved him. The thieves ran away when they saw all the blood. When Roberto came to a few minutes later, blood was still flowing from a wound on his forehead and streaming down his face.

He had to go to the hospital. The policeman on duty took him to the station so he could file a report. Then people were running around taking fingerprints and reenacting the crime in Roberto's apartment. All of that made him very nervous, and he was still frightened, frozen, in a state of emotional shock. He had never thought such a thing could happen to him. He locked himself up in his house, afraid that the men would come back to get revenge on him for denouncing them. He was petrified. All day he'd sit rocking back and forth in an armchair, smoking cigars, trapped by nostalgia, fear, terror, nerves, depression, wanting never to get up. Next to him sat a little Moorish chest. Inside he kept a photo of a pretty teenage girl, inscribed on the back: "For Roberto, with love from your fiancée Caruca. Havana, September 12, 1932."

They were both sixteen then. He liked her very much. Though they had been engaged for three months, he would only give her little kisses. She wanted more. At the very least she wished he would grab one of her breasts. Then she decided to take the initiative. At the movies, they were watching Greta Garbo in *Mata Hari*, and she put her hand on his crotch, sliding downward, exploring, probing carefully. She couldn't find anything. Roberto had broken out in a cold sweat, and he was trembling. She kept prodding hopefully. There was nothing there. Then she decided to go all the way. She was a determined girl. Unbuckling his belt and unbuttoning his pants, she slipped her hand inside. There were no hairs. Down below, wrinkled and shy, she found a penis and tiny testicles, like a newborn baby's. For a moment she was at a loss, but when she recovered, she got up without saying a word and left. Roberto burst into tears, sobbing as if his heart would break. He couldn't help himself. He was crushed. A man who saw that he was alone and crying came over surreptitiously and sat down beside him. A little while later, he pulled out his good-sized tool and started masturbating. In the half-light, between sobs and Garbo's husky voice, Roberto saw what he was doing. At first he was terrified. Then he calmed down and wiped away his tears, pretending to be very interested in *Mata Hari*. The man took his hand and placed it on his prick. Roberto liked how it felt and squeezed hard. He had never seen, much less touched, anything so big and meaty in his life. He liked it a lot. And that was how he discovered his true earthly calling.

He never found out what happened to Caruca. Still, whenever he felt lonely and sad, he would look at her picture. For three months, they were in love. He'd never loved anyone since, and he couldn't forget her. Or rather, he didn't want to. He clung to the picture and to two short love letters Caruca had sent him back then. They were all he had.

Days passed, and his depression deepened. All he did was smoke cigars, make coffee, and drink many cups of it. He wasn't even thinking anymore. Six days later, a neighbor lady knocked at the door. He didn't answer.

"Roberto, are you dead or alive! Let me know, or I'll get the police to knock down the door."

Roberto smiled. Heaving himself up, he went to the door and opened it. His neighbor was surprised.

"Roberto, my God, you're wasting away. What's wrong with you?"

"Nothing, nothing."

"Are you scared of those hooligans? Oh, honey, they're not coming back. I'm going to bring you a bowl of soup."

"No, no."

"I made it just so I could bring you a bowl. I'm not going to let you starve to death in there all alone. Wait a minute."

She came back right away, bringing the bowl of soup and Glenda, a niece of hers who had just arrived from the country. Glenda was a rail-thin, malnourished-looking girl, with an expression on her face that was part sweet and part lewd, her skin blotched from a parasite called *wity*. Her hair was long, tangled, and dirty, her clothes were stained, and her hands were raw. Overall, she looked filthy and dirt-poor. But despite everything, she was cheerful, talkative, friendly. She stayed for quite a while and kept Roberto company while he had his soup, chatting about many things, and telling him all about herself.

"I had a boring life in the village until I ran away with the circus. I worked with them for four years."

"What did you do?"

"At first I was a rumba dancer. I danced rumbas. There were three of us, "The Hot Mulattas." We were the filler between acts, taking turns with the clowns."

"Four years dancing rumbas."

"No. That was at first. Then . . . I teamed up with the Fox, who was an old son of a bitch. And I started working with him. With the whip. We called ourselves 'Fox and the Silver Woman.' "

"Nice. Did you come out naked, painted silver?"

"What an idea! No. I came out in a tiny little bikini, wrapped up in a big silver cape, silver lamé. In the middle of the ring, I'd let the cape drop, like I was teasing the Fox. Then he would chase me, cracking his whip, and I would run. I'd hold out paper cones, cigarettes, or little pieces of cardboard, and he'd switch at them with the end of the whip. Sometimes I'd get lashed too, don't think I didn't. His aim wasn't that good."

"Damn, what a great act. I like that."

"It had its thrills. I was more filled out then. My ass and my tits were bigger."

"Now you're a mess."

"I am. I need a sugar daddy like you to take care of me."

"Oh, child. Are you out of your mind? I like men, just like you. Can't you see we're two of a kind?"

"We're not. I could get you off a million different ways. Ways you can't even imagine."

"Ugh, no. Women disgust me."

"Oh, you'll see . . . wait a minute, I'll be right back."

Glenda went back to her aunt's and returned a minute later with a plastic bag. She took out a whip and a rubber dildo.

"Look. This was the Fox's. I'd whip him with this, and then he'd get off with the dildo."

"What happened to him? Did he die?"

"No. I stole it and left. I was tired of him. Every night after the show I had to whip him and fuck him with the dildo. He was an addict. He could never get enough."

"You're such a wild thing."

"I have been ever since I was little."

Glenda went over and locked the door. Taking her clothes off, she made a sexy face, sticking out her tongue. The look was cheap whore, but it suited her. She stripped Roberto and gave him a few gentle lashes with the whip.

"Oh, nobody's ever done anything like this to me before! I love it!"

The whip and the Fox's dildo had Roberto crying in pain and pleasure. The next day, Glenda came to live with him, and little by little, she took charge of his affairs. The old man was tired, and he put his trust in the woman with the whip. And that was how they lived. Glenda had her lovers, men and women, and she brought Roberto to new heights of pleasure, orchestrating everything like a symphony conductor. They were a perfect match. They were happy together.

3·16 / The Triangle of the Pythonesses

My life is always being wrecked by the cursed trio: love, health, money. Love is a lie, money slips through the fingers, health is ruined in a second. That's the way it is for me. I'm always having to find my way home from my wanderings. You live in a fantasy world, and the fantasy world collapses. It's not the fantasy's fault; after all, salvation was always being promised for the future, the next generation, tomorrow. It's not your fault either. It's collective karma, that's all. But it happens anyway. And then you ask yourself, what should I do? I could run away, or I could stay and live on in the ruins, persist, rebuild myself; or try something new, something different. Only those who admit defeat run away. See, I take things seriously. But it's all a big pipe dream, the fumes filling your lungs. After a few shots of *aguardiente*, you suck in the smoke until you stop thinking about the collapse of the fantasy world and your own collapse and about what else you could do to save yourself. You think maybe God might help. But God's way isn't easy to find. Sometimes you sense it, but that's as far as it goes. You sense it, and you say to yourself, "Oh, my faith can be restored." That's something, at least. A lifetime thrown to you in the middle of a storm on the open sea, while everyone devours each other on a raft surrounded by stinging jellyfish.

So, yes. I smoke weed two or three times a day, drink rum,

smoke cigars. And have some group sex. Nothing fancy. In the ruins, nothing is fancy. It's all very discreet. Isabel likes it too, and there are usually three or four of us, depending on who comes up to the roof. But I won't tell those stories; they're too dirty. Though they're absolutely true. That's the way it is: forbidden fruit is the most appealing. One August night Isabel and I were sitting peacefully on the Malecón, the night breeze blowing. We were quiet, listening to the little waves whispering against the reefs along the coast and looking out at the black sky and the black sea rushing in and running out. We were submerged in it all: the immense darkness like a distant abyss and the limpid murmur of the water at our feet. I was empty inside, and that black abyss and the whisper of the waves washed straight through me. Nothing lodged itself inside. Everything just passed through me and kept going. But at least I was a little refreshed. Taking a deep breath, I could feel the freshness of that wide world fill me. But there was no peace. It was a quick fix, that was all.

Next to us was a fat black woman. She was very jolly, grinning from ear to ear, as naughty and sexy as a nymph, an old whore, sixty years old at least. And we could hear her talking to the girl next to her.

"I don't care if they're white or black. When I'm this horny, I can come just sitting here."

Six feet away from the old lady and her friend, there were three white kids, clearly not from the neighborhood. They didn't have the look of slum dwellers. The girl exchanged a few words with them in a low voice. Then she whispered something to the devilish old lady, who cackled maliciously, "Seventeen years old? Perfect. They can all put their wee wees right here. Scared of black pussy, are they? Ha ha ha. Bring them over to me."

The girl relayed her message again, but the boys must have thought the old lady was crazy. Either that or they were scared, I don't know. They looked like mama's boys, with change for the bus home in their pockets. Anyway, they left very politely, even waving and saying, "Goodbye, ma'am," then hurrying off. The fat old woman rocked with laughter. She had scared them away. If she had gone after them differently, they would never have escaped. I had never had sex with a fat old woman. Thin ones, yes. But the thin ones are always spry and lively, eager, bold, and uninhibited. The older they get, the more uninhibited they are. A skinny old woman is sexier and more exciting in bed than any girl.

Looking over at the old woman, I grabbed my balls and plumped them a little to make them look bigger. Blatantly checking me out, she said, "Hmmm . . . that's what I call the real thing. What do you want, baby?"

"Let's do it."

"You look like a wild one. Her too? Hmmm . . . now you're talking."

The girl didn't want to come with us. She was the old woman's neighbor, and she said she loved her like a mother. She didn't look like the kind of person who loves anyone, but she was theatrical about it. Her loss. The old woman lived alone in a big room in a building near the Malecón. We followed her inside. She had a bottle of rum. We were having a fine time. She would try anything, and she could never get enough. Even after three or four hours, she still hadn't had her fill. She kept wanting more, but we were tired. It was too hot. Everyone was sweating. The water supply to the common bathroom was cut off at night. We got the hell out of there, the old lady calling after us to come back, telling us we were two wild things. But we went back to the Malecón.

For a while we sat there in the cool breeze. There were lots of people out getting fresh air. We were exhausted. Going up to the roof, we showered and then slept like logs. In the middle of the night, someone knocked at the door. Isabel was asleep, snoring, screaming, having nightmares, laughing, snoring some more. I woke her up.

"Are you having a bad dream?"

"No, grrff, leave me alone, damn it, don't wake me up."

I got up. Someone was still knocking.

"Who is it?"

"Susi."

"What do you want at this time of night, Susanita, for God's sake? Leave us alone, girl."

"Come on, open up. Is Isabel there?"

"She's snoring like a pig."

"Open the door, open the door."

I opened it and the slut came in, still dressed to go out, in tiny shining gold shorts with half her butt hanging out, a tight little see-through shirt showing off her beautiful naked breasts, and white spike-heeled boots. The girl was a trip, with her black hair hanging loose. But the bitch is like a cash register. She won't sleep with anyone unless she gets money for it. Lots of times I've tried to recruit her for our little rooftop orgies, but there's no way. She's hypnotized by Yankees and dollars. The only time she has an orgasm with a client must be when they push a rolled-up bill into her cunt.

"What do you want, tits?"

"Show some respect, Pedro Juan."

"Respect for what?"

Going over to Isabel, she prodded her awake.

"Come on, Isabel. The plastic man arrived yesterday."

When Isabel heard that, she shot right up:

"When, girl?"

"Yesterday. And he told me to tell you to come over."

I tried to butt in, since there was money involved.

"What do you mean, plastic man?"

"He's an American who comes here every few months. I'll explain later."

In ten minutes, Isabel was dressed in her white bodysuit, carrying a little leather backpack, wearing lots of perfume and cheap jewelry, her hair combed out big. Happy and laughing, she gave me a kiss, saying, "Don't wait up for me, sweetie. I've got my work cut out for me tonight. I won't be back till tomorrow at the earliest."

"All right, goodbye. Take care of yourself."

The day passed, quiet and stifling. It gets hotter every year. I sold some cigarettes I had and bought a pizza and a soda. Great diet. I was down to 150 pounds from 200, which is what I should weigh.

The night passed, me sitting slumped on the Malecón, not a cent in my pocket, no rum, no food, no joints to puff and get high on. Luckily, that crazy, old fat woman didn't show up again. I went to bed early, but I slept very badly; it was anxiety, hunger, cockroaches wandering around, a rat gnawing, and a presence in Isabel's room. The place needed to be purged, cleansed with coconut and herbs. It isn't clear exactly what's wrong, but Isabel is bad about caring for the *santos*, and that's why it's so murky in here. Finally I slept a little, troubled by nightmares, fears, and a terrible stink of shit coming from the bathroom; for two days there'd been no water. People haul it up in buckets for cooking or washing, but shit floods the toilet in the bathroom and there are—how many of us? I don't know. The count is always shifting, but there are fewer now. In the seven rooms, there must be forty of us, more or less. It's enough. There's still plenty of shit and piss. At last the sun came up. I lay in bed a little longer, exhausted, and I fell asleep again. Then Isabel came home, dead tired.

"Oh sweetie, that American kept me up all night, and now I'm exhausted and my cunt stings. My God, what an idiot; he's a moron!"

"So, explain: does the guy have a plastic dick?"

"No, no. It's the head of it, that's all. The whole head is plastic. It's a prosthesis. But he couldn't come, not with Susi or with me."

"Both of you at the same time?"

"Yes, yes. We spent all night trying and he didn't come. I left him with Yakelín. It'll take him ten days."

"Is it because of the plastic head?"

"Of course, since the only feeling he has is in the little piece of shaft. And you should see the tantrums he throws. The things we have to put up with . . ."

"How much did he pay you?"

"One hundred bucks. He pays a hundred a night. Haven't I ever told you about him?"

"No."

"Oh, I guess it's been a year since he was here last. That American . . . well . . . there are six of us . . . Susi, Yakelín, Mirtica, Lili, Sonia, and me. And we call each other up and take turns until finally he comes with one of us. And then we start all over again, because the guy never wants to stop. Sometimes he's here for three weeks, and it's night after night, without a break. When he finally comes then he relaxes, and he takes us out to dinner and we go dancing."

"And you got your hundred bucks?"

"Yeah, baby. Here it is. But it'll be my turn again in three or four days. We stick to that Yankee like glue and don't let anybody else near him. He's our meal ticket, honey."

"Isabel, I've got to eat something now before I pass out."

"I'm stuffed. I ate a breakfast fit for a queen, even toast and butter and pastries. Here, take five dollars and see what you can find."

"You already changed the hundred?"

"Oh, and what exactly were you expecting? You want me to let you have the big bill? So it'll be gone by the end of the day? No way, sugar. I had to sweat too hard with that piece of plastic stuck inside me for you to waste it all in one day on weed and rum. None of that. Do what you can with what I gave you. I'm going to sleep. And don't wake me up . . . Fuck, the bathroom reeks . . . it stinks like shit! . . . a person can't sleep in here."

"There hasn't been any water for two days."

"Well, to hell with it. I'm dead. Don't wake me up just because you feel like it, sweetie, or you'll be sorry."

I went to get pizza and a soda. Thank goodness for the windfall. God may punish us, but he never forsakes us.

3:17 / The Cannibals

Day was dawning, a red-orange stain behind heavy, dirty-gray clouds. At the mouth of the bay, the water was calm but very cold. And I was almost frozen.

I had been fishing all night, floating thirteen hundred feet from shore, sitting in the hollow of a little raft made from an inner tube. Floating nearby were at least twenty other fishermen like me, but September and October aren't good months. It had been sixteen days since I'd caught anything. I was like that old man from Cojímar who went fishing alone in his boat on the Gulf Stream and didn't catch a fish for eighty-four days.

Except that old man was a hero in the classic sense, worn down to the bone but never vanquished. There's no heroism in me, or in anybody else anymore. These days, no one is as stubborn as he was or has such a sense of duty or devotion to their work. The spirit of the age is commercial. Money. And if it's dollars, all the better. The stuff heroes are made of gets scarcer every day.

That's why politicians and clergymen talk themselves hoarse urging loyalty and solidarity. They have to keep trying or else change professions. But those of us who are hungry stay hungry, and nothing changes. The politicians and the clergymen think they can make everything change by sheer force of will, by spontaneous generation. But that's not the way things work. We human beings are still savages, treacherous and egotistical. We like to break off from the pack and keep watch from a distance, eluding the snapping jaws of our fellows. Then someone comes along asking us to be loyal to the pack.

The wisest doctrine I've ever heard was preached by an old anarchist recluse who lived near me when I was little, in San Francisco de Paula. The old man worked as the night watchman for a big American with sideburns who drove a black Cadillac and lived on a fine country estate. Sometimes I'd go there for the view of Havana; you could see the city from the hill where the house sat. I'd sneak in because the American was bad-tempered and he didn't like trespassers. I'd sit down and talk to Pedro Pablo, who helped in the garden during the day, and he'd say to me, "Life should be governed by two basic laws. The first: every human being has the right to do whatever he wants. And the second: nobody is required to obey the first law."

I've always remembered old Pedro Pablo's laws. But I haven't been able to live by them very often. Most of the time I've had to follow the crowd. Anyway, back then, forty years ago, people had lifelong occupations and they were able to make a living working at them. I get the impression everybody knew their places and kept to them, without being so ambitious and making life difficult for themselves.

Now everyone is scattered. No one knows where they belong or what they should do. They don't even know what they really want, or where they're headed, or where they should settle down. We're all scrambling desperately for money. We do whatever it takes to get a little bit of it, and then we move on to the next scheme and the next. All we've accomplished in the end is to become part of a huge, messy free-for-all.

Oh, I was thinking too much. Anyway, my butt and balls were wet, and I could feel twinges in my aching joints. It was bad for me to spend the night alone, fishing on this little raft. After all, what did I care if people were mixed up or not. My job was to catch big fish, and if there weren't any to catch, then to deflate the inner tube, pack it up with all my other gear, work at something else, and wait until December. When the wind started blowing from the north, there'd be fish again. Porgies and grouper especially, which are tame and easy to catch. Not like the noble blue marlins, the brave, crafty fish old Santiago chased right around here, near Havana.

Now the sun was all the way up, yellow and blurred in the haze. There were too many threatening clouds. Hurricane season: sticky humidity, heat, and strong winds from the south. Terrible weather that wears me out and gives me a headache.

Gathering up my gear, I swam back to Havana with my flippers on. The buyers didn't even glance at me. When I'm loaded down, they come running up to me, all smiles, like I'm their best friend. I went back to the building. I climbed up to the roof and deflated the tube. Isabel was just getting up.

"What are you doing that for, Pedro Juan? Aren't you going to fish anymore?"

"I haven't caught anything for almost twenty days. I'll have to wait until the wind's out of the north. This south wind . . ."

"Then what will we live on?"

"You can hustle a little on the Malecón. Go out tonight."

"Oh right, that's easy for you to say. Remember I already have two warnings from the police. If I'm picked up again, I'm doing time."

I didn't answer. I didn't feel like getting into a stupid argument. Isabel is a fighter and a hard worker, but sometimes she makes me tired with all her idiotic babbling. I poured a little fresh water over my head. It had been days since we'd had soap. If we lived like this much longer, we'd get scabies. I ate a little piece of bread, drank some sugar water, and went to bed. I fell asleep the minute my head hit the pillow.

When I woke up, it was two in the afternoon. I opened my eyes and lay there for a while staring up at the ceiling, my mind racing:

What to do now? The guy next door was still making tin buckets, but he didn't want a helper. I didn't have a cent. So long as Isabel kept hustling, we could make it until December. Even better, maybe she'd take off with some Yankee. That way she could support me from far away. And if she forgot about me, it wouldn't matter. Deep down, I don't expect anything from anybody. I'd have to go work on that damn garbage truck again. It seems I was born to work at night. If only I could get a job riding with a truck driver, that would be pure happiness. Then, after a while, I'd become a driver and get my license. That's the job for me. Always on the road, always moving. Well, at least this afternoon I'd go looking for Pollo. He'd have weed. I'd sell a few joints for him and that way I'd make enough to keep on until who knows when.

Isabel wasn't home. There wasn't any coffee. I went out on the roof for a while so I wouldn't have to think. The sky was still hazy and gray. It reminded me of the country, when I was little. In San Francisco de Paula we had two cows, chickens, goats. If I live to be an old man, I'll go back to the country. I'll find myself an old woman and go. And if there's no old woman to be had, I'll go alone. In the hills there's more than enough land, but we all want to be here, piled up on top of each other. If God grants me good health, when I've had enough of the rat race I'm going back to the country.

So there I was, staring out at the Caribbean, with no idea what the fuck I could do to make a few pesos. A new guy on the roof came up to me. He was from the provinces, from the country. We're all from the country, where things are bad. Much worse than in Havana because there are no pesos to be had out there. Here at least I would probably scrape something up this afternoon, even if it was selling weed. The guy started a conversation with me, speaking with a pretty lilt. He had to be from the east.

"Hey, man, I haven't seen you before. You live here?"

"I've lived here forever."

"Oh . . . well, I guess I'm the new guy then. Let me introduce myself. Baldomero."

And he put out his hand, tough and callused. He was a working man, a skinny, dirty guy, with sideburns and ruined teeth. He kept laughing; he was trying to make me like him. I stretched out my hand.

"Pedro Juan."

"Oh, well, we're neighbors, brother. I live with Vivian."

"With Vivian? Since when?"

"Umm . . . well . . . for months now, but . . . I've only been here, here in Havana for a few days."

"Ohh."

Vivian is a big, tough, white girl with bleached blond hair; a slick operator. She knows how to handle herself, and she's always clean, smelling of perfume, well-dressed, with a gold chain around her neck. She had nothing in common with this pathetic specimen, who looked like he should be out on the street begging.

"Is Vivian home?"

"Yes. She's listening to a soap opera on the radio, and I came out to get some fresh air."

"My man. Let's go see if she has any coffee."

Vivian let me have some coffee and then returned to her soap opera. I went back out onto the roof with Baldomero.

"So what do you do here, brother? How do you make ends meet? It's tough in Havana. It wasn't easy for me back home, either, but this is even worse," Baldomero said.

"No, it's the other way around. Here at least there's some action. But you just got here."

"Maybe that's it. It's my first time in Havana. And I can't go back. I have nowhere to go."

"What do you mean?"

"Ah."

"You're strong, Baldomero. You could do any kind of work."

"Yes. I'm thin because I always have been, ever since I was little. But I'm strong. In the country I did all kinds of things."

"Well, man, get a move on, because up here on the roof, you'll starve to death."

"Vivian says she knows some guys in the market at Cuatro Caminos. I'm going to see them tomorrow. If they give me a job . . ."

"I worked there for a while, and they paid me thirty pesos a day. But just so you know: it's Monday to Sunday from six in the morning or earlier until six or seven at night. It's rough."

"But there's always money to be made."

"Sure. You get a little business going on the side and you pull in something extra."

"That's my plan. I think I'll go over there right now. Is it far?"

"No. Head up Belascoaín, walk ten or twelve blocks, and you'll see it."

For the next few days, the guy was everywhere at once, always filthy, bristling with sideburns, and talking up a storm. He did everything from clearing rubble to hauling sacks at the market. But he was always smiling, always cool. A month later we ran into each other on the roof, and he raised his glass of rum to me.

"It's been days since we talked, brother. Hang out and have a drink."

Going into his room, he came back out with a full glass.

"I've got a bottle in there. When it's empty, I'll buy another one."

"Damn it, Baldomero, have you made your fortune already?"

"Not exactly. I'm making a few pesos . . . I have a business that's bringing in a little cash."

"Ah."

"I'm selling pork liver."

"Ah."

"It doesn't do well at the market. I get it for cheap and I sell it on the side."

"Ah."

"I have some in the fridge. It's great. If you hear of anyone who wants some, send them to me."

"Pork liver is good."

"And good for you too! I'm going to give you a piece. You're a good guy."

"No, no, Baldomero, that's your business you're talking about. You can't give away your livelihood."

"Listen, friend, one little piece of liver isn't going to make or break me."

He went into Vivian's room and came out with a big piece. Isabel cooked it Italian style, with lots of garlic, and it was delicious. It was so big we had it for two meals. Later I bought some from him twice. He didn't charge much.

In a few months, Baldomero had moved up in the world. He bought clothes for himself, but he still looked like a filthy, pathetic slob. A shadow had fallen over Vivian, as if Baldomero's filth and grime had settled on her skin. She didn't work deals anymore, and she never left the house. She had always been a cheerful, friendly woman, married many times, throwing parties that lasted late into the night. Now she was quiet, withdrawn. Baldomero brought home more liver every day. He had regular customers and—to get himself in people's good graces—he'd often give a piece to one or another of the neighbors.

December came, and I was waiting for the first wind from the north to set out to sea again. I had a little marijuana hidden in my room. We were getting along selling that, because Isabel had decided she wanted to play wife, claiming that Yankees made her sick.

"Who cares if they make you sick? Unless you go fuck one of them, we're going to starve to death."

"Oh, honey, don't be mean. The only man I want is you."

"Don't blink those big eyes at me. You've been playing house for three months now, but when I met you, you were the biggest slut around."

"Nothing lasts forever. And I've had enough. Just drop it. Every day it's the same old story. Roll us a joint; there's nothing else to do."

"All right . . . fine, that's better . . . so why don't you wash and iron for someone or look for a job in Miramar?"

"I told you to drop it, or we'll just end up fighting."

"Close the door."

We like to smoke together and drink rum. When we're high, we fuck for hours and hours without stopping. My prick gets like an iron rod. I pulled out the weed and started rolling a joint. There was a loud knock at the door.

"It's the police. Open up."

My balls shrank. I hid everything under the mattress. It was the only thing I could think to do. Now I was in deep shit! I had two kilos of weed!

There was no time to think. They knocked hard again. Isabel started to shake. But she opened the door. A policeman looked in.

"Do you have a refrigerator?"

"No. Why?"

They had Baldomero handcuffed. He was carrying a plastic bag. Grabbing him by the neck, they shoved him forward.

"Has this citizen ever sold you liver?"

"Sold us liver? No."

"Are you sure?"

"Sure."

"Have you ever eaten liver provided by this citizen?"

"No."

"Lucky for you."

My balls dropped back down into their usual position. I stayed in the doorway taking in the scene. The policemen went asking from room to room. Everyone denied it. No one had eaten liver provided by the citizen in question. The two policemen decided to change their tactic. They stood in the middle of the roof with Baldomero in his handcuffs carrying the plastic bag. All the neighbors were watching nervously and suspiciously from their doorways. The same policeman spoke. The other one never said anything. He just put on a watch-it-I've-got-a-big-stick face.

"People, listen up. This citizen here was caught by a guard this afternoon just as he was coming out of the morgue with a bag full of human livers . . ."

A murmur from the neighbors interrupted the policeman.

"Let me finish. This citizen has been working at the morgue for two months, and we suspect he's stolen livers from the corpses on other occasions to sell them on the black market, passing them off as pig livers. We need witnesses . . ."

Another murmur from the crowd. An old lady was the first to take the plunge.

"You son of a bitch! You've brought shame upon me! It's true, officer, it's true he was selling us liver! The son of a bitch deserves to die!"

Isabel and I looked at each other. I couldn't help laughing. Isabel was screwing up her face in disgust.

"Listen, Isabel, it's already been eaten and crapped. Forget about it. Anyway, the way you fixed it, it was delicious. It tasted great."

"Don't be an animal, Pedro Juan!"

"Let the old ladies have Baldomero. I'm not going to testify against anyone. What I am going to do is blow up the inner tube and fix up my gear. I think tonight I'm going fishing."

"Oh, thank goodness. I'll light a candle to the Virgen de la Caridad for you."

I picked up the inner tube and went downstairs to blow it up. Baldomero watched as the policemen took notes and the indignant old ladies presented their accusations. And he smiled. The idiot smiled. I don't know why. It must have been out of fear.

Cancer rotted his insides and killed him in a matter of months. He was barely thirty-two, and people called him "Santico," or Little Saint, though he was a diabolical son of a bitch. He sold avocados, mangoes, onions, anything, from a two-wheeled cart, making a few pesos each day to spend on women, rum, and cigars.

His wife, Danais, was twenty, and she was beautiful, an adorable mulatta. She fell madly in love with Santico. When he died, she almost lost her mind. Thirteen people were all living in the same room, blacks, mulattos, and mestizos. Things were a little calmer for them once Santiago died, because he used to come home drunk at all hours of the night. First he'd beat Danais, then fuck her later. He liked to see her cry. And he was just as rough with everyone else. Almost every night it was the same: blows, tears, shouts, and then sex and gasps. The rest of the brothers, sisters, cousins, nieces, and nephews would pretend to be asleep and let them do their thing in the dark. Thirteen people living together in a damp, ramshackle sixteen-by-twenty-foot room, reeking of sweat and filth, the bathroom and kitchen outside shared with fifty other neighbors. Living that way, it was impossible to keep secrets or have a private life. But no one got upset. It was the way things were.

Santico had always been a bastard. He liked blood and knife fights. He was a fighter, and he was brave. His *santo* was Oggún. In a corner of the room were Oggún's iron pot and his miniature tool irons, warrior figurines, the glasses of *aguardiente* and the cigars, the plates of avocado, cassava, pepper, garlic. Thunderstones, rods of ironwood and *camagua* and *jagüey*, stewed greens. A chain, a machete, an anvil, a knife.

Santico died before he was ready. He didn't want to go while he was still so young, so strong and virile. The end came quickly, but he suffered horribly, vomiting up dark blood. It was a wretched, disgusting death. Danais was left with the tool irons and necklaces of green and black beads. When she came back from the cemetery, she cried for two days without stopping, until Santico's mother managed to console her. The old lady had nine children—now there were eight—and seven grandchildren. She knew a thing or two about life.

When Danais felt better, she went to the market. She came back with a rooster, a pigeon, and a dog, all alive, and tied them up in a corner of the room. Each week, on Monday or Friday, she would kill a chicken and sprinkle the blood on the iron pot, mixing in a little bit of honey for sweetening. Danais was still very sad. She wouldn't talk to anyone. Men's compliments upset her, and whenever a man approached her, even with the best of intentions, she'd be rude to him. One night Santico came to her in her dreams and murmured in her ear, "Come with me, Danais. I've come to get you."

She saw him laughing and walking toward her. Opening her eyes, she woke up trembling with fear. Above her, in the darkness of the room, a hazy red light was spinning. Danais shivered as she crossed herself, and she prayed.

"Have mercy, Lord, make his soul be lifted up, Lord, have mercy."

But his soul was not free to rise, because though no one knew it, Santico had killed three men in late-night, back-street brawls, and he had wounded many others. He had caused too much pain, and now he was paying for it. Danais didn't tell anyone, but Santico kept appearing to her. Every day she was more obsessed with him.

She put out flowers, glasses of water, and candles, and she prayed for his soul, but Santico kept tormenting her even in death. He wanted Danais with him.

Santico's mother tried to get her to go back and live with her parents. Danais was from Guantánamo. But she wouldn't go. She wanted to stay a while longer.

"Let me help him to rise up, grannie. Let me help him. I love him so much."

The old woman understood and let her do as she wished. Danais wasn't afraid anymore, and now she liked it when he came to her at night while everyone was sleeping. He'd appear, take off his shirt and pants, and with his cock already stiff, he'd penetrate her. She'd come many times, panting, and he'd fade away. Danais never woke up; she'd be exhausted. The next morning, she'd feel damp, and that was proof it wasn't all just a dream. She had many orgasms while she was asleep. She liked it. Santico hardly ever spoke on his visits.

She'd leave a glass of *aguardiente* and a cigar next to the iron pot. Sometimes he'd walk toward her, smiling, and sit down next to her on the floor, without speaking. Danais would wake up, and the hazy red light would be spinning overhead. She wasn't afraid of it anymore. Once she got up and went over to the pot, picked up the glass of *aguardiente*, and drank it down in one gulp. She fell exhausted again onto the mattress on the floor where she always slept. And there was Santico, laughing and happy, savoring the alcohol. Then he got in bed with her and mounted her as if he were a wild pony and she were a mare. An hour or two went by. He came three times and still his penis was stiff. When they finished, he wanted to have more *aguardiente* and smoke his cigar. They didn't talk. There was no need. But they understood each other. She got up again and went over to the pot, picking up the cigar and lighting it. Sitting on the floor and leaning against the wall, she smoked it, half-asleep and half-awake. Santico was smoking, but he didn't have any *aguardiente*, and he liked to drink hard after fucking. His mood had changed. He hit Danais, and she cried. He hit her more. Getting excited again, he took her once more right there on the damp, dirty floor, next to the irons of Oggún, on the rooster, dog, and pigeon droppings. She thought she was asleep, and she didn't realize what was happening. She could feel him pushing deep into her with his big, long, powerful prick. Everyone else heard her rolling around and panting in the dark. They turned on the light and there she was, naked on the floor with her legs spread and raised, her sex quivering, radiant, making love to the air, buffeted by blows to her face. Everyone was afraid. Santico's mother took charge. Grabbing a jar of holy water mixed with perfume of seven powers, she went to Danais and sprinkled her with the liquid, praying, "Have mercy, Lord. Have mercy. Give her peace, Virgen de las Mercedes. All powerful Obatalá, give her peace. Have mercy, Lord. Let her be lifted up, Obatalá; don't make her suffer anymore."

She rubbed Danais's head and neck with the holy water, then her arms and legs. At last the girl came back to herself. She didn't know what had happened. She threw her arms around the old lady, crying, "Oh, he comes every night! He comes every night! And I like it when he comes."

"It's over now; it's over now."

The old woman soothed Danais, and she understood exactly what the girl meant. But she kept quiet. When everyone had calmed down, she turned off the light, and they all went back to sleep. After the first shock, no one was surprised. They all knew Santico wouldn't go quietly, without a fight. A ceremony would have to be held for him: two, three, ten rites for his soul, as many as were necessary to make it rise up. Everyone was thinking the same thing, but no one said anything. It's best not to cross the dead. Only Santico's mother, as she got back into bed, said very softly to herself, "He thinks he's still alive. Poor thing. We've got to help him rise up."

The next day she got up early to arrange for the ceremony. She went to see a friend of hers who would make a good job of it. When she came back two hours later, she found Danais lying on the floor next to Oggún's pot.

"Danais, we're going to have the ceremony on Monday, which is when my friend can do it. So there are five days to go. But what's wrong with you? Why are you on the floor?"

"I don't know. I don't feel like going out."

"Stop being silly, girl. Take your box of avocados and go sit out on the sidewalk and sell them. Or do you expect me to support you now?"

"No, grannie, no, I'm going. I'm just so sad and tired . . . I don't know what's wrong with me."

Danais willed herself to get up. Gathering the avocados and some lemons, she arranged them on a wooden stool on the sidewalk in front of the building. That was how she made her living. Every day she'd be outside selling something. She was busying herself at her stool when a neighbor lady called out to her, "Danais, look how swollen your legs are! What's wrong with them?"

Danais kept working and didn't pay much attention. Young people never give a thought to illness. By evening, her feet, calves, and thighs were red and irritated. She picked up her stool and went inside.

"Tomorrow I'm going to the doctor. This looks like an infection."

That night Santico didn't come to her. She saw him in the distance, walking through the hanging vines. He was avoiding her; he wouldn't look her in the face. She was standing naked in a clearing, at the foot of a sacred *ceiba* tree. Santico circled around, but he didn't come close. He showed her his beautiful erect penis, and then he was gone, laughing in the bushes. After that, she walked all night. It was damp and cold until the misty dawn came, and she was naked and barefoot, gorgeous with her hair hanging loose, but exhausted from walking for so long, her skin scratched by thorns and the underbrush. Danais knew she was alone and lost in the forest. The next day, she could barely stand. She was tired and her legs were even more swollen. Her skin was irritated and stretched tight, and her scratches burned. She had always been a beautiful mulatta, with dark cinnamon-colored skin, but now she was dazed, and she had dark circles under her eyes. In just a few days, she had grown very weak. Santico's mother was alarmed; not for nothing had she lived so long.

"No, Danais, you're not going to the hospital. You and I are going somewhere else together."

Rómulo, a sixty-five year old *santería* elder, lived in the room next door. He was a learned and dignified man, not a huckster like those ignorant, crafty kids who fool the unsuspecting and pocket their money. People respected Rómulo. When he saw the two of them coming, he nodded hello. To the old woman, he said, "I knew you were coming. But you waited too long. Why didn't you bring her in sooner? You should know better. You're not twenty years old."

"But Rómulo, your cures are expensive, and I thought . . . ."

"Quality costs money. Let's see what we can do. Come over here."

Rómulo had his *santos* behind a screen. The three of them sat on the floor. In the middle of the circle, he placed the chart of Ifá. He tossed a handful of cowrie shells, without speaking. He tossed them again, slowly, twice, then three times, meditating all the while. And still he didn't speak.

"What will be, will be. Take her to the doctor and see what he can do for her."

"Rómulo, by God!" said the old lady.

"Don't be afraid, but pray for her. Take her to the doctor. There's nothing I can do."

Danais didn't understand what was happening. She was too young to understand. She wasn't very worldly. Santico had fallen in love with her and plucked her from the wood and guano hut where she lived with her parents and eight brothers and sisters on top of a hill surrounded by neglected coffee fields thick with weeds. She was eighteen years old. She had been out of school for nine years, and the only work she could get was picking coffee at each harvest, side by side with her parents and whichever brothers and sisters were still around. Most of the men left the mountains near Baracoa to look for work elsewhere. It was thanks to them that the family didn't literally starve to death. Each year there was less money to be made picking coffee. When Santico met Danais, it had been a very long time since she had shoes or underwear or soap or anything at all. Half-wild and innocent as she was, he fell in love with her, and she was ready to fall in love with the first person who would take her away from that place forever. When Santico made love to her in his fashion, furiously, battering her relentlessly like a four-day rainstorm, she was left speechless. She had been with her three or four other boyfriends many times, but it had never been like that. She was caught forever in that beautiful black man's steely nets; he was the most macho of men. She had been taught to worship men, to surrender herself wholly and enslave herself to them. That was the way it had always been in those mountains, and it would be that way forever.

Danais went away with him. Santico brought her to Havana and shut her up in the family's room. The girl from Guantánamo was too pretty to be allowed out much in the neighborhood, which was full of predators. Anyway, she was too naïve. She didn't know anything about anything, and anyone could have told her some story and wheedled her away from Santico. As a result, she was only allowed to go out with him. The rest of the time she had to stay in the room, safe within its four walls. He covered her eyes with his hand and wouldn't let her budge. And she gave in without making a fuss. In fact, she was happy. She was satisfied with his confining love. It was what she had always known.

They went straight from Rómulo's house to the hospital. The old woman was skeptical. The doctors' diagnosis was late-stage phlebitis. They admitted Danais so they could put her through a course of antibiotics. The antibiotics weren't quite the right ones for such a serious case. But there wasn't anything else at the hospital, so they had no choice. That night Danais swelled up even more: her hands, her arms, her whole torso. The next morning, she was moved to an intensive-care ward. The doctors wouldn't say exactly what was wrong with her. Sidestepping the old lady's questions, they would only repeat, "It's a difficult case. We're studying it."

They injected antibiotics directly into her veins. A few hours later, she fell into a coma. They gave her oxygen. Santico came to her, laughing, and moved up close to her. When she saw him, she started to laugh too, and she took off her clothes. The nurse sitting next to her couldn't understand why she was laughing, and he tried to hold her down so she couldn't strip. If she was really out of her head and unconscious, why and how was she moving that way?

Danais and Santico are in the forest, in the shade of a huge old fig tree. Santico strips and puts on a necklace of black and green beads. He puts another around her neck. His organ is like a bull pizzle, big and hard. Santico is in good spirits but restless, as always. He can never be still, night or day. From behind some bushes, the ever-vigilant god of roads and evildoing keeps watch with his snail eyes. He is Oggún's friend. They travel together, doing as they please, raping the women whose paths cross theirs and starting fights wherever they go. Santico buries a bloody nail in the earth. He is valiant, drunk, stormy. He has spilled rivers of blood. He has hurt many people. Wary, he fears he will be made to pay. He always faces forward, and he watches his back. He fears, and he is feared. He lives in a rage. Eternal and magnificent chief of warriors, he has never been happy. When he touches Danais, she feels his cold, hard hand with its metallic promise of death. He smells like furious steel, lord of metal and of the forge, iron and fire. He penetrates her without warning, no gentle first touch, and she surrenders, swooning like a maiden, abandoning herself to pleasure. The tip of his penis has barely touched her when she comes, and she comes again and again. They are rolling on the ground and in the damp grass. Oggún demands the juices of this beautiful, innocent maiden, who has given herself up to love. She convulses. The nurse tries to keep her on the bed, but the girl is possessed by a supernatural force. She bucks and jerks her hips as if she is making love, and she sighs and snaps her teeth and screams, finally rolling with a crash to the floor. Death sweeps her up in its embrace, and everything is over. Panting, her face transfigured, she is pierced by a wind that suddenly sweeps through the dense forest. Santico withdraws, his penis still engorged, leaving her lying on the ground; he beats her. Then he goes, passing between the *ceiba* and *jocuma* and *camagua* trees. A dog, a rooster, and a pigeon run and fly behind him, howling and screeching. He leaves her defenseless and abandoned, crying, suffering cruelly, alone in the terrible forest, caught up in a storm, and overwhelmed by the wind, rain, thunder, and lightning. She doesn't understand what has happened, and she never will.

All night, Chicha could hear a big rat rattling her pots and pans, and she practically pissed herself she was so scared. The rat was bold; it felt right at home. It had come up an old rotten pipe from the basement. Eight floors it would climb until it came out into the open. Then it would jump down onto the roof and forage in piles of garbage or slip into one of the rooms.

Since at least fifty people were crowded into the seven rooms built on the roof bit by bit over the past thirty years, enough odd corners and food scraps were guaranteed. Chicha thought there was only one rat, because one afternoon at dusk she had seen where it came up and how it neatly jumped three feet up. In fact, many others followed that athletic rat, and at night they ruled the roof. In the basement there was only damp air, mud, rotting boards, rusting iron and wires, pipes, nothing at all appealing. Some of the rats dared to prowl the doorways and filthy sidewalks of the Malecón, and they'd always find something, though they were continually being startled by other nocturnal fauna: whores, drunks, police, panhandlers.

At last it was morning, and Chicha got up fearfully to assess the damage. The rat had knocked the lid off a pot holding leftovers of beans and potatoes. He had eaten almost everything; he had even shat on the table. There were little puddles next to the pot. Chicha had always been sloppy and careless, but this was too much. She opened the door to her room, put the pot on the ground outside and filled it with water. Just then, her sister Tita came bustling in, her wide smile revealing enormous plastic teeth that didn't quite fit her gums and threatened to shoot out of her mouth and hit whoever she was talking to.

"Good morning!"

"What do you mean, good morning? Don't start."

"What, you're already in a bad mood?"

"Bad mood or good, leave me alone."

"A person should be polite and treat others courteously no matter what."

"Enough, Tita. Don't play schoolteacher with me."

"Didn't you sleep well?"

"I couldn't sleep all night. Do you remember the rat that came up in the pipes and jumped out onto the roof?"

"Yes."

"Last night he got in my room. And he went through all the pots looking for food. It was awful!"

"Awful? Not so awful. Worse things have happened to me. Why didn't you get up, turn on the light, and beat it to death? What you are is helpless, woman."

"All right, all right!"

"When my husband left me and I was all alone with four children . . ."

"Tita, enough, for God's sake. You're a fucking lunatic."

"And you can't even talk without being rude and swearing. But you can't hurt my feelings. Because what you just said really is something a crazy, mixed-up person would say. Somebody who's scared, immature . . ."

They kept arguing, just as they always had, exasperating each other. Chicha had been alone for six years, ever since her husband died. Now she was sixty-nine. Tita was her younger sister, and she'd come over a few times a week to look after Chicha. All she really did was drink coffee and chain-smoke and shout and get into fights with her. They couldn't stand each other.

"Tita, are you going to clean the room today?"

"Don't boss me around! I'm not your maid."

"Oh, Tita, for God's sake, you're driving me crazy. Aren't you here to help me? What do you come for?"

"To keep you company since not even your daughters can stand you. Somebody has to do God's bidding."

"The hell with God! You come just to torment me acting crazy the way you do."

"You see? That's why no one wants to be around you. Because you're rude and disrespectful. Show me some respect. I'm a good Christian, you know . . ."

"That's crap. God doesn't exist. If he did, people wouldn't be as hungry or as poor as they are . . ."

"It's the same old story. There you go again with communism and politics and insults. And where has all that gotten you, girl, tell me, where? God hasn't solved our problems, it's true, but communism hasn't either. Just look at the way we live."

"Tita, it's impossible to talk to you, you're such an illiterate."

"And you're so wise and full of learning. La Capitana . . . ahhh . . . fancy that."

"Enough, enough. Go on, go, even if it's just out to get bread."

"I will go, because sitting up here in this pigeon coop listening to you bad-mouth God and everybody else . . ."

"All right, enough, go out and get some bread."

After Tita had gone downstairs, Chicha remembered a dream she'd had the afternoon before when she dozed off in her armchair. Her sister was begging for change on the street, filthy, barefoot, and ragged, clutching a tiny statue of the Virgin in her left hand and holding out her right, sleeping on park benches. She was sure it was a premonition. She had always had these visions. She had seen how everyone she knew would die. Before her father hanged himself, she had seen him hanging himself with a heavy rope in recurring dreams for ten years. The same thing happened before her husband died. He was still in good shape, even though he was sixty-four years old, but in a dream, she saw him climbing an avocado tree. He was happy and laughing, without a care in the·world, and then he slipped trying to reach some fruit and fell headfirst to the ground. When he really did fall, he suffered a fatal concussion.

Chicha paid no attention to her premonitions. "Coincidence," she'd say. She had been hungry too often and suffered too much. When she worked in rich people's houses as a cook, she was humiliated beyond measure. If God could let such things happen, there was no God. When the Revolution triumphed, she got a job on the police force. She was given a pistol and a uniform, and she said to herself, "Now it's my turn; I'll show them." So that's what she did. She devoted herself to imposing iron-fisted order and discipline on everyone around her. Eight years ago, she retired. A little while later, her husband died. And it was then that she was seized by an uncontrollable fear of leaving her room, of going out on the stairs, of her neighbors, of everything. She was convinced she would be murdered if she set foot outside her room. It was only within her own four walls that she felt safe. She didn't have enough money or food, and she turned sickly, skin-and-bones thin, with a permanent cold that caused her to hawk smelly phlegm in every corner. Then she realized that she was absolutely alone. Her family couldn't stand her and neither could her neighbors. Nobody even wanted to go and buy her daily ration of bread for her. Instead of calling her Chicha, they called her "La Capitana." And they avoided her. There she was, all alone, hungry, sick, living in filth, with her two sagging armchairs and a mattress losing its stuffing, in her squalid twelve-foot-square room. She had never milked the Revolution for her own profit. She was utterly honest, convinced that the only way to behave as a righteous revolutionary was to uphold honor, authority, order, discipline, self-control, and austerity. Now, penniless and starving, sometimes she despaired. In one corner stood a little bookcase crammed with the works of Mao, Lenin, Marx, Kim Il Sung, speeches, *Sputnik* magazines, old *Selecciones*. Looking at all those dusty books, she sighed deeply, picked up a magazine from 1957 and opened it at random. An interview with Frank Lloyd Wright: "How long will we last if we are stripped of our poetic principles? How long can a civilization last without a soul? Science can't save us: it has led us to the edge of the abyss. It will have to be art and religion, which house the soul of civilization."

Snapping the magazine closed, she tossed it aside.

"Spineless Americans!"

She sat for a while in the doorway, in her ragged armchair. A man was going back and forth hauling bricks. He'd climb eight flights of stairs carrying ten bricks, drop them in his room, and go back for more. He was only wearing pants cut off at the knee, and he was barefoot. A fine white-gray dust of lime and cement had settled on his black skin, shiny with sweat. To Chicha he looked like a living sculpture, a sculpture of plaster or cement or rough stone. He was a young man, tall and well-muscled. A strange sight, a walking sculpture. The man was hauling bricks from some demolished building and stockpiling them in his room to build an illegal wall or a loft. Everyone did it, adding partitions here and there. They tore down walls, knocked holes, and added rooms, using rotting boards, sheets of plastic, loose bricks, whatever they could find. More and more people were always moving into the little twelve-by-fifteen- or fifteen-by-fifteen-foot rooms, like roaches. Sometimes twelve or thirteen people managed to cram themselves into those dark little holes. It was forbidden to make changes to city buildings. But everybody did it without asking permission. They filled up every available space and they sent away for more relatives from the country. Or they had more and more children and they all piled up on top of each other.

Chicha said nothing. A few years ago she would have gone to see what they were doing, so she could lay down the law and demand that they apply for official permission from the city for their renovations, or else she would get the police and the inspectors from the Municipal Bureau of Architecture and Urban Affairs to tear everything down. Everything had to be done with the proper documentation and organization. Not anymore. Now she just let things happen. She didn't care. None of the neighbors on the roof would look at her or talk to her. And she never looked at anyone or talked to them either. It was as simple as that.

She picked up an old *Sputnik* magazine from 1982 and started to read a soothing article called "The Project of the Century: The Baikal-Amur Railroad," losing herself on the frozen steppes where young heroes unfurled red flags at their work camps.

At the bakery, Tita discovered she didn't even have the five cents she needed to buy bread. And she was overcome by a depression that made her feel like the most wretched person in the world. A few tears ran down her cheeks. And the girl behind the counter gave her the bread for free.

"You don't have five cents? Take the bread, but don't cry in here because it'll bring me bad luck."

Tita took the bread, but when she heard that, she started crying in earnest, sobbing and sniffling.

"Go on. Go on."

The girl hustled her out. Everybody in the neighborhood knew Tita was half-crazy. What nobody knew was that her husband had abandoned her and her four children when she was young and pretty, back when she still wore perfume and washed her face, but now she never bathed or cleaned the house or looked after her children. She was a pig with the face of a butterfly. She spent all her money on coffee and cigarettes. When she realized she had been abandoned, she went mad and she spent three years in bed, utterly depressed. The psychiatrists thought the only way to save her was with electroshock treatment.

Now, thirty years later, Tita would flash her best smile, push her big plastic teeth forward, maneuvering them with her tongue so they didn't come detached from her gums, open her eyes wide, and delight in telling her story to anyone who would listen.

"They gave me thirty-two shocks, but I feel fine, just fine, just fine. And if they have to give me more, they can, though I'm fine, just fine, just fine."

She left the bakery crying and terribly depressed, forgetting all about Chicha and the bread. Walking slowly along, she stopped crying, blowing her nose straight onto the sidewalk, pressing one of her nostrils closed with her index finger and clearing the other. She went down Ánimas toward Galiano, walked a few blocks farther, and sat down in the park at Galiano and San Rafael, her gaze lost in the distance. For a second, the old Ten Cent at Galiano and San Rafael caught her eye, and she remembered the ten happy years she spent as a young salesgirl there, selling cosmetics and perfume. She was pretty, tall, and dark, and she had beautiful breasts. With her good looks, her constant smile, and her perfect manners, she radiated calm, sweetness, and candor, and she sold a lot. She had boyfriends, dozens of boyfriends, who brought her flowers, chocolates, perfume. How could she have fallen in love with that bastard? She was in the militia, the Ten Cent was closed, the Americans went shuffling home, and she got married because she was pregnant. How that idiot beat her! Even when she was pregnant, he beat her. She had never been able to explain to herself why she didn't have an abortion. What ever happened to the Ten Cent?

Around her were other crazies, homeless people, panhandlers, women trying to sell whatever trash they could to the passersby, two or three flashers exhibiting their half-erect equipment to the crazy women and the female beggars, and being aroused by them. Tita didn't notice any of the rabble. She was in a stupor. She held out her hand and begged from the people walking by, wanting to buy herself cigarettes and coffee. That was all she needed. And she kept repeating very softly, "Give me a few cents, for the love of God, for cigarettes and coffee. Be kind. People should treat each other with respect. Give me a few cents, but be polite about it. Be nice. Don't hurt me."

No one heard her. She was talking very softly, pronouncing each word properly and smiling the constant and relaxed smile she had been taught in the training sessions at the Ten Cent.

Chicha finished reading the heroic account of the Baikal-Amur and wondered why Tita hadn't come back with the damn bread. She thought about telling her to stay away once and for all:

"I have to make up my mind to drive her away so she never comes back again. She'll make me crazy just like she is. She drives me insane, and she sits there as cool as can be, like nothing's wrong, smoking and drinking coffee. Enough! I have to get away from her! I'll turn this room over to the state and move into a home."

She stood still for a while, in the middle of the room, thinking. She had been considering the move for months, but she hadn't dared. "I will go. After all, I don't need her anymore, and I don't have the strength to deal with her." She went over to a small cupboard and opened a drawer. At the back of it, under some dirty clothes, she found an American pistol, a Colt. A high-ranking officer had given it to her at the very beginning of the Revolution. It was a gun that wasn't used anymore, an old regulation piece from before the Revolution, but it was in perfect condition. She kept it clean and oiled, and she had thirty bullets in a cardboard box. She put them in a jar and covered them with water so they would rust and slowly be ruined. She hid the jar under the bed and it occurred to her that she needed a hammer to pound the pistol into pieces. But where could she get a hammer? She put the gun away again, burying it under some clothes, closed the drawer, and sat down in the ragged armchair in the doorway. The same man was still hauling bricks, a walking sculpture carved from stone and cement, a statue ceaselessly carrying bricks.

3:20 / There's Always Some Bastard Out to Get You

Old Cholo finished gathering up his books from the floor of the entryway, thousands of used books. He put them away in boxes and carried them into his ramshackle room. Picking up a dirty, rusted can, he closed the door, padlocked it, and went to get his dinner. It was twenty-six blocks from Carlos III and Belascoaín to Cuba and O'Reilly. He walked them fast, in less than half an hour. Going down Reina to Monserrate, he turned right onto O'Reilly, walking until he hit Cuba. It was seven at night when he arrived. The girl, in a bad mood as usual, shouted what she always shouted at him, "Late again, Cholo, you're always the last fucking one. Here, this is all that's left."

She dumped a little bit of rice and chickpeas in his can and marked off his name on a list of 342 people with dining privileges at the free state-run kitchen.

"Isn't there anything else? Look and see if there's more, girl, go on."

"That's it. Today you got screwed. Come earlier tomorrow."

He went outside and sat on a doorstep. Taking a spoon out of his pocket, he ate the insipid mess. He was still hungry. He thought about the cheap cafeterias that had recently opened on Belascoaín. But it was already dark. By now, if they had anything left, it would be rum and cigarettes. He put his hand in the left pocket of his pants and felt a roll of bills. A fat roll. Today he had made at least five hundred pesos selling the old books. He had thousands of pesos hidden in a cardboard box in his room. Many thousands, more than he could count.

A woman came up to him with paper cones of peanuts. She offered them to him. No. He never wasted money on frivolous things. He didn't smoke or drink rum or coffee and he only ate two meals a day, frugal ones. Women were his only vice. Though he was seventy-six, he didn't look any older than sixty: he was strong and well-built, short and white and quite blond, with light-colored eyes. His mother told him he looked just like his father, a Basque as strong and crude as an ox who lived with her for a few months; when he discovered she was pregnant, he dropped off the face of the earth, and she never saw hide nor hair of him again. Cholo never knew him. His mother gave birth to him and died when he was four. Now he can't even remember her.

Cholo grew up on the street all alone, without a father or a mother or brothers and sisters, sleeping in doorways or wherever he could find a place and working at whatever turned up. He had been a porter, sewer cleaner, garbageman, boxer, newspaper salesman, shoeshine man, construction worker. Everything. There was no dirty manual labor he hadn't tried. Ever since his mother died, he had worked in garbage dumps, slaughterhouses, at the market, in factories, without a break. He had never had a home or a steady woman. He liked to be with one woman for a while, but right away she'd start to ask for more and more money. She'd get jealous. She'd try to keep things too neat. She'd want to have kids. She'd want Cholo to spend money on soap for washing clothes and she'd want him to shower every day. No, no. It was impossible to live with a woman for more than a month!

And Cholo was a healthy male. Two or three times a week his shaft would get as hard as a breeding bull's. To take care of that, he did need money. The woman with the peanuts stopped a few feet away from him, waiting for customers, but no one came by. He looked at her more carefully. She was a skinny woman, close to thirty, her dyed hair half-blond and half-black, a little dirty, her heels grimy and callused. She looked at him again and smiled. Her teeth were just like his: crooked and black.

"Buy some peanuts, old man. Only one peso."

"No, no peanuts. But come here. Sit down."

"Why would I sit down next to you? Are you crazy?"

Then Cholo got up and went over to her.

"Do you want to make twenty pesos?"

The woman got defensive.

"Doing what?"

"Let me suck your pussy. That's all."

"No, man, no. You're too repulsive. I'd probably get some disease."

"I'll give you thirty. And if I feel like screwing you, I'll give you ten more."

"No, no. You're a disgusting pig. Forget it."

"You'd make forty pesos, easy. In a second."

"I wouldn't let you touch me for one hundred, never mind letting you screw me. Are you crazy?"

"Come on, girl. It'll just take a minute."

"No, no. Leave me alone."

And she walked away with her paper cones of peanuts. Cholo stared after her, smiled to himself, and shouted, "I'll give you a hundred."

She stopped. Retracing her footsteps, she looked at him with a broad, friendly smile on her face.

"Really? Well, that's a whole different story."

"No, I'm not giving you that much. But look, forty today and forty tomorrow and forty the next day . . ."

"Oh, screw you, old man. You've got a lot of nerve, you really do. Leave me alone or I'll call the police."

Cholo got excited. His prick was half-erect, making a bulge in his pants. It made him proud. He knew he was the only old man in the world who still got as stiff as a rod. He knew he was a stud. And in the middle of the sidewalk, in the dark, he bounced on his heels. Putting up his fists, he lowered his head and threw a few tight punches at his opponent's face. "Hard and short. Your right arm is a powerhouse. Use your right," his trainer at the America Gym used to tell him. In three years he had ninety-seven wins and twenty-three losses. "Cholo Banderas." That was his boxing name. The trainer added "Banderas" to make it sound better: "It's catchier, it's got more of a ring." Until that black bastard KO'd him. Knocked him to the mat, plus cracked his skull. He couldn't fight anymore. Then he was in prison for two years, for practically nothing: an obnoxious loudmouth of a policeman provoked him, and Cholo beat him to a pulp. All he got was two years. He was comfortable in jail. No work to do. He sat quietly in a corner. Everybody else talked shit and told stories about how tough they were, except for him. He never opened his mouth, and he had no friends. None at all. He was on his own, just like always. Until it was time for him to hit the streets again.

That was many years ago. He couldn't even remember what had happened back then anymore. The truth was, he never remembered anything. "You have to live in the present. Yesterday's past, and tomorrow hasn't come yet," he often said to himself. Anyway, when it came down to it, it made no difference to him whether he was a boxer or whether he cleaned drains, whether he was in jail or out on the street. That's where he was now, standing on that dark corner with his prick half-erect. He threw the can into the street. Hard, so it would make a noise. He felt relaxed and powerful. He flexed his dorsal muscles, his biceps, his triceps. "You're a he-man, Cholo. You've got to get yourself a girl tonight."

And he moved on, bouncing up and down and shadowboxing. He was heading toward Avenida del Puerto, in a neighborhood he had always liked. It used to be easy for him there. Down Muralla, on the way to Avenida del Puerto, lived three whores. Each one had a little room with a red door. And in gold letters: Berta, Olga, Lola. It was the best memory he had. Three whores, five pesos the fuck. They'd talk to him, smile at him. As time went by, they became friends, and when he arrived, they would even make him a glass of lemonade or bathe him and shave him. When that happened, he always gave them a few more pesos. Nothing is free in this life. But the three of them had been dead for a long time. They were probably close to sixty when they died, young enough.

That wasn't his story: he felt like a boy. The protective shell he had built around himself when he was almost still a baby was tougher than ever. Nobody had ever protected him. He knew no one could touch him. Like a jungle beast, he was solitary, separate from the pack. He'd had many women and many children. But it had been a while now since anyone had come up to him to say, "You're my father. My mother is so-and-so, do you remember?"

He used to drive them away. He never remembered who so-and-so was, much less whether she had had a child. No woman ever gave birth while she was with him. When they'd tell him they were pregnant, he'd disappear. Who could prove the child was his? Women were all the same: they'd sleep with anyone for four pesos, and then they'd try to find some idiot to raise their child. That trick never worked on him. It certainly wouldn't work now. It had been years since anyone claimed him as their father, though he was more prosperous than he'd ever been. He had the last laugh. People said this was the worst crisis in all of Cuba's history. "Well for me, it's the best," he often thought to himself. When people really started to be hungry, in 1990, he had a shoeshine stand outside his room, in the same entryway. Then he realized he could buy used things and sell them there. All kinds of things, from sections of pipe and lengths of electric wire to hangers, old shoes, magazines, books, glasses, old toys. There was nothing in the stores, absolutely nothing. People had money in their pockets, and they couldn't even buy cigarettes.

There came a time when he was making more selling things than shining shoes. And anyway, shoe polish had vanished too, so he had to stop. He bought very cheaply and sold cheaply too. He was centrally located, and lots of people passed by. They all stopped to look and ask how much things cost. Some of them bought things. Finally, he realized that the books and old magazines were selling much better than everything else. So he gave up the rest of it and put up a sign someone had made for him on a piece of cardboard. "I buy books and old magazines. Hoam vizits." He covered all of Havana on foot carrying four huge cloth sacks. And he'd come back loaded down. He couldn't read, so he bought in bulk. Everything. Thousands and thousands of books stacked in the entryway, on the floor. And hundreds of customers every day. He had never made so much money. He hid the cash in a cardboard box, tossing old books on top of it. No one would ever imagine a fortune was hidden there.

He never talked to anyone or smiled at them. People weren't to be trusted. If you gave them an inch, they'd take a mile. Days and days would go by and he'd only open his mouth to say "yes" or "no" when some customer asked him a question. He understood very well what was going on. He'd lived long enough to figure it out. "The problem is, people scare easily. The Americans turn the screws, people get a little hungry, and right away everybody's shitting their pants. There you see them, skinny, whipped, talking to themselves on the street, half-crazy, I don't know why people are such jackasses. It's always been this way in Cuba: three or four years of prosperity and then twenty of poverty. It's been that way ever since I can remember. So there's no reason to go around scared all the time. People have got to stop being scared and keep moving ahead." Those were his thoughts, but he never put them into words. Mostly because he had no one to talk to. Anyway, he wasn't any good at talking, and he didn't like to, either. It was safer to keep quiet.

At last he came to Muralla, and he sat down under the arch standing where the street turned toward Avenida del Puerto in the dark. It was quiet. A little farther down a black man and woman were fucking furiously, leaning up against a column fifteen feet from him. He could hear them straining and panting, and he could see how frenzied they were. It got him even hotter than he was before. There were very few people walking by on the sidewalk, hardly anyone at all. He pulled out his cock and jerked off a little on account of the black couple. Just a little. He hadn't wasted his semen in years. After all, he couldn't produce the same kind of jets that used to fill a glass and astonish women anymore. There was much less there now, and it couldn't be wasted.

Cholo was happy. Mmmm. He tucked his equipment back in and began his search for a victim. "Tonight this prick of mine will get pussy for twenty pesos or my name isn't Cholo," he said to himself. And he bounced up and down and boxed at the air. He went walking along Avenida del Puerto toward the Malecón. Hustlers, taxi drivers, bars, three ruined old buildings which had just recently collapsed. The rubble hindered his progress. The mouths of the sewers were clogged where they opened onto the bay and shit was flooding the street in front of the Los Marinos bar. Cholo didn't notice anything. He had always lived in the middle of decay. All he wanted was a cunt for twenty pesos. In front of Los Marinos, a group of baby sluts were waiting for customers, very young, pretty, flirtatious, smelling of perfume. It had been a while since Cholo came by this way, but he supposed that one whore was the same as the next, just as it had always been. He hailed a little mulatta. The girl was surprised that such a disgusting old man would call for her. She stayed where she was. From a distance, she shouted, "What do you want, grandpa?"

"I'm not your motherfucking grandfather. Come here!"

"Eh? What's wrong with the old man? Your mother's fucking cunt, asshole. Don't fuck with me or I'll cut you up."

Cholo, unruffled, called to another one. She was friendlier and came within six feet of him.

"Tell me, grandpa, what do you want? Change? We're broke. We don't have any money. Ask a tourist."

"No, I have something for you. Come here. Come closer."

"Nooo. Tell me what it is."

"I'll give you twenty pesos if you let me suck your pussy . . . Come closer . . ."

"Twenty what? Cuban pesos?"

"Of course. Twenty Cuban pesos."

"You must be crazy. Did you just escape from Mazorra?"

The girl turned toward the group of eight or nine whores, and, making fun of Cholo, she shouted, "He says he'll give me twenty Cuban pesos to suck my pussy. Ha ha ha, the senile old fool, ha ha ha. Hey you, heads up. Fifty bucks, dollars, for a session with us. And stinking the way you do, not even a hundred would be enough. Not to mention you've never seen a dollar in your life. So get a move on, get out of here."

The other girls laughed and laughed, mocking him.

"Go on, you stinking old fool, get lost."

Cholo got up and walked away. They were the crazy ones. He made a quick calculation. The dollar was at 23, times 50 was, 1,150. Goddamn it! It couldn't be. How could a little slut like that earn in one fuck twice what he made in a day? They'd be millionaires in . . . no, because they wouldn't save. They'd spend all their money on perfume and stupid makeup and purses. That's what was wrong with people. No one saved at all.

He kept walking. He passed a few little bars. People were drinking beer from cans, listening to music, laughing. He didn't even glance at them. The truth was, it made him angry to see people throwing money away like that. He sat down alone on the wall a little farther along to watch the few people walking by. A mulatto came along pedaling a pedicab. He braked in front of Cholo. Seated behind him was a white slut with her hair dyed blond. The guy wheeled the pedicab onto the sidewalk and pushed it close up against the wall, and they sat down very close together. He was facing the sea, and she was facing the city. The man was high. He unzipped his fly and pulled out his prick, and she grabbed it with her left hand and jerked him off without looking at him or making a sound. Some people walked by, but they didn't notice how her arm was moving. All of this just a few steps from Cholo, who was building up steam like a pressure cooker. The guy came in less than five minutes. He was breathing hard. She pulled her hand away fast so as not to be splattered. The guy gave her a few bills, saying something under his breath. He got back on the pedicab and rode away singing happily. She stayed sitting on the wall. Cholo eyed her carefully. She had a good body, though she looked battered and dirty. Cholo went up to her and got straight to the point.

"Listen, I'll give you twenty pesos if you let me suck your pussy."

"No, old man, no. Cool it."

"Well, you tell me."

"Tell you what?"

"How much do you want?"

"For you to suck my pussy?"

"Yes."

"Oh . . . well . . ."

"Thirty pesos. Come on, let's go."

"Well, all right."

Across from them were some shrubs alongside a small amusement park, which was closed and dark. There was no one around. They went into the bushes. Cholo was as horny as a boy. She took off her shorts and panties, laid them on the ground, and sat on them with her legs spread.

"All right, go ahead. Only for a few minutes. Don't think you're going to be down there for an hour."

The old man sniffed, prodded, licked at her with his raspy, dirty, expert tongue. She had never imagined he would be so good. He was like a calf, sucking with devastating force. He knew lots of tricks, and he went through his whole repertoire, almost driving her out of her mind. When he bit lightly on her clit, she couldn't stand it anymore; she came in a long, drawn-out spasm. Oh, she almost lost herself. Coming back to her senses, she counseled herself, "Don't lose your head, Marisela, with this disgusting old man. Self-control, Marisela, self-control."

"Enough, old man, enough. Stop. Stop."

The old man kept sucking, and meanwhile he was jerking himself off. Marisela saw that he had a big, heavy prick, as stiff as a rod.

"What are you doing? Stop it, stop it!"

But the sight of that beautiful prick softened her. Unconsciously she spread her legs wider. The old man mounted her and pushed inside her.

"Ay, gently, damn it, gently, you're so big. Be careful."

She came again and again. Then Cholo couldn't hold back any longer, and he let himself go. As soon as he had finished, he got up, bouncing up and down like a boxer, throwing short, tight punches. He was cheerful, frisky, not tired at all, ready and willing to go another nine rounds. She couldn't get over her astonishment.

"Come here, man, how old are you?"

"Seventy-six."

"Impossible."

"What?"

"You're all there. Just like a twenty-year-old."

"Oh, yes. That's me. Here, take your money. I've got to go."

"Listen, wait, don't be an asshole. Thirty pesos? It was thirty just for you to go down on me."

"Did I ask you to spread your legs so I could fuck you? I didn't, did I? That's your problem. I'm out of here."

"Wait, wait, don't try to get away, because if you do, I'll split your head open and leave you here to rot."

"Oh really? Is that a fact? You think you're tough?"

"I'm more than tough. Believe me, you don't want to find out the hard way! Give me thirty more for the fuck."

"No, no."

"Give me thirty pesos or I'll scratch your eyes out."

She was as good as her word. Marisela had a piece of wire with a sharpened point in the pocket of her pants. She whipped it out and lunged at Cholo, trying to slice one of his cheeks. He dodged in time and jumped back.

"Well, well, what a little wild thing. Now, now. Calm down. Here, thirty pesos."

Cholo pulled out his wad of bills in front of her and counted out the sum. Marisela was amazed.

"Damn it, sweetie, you're loaded!"

"Oh, so now you call me sweetie. Here, take this before I regret it. This has been the most expensive fuck of my life."

"What's your name?"

"Cholo."

"Cholo what?"

"Cholo. Here, follow me."

"Where?"

"Oh, you ask too many questions. Come on, it'll be worth your time."

Crossing over to Reina, then Carlos III, they came to the damp, dusty little room crammed with books. Cholo turned on the dim light, a single bulb. He slept on the floor, on a mattress and some dirty pieces of cardboard. When Marisela saw the place, she stood there with her mouth hanging open. Pulling a pack of cigarettes out from between her breasts, she lit one and smoked it, keeping her distance, watching Cholo, who was taking off his clothes. He was soon completely naked, and he had another erection.

"Come on, Marisela, take your clothes off."

"I can't believe you live here."

"Why not?"

"For someone with a roll of bills like yours, you live worse than a dog. Do you think I'm going to lie down here with the rats and the roaches and all this shit?"

"Don't lie down. I'll fuck you standing up. It makes no difference to me."

"No, no. Enough. Forget it . . . I'm leaving."

"Come here, girl. Do you live in a palace? Are you a princess? Where do you come from?"

"You really want to know where I come from? All right, I'll tell you. I spent twelve years in jail. I was sentenced to twenty because I hit my husband over the head with an iron pot and then I cut him up into little pieces and scattered them all over the place."

"Shit!"

"Shit, huh? I'm telling you all this so you understand that tough as you may think you are, I'm tougher. You play with me and I cut you. But you know what? In jail I lived much better than you live here. You live like a pig, and I'm not a pig. Why did you lock us in? Unlock the door now, because I'm leaving and you better not try to stop me. I've had enough. This party's over."

"I wasn't trying to lock you in. I always lock the door so no one surprises me while I'm asleep."

"I don't care. Open the door."

"Come on, look at me. Let's fuck again. I'll pay you. And then you can go."

"No, I'm leaving. And don't make me angry. I just got out of jail three days ago. Do you know what that means? I wouldn't trust my own mother."

"That's the best way to be. There's always some bastard out to get you."

"Believe me, I know it. Don't try to give me advice."

"I'm going to make you an offer. You might like the sound of it. Do you know how to read?"

"Of course."

"Help me here with the books. I sell them there, in the entryway. But sometimes someone asks me for a certain book and I tell them I don't have it and that's that."

"You don't know how to read?"

"I don't need to know how."

"Sure, if you have to, you can eat grass and go around on all fours for the rest of your life."

"Look who's talking. You're more of an animal than I am. At least I've never cut anyone into little pieces."

"Because you've never had to."

"Maybe."

"Let's leave it at that, Cholo. How much would you pay me?"

"I don't make a lot. I could let you have ten pesos a day."

"Don't make me laugh, old man. Just giving two hand jobs a day I make forty or fifty. Can't you see I'm white? Dark-skinned guys are dying to be with girls like me."

"And where are you living?"

"What the fuck do you care? Unlock the door, because I'm going to get me some cock. I've told you too much already."

"I've told you too much too."

Cholo unlocked the door. Marisela went out into the night air and was gone. Cholo went out into the entryway and sat down on the floor. It was cool. There was a nice breeze. He wasn't tired. It must have been close to midnight. Springing up, he started to bounce and throw short, tight uppercuts and jabs to an invisible midsection.

"In the red corner, Cholo Banderas from America! Ding-ding! A mighty right arm! Ninety-seven victories!"

The dark city slept in silence. No one was watching Cholo Banderas. He got tired of boxing his invisible opponent and laughed a genuine, heartfelt laugh.

"What a wonderful night, damn it, what a wonderful night! What time is it? Any minute the sun will come up, so I might as well go bring out the books and get back to work. Back to work. You can't let your guard down. That's how they used to knock me out, when I let my guard down."